Sasha Wagstaff

WICKED GAMES

headline review

First published in 2010 by HEADLINE REVIEW
An imprint of HEADLINE PUBLISHING GROUP

2

Cataloguing in Publication Data is available from the British Library

ISBN 978 0 7553 4890 9 (Hardback)
ISBN 978 0 7553 5619 5 (Trade paperback)

Typeset in Garamond by Avon DataSet Ltd,
Bidford on Avon, Warwickshire

Printed and bound in Great Britain by
Clays Ltd, St Ives plc

Headline's policy is to use papers that are natural, renewable and recyclable products
and made from wood grown in sustainable forests. The logging
and manufacturing processes are expected to conform to the environmental
regulations of the country of origin.

HEADLINE PUBLISHING GROUP
An Hachette UK Company
338 Euston Road
London NW1 3BH

www.headline.co.uk
www.hachette.co.uk

For Phoebe
(but please don't read this until you're much, much older)

Prologue

Ignoring the naked blonde making eyes at him from the four-poster, Judd Harrington strutted out of the bedroom. Barefoot with his made-to-measure Savile Row trousers loosely fastened around his muscle-packed midriff, Judd padded downstairs, his hard blue eyes taking in each pleasingly symmetrical room and perfectly restored sash window.

Brockett Hall was a lavish Georgian-style property with gleaming marble floors and Wedgwood-pastel walls. Judd loved the ostentatious moat that surrounded the property and the heated, oval swimming pool that lay in a conservatory beyond the sitting room. His eyes lingered on the pool momentarily, the turquoise water shimmering innocently at him as a torturous memory he'd buried long ago swam vividly to the surface. *New Year's Eve . . . 1984 . . .*

He shrugged the memory off, reminding himself that this was a moment to be celebrated. After twenty-five years, he had finally reclaimed the Harrington family home and his nerve endings were virtually buzzing with anticipation at the thought of owning it once more. After all, it was about fucking time.

Judd stared out of the window moodily, barely noticing the rambling Chiltern Hills, chalk beds and famous beech trees. Situated close to London but still managing to offer a rural idyll to commuters, Meadowbank was a pretty village in the area described as 'leafy Bucks'. But Judd wasn't interested in the undeniable charms of his childhood village. Fixing his gaze on a picturesque old house in the distance, he felt his stomach tighten as the old feelings of resentment and fury stirred inside him. There it was, he mused, larger than life and twice as beautiful as he remembered.

Pembleton, the Maguire family's breathtaking Elizabethan house, with its terracotta bricks and romantic, turret-like chimneys, was set in acres of tangled woodland. Judd could practically smell the powdery aroma of the deep blue irises he knew sprang into life at this time of year and for a second his heart ached. The feeling was swiftly replaced by something else: a powerful desire for revenge. Revenge on the man responsible for making the Harrington family lose everything – their money, their home . . . their good name.

Not to mention the only woman Judd had ever loved, he thought bitterly, his fingers turning white as they gripped the window sill. He squinted as bright shafts of summer sunshine filtered through the clouds, drenching Pembleton in glorious technicolour. It was as if the house was taunting him, gleefully showing him everything he'd missed out on and reminding him brutally of everything he had lost. Suddenly, Judd's life shifted sharply into focus.

'So, what do you think of the house?' Laura Preston, senior estate agent at Fulmark and Green, asked, sashaying up behind him in a rather grubby sheet she'd whipped from a decaying sofa. She slid her hands around Judd's rock-hard stomach enticingly, pressing her ample breasts against his back.

Judd glanced over his shoulder at her, filled with distaste. She had been a good enough shag but he couldn't be bothered with pleasantries, not now.

'Get out,' he snapped at her.

Laura reddened as she yanked her hands away. 'Hey, there's no need to be—'

'Whatever,' Judd interrupted her, his jaw tightening impatiently. 'Look, I'll wire you the money for the house in the morning and I'll leave details of the decorators I'll be using.' He turned away. 'I expect everything to be ready in six months' time, is that understood?'

'Will your wife and family be joining you from the States then?' Laura tugged the sheet higher up under her chin in an attempt to regain some professional dignity. She knew he had a wife because he'd mentioned her in passing, but he didn't wear a wedding ring . . . men like him rarely did. Judd didn't answer her. He simply stared out across the hills as if he had forgotten she was even there.

Laura turned on her heel, sincerely regretting falling for Judd Harrington's arrogant charms in the first place. Why on earth had she allowed him to sweet-talk her into bed – or, more accurately, bend her over the rickety old dresser in the upstairs box room? She didn't even *like* redheads, for heaven's sake!

Arrogant bastard, Laura thought sulkily as she retrieved her bra from a dusty lampshade. Judd Harrington might still have an attractive public-schoolboy accent in spite of all the years he had spent in America and a certain butch appeal, but she had never been treated so shabbily in her life! Thank God she'd nailed the sale. Houses like Brockett Hall didn't come along every day and her commission on a house like this would more than make up for her wounded pride. Laura hurriedly pulled on her Jigsaw suit and left Judd to it, wondering what the hell was so bloody fascinating outside that window.

Lost in thought, Judd didn't even register her departure. As an image of Lochlin Maguire's ruggedly handsome face swam in front of his eyes, he clenched his fists at his sides. His nemesis was going to wonder what the hell had hit him. Oh yes, this time next year, things were going to look very different for the Maguire family because from this point onwards, all Judd cared about was bringing Lochlin Maguire to his knees and taking everything from him. *Everything*.

And that, thought Judd, his body twitching with longing, included Tavvy.

Chapter One

Six months later

Pulling the collar of her lumberjack shirt around her chin for warmth, Iris Maguire crunched through the remains of a harsh January frost. Her arms were almost yanked out of their sockets by the swarm of dogs straining to break free.

'Get *back* here, Nutmeg!' she shrieked, dragging a mischievous Beagle out of a rabbit hole. 'Naughty thing,' she scolded him affectionately as she led the dogs into the village. She spent her life with animals and loved every single one of her mother's rescue dogs, however ugly or badly behaved they were. Nutmeg, with his battered nose and exuberant manner, unfortunately suffered from both afflictions. Tying him and the rest of the yelping dogs up outside the local store which still had Christmas lights twinkling in its windows, Iris headed inside, blowing on her fingers.

'Did you get a good look at them?' Mrs Meaden, the shop's owner was asking eagerly.

Ian, the shop assistant-cum-delivery boy, shook his head with obvious regret. 'Not really. But, judging by the cars and the clothes, I'd say they were loaded.'

'Who?' Iris asked, eyeing a shelf of chocolate bars longingly. With an effort, she strengthened her resolve; she'd eaten far too many mince pies this Christmas and she had a very tight gown to wear in a few weeks' time.

Ian leant on the counter and gazed at Iris adoringly. 'The family who've moved into Brockett Hall – you know, the old Harrington residence.'

Even with her wild cloud of tawny-blond hair pulled into a messy ponytail and an oversized, tomboyish shirt pulled up to her nose, Iris was devastatingly attractive. Her thighs were slender and coltish in her skinny jeans and not even the chilly weather could diminish the rosy glow in her cheeks or the bee-stung lips that Ian felt begged to be kissed. He sighed blissfully, grateful to be mere metres away from the object of his unfulfilled fantasies.

'What, that flashy house at the other end of the valley?' Iris asked, fixing her sleepy amber eyes on his with interest, unaware she was making his knees go all quivery behind the counter.

'That's the one.' Ian groaned inwardly, wishing Iris hadn't snogged Ollie Ramshaw under the mistletoe in the Forgers Arms on Christmas Eve. A sickeningly handsome scrum-half, Ollie was, if rumours were to be believed, an arrogant womaniser and a fully paid-up member of the Twat Society, hardly worthy to kiss the ground Iris walked on. If only I had the courage to tell her how I feel about her, Ian thought dreamily.

Iris frowned. 'The Harrington residence? There hasn't been anyone in there for years, I don't think. What's the big mystery about them anyway?' She was intrigued; the Harrington name was mud in her family, so much so that a mere mention of it could send her father into a black mood of epic proportions. Iris had no idea why because her parents always clammed up and changed the subject whenever Brockett Hall was mentioned.

Mrs Meaden averted her eyes and ignored the question. 'Isn't it *exciting*?' she steamed on. 'We're all dying to know who our new neighbours are and Brockett Hall is such a *grand* residence.' She nudged Ian, wishing he didn't always end up looking like a lovesick fool every time Iris Maguire was in the vicinity. She was stunningly beautiful as well as talented but Mrs Meaden had a feeling Iris wouldn't stick around in a village like Meadowbank for ever, not with a voice like hers.

'Here's the money for the papers.' Iris smiled, pulling a twenty-pound note out of her purse. 'Ooh, look, here's Old Mrs Stafford, she's bound to know something.'

They all perked up as the village gossip pushed her tartan trolley into the shop.

'If you're talking about the new people in the Harrington residence, I have nothing to report,' Mrs Stafford said, her beady eyes surprisingly lacklustre. 'I asked that tarty estate agent about them and she was *most* unforthcoming! Snapped something about an obnoxious American family and got very uppity indeed.'

'Americans?' echoed Mrs Meaden, somehow making the word sound as appealing as leprosy. 'How . . . er . . . thrilling.'

Iris left them to it. Clearly no one had a clue about their new neighbours and she didn't have time to hang around and find out. Rounding up the impatiently yapping dogs, she stared at a flashy vehicle with blacked-out windows that was parked at the side of the road. The sleek red sports car looked incongruous next to the mud-splattered Land Rovers; it was the kind of car Iris would have expected to see in Monaco, not Meadowbank. Spotting the trademark prancing stallion on the bonnet, Iris wondered what sort of tit drove a Ferrari down to the village store to buy their daily papers and pint of milk, and suppressed a grin.

Remembering she only had a few weeks before her big performance at the Valentines' Ball, Iris strode past the car and started to sing. She didn't notice the window of the Ferrari silently sliding down or the flash of red hair that appeared over the top as her voice filled the air. The full, rich tones were unexpected from someone so slight and Iris gave it everything she had, her head flung back and her free arm spread wide as the ballad burst forth. Struggling to keep the dogs under control, Iris felt her stomach exploding with hope as she remembered her father promising to review her career again soon. He had assured her that he really was serious this time and had even talked about finally giving her a recording contract.

Iris hugged herself. She loved living at home and didn't mind her job at the local vet's, but singing was her dream and she could think about nothing else. She'd been knocked back twice by her father for being too young and unprepared for the harsh realities of the music business, so she'd gone out of her way to prove how much her career meant to her by practising in every spare moment she had. She'd studied the music industry by devouring magazines like *NME* and *Q* and had badgered her brother Shay, who worked for a music magazine, for information. Surely this time her dad would give her a chance. Iris sighed, despair washing over her for a second. What was the point of having a father who owned a record label if he wouldn't give his own daughter a taste of the limelight? Realising high-spirited Nutmeg had got himself tangled up under the other dogs, she pulled the unruly gaggle to a standstill and dropped to her knees.

'What do you think, old boy?' Iris asked as she unwound Nutmeg's lead from Mickey the Alsatian's. 'Is Dad finally going to give me a record deal?' Nutmeg barked happily, hopeful for a biscuit and not in the least bit bothered about his mistress's woes. Dad *has* to listen to me this time, Iris thought, rubbing Mickey's silky black nose absent-mindedly. He has to . . . otherwise, what else could she do? Singing was her life – she needed it like she needed to breathe. Feeling depressed as she opened her mouth to practise her song once more, Iris headed home.

Emerging from his Ferrari and staring after Iris, Judd turned up the collar of his Armani overcoat thoughtfully. What a voice, he thought, absolutely staggered. He simply had to know who the girl was; he hadn't heard a voice that incredible in a long time. And God, she reminded him of someone – achingly so! The cloud of wild blond hair, those unusual, cat-like amber eyes . . . Seeing old Mrs Stafford emerging from the village shop with a deep-filled steak and kidney pudding for one in her wizened hand, Judd stopped her by clutching her arm.

'Ooooh, you scared me!' she cried, looking up at Judd in awe.

He must be at least six foot four, she thought, transfixed by his flinty blue eyes and short red-gold hair. He wasn't handsome as such – he was too muscle-packed for that – but he had a charm of sorts. Dazzled by his perfectly aligned white teeth bared in a wolfish smile, she didn't even realise she was patting her hair coquettishly like a groupie meeting Mick Jagger for the first time.

'That girl who just left the shop . . . the one with all the dogs?' Judd jerked his head towards the door as he watched the red and black lumberjack shirt disappearing into the distance. 'Who is she?'

'Iris?' Mrs Stafford offered, squinting across the fields. 'That's Iris Maguire.'

'Maguire?'

'Lochlin Maguire's daughter.' She nodded, wondering why his eyes were suddenly gleaming like polished sapphires. Something occurred to her and she blinked excitedly. 'You're not . . . are you the new owner of Brockett Hall?'

Judd nodded, feeling adrenalin flooding through his veins. Brusquely thanking the old lady, he jumped into his Ferrari. His nemesis was about to find out exactly how much it hurt to have his family torn apart, Judd thought to himself savagely as he roared into the distance.

In her much-loved mansion in LA, Kitty Harrington was reluctantly packing up the last of her belongings. She glanced round at the vast sitting room with a sinking heart, hating seeing it stripped of its pastel furnishings and lavish furniture. What on earth had possessed Judd to uproot the entire family and move them to the depths of the English countryside? Her grey eyes filled with tears and she dashed them away quickly before anyone saw.

'I'm really gonna miss this place,' Martha said, her usually timid voice echoing around the empty room. She plastered tape across the top of one of the boxes and wrote across it in shaky writing.

Kitty smiled tightly, doing her best to look enthusiastic. She knew exactly what her daughter-in-law meant. Leaving this house was going to be a huge wrench. She knew it was vulgar and ridiculously over the top – Judd wasn't known for his discretion or his taste – but she couldn't help being attached to it. It had been home for so long now.

'I can't believe Dad is making us leave,' Sebastian said, kicking one of the boxes petulantly. He stuck his bottom lip out, looking more like a stroppy teenager than a twenty-four-year-old lawyer. 'Why the hell would anyone in their right mind want to leave Los Angeles and move to fucking England?'

'I haven't the faintest idea, Seb,' Kitty told her eldest son, her shoulders drooping wearily. 'You know Judd makes the decisions around here. I don't have a say in anything.' If she did, she'd have pleaded with Judd not to uproot his entire family on a whim. Well, maybe it was a little more than a whim, she admitted to herself, knowing how much Judd's childhood home meant to him. He had always intended to go back and reclaim it when the time was right; he had told her that from the start.

Elliot heaved the box Sebastian had shoved aside back against the wall with the others. 'Dad's bought a business and his old family home over there,' he said in a flat voice as he pushed his strawberry-blond hair out of his doe-like eyes. 'So, as usual, we all have to follow him while he takes over the world, regardless of what we might be leaving behind.'

'And what exactly are you leaving behind, little brother?' Sebastian jeered, his chin tilted upwards. He enjoyed taunting his sixteen-year-old brother because he knew Elliot was far too gentle to shout back at him. 'Your posh school and girly little friends? Boo hoo, poor Elliot. Some of us have our families here,' he jerked his thumb belligerently in Martha's direction, 'and a business to attend to. Think yourself fucking lucky.'

Elliot said nothing. He was fully aware that his brother didn't care one jot about his wife, and as for having a business to attend to, Sebastian was their father's lawyer, a role he performed as lazily as possible. He had a job for life purely on the basis of nepotism and blithely took full advantage of the preferential position he held in his father's multimillion-dollar businesses.

God, Sebastian was like Judd, Kitty thought, leaning against the wall as tiredness overtook her. He might be her eldest son and she loved him dearly but he was an arrogant bully and, at times, just like his father, he was rather difficult to like.

'I'm off for a swim,' Sebastian said abruptly, leaving them to it.

'He's so selfish,' Elliot grumbled once his brother was safely out of earshot.

Out of the blue, Martha burst into tears and Kitty and Elliot rushed to comfort her.

'Oh, honey, don't cry,' Kitty soothed. 'I'm sure we'll be all right in England once we're settled.'

'It's not that.' Martha snivelled into her sleeve, her mousy head bowed. 'It's Sebastian . . . he's disappointed in me . . . again. I'm not pregnant,' she explained in a woeful voice, lifting her big brown eyes to meet theirs. 'Again.'

'There, there,' Elliot comforted her, offering his sleeve gallantly. His sister-in-law was like a nervy colt and he simply couldn't imagine what had prompted her to marry his idiot of a brother in the first place. He treated her like dirt and she deserved better. 'Ignore him. Sebastian can just be a bit . . . domineering sometimes.'

Just like Judd, Kitty thought again. They all stared out of the window at the azure blue swimming pool and gently swaying trees. Why didn't one of them have the guts to challenge Judd and tell him that leaving was out of the question? Kitty almost laughed at the mere thought; as if *that* would ever happen. She knew better than anyone what happened when Judd's authority was questioned and, unconsciously, she lifted a hand to her left cheekbone which still felt tender after all this time. Deeply ashamed, she had never told a soul about it, although she suspected Elliot might have guessed. It had only happened once and even though Judd had been resolutely unapologetic afterwards, Kitty had realised that leaving him wasn't an option. Judd held on to all of his possessions; it was a strange obsession of his.

LA was in the throes of a heat wave, even though it was January, and Kitty bleakly wondered how she was going to cope out of her comfort zone. She had grown up in Boston; indeed, she was one of the 'Boston Delawares', an incredibly wealthy family who owned several businesses and most of the city itself. But since marrying Judd at the tender age of eighteen, LA had been her home and her family were the most important thing in Kitty's life.

'Are you going to be all right, Mom?' Elliot asked, staring at her in concern.

Kitty nodded, doing her best to look convincing. She was going to be all right – she *had* to be. Judd wasn't the man she had married; he was charismatic, commanding a room like a film star and, like most Americans, she was still bowled over by his upper-class English accent, but she had long ago faced up to the fact that Judd was also an unfaithful bully who had quite obviously married her for her money. At least she had her children, Kitty thought, wishing her middle son Ace could join them in England. His career as a NASCAR driver meant he had to stay in America but she hoped he'd be back in time from the racetrack to say goodbye to them all. Out of all the things she was going to miss about home, Ace was at the top of the list. Damn Judd for uprooting them all, Kitty thought as tears blurred the view of her beloved LA garden.

Feeling the adrenalin kick in like a cocaine high, Ace Harrington gripped the steering wheel of his beloved stock car and hit the gas hard. Taking the corner at high speed, he heard the tyres screech in protest but held his nerve and skilfully zipped past the other practising cars on the track, weaving in and out of the pack with ease.

Ace let out an excited whoop as the driver of a car alongside him spun off course and ended up back to front with smoke spiralling out of the engine. The cocky bastard had taken the corner too tight, Ace thought, spinning the steering wheel sharply to avoid a collision with a frantically zigzagging car. He'd ended up that way many a time in his NASCAR career but this year, things were going to be different. He knew he was seen as an irresponsible rich kid, with his father funding his team sponsorship as well as his swanky Bel Air apartment, and undeserving of his high profile on the NASCAR circuit. His love of danger and crazy addiction to speed had earned him the reputation of a wild child, someone who drove for the fun of it, rather than taking the sport seriously.

But, contrary to popular opinion, Ace wanted nothing more than to break free from his father's iron grip by winning some of the million-dollar prize money up for grabs. More to the point, he wanted to please his father and finally make him proud, a seemingly impossible task. In fact, Judd was demanding nothing less than perfection from him this year and he was unwilling to accept excuses of 'bad form', nor did he believe the spectacular crash Ace had suffered at the end of last year should stand in the way of his making it to the number one spot. Judd had bawled Ace out ferociously for his lack of concentration after the accident and Ace had chosen not to reveal the real reason behind the crash, knowing how unforgiving his father was.

He tightened his grip on the steering wheel and focused his grey eyes on the track. This year, he was determined to prove himself: to his team, to his fans – but most of all to his father. Hence driving an hour east of Los Angeles to practise repeatedly before the big races began and, for once, being one hundred per cent focused on driving without playing the fool.

God, he loved racing! Ace thought, nodding to his best friend and team mate Jerry, who was watching from the seating area. Charging down the final straight at breakneck speed, a Ace felt elated and alive. As ever, the sense of danger sent the blood pumping madly through his veins and in exhilaration he shot over the finish line and slid to a halt in a swirl of dust.

Ace eased himself out of the car window. Tearing his helmet off to reveal dishevelled mahogany hair and a tanned face, he checked his tyres intently. They could withstand high temperatures and speeds but the way he drove his cars, they frequently needed replacing, much to the fury of Joe Wilson, his team boss. Finding a slight bald patch, Ace crouched down to inspect it.

'Hey there!' cooed a voice loudly.

He jumped up, clutching his chest. 'Allegra! Jesus, you scared the fuck out of me.' He was astonished to see his on-off girlfriend leaning over the barrier at the edge of the racetrack. He hadn't expected to see her for another two weeks. An exotically beautiful model with long, tanned legs and a mane of wavy chestnut hair that hung past her shoulder blades, Allegra was as sleek as a Siamese cat. She was also wearing a crotch-skimming turquoise dress that made the most of her sensational figure and she had clearly forgotten her underwear.

Ace raked his dark auburn hair out of his eyes tiredly. 'What are you doing here? I thought you were in Milan being chased by randy Italians.'

'I was in Rome, not Milan,' she corrected him, frowning slightly. She pouted, meeting his sexy grey eyes. 'But I missed you so much I flew back early to see you. You weren't at the apartment so I guessed you'd be down here practising.' She ran her eyes over him lasciviously, knowing that under his suit, Ace's body was tanned all over and as well honed as a thoroughbred racehorse. 'Isn't it a wonderful surprise to see me?'

'Wonderful,' Ace murmured.

'When's your next race?' Allegra asked, feigning interest in his career as she leant in towards him with her cleavage on display.

'Not until February . . . Daytona.'

Hiding a smile, Ace unzipped his suit and climbed over the barrier. He was well aware Allegra didn't understand the first thing about NASCAR racing; she simply saw his job as glamorous and dangerous. She didn't have a clue that in terms of television ratings, it was one of the most viewed sports in the United States, second only to professional football.

Arriving at his prized car, a red Corvette C3, an original 1965 'Mako Shark II' his father had bought him for his twenty-first birthday two years ago, Ace and Allegra found Jerry leaning against it. With his preppy blond hair and chiselled chin, Jerry, who also worked as a model to help pay his way, looked as if he'd just stepped off a photo shoot.

'Good round?' he asked Ace, giving Allegra a cool stare. 'You picked up some impressive speed at the final stretch.'

'I'm on good form, can't wait for the Daytona. What about you?' Ace was taken aback when Allegra gave him a juicy kiss in front of Jerry, obscuring his view.

Jerry rolled his eyes. 'Not bad at all. Joe reckons I've got a good chance of really making my mark over the next couple of months if I keep practising.' He grinned. 'I can't believe how much practice I have to put in compared to you.'

Ace protested. 'Hey, I'm working really hard!'

'Yeah, for once!'

Jerry had met Ace at the Los Angeles Kart Club when they were kids. Jerry had gone to longingly watch the other kids racing, unable to afford it but dreaming of one day becoming a NASCAR driver. Having dismissed Ace as one of the lazy rich kids he despised so much, Jerry had been taken aback when Ace had stepped in to defend him against some boys who bullied him for being a pretty boy from the wrong side of the tracks.

From a very early age, Ace had been told he was simply too charming to be annoyed with for long and he had carried that mindset into his teenage years. Humorously telling the bullies to fuck off and pick on someone ugly, he joked to Jerry that being poor, he needed to preserve his beautiful profile in order to make some money. He had then generously shared his kart at the racetrack so that Jerry could practise too and they had been firm friends ever since, now sharing Ace's Bel Air apartment.

'What are you *doing* here?' Jerry narrowed his eyes at Allegra as she wound her sinewy body around Ace like a snake.

She gave him a withering stare. 'Well, I'm not here to see *you*, that's for sure.' She turned to Ace. 'I have my car. Shall I meet you back at the apartment?'

He nodded, watching her undulate away and climb into her flashy silver convertible. 'You could be a *bit* nicer to her, Jez,' Ace chided, giving his best friend an affable smile.

Jerry shuddered. 'Allegra's such a fucking pain in the ass! She's like an irritating wasp, always turning up and spoiling everything when you're having fun.' Truthfully, he had other reasons for detesting Allegra but he wasn't about to enlighten Ace about that. 'Hey, aren't you supposed to be saying goodbye to your folks before they fly to England tonight?'

Ace looked stricken. 'Shit, Jerry, I totally forgot the time!' Jumping into his car, he shot off in the direction of his parents' LA mansion without a second thought.

Jerry stared after him, wondering how long Allegra would sit in Ace's apartment before she realised she'd been stood up. Shrugging and knowing it was none of his business, Jerry jumped into his own car and headed for the nearest bar.

Savannah Summers climbed the fifth flight of stairs to her New York apartment, almost dropping the box she was struggling with. She groaned when she saw her mad old neighbour Rhea shuffling out of her doorway, clutching the grubby shopping bag that was as much a part of her outfit as her oversized puffa jacket and navy ankle boots. Savannah just wanted to be alone right now.

When Rhea caught sight of Savannah, her rheumy eyes softened in sympathy. 'How'd it go, kid?'

'I can safely say I've been to better funerals,' Savannah replied. She wasn't lying. Funerals were never a barrel of laughs but the cheap coffin, the absence of flowers and the small huddle of mourners had made this one the pits.

Rhea scratched her hairy chin. 'Not much of a turnout?'

Savannah shrugged, her dark red hair hiding her eyes.

'Poor thing,' clucked Rhea, shaking her head. Savannah was a tough, sassy girl with an attitude the size of Manhattan but underneath it all, there was a big heart in there. She waggled her finger. 'You should try and find that father of yours.' She nodded to emphasise her point. 'He owes you. And let's face it, kid, you don't have anyone else now.'

Heading inside her apartment as Rhea traipsed downstairs mumbling under her breath, Savannah set the box down on the bed. It was full of her mother's belongings – such as they were – and she peered into it dejectedly. A couple of tired-looking stage outfits with torn sequins and faded feathers, a bundle of photographs and the odd piece of cheap costume jewellery, the box was a sad collection of effects, a paltry representation of an otherwise colourful life.

Stamping angrily on a cockroach that had scuttled out from under the bed, Savannah stared out of her tiny window at the distant view of the Empire State Building. Rising majestically out of the misty New York skyline, it was lit up with twinkling red and yellow bulbs which provided a warm glow in the darkening sky.

She threw herself on her bed. What if she ended up like her mother? Alone and miserably drunk, Candi had barely known what day it was at the end. The mere idea chilled Savannah to the bone, particularly since it wasn't impossible, the way she was carrying on. What had her mother ever achieved? Savannah wondered critically. A lifetime spent chasing a dream; always an 'aspiring' singer-dancer and never a successful one; disappointment, loneliness and poverty driving her to drink herself to death in dodgy strip clubs as she drunkenly peeled off her clothes in front of perverted losers. Not that Savannah had sunk that low . . . yet.

Tugging a torn photograph she'd never seen before out of the box, Savannah's mouth tightened as she looked at the unsmiling, red-haired man she'd seen in other photos. She knew it was her father. Her mother had obviously kept some of the photos back for herself, no doubt mooning over them when she was drunk, wondering what might have been if they'd stayed together or some such romantic nonsense.

Daddy dearest, Savannah thought scornfully. What a useless asshole! She'd never met him, she didn't know his name and she had never been remotely interested in making contact with the man she knew had dropped her mother when she was pregnant. About to rip the photo into shreds and toss it in the can with the rest of the rubbish, Savannah couldn't help thinking of Rhea's earlier words. 'Find that father of yours . . .' she had said sagely. 'He owes you.'

Did he? Savannah supposed in some ways he did, especially after what her mother had sacrificed to bring her up. He had certainly had nothing to do with her for the past twenty-one years but she wasn't sure how he would respond to her appearing in his life out of the blue. Would he refuse to see her? Deny her existence? She had no idea. Until now, she had never cared.

About to screw the photograph up, she noticed the name '*J. Harrington, Bucks*' scrawled across the back of it. She paused. So that was his name, was it? But was he a Jack? A John? And what the hell was Bucks, anyway? Savannah had never known anything about him apart from what he looked like; to her irritation, his butch jaw and arrogant features were imprinted on her brain even though she had tried to obliterate him from her memory. And she could hardly ignore the red hair, she thought, touching a rueful hand to her own auburn tresses.

But now that she knew his name, Savannah was intrigued. Thoughtfully, she wound her mother's favourite pink feather boa round her neck, finding the stench of cheap perfume strangely comforting as she inhaled it. Abruptly, she made a decision. She lived alone in her apartment with dirty cockroaches for company and the few friends she had were all in the same boat as her – waitressing to make ends meet while they attended endless auditions. Savannah realised she had nothing to lose – not now her mother was dead. Shocked to find a solitary tear trickling down her cheek, Savannah hastily wiped it away with the feather boa and threw the pink fluffy thing back in the box.

Whacking another cockroach soundly with a book, she curled up on her bed and thought about what she would say to her good-for-nothing father when she met him. What did he do? she wondered. Knowing her luck, he was most likely a low-life on benefits but maybe he could throw her a few dollars . . . or maybe he lived in a slightly better part of the city and could offer her shelter. Or maybe 'Bucks' wasn't even in New York City. It sounded faintly British but she was probably way off the mark.

Either way, he was her only living relative now and Rhea was right, Savannah decided grimly as she watched the bright lights of New York twinkle and glitter in the darkening sky. He *owed* her.

Chapter Two

In his spacious London office, Lochlin Maguire looked up as his efficient PA Erica strode towards his desk.

'Thought you might want to see this,' she said, handing him a printed announcement. She watched him scan through it, his jet-black hair falling forward as he concentrated. He was an incredibly handsome man, she thought neutrally, studying the discreetly expensive grey and white shirt that somehow brought out the green of his eyes.

Ruggedly Irish, she decided, the thinking woman's crumpet, if you like, with a deliciously soft Irish accent that could melt the coldest of hearts. Not her cup of tea, naturally; he was in his mid-forties and she preferred her men rather more young and vibrant. Like Shay, Erica thought dreamily, staring at the family portrait on the wall and homing in on Lochlin's good-looking son.

'The Jett Record Corporation,' Lochlin read, leaning back in his chair. He prided himself on knowing the client list and key staff of every other record company in existence but he had never heard of this corporation. He shrugged, his green eyes twinkling at her. 'I can't say I know anything about them.'

Erica tore her eyes away from Shay's achingly perfect cheek-bones with difficulty. 'No one does. I've called all my contacts but none of them seem to have a clue.' She consulted her notes. 'My friend Marissa says that some sort of clandestine takeover has taken place but there hasn't been a formal announcement in the press yet.'

Lochlin glanced at the piece of paper again, deep in thought.

Jett, he thought tremulously, feeling a shiver go through him. That had been the childhood nickname of someone he would rather forget, someone whose memory lay deeply buried.

'Would you like me to do some digging?' Erica offered, wondering why Lochlin had turned pale.

Lochlin recovered himself and gave her a warm smile. 'Can't hurt,' he said. What were the odds? he asked himself. Surely it was nothing to do with the past; it couldn't be.

'You have that meeting with Darcy Middleton in five minutes in the boardroom, remember.' Erica paused by the door. 'Oh, and Charlie Valentine called again.'

Lochlin groaned guiltily. 'Oh God. Put him off for a bit longer, if you can, Erica. I really need to have a think about this.' He sighed. 'Charlie's a great friend but his career has pretty much ground to a halt.'

'I'm sure you're aware but his contract is up shortly,' Erica informed him helpfully as she withdrew. Frankly, she thought Lochlin was far too nice to Charlie Valentine. He might be a friend but his career was in the shitter. Still, that was Lochlin all over, loyal to a fault, even if it did occasionally affect his normally superb judgement, Erica mused wryly.

Lochlin stared at the imposing family portrait that dominated one wall of his mahogany-lined office, his knuckles turning white as they gripped the arms of his chair. His father Niall had moved the entire family from Dublin to Buckinghamshire to realise his dream thirty-five years ago and had built Shamrock, a successful record company, from scratch. Starting off by looking after a couple of incredible jazz artists he'd spotted in a dingy club in Soho, Niall had worked every hour of the day and sometimes the night, toiling away until he had created something he could be proud of – something he could leave to his sons or, as it turned out, Lochlin thought despairingly, his only son. God, it had all been such a mess back then. And as for his mother . . . who knew it was possible to die of a broken heart?

Lochlin sighed and glanced at all the gold and platinum records in glass frames that took pride of place on the wall opposite the Maguire family portrait. He was so proud of Shamrock and everything it had achieved, both in his father's lifetime and under his own direction. The company was doing fantastically well and he was about to sign up one of the hottest girl groups since the Spice Girls had strutted across stages in leopard skin and Union Jacks, as well as having his eye on a number of other undiscovered talents.

Including Iris, Lochlin thought tenderly, wondering if he would ever have the guts to send his stunningly beautiful, ferociously talented but rather vulnerable daughter out into the dangerous world of showbiz. After all, look what had happened to Tavvy all those years ago when she had fallen in with the wrong crowd . . .

Lochlin wondered if that was the reason he kept shooting home from his Kensington office earlier these days – a desire to spend more time with his family. Lochlin had always loved his job but recently, and with increasing frequency, he found himself thinking longingly of Tavvy's warm, welcoming body and the safe, cosy sanctuary of Pembleton. He loved being at home and always had done; the rambling, overgrown garden and surrounding bluebell woods filled his heart with joy. But so did Shamrock . . . didn't it?

Christ, what was wrong with him? Was he losing his touch? Frustrated at his whimsical thoughts, Lochlin pulled himself together. Darcy Middleton was waiting for him next door and he had to go and wow her with a dazzling pitch that would hopefully impress her enough to sign up with them for the year. She was the most sought-after PR consultant in the music business, with a reputation for tough talking and shrewd business sense. Having already put a number of flagging businesses back on the top spot, Lochlin had no doubt Darcy could put Shamrock streets ahead of its competitors.

He cast his eyes down to the announcement about the Jett

Record Corporation, then put it to one side. Gathering up his paperwork in preparation for his meeting with Darcy, he hoped to God for the first time in his life that his gut instincts were totally off the mark and that the Jett Record Corporation had nothing whatsoever to do with Judd Harrington.

At Brockett Hall, Kitty Harrington was freezing cold, and bundled up in several thick jumpers in a redundant attempt to recreate the warm glow of the LA sunshine. Sorting through her wardrobe despondently, she wondered if, along with her home and her heart, she had somehow left her favourite Caroline Herrera cocktail dress behind as well.

Kitty sank down on to the bed. She missed her bridge and coffee-morning friends more than she had imagined she would and suddenly realised how much she had relied on them to keep her sane. Now she felt like the proverbial fish out of water. Kitty knew it was February, but why was it so horribly dark here all the time?

Grey, shapeless clouds hung over Brockett Hall like harbingers of doom and a relentlessly dismal drizzle trickled down the windows and made Kitty want to dash around turning all the lights on, even though it was only ten o'clock in the morning. She caught sight of a ravishing house in the distance which managed to look warm and inviting in spite of the turgid weather, its russet bricks and slatted roof resembling something out of a Victorian novel. Kitty wondered who lived there. Someone terribly glamorous, she decided.

Kitty read the invitation again anxiously, wondering what the hell she was supposed to wear to a ball. The Valentines' Ball, no less, hosted by Charlie and Susannah Valentine, who were, by all accounts, their neighbours. Kitty had no idea what the party-going etiquette was in the depths of the English countryside. Did the women dress up to the nines in glittery ball gowns and fur stoles or did they just throw on their tweed skirts and twinsets and rough it, corgis in tow? She cursed Judd for accepting the invite without even consulting her but guessed he had been impressed by the heavy ivory card with its scarlet edging and Gothic lettering.

As Kitty fretted over the minefield of potential social faux pas, she paused and thought about Ace, thousands of miles away in LA. Being born three months prematurely whilst Kitty was on a business trip in England with Judd, Ace had nearly died and the image of him curled up in his incubator as tubes breathed for him was imprinted on Kitty's brain for ever. As a result, Ace had always been terribly spoilt but, being lovable by nature, it wasn't exactly a hardship for any of them.

Kitty sighed. She missed Ace enormously already but she detested the way Judd showed his middle son such blatant favouritism. He showered Ace with cars and apartments and kept his NASCAR team up and running with sponsorship deals and donations. Still, even though Ace's racy lifestyle and flagrant womanising delighted Judd, the critic in him still managed to find fault. Poor Ace's attempts to impress his father seemed doomed to failure, Kitty thought sadly.

Taking some of her dresses downstairs to show Martha, Kitty wondered how her daughter-in-law was coping with the upheaval. It troubled Kitty that Sebastian made his wife's life hell with his critical putdowns. Gentle Martha was too soft to tell him where to go, which was exactly what he needed. Mind you, she was a fine one to talk, Kitty reminded herself unhappily. When was the last time *she'd* put Judd in his place? In fact, when had she *ever* told Judd he was in the wrong?

Heaving the dresses on to an armchair in the sitting room, Kitty resolved to be more supportive of Martha in the future. Women like them should stick together.

'Where's Martha?' she asked Elliot as he looked up from his book. He looked uncomfortable sitting in one of the sparse chairs covered in eau-di-Nil silk Judd had ordered.

'In her room crying, the poor thing,' Elliot said with a frown. He held up *The Beautiful and the Damned* by F. Scott Fitzgerald. 'This would make an amazing play.'

Kitty smiled. Elliot, with his brooding grey eyes and floppy blond hair was a heartthrob in the making, as well as being the academic of the family. It was a well-known fact that Sebastian's law degree had been granted on the basis of Judd's hefty donations and, even at a young age, Ace's head had been too full of dreams of racing cars to concentrate on his studies for more than a few minutes. Elliot, however, was intellectual and completely oblivious of the giggling group of girls that had always followed him around in LA.

Why he didn't have a girlfriend was beyond her, Kitty thought, hoping some pretty English girl might take his fancy. Elliot hadn't uttered a single word of complaint since leaving the States, but she knew he was floundering as much as she was in their new surroundings and dreading starting a new school. He was sixteen years old and he must be missing his friends and his days surfing at the beach. Judd hated the fact that Elliot wasn't into more macho sports and Kitty remembered with absolute clarity the day Judd had cruelly questioned Elliot's paternity, unable to believe he had sired such a sensitive, artistic boy.

Sensing her scrutiny, Elliot closed his book and gestured to the dresses. 'Deciding what to wear to that party?'

'It's not a party, it's a *ball*.' Kitty handed over the invitation and raised helpless grey eyes to his. 'I haven't the faintest idea which dress to choose.'

Elliot frowned as he read the invite. 'Mom, this is a party hosted by Charlie Valentine!'

'I know. He's our neighbour. So what?'

'He's also a famous rock star.' Elliot laughed. 'You must know who he is, Mom! He sings kinda cheesy nineties rock and wears tight leather trousers and eyeliner. Pretty dated but still, he's a proper celebrity. We didn't really get to meet any of those in LA, apart from some of Ace's glitzy friends. My friends are gonna be sick with envy when they hear about this!'

'I didn't even realise,' Kitty murmured, gripped by a new wave of insecurity. She had been worried enough about going to an English ball, she hadn't realised it was hosted by British rock star royalty.

Elliot grinned. 'We're in the back of beyond but there are pop stars on every corner here, can you believe it? The lady in the village shop told me Tavvy Edwards lives in that amazing house across the fields – she sang that famous song, "Obsession", remember? Apparently she gave up singing years ago and married some guy called Lochlin Maguire.'

Kitty's blond eyebrows knitted together as she tried to put a face to the name. The song sounded familiar but Tavvy's name didn't. However, she did know Judd had mentioned a man called Lochlin Maguire years ago. For some bizarre reason, he detested Lochlin with a passion and when she'd quizzed him on it, Judd had yelled at her, telling her never to mention Lochlin's name again. Kitty guessed Judd had some unfinished business with this Lochlin Maguire, whoever he was, and she felt a tremor of unease. Judd held grudges more than anyone she knew; look at the way he'd cut himself off from his family all those years ago!

All of a sudden, the move to England felt significant. It couldn't be a coincidence that an arch enemy of Judd's lived so close. Kitty sat down abruptly, wincing as her bottom made contact with the hard chair.

Elliot didn't notice his mother's discomfort. 'I have to call my friends. They're gonna think I've been invited to Hugh Hefner's place. Where's my cell?' He stopped himself. 'I mean, my *mobile* phone. Have to pick up all the new lingo.' He paused in the doorway. 'I wouldn't worry too much about clothes, Mom. I reckon the flashier the better.' Elliot gave her a reassuring smile. 'Hey, maybe this place won't be so dull, after all.'

Kitty nodded brightly as he disappeared. Elliot was probably right but learning that Lochlin Maguire lived only a few miles away, she now felt certain the move to England had a much more sinister agenda than she'd imagined. What the hell was Judd up to?

Darcy Middleton shrugged her arms into the luxuriously fluffy hotel robe and helped herself to another glass of champagne. She surveyed the hotel room, her hazel eyes giving the suite a practised once-over. It was as opulent as she would expect for the extortionate prices the hotel charged and handsomely decked out with the prerequisite plasma TVs and MP3 ports, as well as an abundance of Thassos marble in the bathrooms. The trouble with these sorts of suites, Darcy mused, was that they soon became rather samey.

God, I'm *bored*, she thought brusquely. Of this affair, and of the dead-end job she had tired of within weeks. She thought about her meeting with Lochlin Maguire at the Shamrock Music Group offices the other day. She hadn't made a decision to take him up on his very generous job offer but she was intrigued that Lochlin had approached her in the first place. The record label had a fabulous reputation. Lochlin was renowned for having the Midas touch when it came to acquiring new acts and his loyalty and professionalism were legendary.

He wasn't unattractive either, Darcy mused, stretching luxuriously. Married, of course – they all were – but that was hardly an impediment. Rumour had it that Lochlin was still hopelessly besotted with his wife Tavvy, but in Darcy's experience, even the most devoted of men could be lured away with the right persuasion. She stretched out one of her long legs and smirked. Cocking her ear towards the bathroom, she became aware of her hapless lover's voice talking into his mobile phone, his tone frantically apologetic.

'I do miss you, darling,' he was saying, sounding whiny and adolescent, in spite of his years, 'you *and* little Horatio. It's just that I have this really important business meeting and I can't possibly get away just yet.' There was a pause. 'Horatio, my little prince! Who's Daddy's favourite boy? Oh, don't cry, my brave soldier, you're making Daddy so sad . . .'

Darcy's lip curled with contempt and she almost threw up her vintage champagne. This is *so* over, she decided, knowing she had actually made that decision a while ago. God, how could Darren be such a bloody hypocrite? *Business meeting* indeed . . .

Darcy tore the robe off and quickly slipped her black lacy La Perla thong back on. She wondered if Darren's wife knew the 'business meeting' in question had actually involved dining out at the absurdly expensive new restaurant of a famous TV chef, followed by a three-hour marathon of screwing his mistress senseless in a penthouse suite in one of the most sought-after hotels in London – the cost of which could probably pay for a family of four to go wild at Disneyland for a week.

Married men were all the same, Darcy thought scornfully; they wanted a bit on the side as well as their dutiful wives at home and the lengths they would go to in order to hide their deceit never ceased to amaze her.

Enough was enough, she thought as she hunted for her bra, her mouth tightening. Her affair with Darren was well and truly over and it was about time she got the hell out of his life – and his crappy job. Abandoning any thought of finding her bra and lamenting the loss of such an exquisitely expensive piece of lingerie, Darcy shrugged her arms into her navy Diana von Furstenberg dress and tied it smartly around her narrow waist. She had known Darren was married, of course, but that wasn't her problem! Darcy was an intelligent, successful music consultant in her early thirties with a fabulous flat in Kensington. She dated rich, powerful men and had affairs indiscriminately. The martial set-up of her chosen partners was none of her business, she was a free agent and able to do whatever she pleased without conscience.

And that was just the way she liked it, Darcy thought, pushing her feet into her four-inch navy heels; short and sweet, and when the fun was over, the man in question could go back to his unsuspecting wife with his sex drive rejuvenated and his tail – or rather his *dick* – firmly between his legs.

'Where are you going?' Darren demanded, emerging from the bathroom. His sheepish expression turned thunderous as he watched her scoop the tasteful Cartier jewellery he'd given her the night before into her handbag.

'I'm leaving. Look, go home to your wife,' she advised him shortly as she twisted her long cinnamon-brown hair up into a chic chignon. '*And* your son.' She touched up her make-up, noticing that Darren had turned the exact shade of her scarlet lipstick.

'You . . . you can't do this,' he spluttered. Even as their relationship crumbled, he couldn't help noticing Darcy looked sensational; her fantastic body sheathed in the expensive dress, her hair and make-up immaculate. She was ballsy but incredibly feminine, not a patch on his plain wife. 'I have the room booked all night . . . I've told my wife I won't be home until tomorrow lunchtime . . .'

'I'm sorry, Darren, but that's not my problem, is it?' She raised her eyebrows at him. 'Seriously, maybe you should just tell your wife you like your ass whipped like a naughty schoolboy and then you wouldn't need to go elsewhere for it.'

Mouthing furiously like a gormless goldfish, Darren took a step towards her but she halted him with an icy stare.

'And before you dare to fire me, don't worry . . . I quit.' She let out a sigh of resignation, well versed in the required etiquette as an affair with a married man with a reputation to protect came to an end. 'And you have my word that no one will ever know about our non-professional relationship, so you have nothing to fret about.' She headed out to the lifts, glad the deed was done. The affair had become dull and the sex even duller, and her minor role at the company was hardly going to set her CV on fire. *People Records* were small fry and even though they had presented her with an interesting challenge at the outset, it was about time she put her substantial skills to the test once more. Inside the lift, she noticed in the mirror that a full, creamy breast had almost escaped and, languorously, she rearranged her neckline.

God, was it *that* difficult to find a strong, successful man who didn't waste time regretting his choices or apologising for his behaviour? Darcy supposed she was after someone like her father; Christ, what would fans of Freud make of *that*? Her father had been an attractive, successful businessman and an authoritarian presence and, truthfully, he had frightened the life out of her but she had idolised him with something close to hero worship. At least *he* showed her attention, unlike her mother who never seemed to take an interest in her daughter's achievements.

Darcy stabbed the lift button impatiently. Her father had instilled in her a need to be self-sufficient and at the age of sixteen when he had died suddenly of a heart attack, she had left the family home for good, severing all contact with the mother who'd never been there for her. Darcy had resolved not to become a needy housewife, stuck at home with the kids and, in honour of her father, she had set out to become successful and independent. Striking and good-looking rather than conventionally pretty, Darcy acted like a man in the bedroom as well as in the office and she had soon gained a reputation for being a ball-breaker – a nickname she welcomed.

It was only at night that Darcy's conscience occasionally troubled her and she allowed herself to wonder why her mother had always flinched when her father had come into the room and why she had never offered an opinion on anything. Darcy had long since learnt to shake such uneasy feelings off, however; and in her waking hours, she refused to linger on the possibilities. She and her mother hadn't spoken since her father had died and Darcy preferred it that way.

Her eyes lit up as she read a notice on her BlackBerry about a new company called the Jett Record Corporation which apparently had the music industry bubbling over with speculation and excitement. She tapped her chin thoughtfully, deciding to keep Lochlin Maguire waiting a while longer while she did some research.

Aware that two fat cats in ill-fitting suits were admiring her protruding nipples as she stepped out of the lift, Darcy extinguished their ardour with a frosty stare. They weren't handsome enough or rich enough for her to waste her time with but, knowing how tricky it could be to get a cab at this time of the day, Darcy gave the doorman a full-on smile and a discreet eyeful of her fabulous bra-less breasts that had his trousers pitching a tent and his fingers snapping feverishly to bring a taxi to her side.

Darcy settled herself in the back of the cab and read the notice about Jett again. Something about this new company had sparked her professional interest and the thrill of something new and exciting was almost sexual. Squirming slightly, Darcy felt a throb between her legs that Darren had *never* been able to achieve and she grinned.

Tavvy Maguire winced as a biting wind whipped her hair around her face. Dressed in a pair of faux leopard-skin boots from her pop star days, woolly tights and an old black sweater of Lochlin's that reached her knees, she lovingly rubbed a flea-bitten old mare on the nose.

'There, there, old girl,' she soothed, feeling the horse shivering with fright beneath her fingers. 'You're safe now.' How dare that *bastard* of a farmer treat horses like this, Tavvy thought furiously. Saving animals was her passion; she had set up her charitable organisation, Noah's Ark, a few years ago to rescue abused animals and it kept her extremely busy. Although funded by royalties from Tavvy's pop career and donations from wealthy locals, the charity brought in the bulk of its income at fundraising events such as the Midsummer Ball Tavvy hosted every June.

She frowned as a haunting melody that had been tantalising her for the past few days popped back into her head again. This hadn't happened to her for years, not since she had given up her pop career, and Tavvy was far too busy looking after her family and her animals to be writing songs these days.

'Oh, the poor thing!' Caitie panted as she joined her mother at the gate. Sporting tights patterned with pink hearts that were most assuredly *not* regulation school kit, teamed with her favourite biker boots, Caitie wore the rest of her maroon and white uniform with panache. 'Christ, don't let Iris see this mare; she'll be in bits like she is at the vet's.' She pulled a face. 'Iris is too soft-hearted to work with animals. Still, as soon as Daddy pulls his finger out, she'll be a famous singer, won't she?'

Tavvy grimaced. She didn't want to think about the possibility of Lochlin putting Iris's pop career on hold again because Tavvy knew it would destroy her eldest daughter. She handed the mare over to Petra, her part-time assistant, and watched as she tenderly guided the damaged horse into a stable. 'I've named her Moccachino,' Tavvy added, her jerky movements indicating how angry she was. 'That bastard of a farmer didn't even give her a name.' She linked her arm through Caitie's as they walked back to the house.

Caitie suppressed a smile and glanced at her mother approvingly. With cheeks the colour of Pink Lady apples from the cold, Tavvy was much prettier than any of her friend's mothers.

'Now, what on earth am I going to wear to the Valentines' Ball?' Caitie demanded as they strode back to Pembleton. 'Jasmine can't come because she's still in Italy with her parents so I'll be at the mercy of the Valentine twins. I need to look my best.' She called on her considerable acting skills and widened her eyes. 'I guess I could always wear my school uniform and go for early Britney chic . . . although I'll probably catch the eye of some dreadful old perv.'

Tavvy eyed her daughter with a twitching mouth. The Valentine twins had blond hair extensions and over-padded bras and, compared to Caitie, who was naturally pretty with merry green eyes and a mass of dark ringlets, they looked like plastic dolls. Passionate and outspoken, Caitie fell in love on a daily basis and always seemed to find the good in everyone she met. Keen to emulate the career of her idol, Kate Winslet, Caitie was determined to become a serious actress but, even though her acting was superb, Tavvy had her own methods of dealing with her daughter's dramatic declarations.

'What a *shame*,' she murmured. 'Me and Iris were planning to lend you something but if you're planning on bagging a geriatric, you might as well go in your wellies and a waxed jacket, darling.'

Caitie looked panic-stricken. 'No, I'll borrow something from you or Iris!' she assured her mother, as they approached the front door.

Smiling, Tavvy gazed up at Pembleton distractedly, thinking how glorious it looked in the dying rose-hued light, its timber frames neatly edging the slightly rundown terracotta brickwork. Lochlin's father had bought the dilapidated home years ago when Shamrock had finally turned a corner and made some serious money, and Niall and Colleen Maguire had spent years lovingly restoring it until the terrible tragedy had rocked their solid, close-knit existence. Then, after Colleen's subsequent and very sudden death, Niall had moved back to Ireland with Lochlin's three sisters, leaving Lochlin in charge of both Shamrock and Pembleton. Now full of random memorabilia from Tavvy's pop star days, CDs and records stacked from floor to ceiling and souvenirs from holidays all over the world, their home was cosy and homely and Tavvy's favourite place in the world.

Opening the creaky kitchen door, Tavvy came face to face with a hot and bothered Iris.

'We can't have toast for supper,' Iris panted, sheepishly holding up a horse comb. 'I've buggered this up totally.' She pushed the toaster to one side before smiling dreamily. 'Did I tell you Ollie Ramshaw's taking me to the Valentines' Ball?'

'God, I'm jealous. He's so handsome.' Caitie pouted, wondering how Iris managed to look so beautiful with her tawny-blond hair held up with a pencil and her long legs hidden under a pair of

Shay's old jeans. 'Mind you, those carnations cost the same price as a Toblerone,' she commented, glancing disparagingly at some squashed pink flowers in a jug.

'I don't care. Since Claudia buggered off to Sweden to become an au pair, I'm like Billy No Mates. Ollie's my only friend.' Iris gave a regretful shrug. 'I suppose I could have moved to London with Emma and Daisy . . . just think, wild parties every night, gorgeous, unsuitable men . . . but I was hoping I'd be singing professionally by then.' Her face fell.

'How are your rehearsals going?' Tavvy asked, studying her daughter. Iris always gnawed her bottom lip when she was nervous; an unconscious habit she'd developed as a little girl.

Iris shrugged. 'Not bad. Just worried about doing your song justice. It's such a well-known number . . . everyone loves it. I-I'm worried I won't be up to it. Oh God! And there's my stutter! What if I do that during my performance?' She clutched her hair in frustration and the pencil fell out, her tawny hair tumbling to her shoulders.

'You won't,' Caitie assured her, exchanging a look with her mother. She knew how hard Iris had worked on removing all traces of her speech impediment but it still emerged when she was nervous. She adored singing but performing petrified her. Caitie, along with the rest of the family, felt absurdly protective of Iris; she was incredibly talented but she possessed a vulnerable quality that had the whole family wishing they could keep her from harm. Bullied for years for stuttering and stammering in class, Iris had bravely, on her last day of school, made a speech about overcoming adversity to a packed assembly hall. Having practised it tirelessly, the speech was made without a single mistake or stumble and Shay and Caitie whooped triumphantly from the back of the hall. It had been a small but poignant victory and Iris hadn't looked back since.

'Just stay calm,' Tavvy advised Iris. 'Your voice is far better than mine ever was.' She meant it. In her pop star days, she had found performing difficult – the attention was overwhelming and her nerves had been crippling, far worse than Iris's. She had always been far happier tucked away in a room writing songs, something she longed to do now, especially when she was haunted by a gorgeous melody that wouldn't leave her be. Tavvy pushed the thought aside; she simply didn't have time for such things these days, not with a family to look after and her animal charity to run. Just as she was about to reassure Iris that her father would come round about her career soon, Lochlin arrived, blowing on his cold hands and taking over the room with his broad shoulders.

'Fuck, it's freezing out there!' He tore his coat off to reveal a green, threadbare jumper.

'You didn't go into work like that, did you, Dad?' Iris giggled, poking a finger through a hole in the elbow of his jumper.

The green eyes Caitie and Shay had inherited from him danced merrily. 'Don't be daft, I'm not *that* senile! I've just been outside on the phone to Erica. She was telling me about this new record company.' He pulled Tavvy into his arms and felt her shiver with pleasure.

Caitie tutted. Her parents were so embarrassing! They were always making out and they had a maddening habit of being secretive, as if they shared some special bond no one else was part of. 'I think Shay was going on about that the other day. The Jett Record Corporation or something?'

Lochlin and Tavvy exchanged a pointed glance.

Caitie pounced on them. 'What was *that*?'

'What?' Lochlin answered evasively.

'That look! As if you've both got a secret you don't want us to know about.'

'Don't be silly,' Tavvy snapped, uncharacteristically sharp. She turned away and bumped straight into the broad chest of her son Shay.

Tall and imposing, Shay strode across the kitchen. 'God, I'm starving. I haven't eaten a bite all day.' Flinging his wide-shouldered frame into a chair, he sniffed the air, hoping one of his culinary-challenged family had started preparing supper before sighing and picking up a copy of the latest *NME*.

'I heard the twins are wearing Dolce and Gabbana to the ball,' Caitie informed him with a doleful expression. She couldn't believe her brother could look so sickeningly stylish in an old grey cashmere jumper and a pair of battered black jeans.

Shay shuddered comically. 'Urgh! Just thinking about those two brings me out in a rash. They're like a walking advert for STDs.'

Iris looked shocked. 'Don't be mean, Shay, they're just rather . . . over-spirited.'

'Over-sexed more like,' Shay retorted. 'You're far too nice, Iris. Those twins are toxic.'

Caitie gave him a wicked smile. 'So, how is sloaney Saskia?' Saskia was Shay's current girlfriend but considering he went through relationships the way other men went through under-pants, Caitie was astounded her brother hadn't tired of Saskia already.

'Lovely.' Shay yanked one of Caitie's jet-black curls. 'Much nicer than you, for a start. You'll never get a boyfriend if you keep being such a bitch.'

'God, really?' Caitie paused then narrowed her eyes. 'Hang on, that can't be right. Tons of your girlfriends have been absolute cows!'

Shay roared with laughter. He wasn't about to enlighten Caitie about Saskia who, aside from having a surprising fondness for slightly kinky sex, had in the beginning shown real signs of being 'the one'. But as time had gone on, Shay had realised they had less in common than he'd thought and he knew he would have to end it soon before things became more serious.

Shay frowned. It wasn't Saskia's fault, but he wanted more. He wanted someone who loved music as much as he did, someone he could endlessly discuss jazz and Louis Armstrong with, a woman who was intellectual and exciting. Shay wanted to feel real passion and, sadly, Saskia didn't make him feel that way.

'Charlie's sent me another text!' Lochlin howled in utter vexation. 'He's badgering me about his flagging career and I haven't a clue what to say to him. I mean, Jaysus, I think the world of Chas, but I'm not a fucking magician!'

About to offer some advice, Shay closed his mouth and disappeared behind the *NME* again. His father didn't seem to take kindly to his recommendations at the moment so he might as well keep his mouth shut, even if he *did* think he knew how to breathe life into Charlie Valentine's lacklustre career.

Bright but bored by school, Shay's business acumen was instinctive rather than academic. Flying by the seat of his pants in each job he'd had, including his current one at a music magazine, Shay had recently and rather unexpectedly felt increasingly keen for people to take him seriously. Especially his father. Belatedly, Shay had realised he only had himself to blame for his playboy profile but still, it was exasperating when he knew damn well he could solve his father's problems in a matter of seconds.

'What's for dinner?' he asked suddenly, feeling them all staring at him. 'Oh, I get it, you're waiting for *me* to cook. Again.' Jumping up and yanking open the fridge, he was soon expertly chopping shallots and ordering Caitie and Iris around as he swiftly cooked steak Diane for five.

As he opened a bottle of Chateauneuf-du-Pape, Lochlin couldn't help wondering why he felt such a sense of impending doom. He longed to talk to Tavvy about his ludicrous fears surrounding the new record label, Jett, but he didn't want to worry her.

Feeling Lochlin's arm snaking around her waist, Tavvy's attention began to drift. Staring out into the darkening sky as it turned the garden into a magical inky wilderness, she was again reminded of the bewitching melody that had been haunting her for days. It had light and shade and exquisite chord changes that wound themselves around her like old friends . . .

If only she could shake it off, Tavvy thought distractedly, wishing for the first time in years that she could just have five minutes to herself to capture the song on paper . . .

Chapter Three

'Now, for the party, do you think the black leather or the white jeans?' Charlie Valentine wondered, preening himself in front of the huge Gothic mirror that almost obscured an entire wall. His chest was bare apart from the heavy cross he always wore and he puffed as he struggled with the zip of the black leather trousers.

'Well, the white jeans went down a storm at your sell-out tour in two thousand and four,' Susannah told him, hoping he'd take the hint. Aside from being too tight, the jeans had a nasty sweat stain around the crotch and really shouldn't be worn by the over-forties.

'You're right,' Charlie murmured, missing her point as he struck another pose in the mirror.

Susannah suppressed a sigh. God, it was difficult living with an ego maniac! In his day, Charlie Valentine had been an absolute heartbreaker, sex on legs with a gravelly voice and a career in the stratosphere. These days . . . Susannah tried not to roll her eyes as Charlie gyrated his skinny hips in the mirror, his face contorted in what he called his 'rock star orgasm face'. These days, as much as she adored him, Susannah couldn't help thinking Charlie was more like a dad dancing at a wedding – dated and ever so slightly embarrassing.

Their home, a rather vulgar, Gothic-style mansion Charlie had bought years ago with his first million, was stuffed full of garish rock and roll paraphernalia and overpriced antiques. It had become as famous as Charlie himself after a series of high-profile parties back in the eighties and nineties but as much as he loved his home, Charlie was driven less by his desire for wealth and more by his love of being on the road and singing to crowds of screaming women. Loving his career as much as he did, it was killing him that interest in his music was waning and that his most popular tracks hadn't been downloaded on I-Tunes half as much as he hoped they would be.

'Bloody Lochlin wouldn't even give me the time of day when I phoned him about my career again,' Charlie griped, drawing a smudgy blue line round his eyes with one of Susannah's long-last pencils, the latest product in the make-up line she'd developed five years ago. 'I've left him countless text messages too, but I don't think he's going to arrange a comeback tour for me, even though I'm his fucking friend.'

Staring at her husband in the mirror, Susannah wanted to tell Charlie he was far too old to get away with 'guy-liner'. She'd met Charlie when she'd been the make-up artist for him and his band and, a charmer with practised lines and come-to-bed blue eyes, it hadn't taken Charlie long to sweet-talk her into his trailer. Four weeks later he had proposed to her. Happily accepting, Susannah had been stunned when Charlie had blithely continued shagging young groupies, barely stopping to buy her a chunky emerald engagement ring before ducking back into his trailer with a fan.

Loving Charlie as much as she did, Susannah had learnt to make peace with that aspect of their marriage and he always came back to her. Charlie was simply addicted to the rock and roll lifestyle he had dreamt of since he was a boy. The trouble was, those crazy days were over and Susannah wasn't sure Charlie's career had any life left in it.

She went out on a limb. 'How's this for an "out there" idea? Why don't you just hang up the spangly neck scarves once and for all and kick back?' She wondered if Charlie knew how much the harsh lighting was showing up his wrinkles, and made a mental note to slip some of the new wonder foundation she'd created into his bathroom cabinet.

Wincing as Charlie's expression turned thunderous, Susannah pushed ahead. 'You know I'm your biggest fan, but you haven't written a new song in ages and if you keep churning out the same old stuff, you're going to end up looking like a has-been. Even though you're not, Chas, of course you're not,' she added hurriedly.

Peeved, Charlie ran a hand through his bleached blond hair. Susannah was right, of course. He hadn't written any new material in years and his records weren't selling as well as they had done in his heyday but he wouldn't dream of giving up and 'kicking back'. What the hell would he do with himself?

Charlie made a private decision to ambush Lochlin at the party. Surely if he persisted, Lochlin would relent eventually. Their friendship went back years, they had always had each other's backs.

Changing the subject, Charlie told Susannah that he had invited their new neighbours at Brockett Hall to the party. 'I also invited Darcy Middleton, that PR chick who worked at my old record label years ago. She's a total ball-breaker but Lochlin's interested in her working at Shamrock so I did him a favour and invited her.' Charlie pursed his lips as if to say that Lochlin definitely owed him at least five minutes of his time at the party. 'Anyway, I haven't a clue who lives in Brockett Hall but I invited them so they could get to know us all. They're probably old and dull but they can have a glass of vino and a vol-au-vent, can't they?'

Susannah bit her lip, wondering if the number of crates of Krug she'd ordered would be enough. With all the extra guests Charlie kept adding to the list, they were going to run out before the supper buffet at this rate and as the champagne was all being dyed red to fit with the 'Valentine' theme, Susannah couldn't exactly leave it to chance. And, contrary to Charlie's joke about vol-au-vents, the bill for the upmarket catering company she'd hired was already astronomical.

Catching sight of their twin daughters strutting around outside in matching crotch-skimming dresses, Susannah forgot about the party arrangements and exploded.

'Bloody hell, what *do* they look like? Abby, get back here at once! And Skye, if you think you're attending the party dressed like a prostitute, you've got another think coming!'

Leaving Charlie to his preening, she dashed out after her wayward daughters, beginning to think this party was going to be a disaster.

'Wow, second place!' Jerry cuffed Ace's helmet. 'Good for you!'

Ace tore off his helmet and whooped. 'Fuck, I've never driven like that in my life before! Jerry, you really helped me out there, blocking those two for that last half mile.' He raked his mahogany hair back with tanned hands. 'What a wing man, I really owe you one.'

Jerry inclined his blond head graciously. 'Hey, that's what team mates are for. I still got a fifth.'

'You were fucking awesome, Jez. We both were!'

His grey eyes sparkling with elation, Ace relived the race in his mind, seeing himself tearing round each corner with precision, swiftly edging in between the other cars to jostle for one of the top spots. He wondered when he had last completed a circuit like that. His sense of timing had been impeccable, his focus unwavering.

The only reason he hadn't won was because NASCAR's best driver, Kyle Stewart from the Toyota team, had managed to barge Jerry into the backstretch wall, something he probably should have been cautioned for, and had then nipped in front to take first place. Ace didn't care. It was his best race to date and he was proud of himself. This was the boost he needed after his bad form last year and after the accident. Maybe, finally, he could put it all behind him.

'Ace, you're needed up on the podium,' Jerry called.

Leaping up on to the stage area, Ace punched the air as the crowd cheered. He didn't think he'd ever felt more alive. Unexpectedly, he felt tears pricking at his eyelids. This was the start of it – this was what he'd worked so hard for all these years. Even his father couldn't fail to be impressed now. Ace enjoyed the moment as the places were called out and he clapped the winner on the back, congratulating him on a good race.

'Hey, it was a close thing,' Kyle Stewart told him. 'You might just beat me next time.'

'Might? It's a dead cert,' Ace returned, laughing.

Staring out at the crowd and hearing them chanting his name, he felt a rush of gratitude for their support. He wondered what it was going to feel like when he finally won and, for the first time, Ace actually allowed himself to believe it was going to happen.

Seeing a microphone thrust in front of his face, he did his best to pull himself together. 'It feels fantastic; who cares if it's a qualifying race, it was great out there.' Ace shook his head. 'I can't really remember all of it, it's a blur, but it was one of the best moments of my life.' Suddenly overcome, he thrust his sunglasses on to hide his eyes. Jumping down from the podium, he took his phone out of his pocket and quickly read a text.

Jerry flung his arm round Ace's shoulders and rolled his eyes. 'Christ, it's not Allegra again, is it? She's such a bunny boiler, you're gonna—'

'It's not from Allegra. It's from my father.'

Hearing the flatness in Ace's voice, Jerry withdrew his arm. 'What's he doing texting you now? I thought he was going to some fancy English party?'

'He is. But he still found time to text me and tell me that second place isn't good enough.' Ace chucked his phone to Jerry with shaking hands.

Jerry read the message incredulously. 'I can't believe he did this. That was your best race . . .' His face darkened. 'Fucking bastard. Ace, don't listen to him, you were amazing out there and you only just missed first place, anyway.'

Ace's mouth twisted bitterly. 'You know, even the best isn't good enough for him, Jez. What did I expect? A fanfare?' He balled his hands into fists. 'I should have known he was gonna kick my ass this year. Since my accident, he's been on my back like a fucking viper.'

'That accident was his fault,' Jerry responded furiously. 'If Elliot hadn't told you what your father did to your mom that time, you wouldn't have ended up wrapping your car around the fucking barrier. He's a bully. He never tells you he's proud of you, the asshole . . .'

Feeling weary all of a sudden, Ace held a hand up. 'I know all this. Just forget it. I'm used to my father shitting on me from a great height, it's what he does.'

'I thought you were supposed to be his favourite,' Jerry snapped. He wished he could make Ace's pain go away, but he knew it was pointless even trying.

'Oh, but I am,' Ace said, heading into the hospitality tent with a grim expression. 'You should see how he treats my brothers.' Grabbing a bottle of champagne, he glugged it down until the bubbles made his eyes water. Spotting two identical girls wearing bright red mini dresses, their dark hair hanging past their waists, he gave Jerry a crooked grin. 'Hey, our luck's in, after all, Jerry. It's those Brazilian twins from the bar. Come on, let's get wasted!' Sliding his arms round the waists of the twins, he laughed his head off as they tipped champagne down his throat.

Pushing aside the bitterness he'd felt at his father's crushing text, Ace proceeded to do the only other thing his father seemed to think he was vaguely good at and got well and truly laid.

Shaking with nerves, Iris clung to the microphone stand, her hands sweating and slipping on the stand.

The Valentines' Ball was in full flow and hundreds of guests were gathered around the small stage that had been erected in Charlie and Susannah's lavish ballroom. Its vast gilt walls were swathed with scarlet material and glittering hearts. Colourful streamers dangled from the ceiling, almost touching the marble floor which was festooned with red and white confetti. Waitresses dressed in teeny red leotards with white hearts stuck on their nipples and crotches teetered around in Vivienne Westwood heels as they handed out flutes of bright red champagne. Trays of miniature cupcakes topped with red frosting, heart-shaped cookies and chocolate-dipped strawberries were doing the rounds alongside platters of miniature cones containing fish and chips, lobster cakes and filet mignon skewers.

Pushing her stutter to the back of her mind, Iris opened her mouth and began to sing. Hearing the familiar opening notes of 'Obsession', the number one hit song Tavvy had made famous twenty-odd years before, the audience cheered loudly. Iris had worked hard to make the song her own, slowing it down and giving it a throaty, bluesy feel, and the crowd roared their approval, stamping their feet and clapping their hands.

Iris smiled as she stared across the tops of their heads and allowed her voice to caress the notes, barely aware of the cheering people gathered at her feet. She had found that the only way to combat her nerves when she performed was to act as if the audience simply wasn't there. Iris was desperately worried about doing her mother's song justice but all she could do was sing it with all her heart.

Iris closed her eyes as she headed towards the money note, her husky tones handling it with ease. '*Have to . . . I have to, I have to have you . . . my obsession, you're my obsession . . .*'

The crowd roared in delight, cheering her to the end.

'*Have to be with you . . . my obsession . . .*' Iris finished softly. She opened her eyes, almost taken aback to find herself in front of so many people and blushed to the roots of her hair as the riotous applause hit her.

Lochlin was whooping and cheering at the top of his voice and Tavvy was wiping away tears as she clapped proudly. Shay and Caitie were grinning at her at the back and Shay gave her a triumphant thumbs-up.

'Wow, th-thanks,' she said into the microphone, catching Ollie's eye. He let out a cheer that would have been more at home on the rugby pitch. She gave him a shy smile, excited at the thought of seeing him later. Iris caught sight of Ian, the village shop boy, standing with his friends and, startled, she realised they were all making wanker signs behind Ollie's back.

About to go over and give him a mouthful for being so rude, Iris jumped down from the stage and almost fell into someone's arms. 'Gosh, sorry!' she said, blushing as she tried to extricate herself. To her dismay, the man wouldn't let her go.

'Excuse me, I have to go.' Iris recoiled, twisting her arm to get away.

'Where are you going?' the man slurred, practically asphyxiating her with his boozy breath as he leered down at her cleavage.

She realised this must be one of the Americans they had been talking about in the village. 'I-I . . . please let me go.'

'Don't leave Sebastian on his own,' he cooed. 'We could have special fun together, me and you . . .' Lurching at her, he grabbed her bottom, squeezing it hard.

'G-get off m-me!' she shrieked, slapping his hand away.

'Are you rejecting me?' he snarled. An angry flush spread across his cheeks. 'Who the hell do you think you are! You fucking Brits think you're so special but you're all just sluts.'

Iris stared at him in horror. 'I think you've had too much ch-champagne.'

'Oh, d-do you?' Sebastian mocked nastily. Raking his hands through his ginger hair, his eyes crossed as he tried to focus on her. He staggered backwards in fury. How *dare* she push him away as if he was some drunken idiot. He was a successful lawyer and heir to a billion-dollar fortune, for fuck's sake!

Silly bitch, he told himself as he reeled off in the other direction. The girl might sing like an angel and have a body to die for but seriously, he wasn't *that* stuck for a quick shag. Plenty more whores in the mansion, Sebastian told himself as he spotted a pair of slender legs and a short red dress and he swayed after the owner with intent.

Iris shivered and headed in the other direction. Within seconds, she had bumped into another imposing redhead but this one looked much more in control of himself. He wore a well-cut suit that barely contained his broad shoulders, and on closer inspection, his cropped hair was rather more red-gold than carrot.

'Look, I'm not up for any . . . special fun,' she told him shortly.

'Special fun?' He looked bemused. His voice was clipped and upper class and, unlike the other redhead, his accent was most definitely British. 'No, I want to talk to you about a business proposition. It's Iris, isn't it?' He shook her hand briskly, his expression professional.

Judd couldn't believe how staggeringly beautiful Iris looked out of her tomboy clothes. She was a dead ringer for Tavvy with her mane of wild blond hair and those sleepily sensual amber eyes, and Judd was momentarily distracted by her beauty. Aside from her looks, Iris literally oozed star quality and Judd felt his heart skip a beat.

'I'd like to talk to you about your career,' he said, recovering himself. 'I thought your performance was superb but someone with your gift is wasted singing on a stage here.'

'R-r-really?' Iris clenched her teeth; why did her bloody stutter have to surface now?

Judd narrowed his eyes. The stutter was unexpected but as long as it didn't manifest itself while she was singing, he couldn't see it being a major issue. In fact, it could be marketed as part of her charm, he thought, his mind racing over the possibilities.

'You should be on the world stage and to that end I'm offering you a record deal.'

Looking at the card thrust into her hands, Iris held it shakily, not quite able to believe what was happening to her.

'The Jett Record Corporation,' she read. She looked up at him, craning her neck. 'That's so kind of you but my father is going to give me a record deal. I mean . . . he plans to give me a deal soon. H-hopefully.'

Judd raised an eyebrow archly, knowing exactly why Lochlin was stalling. If he had a daughter – one as gorgeous as Iris, at any rate – he wouldn't want to let her out of his sight. Especially not to be let loose into the music business with all its dubious temptations and men out for everything they could get. Look at Britney Spears, for fuck's sake. Judd dismissed the thought grimly. If Lochlin was dragging his heels with Iris for whatever reason, that could only be advantageous to *him*.

Suddenly feeling as if he had more aces up his sleeve than he had anticipated, Judd made his move. 'Well, if you want a record deal with your father, that's entirely up to you and I wouldn't stand in your way if that's what you decide to do.' He played his trump card casually. 'Regardless of that, I'm so convinced of your talent, I'm willing to offer you a trip to LA, all expenses paid. Pia Jordan – you might have heard of her? Well, she is a personal friend of mine and I know she would be honoured to work with someone with a voice like yours. She also has an amazing network of contacts within the music industry and I suspect she would be able to hook you up with some big gigs and major appearances at award shows.'

Judd watched Iris's amber eyes widen with shock at the mention of LA's hottest voice coach and felt a frisson of excitement. This little fish was taking the bait, he was sure of it; record deal or not, his offer of working with one of the best voice coaches in the business was, as he had known it would be, practically irresistible. He brought the meeting to a swift close. 'Think about it. And if you change your mind in the next few weeks, call me.' Judd turned on his heel smartly and walked away.

Incapable of uttering a single word, Iris gawped, her gaze switching between Judd's retreating back and the card in her hand. Had a stranger really just approached her and offered her the most perfect dream imaginable? The chance of working with a voice coach she had respected for years and the possibility of appearing at an awards show? Iris's legs almost gave way beneath her. She had to find her father and tell him. Surely he would *have* to give her a record deal after this?

Stunned at being offered the chance of a lifetime at long last, Iris wove through the crowds, searching for her father.

'Bloody well cover yourselves *up*,' Susannah hissed at her daughters as she caught sight of their outfits. Skye and Abby were wearing matching red dresses that plunged to their navels, showed a glimpse of tanned buttock and allowed their jiggling boobs to protrude alarmingly.

'Don't be such a party pooper, Mummy,' Skye pouted. Older than her sister by just two minutes, she could always be relied upon to defend both herself and her sister. 'You can't argue with fashion, Mummy, and would you really want us to look like frumps?'

Abby nodded vigorously in agreement, almost popping a bronzed breast out of her dress.

'God, just get out of my sight before I do us all a favour and call Social Services.' Susannah sighed in resignation as they wobbled away in their high heels. She wished her daughters hadn't taken after Charlie so much when it came to dress sense. Susannah adored them but she did worry about their futures.

Smoothing down her scarlet Dolce and Gabbana dress, she plastered a smile on her face and prepared to greet their new American neighbours. She wasn't sure what she'd been expecting but Kitty Harrington, with her gentle grey eyes and peaches-and-cream complexion, was much shyer than she'd anticipated.

'It's *so* lovely to meet you,' she enthused, grasping Kitty's hand.

Kitty, suddenly feeling rather drab in her tasteful black dress and diamond choker, smiled back at Susannah, taking an instant liking to her. She was warm and friendly and seemed completely down-to-earth – not at all like a rock star wife, in fact.

'All the locals are dying to meet you, *especially* Lexi Beaument, who lives at Foxton Manor.' Susannah's mouth twitched playfully. 'Basically she wants to have a good old nose round your gorgeous house, whatever she might protest to the contrary.'

Kitty laughed. 'It's really not that special,' she said, thinking fondly of her former home in Los Angeles. 'It's a house, rather than a home, if you know what I mean.'

Susannah smiled ruefully. 'Whereas this . . . this is a monstrosity!' She shook her head. 'It's very Charlie but it's not exactly classy, is it?'

'It's very rock and roll,' Kitty said tactfully, giving Susannah an admiring sideways glance. She had the messy blond hair, the big boobs and the heavy make-up that seemed to be the uniform of a rock star wife but her brown eyes, almost hidden behind all the smoky kohl and glittery eye shadow, were full of understanding and sincerity. Kitty was greatly in need of another woman to talk to and she wondered if Susannah might turn out to be the friend she longed for since she'd moved to Britain.

Lexi Beaument barely waited to be introduced and threw herself into Kitty's arms. 'It's so exciting to meet you! This really is . . . I can't tell you how chuffed I am.' She tugged at the neckline of her glittery gold shift dress, her surgically enhanced breasts balanced high up on her chest like a couple of flesh-coloured bowling balls.

Kitty smiled graciously, not sure how to handle such fervour.

Lexi's words rushed out. 'I've been dying to come over and see the house . . . I mean, to see you all.' Her artfully plucked eyebrows knotted above wide-apart green eyes.

'You're welcome anytime,' Kitty murmured, taken aback by Lexi's glamorous appearance. Remembering her manners, she said, 'You must come over to Brockett Hall during the week, Lexi . . . I mean, for coffee or something. And I can show you around. If you'd be interested, that is.'

Susannah hid a smile as she watched Lexi hop from one foot to the other in excitement.

'That would be brilliant!' Lexi cried. She glanced over her shoulder. 'Leo . . . my husband . . . he's around here somewhere. He'd love to meet you.' She rolled her eyes. 'He's a lawyer which is a bit dull, but apparently he's very good at it.'

Kitty smiled. 'My son Sebastian is a lawyer too. Oh, look, here comes his wife, Martha.' Her smile faded as she realised Martha was lurching unsteadily towards them like a drunken sailor, her tights ripped and her mousy hair all over the place. Wearing a red dress two sizes too small for her, which drew attention to her vast bottom, Martha wasn't looking her best. She had a look of devastation on her face and her hands were clutched to her breasts which were spilling out of her dress like overflowing double cream.

Kitty had seen this look before and her heart sank.

'I can't find him anywhere,' Martha said to Kitty, her eyes darting around frantically. 'Who's he with? What's he doing? Oh dear, I really don't feel very well.' Her face went from red to green and she wobbled on her satin heels. 'Jeez, I think I need to throw up.'

'Come with me, sweetheart.' Susannah slipped her arm through Martha's and, giving Kitty a reassuring nod, headed quickly to the nearest bathroom. She stood aside as Martha was violently sick.

'Why did I drink so much?' Martha moaned, as she bent over and retched again. Looking up, she noticed she was in the gaudiest bathroom she'd ever seen; it had gilt walls, mirrored tiles on the floor and fat little cherubs for taps. And was that a plasma TV screen on the far wall?

'Could you be pregnant?' Susannah suggested with an impish grin, instantly regretting her comment as Martha's face crumpled.

'As if!' Tears gushed down Martha's cheeks as she grabbed at the toilet roll. It unravelled at high speed and fell in a messy heap on the floor. 'Story of my life,' she stated flatly, staring at it.

Susannah carefully knelt down next to her. 'Gosh, I'm so sorry, Martha. That was incredibly insensitive of me. Are you . . . are there . . . problems? You don't have to tell me anything, obviously. I just feel terrible for upsetting you.'

Martha sniffed, her brown eyes brimming over with tears again. 'We've been trying for a while but it's not just that. It's Sebastian . . . he's . . . there are others . . . I'm . . . oh God, I'm not enough for him, you see.'

Looking up and catching sight of the image of Charlie gyrating away in his white trousers on the plasma screen, his crotch wiggling in the face of a groupie Susannah happened to know had ended up in Charlie's trailer later that night, she knew exactly what Martha was talking about. She wondered if the drunken American with the carrot-coloured hair who'd lecherously slipped his hand down the back of her dress earlier was Martha's adulterous husband and guessed it probably was. She felt terribly sorry for Martha, knowing exactly what it felt like to be cheated on over and over again. Even when you were used to it, it hurt and that was the very reason Susannah had given in; it made life far more bearable to let go and accept it.

'Sweetheart, some men just can't help themselves.' She gently pulled Martha to her feet and cleaned her tear-stained cheeks with a damp flannel. 'But if they come home to you, that's what matters, isn't it?' Seeing Martha's shoulder slumping with misery, Susannah realised they were very different. She was a tough cookie but Martha was vulnerable and quite obviously not cut out to be married to a man who felt the need to prove his virility regularly. And sooner or later, this Sebastian would probably break Martha's fragile ego beyond repair.

'You poor kid,' Susannah said gently. As Martha burst into a fresh bout of noisy tears, Susannah welcomed her into the warm, motherly circle of her arms.

He is, without question, the most gorgeous boy I've ever seen, Caitie thought, staring at the stranger across the room. That brooding pose, the sensitive grey eyes – even the way he wore his dinner jacket with baseball boots and a dark grey T-shirt with the name of some unknown band on the front was sexy. Tugging distractedly at her scarlet wig, Caitie wondered how she could get him to notice her. More to the point, who *was* he?

Wishing Jas was here to offer advice, Caitie watched with a sinking heart as her arch enemies, Skye and Abby Valentine, ran lascivious eyes over the gorgeous boy before joining her.

'OMG,' Skye said, running her fingers through the roots of her dyed hair to give it more volume. 'What a *hotty*.'

Abby stuck out her padded chest. 'He's *so* mine, Skye. Hands off.'

'I saw him first!' Skye barked at her twin.

Actually, *I* did, Caitie thought to herself, biting her lip. Not that it would matter to the Valentine twins. There wasn't any honour amongst friends with those two, let alone amongst enemies.

'Fine,' Abby sulked. Her face brightened. 'I'll have Shay Maguire then.' She swooned as Shay swept past in a dinner suit and snow-white shirt. With his black bow tie undone and sloaney Saskia hanging off his arm, Shay looked the epitome of untouchable glamour.

Caitie gaped. Was Abby being serious? She didn't have a hope in hell of getting Shay into bed and neither did her sister. Her brother might be a dreadful slut at times but even he had standards.

'Where's Lady Jasmine tonight, then?' Skye asked, her smile not reaching her eyes.

Caitie glared at her. Skye and Abby were insanely jealous of her best friend because her father was a peer and the twins knew damn well that money didn't buy class. Jas was also impossibly glamorous and chilled out about her title which drove the twins nuts.

'Jas is still in Italy with her parents.'

'With her parents?' Abby tittered. 'How very immature of Jasmine. We *always* holiday without the olds. *God*, your brother's handsome. Let's grab him, Skye!'

Caitie watched incredulously as they made a beeline for Shay who, now that Saskia was in the loo, was far too busy hungrily eying up a confident-looking brunette to notice. Wearing a black silk dress with a high neck and a sexy, scooped-out back that left the dents above her buttocks on full display, the woman was clearly aware she had a killer body. About to pursue her, Shay suddenly caught sight of the Valentine twins heading towards him and, winking at Caitie, he hastily careered off in the other direction.

Caitie turned her attention back to the boy with the floppy blond hair and brooding grey eyes. He had a slight tan that he couldn't possibly have got in England in winter and hands that looked as though they were made to play the piano. Or something infinitely more romantic.

Caitie gazed at him longingly.

I'm in *love*, she told herself, clasping her hands to her chest. And even though she uttered these words on an almost weekly basis, this time Caitie really meant it.

Chapter Four

Strolling around the Valentines' Gothic mansion, Darcy couldn't get over the outlandish decor. She had been in enough rock star homes in her time to be unmoved by extravagance but she had never witnessed such a flashy display of vulgarity in her life. Every nude statue, ornate ceiling and piece of mock period furniture seemed to be sparkling with semi-precious stones, covered in gilt or swathed in designer fabric.

Darcy paused by a dazzling fountain in the hallway. Sculpted from sleek ebony marble was a vast bowl containing a guitar-shaped column which was studded with rhinestones. Spurting from its head was bright red water that resembled frothy blood and there were coloured lights going on and off in the water, sending jewel-like shafts shooting up the walls.

Christ, who *lives* like this? Darcy thought incredulously. Charlie Valentine clearly liked to live out his rock and roll image to the full. It was apparent in every glitzy nook and cranny of the mansion. Darcy grabbed another glass of champagne and decided to check out the men at the party.

She'd already had a brief chat with Lochlin Maguire but she hadn't committed herself to the role at Shamrock because she wanted to keep her options open. Before she'd even had a chance to approach the Jett Record Corporation, she had received an enigmatic text message saying that someone from the company would approach her at the party. So far, no one had so much as mentioned Jett to her but Darcy couldn't help feeling rather intrigued by the secrecy. Still, she thought, glancing at Lochlin, working at Shamrock would definitely be stimulating.

She watched him charming someone at the other end of the room, his jet-black hair overlong on his collar, his intelligent green eyes sparkling as he roared with laughter at something his wife was saying. Disappointingly, the rumours about Tavvy and Lochlin appeared to be true; they looked utterly besotted with one another, finishing each other's sentences and touching each other at every opportunity.

But who was *that*? Darcy marvelled as she caught sight of a tall man wearing a well-cut dinner suit. He had to be Lochlin Junior, she thought, feeling a spark of lust shoot through her. Taking in eyes the colour of shamrocks framed by long, sooty eyelashes that almost grazed his to-die-for cheekbones, Darcy wondered if she'd ever clapped eyes on a more perfect specimen of manhood. So engrossed was she that she almost jumped out of her skin when someone's fingers curled around her arm. About to turn round, she found she couldn't, so strong was the man's grasp. She felt a firm, hard body pressing against her bare back and her skin prickled from the intimacy of it.

'Meet me outside,' he said in clipped tones close to her ear, his breath teasing her earlobe as he let her go and stalked past her without a second glance. Darcy stared after the man. She saw that he had wide shoulders and cropped red hair but then he was gone, disappearing like a phantom. Darcy touched her arm where his hot, firm hand had been, the imprint still visible. Intrigued, she headed outside and navigated a narrow path in her high heels. She found the red-headed man sitting on a wrought-iron bench, thankfully next to an outside heater.

'What's all this about?' she asked, accepting a flute of champagne, and lowering herself on to the cold bench, several feet away from him.

'I'm Judd Harrington,' he replied suavely.

'So?' Darcy shrugged; the name meant nothing to her. She sipped the champagne, wondering how he'd managed to secure the only bottle that hadn't been dyed bright red for the party. She could see that he was packed with muscle beneath the well-fitting dinner suit but she refused to look impressed.

Judd leant forward, his hard blue eyes focused on hers. 'I own the Jett Record Corporation.' Seeing a flash of recognition in her hazel eyes, he got straight to the point. 'I have an excellent team but I need a good PR representative to have control over many aspects of the business. I only work with the best and having researched you in great detail, I know you're fantastic at what you do.'

Darcy's fingers curled around her champagne flute tightly. He was turning her on, both professionally and personally. And that didn't happen to her very often. Not sure if her lust was fuelled by the sight of Lochlin's dreamy son, her skin tingled as she felt Judd's eyes travelling down her body. She coolly met his gaze.

'Can you afford me?' she murmured, raising her eyebrows. She saw his mouth tighten momentarily and she cursed herself for mentioning money. She was expensive and worth it but he probably thought she was crass for making reference to it.

'I can afford you several times over,' he returned, rubbing the slithery silk of her dress between his fingers carelessly. As he barely brushed Darcy's thighs with his fingertips, he felt her involuntary shudder. He breathed her perfume in; it was something heady and exotic, exactly the kind of sexy, overpowering scent a self-confident businesswoman would choose.

Judd paused. The only woman he cared about was Tavvy but Darcy was sexy and he could tell she would be dynamite in bed. She would be a welcome distraction in the meantime, Judd decided, and no doubt extremely useful to him professionally. Taking a chance but certain she would respond nonetheless, Judd kissed her hard on the mouth.

Gasping at his audacity but desperately turned on, Darcy greedily kissed him back, her tongue coiling around his expertly. She pressed her full breasts against him as his hand grasped the small of her back and she hid a smile as he abruptly shoved his other hand under her dress. He was her kind of man. Meeting his gaze boldly, she parted her legs, giving him easier access to her lacy La Perla thong. Sucking her breath in as he probed inside the fabric, Darcy was momentarily jolted when she heard the stunning voice of the girl who had sung earlier drifting outside as she sang her second set.

'Fabulous voice,' she managed, determined not to appear too distracted by Judd's sensual probing. 'Someone should sign her up on the spot.'

'I plan to sign Iris Maguire to Jett,' Judd confided, sucking on Darcy's bottom lip in a most provocative manner. He removed his hand from under her dress, leaving her gasping for more.

'Iris . . . *Maguire*?'

He nodded and thumbed her erect nipple. 'Her father Lochlin Maguire owns Shamrock but he hasn't got around to signing her yet, the stupid fucker. I've already started the ball rolling. She'll have a deal with Jett before the year is out. I'm thinking of offering Charlie Valentine something too.' His eyes gleamed as Darcy unzipped his trousers and circled the head of his bulging erection with delicate fingertips. 'Not that he has an ounce of Iris's talent, of course, but stealing him from Lochlin is all part of the fun.'

Darcy could barely contain her excitement. Judd Harrington reminded her of a classic celluloid villain; sexy, arrogant and ever so slightly scary. She noted the spark of ruthlessness in his eyes and wondered what happened when he was really riled. 'I thought Lochlin Maguire was supposed to be the best in the business,' she taunted him. 'And he's very good looking with all that dark hair and those sexy green eyes.' She gasped as Judd squeezed her nipple hard.

'Things are about to change,' Judd purred. 'There's a new boy in town.'

Darcy didn't know whether to be repulsed or blown away by his cocky self-belief. 'Didn't think much of his wife,' she said. 'Everyone says she's dazzling but I couldn't see it myself. . . . And knee-high boots are so inappropriate at her age.'

Judd removed his hand from her breast, his eyes frosty. 'Do we have a deal?'

Darcy made a snap decision. 'I think we do, actually.'

'Good.' He stood up abruptly and casually straightened his bow tie. 'I've drawn up a contract, you'll find a copy of it at your house when you go home tonight.'

She blinked at him. 'What? But we haven't even discussed terms!' The last thing she wanted was for him to think she was a pushover. 'I'll get my lawyer to check it,' she asserted haughtily, keen to regain some advantage.

'No need,' Judd said, his blue eyes glittering like sapphires in the darkness. 'The salary is far more than you're worth and the terms are absurdly favourable. You'd be mad not to agree to it.' He gave her a curt nod. 'See you bright and early Monday morning. As a heads up, I deplore tardiness.'

Zipping his trousers up smartly, Judd made his exit, leaving Darcy shivering with desire and inexplicably impressed.

As the music pumped out around him, Lochlin listened patiently to Charlie Valentine droning on about his comeback. Feeling his jovial mood evaporate like the scarlet champagne bubbles in his glass, he realised there was nothing more depressing than having to tell a friend their career might be over.

To buy himself some time, Lochlin grabbed another glass of champagne from a passing waitress, averting his eyes from her bulging cleavage. He watched a grinning Shay twirling his girlfriend Saskia around the dance floor and frowned. Why did his son irk him so much? Shay was so headstrong, so impulsive. Hugely popular at the music magazine he worked for, he did just enough to get by. Relying on his gut instinct to spot up-and-coming talent, he wrote pithy, articulate prose to accompany the glossy photographs and was brimming over with confidence and attitude.

And even in his relationships, Shay flitted from one girl to the next, seemingly searching for some elusive romance he might never find. Lochlin sighed. One day, he would be proud to have Shay working alongside him at Shamrock but he detested nepotism and Lochlin felt his son had a good deal of growing up to do before he could take on any serious responsibility in the family business.

'I really think I deserve another chance,' Charlie was insisting, sweat trickling down his forehead and mingling with his lurid eyeliner. Sensing Lochlin was about to piss on his bonfire, he pressed on. 'I've got as much right to be in the charts as any of these youngsters, and I've got a huge fan base who love everything I do.'

'Who love everything you've ever *done*,' Lochlin corrected him softly.

Charlie flinched. 'So what? That proves I can still wow them, given the chance.'

Lochlin pinched the skin between his eyebrows. Why did he seem to spend his life saying no to people he cared about? Shay was frustrated at being held at arm's length and as for Iris . . . She deserved a chance, Lochlin knew that and he was inordinately proud of her. If only he could bring himself to let her go, he fretted guiltily.

'So, what do you think?' Charlie demanded.

Lochlin cleared his throat. 'I just don't know if the timing is right for you. The last thing you need is to put yourself out there and be ridiculed.'

Charlie visibly bristled. '*Ridiculed?*'

'Hip hop is all the rage at the moment . . . winners of reality TV shows, kids with operatic voices, that sort of thing.' Lochlin grimaced. 'Believe me, Chas, I wish the market wasn't the way it is but I have to give the public what they want. Look, all I'm saying is that we should wait a while and pick our moment. Trends change all the time; it's just a case of waiting it out.'

Charlie's brittle ego shattered into tiny pieces. The thought of not performing again, at least not for a few years, was more than he could handle. Where was his management when he needed them? Charlie fumed inwardly. Greg, the fat tosser, spent most of his time stretched out on the terrace of his villa on the Costa Brava, never lifting a finger to further Charlie's career and living off the spoils his outrageous percentage afforded him. Unable to even look his old friend Lochlin in the face, Charlie stumbled away. Accidentally crashing into someone, he apologised without even looking up.

'Lochlin Maguire doesn't always know best,' he heard someone say before a glossy business card was thrust into his hand. Squinting in the dim light, he spotted a flash of red-gold hair and a thick neck before the man strode away. Charlie stared down at the card, feeling a glimmer of hope stirring inside him at last. 'The Jett Record Corporation,' he read in wonder. He didn't know who they were or who the red-headed man was who'd given him the card, but if this was the way for him to get a new record deal, he was going to grab it with both hands.

'Lochlin Maguire doesn't always know best,' he repeated self-righteously, his ego restored. Jutting his leather-clad hips out, Charlie swaggered to the bar to celebrate.

Shay rubbed Saskia's back, wondering at what point his evening had turned from being great fun to being utterly disastrous. Not only was Saskia horribly drunk, she had also decided it was time to have a 'serious talk about their future'. Feeling his good mood plummet, Shay knew this sort of conversation tended to signal the beginning of the end – for him, at any rate.

'The thing is,' Saskia was saying, pleating the skirt of her chocolate-brown silk dress, 'the thing is, we've been going out for a few months now, haven't we?' She let out a delicate burp and put her hand to her mouth with a giggle. 'And I was thinking, maybe we need to take things to the next level.'

Shay gazed past Saskia, staring out into the inky darkness of the night despondently. Why did his relationships always seem to end this way? He adored women and he was never short of a warm and willing body if he needed one but somehow he never seemed to meet a woman who got under his skin.

Still rubbing Saskia's back absently, Shay lit a cigarette. He didn't have a type when it came to women; he dated curvy girls, slim girls, ones who made him laugh, serious intellectuals with letters after their names, but none of them made his head spin and not one of them had managed to jolt his heart yet. He entered into every relationship with hope and romantic expectation only to be hit with the realisation that he wasn't captivated. He wanted to be consumed by passion, bursting with love like it said in all the songs he listened to, and so far, it hadn't happened.

Darling Saskia, Shay thought sadly, taking off his dinner jacket and slipping it around her shoulders. She was a lovely girl but their relationship simply wasn't going anywhere. He had an idea Saskia had done her level best to be the perfect girlfriend to him, thinking that if she did so, Shay would love her more. Saskia had presented herself as a fun-loving sex goddess with a gourmet palate and an encyclopaedic knowledge of jazz music. But it was all for his benefit; it wasn't who she really was; Shay knew that now.

'Shay?' Saskia gulped. She knew that look; this was the end. She burst into tears.

Distressed, Shay held her. He felt deeply sorry but he couldn't lie, not to Saskia. 'Please don't think there's anything wrong with you, Sask, you're an angel, truly.' He wiped her tears away with his thumb and looked away. 'I just can't see myself marrying anyone the way I'm going.' He let out a short laugh. 'Fuck, that almost sounded as if I was saying "it's not you, it's me". But actually, that really is the truth of it. I'm a total fuck-up.'

Saskia gave him a heroic smile, brushing her tears away. 'It's over, isn't it?' She cringed with embarrassment. 'And there I was, wittering on about the next level . . . fantasising about us moving in together . . . getting married even.'

'I'm so sorry, Saskia.' Shay ground his cigarette out on the step, his green eyes full of regret.

Biting her lip, she gave his profile one last, lingering look. Those gorgeous cheekbones, the perfectly straight nose . . . and that sensual, laughing mouth that had given her so many hours of pleasure. Getting to her feet with a slight wobble, she removed Shay's dinner jacket from her shoulders and handed it back to him, hating how brutally final the gesture felt.

Shay wished he'd brought a bottle of whisky out with him.

Saskia paused in the doorway and glanced over her shoulder. 'You'll meet her one day, you know.'

Shay turned his head, puzzled.

She gave him a sweet, genuine smile. 'The one. You know, someone you want to marry.'

Shay gave her the ghost of a smile. 'Maybe I'm just not the marrying kind.'

Saskia nodded. 'Of course you are. You just haven't met the perfect person yet. I wish I hadn't.' Avoiding his eyes, she vanished back inside.

Feeling immeasurably sad, Shay stared out into the darkness before going in search of a bottle of Charlie's finest malt.

'Are you OK in there, darling?' Tavvy called to Iris on the other side of the door.

Poor Iris, she thought. Trying to find Lochlin for some unknown reason, Iris had instead walked in on her boyfriend Ollie with his head buried in the cleavage of one of the Valentine twins and his flies undone. Devastated, Iris had proceeded to down red champagne like there was no tomorrow and currently she was doing her best not to be sick in Susannah's upstairs bathroom.

'He's not worth it!' Tavvy called, wishing she could help. She had a feeling Iris had been on the brink of falling head over heels in love with Ollie Ramshaw, the cheating lowlife, and now he had let her down spectacularly. With Skye Valentine, of all people.

Some people had no class, Tavvy thought. Susannah was her friend but Shay was right: those twins were toxic.

'I should've listened to Caitie,' Iris gulped in response. 'Ollie *is* a cheapskate!'

Tavvy smiled and put her mouth closer to the door. 'That's right. A cheapskate and a total bastard.' She was gratified to hear a chuckle from the other side. 'And he had smelly feet,' she added for good measure. She didn't know if he had smelly feet or not but it was worth a try.

'Worse than that,' Iris mumbled, sounding as though she might finally be sick. 'He used to sing "Swing Low, Sweet Chariot" when we were in bed together. At crucial moments.'

Tavvy shrieked with laughter then stopped as she heard Iris heaving into the toilet. Sinking down on the bed, she turned to find Shay standing behind her, his green eyes dejected. 'Not you too. What's wrong?'

'Me and Saskia just split up.' Shay shrugged. 'It's been on the cards for ages but tonight she started talking about our future and I had to be honest with her.'

'Not "the one" after all, then?'

Shay grinned but his eyes were melancholy. 'It appears not.'

'Shame,' Tavvy said lightly. She worried about Shay. His outwardly breezy, sarcastic persona bore almost no relation to the intense person he was underneath. It was all bluff and barriers with Shay and it was going to take a remarkable woman to penetrate his prickly outer shell.

Shay frowned. 'What did you mean, not you too? Who's in the bathroom?'

'Iris. Ollie Ramshaw did the dirty with Skye Valentine – or rather, he was just about to.'

'Dickhead,' Shay stormed furiously. 'How dare he do that to Iris, the little shit?' He pulled a face. 'With one of the Valentine twins as well. Good God, the man's got more courage than me. I wouldn't go there without full body armour.'

Tavvy giggled.

'There you are!' Lochlin, his dark hair all over the place, burst into the room. 'I've been searching for you everywhere, Tav.'

She stood up, wondering why his face was so ashen. 'Is everything all right?'

Lochlin shook his head. 'No. No, it's not.' His eyes wild, he ran a hand through his hair.

'I feel much better now I've been sick,' Iris informed them as she emerged from the bathroom looking green. Surprised to see most of her family in the room, she frowned. 'What's going on?'

Lochlin was pacing the room like a madman, muttering under his breath. 'I can't believe it . . . not after all this time. The audacity, the fucking *audacity* of the man . . .'

Tavvy was beginning to lose patience. 'Lochlin, what the hell is the matter? What can't you believe?'

He turned to face her. 'Susannah just introduced me to a lovely American lady called Kitty Harrington.'

Tavvy started. That was the last thing she'd been expecting him to say. 'Harrington?'

He nodded, his eyes meeting hers. 'She's Judd Harrington's wife.'

Tavvy started to shake all over, barely noticing as Lochlin took her hands. 'He's . . . he's back,' he told her in an unsteady voice. 'After all this time, Judd Harrington is here, in Meadowbank.'

'What for?' she whispered, her amber eyes wide. 'What does he want?'

Bemused, Shay watched them, wondering why they both looked so shell-shocked.

Lochlin shook his head, his shoulders rigid. 'I don't know. But the Jett Record Corporation? That's him.'

Surreptitiously, Iris drew the crumpled business card out of her pocket and glanced at it. Suddenly, the offer of a record deal she'd received earlier that night didn't feel quite so exciting. 'Wh-who is he?' she asked in a timid voice. 'This J-Judd Harrington, who is he?'

Lochlin swung round, his expression thunderous. 'Stay away from him, Iris, do you hear me? And you, Shay.' His voice was hoarse but he had never looked more sombre in his life. 'Judd is . . . he's a dangerous fucking bastard, that's who he is!'

'Daddy, *do* keep your hair on!' Caitie, her cheeks flushed and her black dress around her thighs and revealing several inches of black opaque stocking, looked absolutely sloshed. Oblivious of the tension in the room, she flung herself on the bed and let out an ecstatic sigh. 'Everyone . . . I'm in love.'

Shay mocked a yawn. 'Again? That's a daily occurrence.' He gave his father a questioning look, wondering what the hell was going on.

'This is different,' Caitie argued. 'This time, I really mean it.' Her eyes misted over. 'He's drop-dead gorgeous and get this! He's *American*.'

Tavvy and Lochlin exchanged a glance. Surely not . . .

Caitie stared up at the ceiling. 'I heard on the grapevine that he's called Elliot Harrington. Isn't that a great name?'

Seemingly speechless for about thirty seconds, Lochlin abruptly exploded. 'Over my dead body will any of you ever end up with a fucking Harrington!'

Stunned, Caitie sat up, her scarlet wig lopsided. Shay put his arm around Iris. Tavvy, overcome with the sheer horror of it all, burst into tears.

'I'm serious.' Lochlin pushed his black hair out of his eyes with an unsteady hand. 'If any of you go near a Harrington, you won't be welcome in this family.'

Shay gave a nervous laugh and took his arm. 'Dad, you're sounding mental. What's this all about? Who's this Judd Harrington bloke, anyway?'

Lochlin shook Shay's arm off, his green eyes cold. 'I don't need to explain myself to you. Just do as you're told for once, can't you?'

Shay stiffened at the barb. He was sick of being treated like a fucking idiot! Christ, what a shitty evening. He already felt like a heel for dumping Saskia, the stunning brunette he'd had his eye on earlier seemed to have disappeared and now his father was treating him like a badly behaved child.

Shay's mouth twisted obstinately. Now obviously wasn't the right time but soon he was going to confront his father. About working in the family business, about this mysterious Judd Harrington – and being treated like a responsible fucking adult. He was twenty-four years old and he'd been nothing but loyal to his family all his life. He deserved more than being chastised and fobbed off.

Lochlin was so blind with rage he didn't even notice his son's rigid jaw. 'That man did more damage to this family than you can ever imagine,' he went on. He threw his arm protectively round Tavvy's heaving shoulders and turned back to his children. 'So if you love me and your mother, you'll keep your fucking distance, all of you.'

Shay stalked out before he said something he might regret.

Caitie looked stricken. 'But Elliot is amazing,' she mumbled to Iris. 'I mean, I barely know him but I really think I might love him. What on earth am I going to do?'

Iris stared down at the crumpled business card in horror. Caitie's crush on Elliot Harrington was the least of their worries. What the hell was her father going to say when he found out Judd had offered her a record deal?

Chapter Five

'Can you tell him I'm here, please?'

Darcy barked the order at Judd's receptionist and waited impatiently by her desk.

Heidi flushed. Highly skilled at acting as personal assistant, chief protector and decorative right-hand woman to many a high-powered man before taking the role at Jett with Judd at the helm, Heidi detested being spoken to as if she was the office junior. Especially by a woman wearing slutty red lipstick and an attitude the size of Africa, she thought, with gritted teeth.

'Do take a seat,' she said, glancing discreetly at her watch. It was eight o'clock in the morning; hardly any visitors arrived this early, although Judd had requested a breakfast meeting for quarter past.

'No need,' Darcy replied coolly. 'He's expecting me. Darcy Middleton.'

So this was the infamous Darcy Middleton, Heidi thought, giving Darcy's outfit a quick once-over. Instead of the bolshy power suit she'd been expecting, Darcy was wearing a cream silk Ralph Lauren shirt with a scooped neckline, a sharply cut black pencil skirt that hugged her curves but not indecently so, and a pair of to-die-for scarlet Louboutins with spike heels. Somehow, Darcy was managing to look businesslike yet desirable and Heidi, like most women, knew how difficult it was to pull off such a classy look.

'Shall I just let myself in?' Darcy inquired slowly, as if Heidi was mentally challenged.

'Certainly not!' Heidi jumped up. 'Mr Harrington detests

people bursting in on him. I'll let him know you're here and then you can see him if it's convenient.' She stalked past her, nose in the air.

Darcy rolled her eyes and put a hand to her cinnamon-brown hair, which had been personally pinned up in a neat chignon for her by Nicky Clarke that morning. She couldn't *stand* receptionists and could never resist ruffling their feathers.

Aware she had alienated Heidi as well as practically every woman in the vicinity by striding confidently through the half-empty building as if she owned the place and throwing hot looks at every halfway decent man behind a desk, Darcy guessed she might already be public enemy number one. It had given her such a powerful boost, she actually felt sexually charged.

As Heidi gestured to Judd's office with an angry flick of her hand Darcy strutted past her without a backward glance. Dialling her best friend to let off some much needed steam, Heidi savagely filed her nails and wondered if she would ever be able to justify Christian Louboutin heels on her salary.

Once inside Judd's office, Darcy headed towards him, undeterred by the sight of his red-gold crewcut bent over some paperwork and not remotely fazed by the vast glass desk he sat behind. He wore a charcoal suit with a lilac silk lining, which looked like Savile Row, teamed with a crisp white shirt and a bright pink tie. Subtlety wasn't his strong point but he had achieved his objective and he looked both imposing and successful.

'Bright and early, as requested,' Darcy said, her body tingling as she remembered their last meeting at the party. 'You deplore tardiness, as I recall.'

Judd raised his hard blue eyes to meet hers. 'What a good memory you have; I barely remember saying any such thing.'

Darcy's mouth tightened. God, he was a slippery bastard! Judd obviously got off on point-scoring – regardless of how petty that point was – and it was clear that maintaining the upper hand was paramount to him. Darcy shrugged inwardly. She was used to men like Judd and, in her experience, there was *always* a better way to get the upper hand.

Unbuttoning her silk blouse, she allowed it to slither from her shoulders before unzipping her skirt and gracefully stepping out of it. Standing in front of him in an ivory bespoke Rigby and Peller corset and a pair of sheer, nude stockings that set off her scarlet Louboutins perfectly, Darcy was pretty sure she had Judd standing to attention. Especially since she had deliberately left her knickers at home that day.

Pushing his paperwork to one side, Judd swivelled round in his chair. 'Come here,' he said roughly.

Obediently, Darcy slowly moved to his side of the desk, noting the bulging erection in his trousers with satisfaction. In her opinion, stripping down to her underwear wasn't remotely unprofessional, nor did it render her vulnerable; in fact, Darcy had never felt so empowered in her life. She recognised Judd as a chauvinistic man who needed to feel dominant, even if in reality *she* was the one in the driving seat, sexually speaking. It was just a question of letting Judd think he was the one making all the moves and being subservient herself at the right moments. Judd Harrington might be a millionaire and he might be smart but when it came down to it, he was a man and that made him somewhat predictable, Darcy smirked to herself.

'Oh, I'm really going to enjoy doing business with you,' she said breathily, enjoying the sight of Judd's eyes turning cobalt-blue with lust. She paused between his legs, allowing him to drink in the view.

Judd let out a growl and nudged her closer with his knee. Putting out a hand, he cupped her narrow waist and stroked the flare of her hip before trailing his fingers down further until he reached the bare flesh above her stockings. He stroked her soft skin, his eyes fixed on hers and reached around to caress her naked buttocks.

Feeling a surge of desire, Darcy straddled his lap and eased his rearing penis from his trousers. He was a well-hung man, she thought, sucking her breath in and noting with amusement that the hair covering his groin was dark red and clipped brutally short. She could feel the rock hard muscles of his thighs beneath hers and, idly, she wondered how much time he spent at the gym.

He pulled the top of her corset down, revealing her voluptuous, creamy breasts. Taking a juicy pink nipple in his mouth, he sucked hard on it, his other hand thrusting two fingers inside her crudely. He smiled as she flinched slightly.

Darcy flung her head back and let out a moan, her mind working overtime. Judd was clearly a man who liked rough sex and, if she had him pegged correctly, a man who might attempt to demean her in some way if the mood took him. Abruptly, she pushed his fingers aside and slid down on to him languorously, noting the spark of surprise in his eyes.

He has no idea who he's dealing with, she thought as she rode him expertly. Nothing was out of bounds with Darcy but the one thing Judd would never get close to was her soul. She made it a golden rule to always, always hold that part of herself back. And with someone like Judd, Darcy felt it would be imperative to keep her distance, emotionally, at any rate.

Giving him the performance of a lifetime, Darcy ground her pelvis like a professional lap dancer and moaned loudly. Keeping himself otherwise under control, Judd grabbed her breasts abruptly and climaxed inside her. Darcy wriggled and threw her head around until her brown hair cascaded down on to her bare shoulders.

Nicky Clarke would kill her for ruining his updo, she thought, letting out a sigh of pleasure. She eased her corset back up and squeezed her pelvic floor muscles rhythmically as Judd's spasms died down. Sex was infinitely more rewarding, she decided, when she had her man exactly where she wanted him. Judd couldn't move from his chair, yet she was sure he was still under the illusion he was fully in charge of the situation.

Second later, the smile was wiped off Darcy's face as she realised that, yet again, she had underestimated him.

'We're due in a meeting shortly,' Judd commented, straightening his pink tie and looking for all the world as if the last ten minutes hadn't happened. 'So you might want to get dressed unless you'd like my staff, including my eldest son, to see you like this.'

Darcy lifted herself off his lap with dignity. She put her clothes back on without any sign of urgency and took a seat opposite him on the other side of the glass desk. Pinning her hair up quickly, Darcy felt an increasing sense of annoyance at being outmanoeuvred and made a mental note to always be on her guard around Judd in future.

Reaching into her Prada briefcase, Darcy drew out a file and rapidly outlined her plans for the company before Judd had a chance to usher her into the meeting.

'So, in summary,' she finished, raising her hazel eyes to his challengingly, 'I believe the Jett Record Corporation could become the most successful record company in Britain.' She efficiently listed her ideas for approaching some high-profile acts for representation, some groups she had heard about on the grapevine that were on the brink of discovery, plus her thoughts about strategic release dates. 'We can discuss image and marketing another time,' she added for good measure. 'But from the research I completed at the weekend, I think what you have planned could be far more dynamic with my help.'

Darcy gave him a disarming smile. She wasn't about to admit that she had barely slept all weekend due to the amount of time she had spent searching the net for information, mapping out her ideas and preparing to make a fabulous impression on Judd. As a final point, she ran through her thoughts on Charlie Valentine, suggesting that if he signed with Jett they pressure him to go back into the studio to record some new material, revamp his image and repackage him as a more serious artist.

Judd listened carefully to every word but remained deadpan. He knew full well Darcy imagined he was scarcely compos mentis after such a mind-blowing performance, but she wasn't to know that sex had the opposite effect on him; it heightened his senses and left him acutely alert. He heard every word, every nuance in her voice and he had a photographic memory when it came to details.

It had been incredible sex, Judd conceded, as he sat back in his chair and watched Darcy, and he was a connoisseur when it came to matters of a carnal nature. He certainly couldn't imagine Kitty mounting him with such confidence or grinding her body in such an overtly erotic manner. But then . . . Judd couldn't even remember the last time he'd had sex with Kitty or, for that matter, the last time he had wanted to.

'You certainly seem to have some good ideas,' he drawled. 'Let's discuss them another time . . . over dinner, perhaps.'

Standing up, he led the way to a boardroom at the side of his office and Darcy had no choice but to follow him, smarting from his patronising response. Realising the room was already full of staff, she faltered, wondering how much they had overheard.

Bastard, she thought to herself heatedly, knowing as he took his seat at the head of the table and caught her eye that Judd knew exactly what she was thinking. He gave her a sardonic grin and she didn't know whether to be furious or amused by his antics.

'This is Darcy Middleton,' he announced courteously, giving the room the benefit of his wolfish smile. He frowned slightly. 'Where the fuck is Sebastian, the useless idiot?'

Heidi came in and consulted her BlackBerry. 'On his way. He got delayed in traffic.' Or in some floozy's knickers, she thought, shuddering as she recalled the way Sebastian always leered down her top. She threw Darcy a bitchy smile to let her know she and the rest of the staff had overheard the goings on in Judd's office.

Darcy, refusing to be intimidated, took a seat to the right of Judd, guessing correctly that she had stolen Heidi's seat. Heidi bit her lip and took the next seat along, her body rigid with dislike.

Judd introduced key members of staff to Darcy, pointing out his A&R executives, the people responsible for observing market trends and sourcing new talent, and his production manager.

Sebastian burst into the boardroom with his tie askew and his shirt tails flapping. Contrary to Heidi's assumption, he actually *had* been caught in traffic, because he'd left the house late after his alarm didn't come on. Knowing such a flimsy, schoolboy excuse would go down like a sack of shit with his father, Sebastian slipped into a chair as unobtrusively as possible and avoided his flinty stare.

'Nice of you to join us,' Judd said tersely. He turned to Darcy. 'My son, Sebastian. Exceptionally young company lawyer with a huge office and use of his father's expense account.'

Glad to see she wasn't the only one Judd liked to toy with, Darcy gave a reddening Sebastian a brief nod. He ignored her and looked at his father. Knowing his father's tastes and recognising the smug look on his face as post-coital, Sebastian fumed inwardly that his father was, as usual, doing better in the extramarital stakes.

Lucky bastard, he thought jealously, giving Darcy's fantastic body a lingering stare. It was about time he got himself a fine piece of British ass. The problem was that all the women *he* approached seemed to be bloody well frigid, he thought, noting the way Heidi was cold-shouldering him.

Judd had already moved on and was striding around the room like a caged tiger. 'Now, as you know, the Jett Record Corporation is a new company,' he said, 'but with me at the helm, I think we can be the biggest record company in Britain. And here's how.'

Listening as Judd aggressively outlined his ideas, incorporating some of Darcy's and making a point of crediting her with them as he did so, Darcy couldn't help being impressed. Judd was a formidable force and a consummate public speaker; his audience were hanging off every word. They were paid to, of course, but without exception, each and every one of them was gazing at Judd with the slavish devotion of an extremist groupie, their eyes shining with anticipation at the powerful message he was delivering.

'If we're going to become the biggest record company in Britain,' Judd paused to afford them all an evil smile, 'there are going to have to be some casualties.'

Sebastian, engrossed in looking at porn on his iPhone until that point, finally lifted his head.

'The Shamrock Music Group.' Judd put a hand to his red-gold hair and Darcy was surprised to see the hand trembling. She'd already guessed Judd had a personal reason for launching a vendetta on Lochlin Maguire from what he'd said at the party but she had no idea what was behind it. She fervently hoped whatever it was wouldn't turn out to be Judd's Achilles' heel because, in her experience, personal issues were the one thing guaranteed to create weakness in any plan.

Wow, he really was hell-bent on revenge, she thought, shocked to see how moved Judd was as he appeared to forget what he was saying. In spite of letting out an involuntary shiver at his malevolent declaration, Darcy couldn't help feeling a grudging respect for Judd's single-mindedness. There was something incredibly dynamic and charismatic about him; he reminded her of Simon Cowell, whom she had met several times.

But there was something different about Judd, a coldness where there should have been warmth. He was like Simon Cowell without his intrinsic air of humorous self-deprecation, Darcy decided. And that, she thought, made Judd incredibly egotistical and seriously dangerous.

'We can tackle the likes of EMI later but for now, Shamrock is our biggest competitor.' Judd cracked his knuckles loudly. 'I have big plans for some of Maguire's artists, and some of his staff, for that matter, but our first acquisition is Charlie Valentine.'

Astonishment registered on the faces of Judd's loyal groupies and he nodded, as if expecting this response. 'I know what you're thinking but this is all about stealth. Charlie is the first of many artists I'm interested in and I happen to know he's very unhappy at Shamrock. So what I'm planning is another greatest hits album and Darcy will be taking Charlie on as her first project.'

Another greatest hits album? Darcy frowned. What a terrible idea! Charlie was already seen as a bit of a joke with his nineties rock look and dated material, how on earth was she supposed to make him look good with regurgitated soft rock and leather trousers from two decades ago? And what about everything she'd just suggested to Judd in his office about Charlie? Had he even been listening?

She opened her mouth to say something but seeing the threatening expression on Judd's face, she closed it again.

Jesus, what on earth had she got herself into? Remembering the way her body had shuddered all over in his office earlier, Darcy knew that wherever it might lead her, right now Judd was far too exhilarating to resist. She was just going to have to bite her tongue for a while, until she had him more under control. She was certain she could be a success at this job and have Judd eating out of her hand by the time she was through.

She inclined her head demurely. 'I'll make sure Charlie's album is absolutely first class. Even with regurgitated material,' she added, to make her point.

Judd stared her down before allowing himself a Machiavellian sneer as he took his seat at the head of the table again. Leaning back in a classic alpha male pose, his hands tucked behind his head, his groin exposed, Judd couldn't help revelling in the feeling of elation rising inside. Charlie Valentine was just the start of Lochlin's problems. There was still Iris – he had big plans for her, bigger than anyone could imagine. There was also that jumped-up little shit Shay to deal with, and of course Tavvy . . .

Before the year was out, Judd thought, his eyes glinting wickedly, unaware that Darcy was watching him in utter fascination, no one in the music business would even remember who Lochlin fucking Maguire was.

Kitty reluctantly poured hot coffee into the lavish Versace Barocco cups Judd had ordered. They were black and gold and rather difficult to hold but Lexi Beaument, at least, seemed entranced by them.

'OMG, it's so fabulous, I don't think I should even drink out of it!' Lexi held the cup up by the tiny winged handle and gawked at it, almost spilling coffee down her Rock and Republic jeans in her excitement. 'I'm going to get my Leo to buy me some of these.' She wandered off to gape at the swimming pool.

Susannah rolled her heavily kohled eyes. 'That girl is such a wannabe!'

Hopeful of fitting in with her new English friends, Kitty had thrown on a navy wool dress and conservative heels but glancing at Susannah in her red jeans, diamante T-shirt and black blazer with the sleeves rolled up, she realised she'd got it spectacularly wrong. Kitty reassured herself with the thought that Susannah and Lexi were perhaps not stereotypical of women who lived in remote English villages.

'Lexi's real pretty,' Kitty sighed, wishing her bum was even half the size of Lexi's.

'She is,' Susannah agreed, checking out Lexi's long slender legs and minuscule waist. 'Do you know, I think I used to look like that before I had the twins.' She held her tiny cup out. 'Seriously, I'm going to need at least ten more of these if we're drinking out of thimbles.'

Kitty laughed ruefully. 'I *never* looked like that, even before childbirth! Hey, did you enjoy your party? We all thought it was great fun.'

'Full of drama, as usual,' Susannah said. Rumours about some feud between Judd and Lochlin were spreading around the village like wildfire but she wasn't about to comment on them. 'How's

Martha, by the way? I put my foot in it dreadfully over the pregnancy thing.'

For her part, Kitty was feeling rather uncomfortable. Without explaining why, Judd had tersely informed them that they should all steer clear of the Maguire family who lived across the valley, which might make things awkward when Susannah and Charlie were good friends with Lochlin and Tavvy.

'Oh, it's not your fault. Sebastian and Martha have a difficult marriage.'

Susannah nodded. 'She told me about the affairs. I sympathise; Charlie's an absolute nightmare when it comes to groupies, he can't resist them. What about Judd?'

Kitty's pink cheeks spoke volumes.

'God, what is it about men?' Susannah nearly knocked her cup flying in her indignation. 'Jesus, it's as if their penises are their favourite toy from childhood; they can't stop playing with them and they simply refuse to put them back in the box.'

Kitty burst out laughing then stopped, knowing the situation really wasn't that funny. She felt she could trust Susannah so she explained. 'Judd's affairs . . . well, it's one of the reasons there's such a gap between the boys. Alistair – we call him Ace – is twenty-three and Elliot is sixteen. Judd was having a fling with someone in New York for ages, you see, when he was working there. Callie, Candi . . . something like that. He thought I didn't know but I found out and I literally couldn't bear to let him near me.' She swallowed, remembering what a terrible time it was. 'I–I almost left him, actually, but he wouldn't have it.' Kitty almost touched her shattered cheekbone again as she said the words but caught herself just in time.

Susannah watched her keenly. She'd seen the signs before and it made her blood boil. 'We should all stick together against our husbands and their wandering dicks. You, me and Martha.'

'What about Lexi? Shouldn't she be in our gang too?' Kitty craned her neck to see where Lexi had got to.

Susannah pulled a face. 'Leo? You're kidding, aren't you? He's the most attentive husband you could ever wish for.' She frowned. 'Didn't you meet him at the party?'

Kitty shook her head.

'Lovely guy,' Susannah commented. 'He fell for Lexi years ago, found her sobbing in a corner at some dinner party and instantly wanted to take care of her.' She studied Kitty. What on earth she was doing with a domineering bully like Judd was anyone's guess but Susannah couldn't help feeling her new friend needed a boost. 'You must come to one of my make-up parties. I own my own line, Valentine Make-Up. Have you heard of it?'

Kitty's open mouth indicated how impressed she was. '*You* own Valentine Make-Up? Wow, you can only buy that in the best stores in the States.'

Susannah looked pleased. 'Good, so you'll come then? We'll have a really girly evening. You deserve to pamper yourself.'

'Do I?'

Susannah nodded. 'Apologies if I'm speaking out of turn but Judd looks rather . . . high maintenance.' She chewed her lip, not sure how far she should go. 'I mean, apart from the affairs, he looks quite . . . aggressive.'

Kitty flushed. 'He's . . . I'm . . .' She faltered, tears springing into her eyes.

'My sister got killed by her husband after years of being beaten,' Susannah informed her in a gentle voice. 'I've seen the signs before.'

Kitty gulped. 'It only happened once before when I tried to leave him after his big affair in New York . . .' Her voice trailed away. 'You can't tell anyone, not a soul.' There was terror in her eyes.

Susannah squeezed her hand. 'Of course I won't! Not even Charlie, I promise.'

They both looked up as Lexi joined them.

'What a beautiful house you 'ave,' Lexi gushed, not even noticing that her accent had slipped. 'I'd love to live somewhere like this. Leo 'as such old-fashioned taste. Foxton Manor is like a hundred years old with all this period stuff in it and it's really musty, but this – this is so bloody *classy*.'

Kitty was rendered speechless but, unable to help herself and far less concerned with demonstrating good manners, Susannah went off into peals of laughter, leaving Lexi staring at her in bemusement.

Savannah tried not to gape at the marble floors and crystal chandeliers as she checked in.

'Will madam require a newspaper in the morning?' the male receptionist asked. He tried not to gape at her fantastic breasts.

'No thanks.' She looked amused at being called 'madam'. It was obviously what they did in the best hotels in London but it felt strange.

His eyes lingered on her glorious long red hair and the curvaceous body, emphasised by tight jeans and a black roll-neck jumper. She was twenty, twenty-one, possibly, yet she oozed that indefinable American confidence some Brits reviled yet secretly envied.

In spite of this, the expert gaze of the receptionist identified that the girl was unused to and, moreover, uncomfortable in such plush surroundings. 'Is madam sure? *The Times*, perhaps? The *Telegraph*? Or if madam would prefer it, the *Daily Mail*?' He gave her a bland smile, only his eyes revealing what he thought of such a choice.

'No thanks.' Savannah paused. 'But *Rolling Stone* would be great . . . if you can get it.'

The receptionist tapped his keyboard. 'Consider it done.'

Impressed, Savannah shivered. It had been snowing in New York when she left but somehow the biting wind and rain made it feel chillier in London. Wishing she'd invested in a warmer coat, she handed over the credit card she'd managed to blag in the States before she left. Daddy dearest was going to be footing the bill for her flight and her hotel once they came face to face so Savannah wasn't prepared to scrimp on luxury. Besides, she deserved it. She took the key card from the receptionist and glanced at the lift he was pointing out.

'Thanks . . . er . . . Lawrence,' she returned, reading the name on his badge. 'Hey, have you ever heard of a place called Bucks?'

Lawrence nodded. 'Of course. Bucks is actually more formally known as Buckinghamshire. It's a county in the south-east,' he explained. He wrote it down for her. 'And don't, whatever you do, pronounce it "shy-er" as in Shire horse. It's "sheer". You Americans always get that wrong.'

'Lucky we have you Brits to put us right then, isn't it?' she said mockingly, taking the piece of paper and heading for the lift. 'Don't forget my *Rolling Stone*, now, will you, Larry.'

Bristling at her familiarity but unable to tear his gaze away from her delectable backside, Lawrence couldn't help smiling once she was out of sight.

Arriving on the twentieth floor, Savannah raced down the corridor to her room and opened the door. Gasping with delight, she charged inside, slamming the door and drinking in every detail. Without a shadow of a doubt, it was the most gorgeous room she'd ever been in. God knows how many square feet she had and, better than that, she had a view of the London Eye. Fuck! She had a four-poster bed all to herself, with a chocolate silk bedspread and a pile of sumptuous vanilla-coloured cushions. There was a vast dressing table lit up by tiny bulbs and in the bathroom she found a tub she could do breaststroke in and a cabinet full of fancy Champneys toiletries. Scooping them into her bag without thinking, Savannah stopped and carefully lined them up on the glass shelf again. She was in a hotel, one of the most fabulous in the whole of London. Even if she somehow managed to use up all that shampoo and bath foam, it would be replaced in the morning.

Savannah whooped and ran back into the bedroom. This was the biggest adventure she'd ever been on and, even now, she couldn't believe she was here. In England of all places. She had always wanted to visit London and here she was. The few friends she had back in New York hadn't believed she would really go through with it and Savannah wished they could see her now, holed up in a swanky room with a view to die for and curtains that cost more than her clothes.

She leant on the window sill and stared out at the view. Her father hadn't been easy to track down, especially with only his surname as a starting point, and it had cost her a small fortune in coffee and laptop time in a cafe back in New York to trace Judd Harrington. Ironically, although he was British, it appeared her father had only just returned to his former home; up until a few months ago he'd been in Los Angeles, just a short plane ride away.

Savannah allowed herself a triumphant smile. What was Daddy Harrington going to think when she turned up at his office? In reality, she knew she didn't really care; in her eyes, he was a cash cow, nothing more. One way or another, she was going to make sure she had a share in the Harrington billions she'd been reading about.

What were the odds of finding out her long-lost father was a *billionaire*? she thought, hugging herself. It was too cool for words. Once she started digging, Savannah had found out about all of Judd's companies. Some had been successful; some had been ill-advised and short-lived. Clearly, her father liked taking risks and he wasn't afraid to invest in an underdog – which might stand her in good stead when they met up. Even though she was determined to get her money's worth out of him, Savannah was less interested in the cash side of things than she was in Judd's latest business venture.

She flung herself back on the bed. She was finally about to realise her dream of being rich and famous. She wasn't going to end up like her mother after all; she was destined for glory, something she had suspected all along. Living a life of poverty and disappointment was no longer part of her future and this – Savannah glanced cheerfully round the room – this was going to be the norm from now on. This and diamonds and Jimmy Choos and an account at that posh shop Harrods, she thought gleefully.

Flipping the TV channels until she found Christina Aguilera strutting around on stage on MTV, Savannah let out a blissful sigh. Life had just taken a turn for the better.

Later that night, wearing Lochlin's reading glasses and a faded red Mickey Mouse sweatshirt to keep warm in bed, Tavvy was bent over a notepad, scribbling furiously. With only the dim light of a candle to work with, her eyes were straining to see the paper but she just needed to get this last part of the melody down and then she could let it go.

Hearing Lochlin stirring in bed next to her, Tavvy ground her teeth and willed the tune to haunt her again.

For Tavvy, the music always came first, the words later. The music would speak to her and the words would tumble out of her like a waterfall, something her pop star friends had envied, back in the day; she made it look easy, they said.

In the eighties, Tavvy had always felt she was lucky because melodies would meander their way into her consciousness, fully formed, soulful in all the right places and intricately beautiful. It was something she'd been lucky enough not to have to work at and, of course, having a number of hit singles worldwide was incredibly lucrative; the royalties paid for her animal charity, for a start.

But these days, it was nothing short of aggravating. Tavvy had far too much going on in her life with her family and her animals to have time to write songs. She had made a decision to become a housewife and to turn her back on her musical career and she had been deliriously happy ever since. She felt far more fulfilled than she had ever imagined she would be and this irritating tune popping into her head was a curve ball she hadn't expected.

She glanced in the direction of Brockett Hall, which on a clear day could be seen from her bedroom window, a section of the roof visible through a crack in the curtains. Judd Harrington was back, ensconced in his former home, far too close for comfort. Tavvy shivered. What the hell was he doing back here?

She tapped the pencil against her teeth thoughtfully. When she'd first met him, Judd had seemed so dynamic. He was forceful and ambitious and he had a brash charm which had been hard to resist. But as she'd got to know him better, she'd realised he wasn't so much dynamic as dangerous and what she'd seen as ambition was actually ruthlessness. Judd had a cruel streak and his reckless behaviour often led to heartbreak – or, as she and Lochlin knew better than anyone else, tragedy. He had led her down a hazardous path and she wasn't the only one.

Tavvy glanced at Lochlin's sleeping form. When they found each other, their lives had changed for ever. The dread and anxiety she'd experienced in her relationship with Judd were replaced by love and heady passion.

'You're infatuated,' Judd had sneered, unable to believe Tavvy could leave him for someone else. Then he had shown her exactly how he felt about her betrayal. She closed her eyes, trying to block out the memories, but it was impossible.

When she'd first started out in music, life had been so simple. The only thing Tavvy had had to worry about was disappointing her parents who, being a famous opera singer and a concert pianist, found her pop star career irksome. Naming their daughter Octavia after the musical note, her parents had dreamt of her becoming a world-renowned classical musician. After their untimely death in a car accident, Tavvy had realised how empty her life was. She desperately needed something to fulfil her. She had always preferred songwriting and, encouraged by Lochlin Maguire, a young, ambitious trainee at his father's record label, she'd started to focus on writing music rather than performing it.

Looking back, Tavvy realised how lost she'd been after her parents died because at first she'd been grateful for Judd

Harrington's reassuringly commanding presence. But soon he'd become possessive and controlling, and when Judd's jealousy over her friendship with Lochlin led to her accidental drug overdose, Lochlin had stepped in and saved her. Handsome, strong and passionate, rather like the proverbial knight on a white horse, Lochlin had nursed her back to health and their romance had blossomed. Shortly after their ridiculously romantic Christmas wedding and the tragedy that had rocked the village, Judd had disappeared from their lives for good. Until now.

Turning back to her notepad, Tavvy focused her mind on the song, knowing herself well enough to realise that if she didn't get it down, she would never be able to rest. She had always been able to ignore melodies in the past, telling herself they weren't good enough and that she no longer needed them anyhow. But this one . . . this one was different. . . .

Letting the song wash over her, Tavvy swiftly transferred it to her notepad. Half an hour later, emotionally drained, she lay back on the pillows in relief and took off Lochlin's glasses.

'Tavvy?' Lochlin lifted his dark head off the pillow. 'Are you all right, darlin'?' He held his arm out to her, concerned.

Shoving the notepad under the bed furtively, Tavvy snuggled back down under the covers, tucking herself into the crook of his arm.

'I'm fine. I couldn't sleep, that's all.'

Lochlin turned to face her, the candlelight exposing the apprehension in his eyes. 'Is it because of Judd?'

Tavvy shook her head vehemently, hating even hearing his name. 'No.' She reached out and stroked Lochlin's face, dismayed at the tension in his jaw.

Lochlin stared past her. 'What he's doing here, Tav? Why the fuck would he come back after all this time? To get revenge on me?' He looked down at her. 'He hates me because I have you, that's it, isn't it? By God, if Judd ever lays a finger on you again—'

'Why would he?'

'Because Judd can't bear to lose. Because instead of admitting to himself that you left him, he'd rather think I stole you.'

Tavvy linked her fingers through his. 'That's his problem.'

'And now it's mine,' Lochlin said grimly. 'He's out to ruin me, darlin', he must be. The Jett Record Corporation, that's not a coincidence. He wants to bring Shamrock down and, if I know him, he'll be after you too.' He sat up in bed, angrily gesturing to Brockett Hall. 'What I don't understand is, shouldn't it be me doing this to him? Shouldn't I be the one who wants revenge?' His eyes clouded over with emotion. 'What about what he did to you, Tav? What about Seamus? He's responsible, everyone knows it . . .'

'Ssshhh.' Tavvy kissed him, wishing she had never got mixed up with Judd Harrington in the first place. 'This is all my fault, I feel so responsible.'

'Don't be daft.' He looked down at her tenderly. 'I'm just worried about the kids. What do we tell them? They're asking questions . . . they want answers, especially Shay.' Lochlin squeezed her fingers. 'Do they really need to know about . . . about what happened? I want to protect them from this, I don't want them to get involved.'

Tavvy nodded, her tawny-blond hair falling forward. 'I know. Sometimes I think it would be better if they knew but then . . . it was all so wicked, do we really want them dragged into the whole hideous mess?' She lowered her eyes. 'But should we shut them out like this? Shouldn't we all stick together now that he's back?'

'I don't know what to do for the best.' Lochlin sighed and drew her closer. 'I can't bear the thought of him near you.'

She touched his chest. 'It's all in the past.'

'But it isn't, is it?' Lochlin cupped her chin and stared into her amber eyes. 'Now that Judd's back, it's bringing it all into the here and now.'

Tavvy gazed at him. Yanking the Mickey Mouse sweatshirt over her head, she pulled him down on to her naked body. 'The only thing in the here and now is you and me. As far as I'm concerned,

Judd Harrington is nothing to do with us, not you, not me and not our children.'

Feeling her warm full breasts crushed against his chest and her sexy amber eyes drinking him in sleepily, Lochlin could almost believe her. Almost. With an aching heart, he bent his head and kissed his wife, the woman he and Judd appeared to love in equal measure. He just hoped to God he didn't lose her.

Chapter Six

Elliot wrapped his scarf around his neck and tried to work out what time it was in LA. Realising the eight-hour difference meant his friends would still be in bed, especially after one of their Friday-night parties, he headed outside for some air. Staring out across the Buckinghamshire countryside, Elliot supposed parts of the English countryside were beautiful in their own way. The gentle slope of the Chiltern Hills was pretty impressive and the silvery-grey bark of the beech trees had an undeniable elegance. But Elliot longed for the cheery sunshine and stretches of sandy beach he had left behind in LA – and all the other things he missed. How could his fucking father have moved them all to England without even asking them what *they* wanted to do?

Pulling his phone out, he read a text from Ace. Littered with mistakes and a lack of punctuation, it looked as if Ace had sent it whilst out partying.

'*Hi little bro*,' it said. '*Miss you and hope uk not too cold? If Seb being a shit – remember his tiny willy has freckles ☺ chickss great here. much love! Ace*.'

Elliot laughed out loud. God, he missed Ace! Just about to text him back, he was accosted by a bundle of energy in a fake fur coat.

'Hello!' the girl panted, her breath making swirly white patterns in the air. 'How lovely to bump into you.'

'It's *you*,' Elliot said, recognising the exceptionally pretty girl he'd spotted at the Valentines' Ball. Flushed from the cold, her dark curls squashed under a cream beanie hat, she was giving him the most dazzling smile.

'I'm Caitie, by the way. Caitie Maguire.' She held her hand out. 'And you're Elliot Harrington. I found out at the party. You do know our parents are arch enemies, of course? We shouldn't even be speaking, let alone touching.'

Elliot shook her hand, feeling nervous. Whoever this Caitie was, she was clearly brimming with confidence and he was suddenly tongue-tied. He realised he was staring at her and rushed to speak. 'Er . . . you must be one of those Maguires my father told me to avoid like the plague.'

Caitie shrugged. Close up, he was breathtaking; his slight tan and incredibly sexy grey eyes made him look like a young film star. 'Isn't it ludicrous? I haven't a clue what it's all about and it's driving me mad. Perhaps you know what the big secret is.' She took a silver flask out of her pocket and took a swig from it. 'Help yourself to Schnapps . . . it's for the cold; I'm not an alkie or anything.'

Marvelling at her long dark eyelashes, cute dimples and mischievous green eyes, Elliot took the flask without a word and winced as the fruity alcohol hit the back of his throat. 'I don't know anything about a secret,' he told her. 'I just know my father hates your father.'

Caitie nodded and, with chattering teeth, lit a menthol cigarette. 'We have to get to the bottom of it. It's exciting but I can't stand all this secrecy. I'm the sort of person who has to get to the truth, you know?'

Elliot smiled. 'Isn't that just another way of saying you're nosy?'

Caitie giggled and blew smoke in the air. 'Of course it is. So, have you met anyone else round here yet?' Before he had a chance to reply she grabbed his arm. 'Hey, you should join my drama group.' She saw him recoil and rushed to reassure him. 'No, no, seriously, it's so much fun! You'll make tons of friends and we have such a laugh. Hugo, the guy who runs it, used to act at the Old Vic, which is terribly impressive, and, for some reason, he seems to think I'm rather good.' She paused for breath. 'I'm going to be an actress, you see,' she informed him gravely. 'A serious actress. Like my idol, Kate Winslet. Or Dame Judi Dench.'

Elliot admired her self-belief. He wished he could see his future with such certainty but, in reality, he didn't have a clue what to do with himself. His father had always told him he was a waste of space and as much as he battled not to believe it, it had, at the very least, made Elliot indecisive about his talents. Acting was hardly the hobby his father would recommend, but Elliot wasn't in the mood to be submissive.

'All right. I'll think about it,' he said, enjoying the spark of rebellion that flared up inside him. He glanced at Caitie. He liked her. He wasn't sure if he liked her in *that* way but then . . . he'd never liked a girl in that way before, not really. Elliot's stomach tightened. For the past few years, he had worried about himself and he hated not knowing what and who he was. Maybe he was about to find out, he thought hopefully.

'Ooh, there's Jasmine. She's my best friend. You'll love her.' A girl with shiny brown hair and a tanned face was heading towards them. 'Look, there's this recital thing on in a few weeks. You could come along and see if you want to join.' She gave him a crumpled leaflet with two masks on the front. 'We're doing *Romeo and Juliet* this year – perfect for us, don't you think?'

Jas joined them and blushed as she gave Elliot a shy smile. 'Hey. Nice to meet you. I see Cait's railroaded you into coming to the recital.'

'Yeah. Well, I'll see if I can come.' Elliot recognised a kindred spirit; Jas was obviously as shy as he was. Watching his new friends head off in the other direction, Elliot took his phone out and sent Ace a much more upbeat text than he'd planned to send earlier.

'See what you can find out about the family feud!' Caitie called over her shoulder to Elliot as she dragged Jas away. 'God, he's gorgeous, Jas! I don't care if he's a Harrington, he's Romeo to my Juliet, I just know it!'

Jas shook her head. She was used to Caitie's madcap ways and Elliot was definitely drop-dead gorgeous, but Jas couldn't help thinking Caitie was in danger of getting her fingers burnt this time.

Dreadfully late for work, Iris was frantically rummaging through her handbag for her phone, hindered by Nutmeg, the Beagle who was doing his best to get under her feet. Hair all over the place, mascara smudged under her eyes, Iris had spent the night thrashing about as she wrestled with telling her parents about Judd's offer.

'Lost something, darling?'

Wearing a honey-coloured silk dress she'd picked up in Oxfam and her fake leopard-skin boots, Tavvy wandered into the kitchen, humming a tune merrily. The words for the song she'd written the other night were flooding into her mind uncontrollably now and, to her consternation, she was actually rather enjoying it.

'*Our love is rare*,' she hummed to herself. '*With you I share, everything . . . yes, everything . . . passion, love and tenderne-eeess . . .*' She glanced at Iris who was tipping a basket of clean laundry all over the floor.

'It's my phone.' Iris frowned. 'I saw it yesterday and now it's *completely* disappeared.' In frustration, she dropped a handful of Caitie's brightly coloured g-strings on Nutmeg's head and he yelped indignantly.

Tavvy calmly stopped Iris hurling pants across the room. 'I hardly think it's likely to have gone in the wash with everyone's smalls, darling. Well, not unless you keep your mobile phone in your bra like Caitie sometimes does.' She smiled, wondering why Iris seemed so preoccupied. Her amber eyes looked troubled and her hands were darting around restlessly, both signs that something wasn't right.

'Everything all right?' Tavvy asked casually, folding up Shay's Abercrombie boxers.

Iris shrugged. 'I'm late for work and my boss has been so understanding lately, what with me having things on my mi—' she faltered. She was dying to tell her mother about Judd's record deal offer and the secret was hanging guiltily on her shoulders like a ton weight.

As a rule, she and her mother were like sisters, gossiping about boys and sex and talking endlessly about music but this, well, Iris couldn't help feeling that this offer from Judd was different. Somehow, Iris didn't feel she could confide in her mother about it, not when both her parents were acting so bizarrely about the whole thing. She busied herself by checking under the kitchen table for her phone.

Uneasily, Tavvy heaved the laundry basket into the pantry. Ever since Judd's arrival, it seemed as if all of them had been on edge; their strong, close-knit family unit suddenly felt disconnected and unsettled, as if Judd's presence had torn a hole in their usually impenetrable circle.

Leaning on the wash basket, Tavvy couldn't help thinking she and Lochlin were making a mistake by keeping their children in the dark about the past. But then an image of Judd's malevolent face swam in front of Tavvy's eyes and the parental lioness in her rose to the surface. No, she wanted to protect her children from him, she didn't want them exposed to his wicked games.

'Oh, Iris, I've found your phone!' Tavvy called as she tugged it out from under a pile of magazines to be recycled. 'And you've got a text message.'

'It's probably just Matt. Can you have a quick look for me?' Iris pulled a fleece over her head, groaning as she realised she'd messed her hair up. She quickly gathered it up into a ponytail.

In the pantry, Tavvy called up Iris's text message and read it. A cold trickle went down her spine and she almost dropped the phone in shock.

'What does it say?' Iris called, using the kettle for a mirror. 'Is

Matt going mental? I promised him I'd be there early because we've got so many surgeries booked in.'

'It's not from Matt.' Tavvy came in and slowly sat down at the kitchen table. She pushed the phone across to Iris. 'It's from Judd Harrington.'

Iris stopped dead, her hands still on her ponytail. Lowering them shakily, she reached out for her phone and read the message. '*Have you made a decision yet?*' she read. '*Time is running out for those singing lessons in LA. Pia has a slot on an awards show if you come. Call me. Judd.*'

Tavvy stared at Iris with fearful eyes. 'What's going on? What singing lessons? And how the hell did Judd get your number?'

Iris slid down on to a chair, her bee-stung lips trembling. 'I-I don't know how he got my number,' she admitted honestly, 'but the singing lessons in LA, Judd offered those to me at the Valentines' Ball.'

'My God, Iris! Why didn't you say anything?' Tavvy stared at Iris. This was so unlike her; Iris was usually an open book.

'I didn't know what to do.' Iris twisted her hands wretchedly. 'Judd spoke to me after I sang and he gave me his card. I swear I didn't have a clue who he was until Dad arrived and told us all to stay away from the Harringtons.' Tears came into her eyes. 'I tried to find Dad so I could tell him about the singing lessons and the record deal but then I caught Ollie at it and the next thing I knew, Dad was throwing a wobbly about Judd.'

'He offered you a record deal as well?' Tavvy put her head in her hands. She remembered Iris dashing around trying to find Lochlin at the ball to talk to him about something but never in a million years had she guessed it was anything like this. Iris's words suddenly hit home and Tavvy's head snapped up.

'Singing lessons in LA. Pia – wow, is that Pia *Jordan*?'

Iris nodded, biting her nails. She couldn't ignore the spark of excitement flickering inside her at the thought of going to LA, even though she couldn't see it ever happening.

Tavvy knew exactly what these singing lessons could do for Iris and how much she must want to go to LA. And so, no doubt, did Judd. She cursed him for making the offer to Iris and, in that instant, she knew for certain that Judd wasn't back to play nicely or to make amends.

'I said no,' Iris said, rushing to explain. 'I mean, I haven't said no but I haven't said yes. I'd never take the record deal, you know that, but the singing lessons . . . look, I wanted to tell you and Dad about it but you've both been so . . .' She stopped, not wanting to sound offensive. 'Well, you've obviously decided not to tell us what happened with Judd all those years ago.'

Tavvy flushed guiltily. 'We didn't know what to do for the best. You have to understand, Judd is so evil. I know that must sound dramatic but it's true.' She grabbed Iris's hand. 'Iris, I'm so sorry. Judd had no right to do this to you – to put you in this position.' She fixed her eyes on Iris fiercely. 'You deserve this, Iris, more than anyone. Judd offered you this opportunity because you're talented and because you're going to be a world-class singer, I'm sure of that. Working with Pia Jordan, what better start could you have to your career? She's the best in the business.'

'But . . . you think his offer has something to do with Dad?' Iris felt crushed.

Tavvy bit her lip. 'I think Judd knows exactly how your father would react to this but he went ahead and did it anyway.'

Iris nodded miserably. 'It's just that I don't know if Dad could ever arrange this for me. Judd obviously has connections . . .' She stood up and headed to the back door, pocketing her phone. She shook her head, her back to Tavvy. 'It's all right, honestly. As soon as Dad said we had to stay away from the Harringtons, I knew this wouldn't come to anything.' She turned back with a sad smile. 'Don't say anything, will you? To Dad, I mean. I'd rather just forget about it.'

Watching Iris's slumped shoulders walk past the window, Tavvy banged her fist on the table. How could Judd do this to Iris? How could he build her hopes up like that, knowing Lochlin would never agree to such a thing? Tavvy almost wished she could convince Lochlin to let Iris go, then at least Judd wouldn't have won. At least they wouldn't be rowing and falling out over this, which had to be exactly what Judd wanted.

Pensively, Tavvy rubbed Nutmeg's nose. An idea popped into her head and with it came a glimmer of hope. She sat up, making Nutmeg jump. Maybe she *could* convince Lochlin to let Iris go to LA after all . . .

Driving to the gym in his black Porsche, Sebastian Harrington gritted his teeth furiously. Martha was driving him insane with her constant whining about babies; even a hard hour on the treadmill had to be less stressful than listening to his wife moaning about periods and fertility.

'Why aren't I pregnant?' she had screamed at him hysterically, as if it was *his* fault she wasn't up the duff. Of course, Sebastian didn't know for sure it was Martha's fault but he refused to believe there was anything wrong with *him*.

Sebastian parked his Porsche with a screech of tyres and grabbed his sports bag from the passenger seat. He didn't have a paternal bone in his body and he certainly had no intention of changing shitty nappies when a baby finally materialised but Sebastian couldn't help wishing Martha would just fall pregnant and be done with it. He hated the thought of everyone gossiping behind his back at work and speculating about their lack of offspring, especially if they might be suggesting his sperm was deficient in any way.

Horrified at such a thought, Sebastian had told Martha they hadn't conceived because she was so fat. She had dissolved into appalled tears and he had made a quick getaway. Heading inside the gym and getting changed, Sebastian felt a flicker of guilt but it was soon replaced by a sense of intense dissatisfaction. Dimly, he remembered Martha being much sexier when he married her.

Sexier, slimmer . . . she had been a glossy young woman other men had salivated over. His father had told him on his wedding day he was a fool to marry her but Sebastian had ignored him, misguidedly envisaging Martha as the perfect wife waiting for him at home in her satin underwear and producing heirs at the drop of a hat. How wrong he had been, but Sebastian was buggered if he was going to admit failure, knowing how much his father would enjoy triumphantly crowing over it.

He took out his aggression on the treadmill, clocking up a ten-mile run in record time. As he climbed off the machine, he caught sight of a stunning brunette in the coffee area wearing a tiny pink leotard.

Giving the girl an admiring once-over, he saw that she had pert buttocks and slender legs with cute legwarmers at the ankles and when she turned round, Sebastian realised with a jolt she was in her early twenties. Not only that, she reminded him poignantly of Martha, the young, attractive Martha he had married, not the chubby, manic depressive she had become of late. As he lusted over her, the girl inspected him, her blunt chestnut hair swinging around her chin. As her wide apart green eyes connected with Sebastian's, the look in them was disappointingly unfriendly.

Sebastian gave her a smarmy smile and strode over. 'Hi there, how are you?' He almost fell into her fake breasts which were jutting provocatively out of her leotard. She gave him a disdainful look and her friends tittered.

'I'm Sebastian Harrington,' he added, wishing he could get her on her own.

In a trice, her manner changed. 'Harrington, you say? Well, how lovely to meet you!' She beamed at him. 'I'm Lexi Beaument.'

Sebastian was taken aback by the abrupt about-turn but he soon forgot about it as she batted her eyelashes at him in the most charming manner.

'We're neighbours,' she went on, gesturing for him to sit with her at one of the tables. 'I live at Foxton Manor, you know, the big old house on the hill?' She leant forward, her green eyes shining. 'I love Brockett Hall, it's so . . . *grand*, isn't it? A really lovely bit of . . . er . . . it's a *lovely* building.'

Sebastian preened. She had a funny accent, sort of posh like many of the PR girls who worked at Jett but with a strange, coarse undertone. He shrugged. All that mattered was that he finally seemed to have hooked one of these English girls, and Lexi Beaument, whoever she might be, was an absolute cracker. She was just what he needed to boost his ego after Martha's tedious whining, Sebastian told himself, pleased. If only his brother Ace could see him now . . .

Lexi was feeling equally pleased with herself and she treated Sebastian to another dazzling smile. Redheads weren't normally her thing, but in Sebastian's case, she could make an exception. For a Harrington or, should she say, the heir to a multimillion-dollar fortune, Lexi could definitely get past his colouring.

'So, what do you do, Sebastian?' Discreetly tugging her leotard down to reveal a fraction more cleavage, she remembered the model's trick of lifting her thighs slightly so they looked thinner.

'I'm a lawyer,' he replied, practically falling down her top. 'In my father's firm. One of them – he owns several companies in America and probably half of London by now, knowing him.'

'My husband's a lawyer too, what a coincidence!' Nothing was more intoxicating to her than money and, until now, Lexi hadn't met anyone who earned more than Leo. But Sebastian's father Judd was rumoured to be worth millions and he had many more millions than even Leo had – at least, he did if dollars were worth more than pounds, and they were these days, weren't they? Lexi could never remember.

She spared a passing moment for her husband. The poor darling believed she loved him to distraction but although Leo was sweetness itself, he was so *old*. In his mid-forties, he was practically a geriatric, for heaven's sake! And he was such a workaholic! He had taken four jobs to put himself through law school, Alan Sugar-style, and now that he had reached millionaire status, all he cared about was that his wife should want for nothing.

Keen to impress Lexi, Sebastian leant forward and put a casual hand on her smooth knee. 'I could show you round Brockett Hall,' he said with a greasy smile. She may be married but the flirtatious look in her eyes suggested she was up for something on the side. 'It would be lovely to spend some time with you, if you'd like that.'

'I'd like that very much,' she murmured in a seductive tone. 'I've already seen Brockett Hall, your mother showed me round there the other day. But I'd love a personal tour.' She covered his hand with her own, subtly moving it closer to her groin. She knew how to charm men like Sebastian. The trick was to come across like the girl next door; wholesome and pure but with a secret longing to be taken dirtily on all fours.

And frankly, Lexi thought hungrily, if Sebastian's bank balance was as big as the bulge in his shorts, he could take her any which way he liked.

Shay paused outside his father's office door. It was late and he didn't know if he'd made the right decision by coming to see him or not, but he was here now so he might as well go for it.

'I didn't know you were coming in.' Erica blushed, pretending to check her diary. Shay always made her feel flustered. As if it wasn't enough that he was devastatingly handsome, Erica felt as if she melted like an ice-cream sundae in a heat wave when Shay laid on the charm.

'Neither did I,' he confessed disarmingly, peering at her well-ordered desk. 'Gosh, you're so fabulously efficient, Erica. My father would be lost without you.' He studied her streaky blond tresses. 'Love the new haircut. Very sexy.'

Smiling, Erica waved away the compliment, distracted by Shay's kissable mouth.

'Now, you remember our pact.' He winked. 'No getting married without me.'

No one was that lucky, Erica thought, nonetheless allowing herself to picture the scene – herself in a stunning Jenny Packham dress, Shay in charcoal-grey tails with a pale pink cravat . . .

Shay went into his father's office and surveyed the gold and platinum discs on the wall with pride. God, what he wouldn't give to work at Shamrock. Ruefully, Shay realised he had spent far too much time mucking about and scraping past with the bare minimum of effort. And the one job he cared about, the only job Shay had ever actually wanted, was slipping out of reach because no one took him seriously.

'I wasn't expecting you,' Lochlin commented, holding up a bottle of Scotch. He could do with a large one himself. That morning, he'd learnt that Judd had signed up the girl band he'd had his eye on for weeks now. Double the money and a flashy image makeover had been too tempting for the girls but it still stuck in Lochlin's throat. More to the point, it had made him suspicious about Judd's sources and he couldn't help wondering if he had spies in his midst. 'Drink?'

Shay nodded, taking a seat across from the desk and thinking how shattered his father looked. He fingered his glass apprehensively, wondering if his timing was off.

Lochlin sank into his chair and necked his Scotch. He was furious with himself for not moving more quickly with the girl band. He'd been so preoccupied with Judd being back, he'd taken his eye off the ball and left the field wide open.

Shay put his drink down. Seeing how demoralised his father looked was the kick up the backside he needed. With Judd Harrington sitting in the wings, Shay figured his father needed all the help he could get. Or rather, if he didn't need Shay now, he never would.

'Did you make a decision about Charlie?' he asked, his green eyes attempting indifference.

Lochlin let out an exasperated sigh. 'Charlie? I guess the problem is that I just can't see him being taken seriously as an artist these days,' he said, running a hand through his unruly dark hair. 'With the current trend for disposable pop and reality TV winners, Charlie doesn't really have a place in the charts.'

'True,' Shay nodded, 'but then it's all about taking someone's strengths and turning them into something profitable, isn't it?

Lochlin shrugged but his shoulders were tense.

Shay sat forward keenly. 'Charlie's written some incredible songs, right? That may have been a long time ago and, yes, he's lazy but he could do it again, he could write new material and take a new direction.'

Lochlin wasn't convinced. Nor did he appreciate Shay barging in unannounced to give him unwanted advice. With Judd turning up, he was stressed out enough as it was; in fact, he'd never felt so on edge in years.

Shay's smile faltered. Obviously it had been a huge oversight on his part to come and speak to his father. Christ, what did he need to do to get his approval? Shay thought, wishing he'd gone out with his work pals instead. And when had he changed from being a laughing, fun-loving father figure into a stern, humourless authoritarian?

'I just don't think the timing works for a relaunch,' Lochlin said shortly. 'And, frankly, I could use your support right now, Shay, not your criticism.'

Shay leapt up. 'That's exactly why I'm here, Dad! To support you!' He gestured to the discs on the wall. 'All this . . . this is what I want to be part of, it's what I've always dreamt of.' Shay bit his lip. 'To work alongside you . . . making this company exceptional.'

Lochlin stared at him coldly, his eyes the colour of frozen moss. 'Oh, and it isn't exceptional now, then? And what do you think people would think if I hired you? They'd think it was nepotism, that you didn't deserve it.'

'I don't give a fuck about "people"!' Shay exploded. 'I only care about Shamrock . . . and . . . and you.' He was flushed with anger. 'You make out you're so principled, Dad, but you don't practise what you preach. You want me to make something of myself but only on your terms, and as for Iris, you're holding her back and you know it. You're pushing all of us away when all we want to do is help you.'

Lochlin recoiled. 'I have my reasons for making Iris wait. You know how vulnerable she is.'

Shay was so furious, the words tumbled out of him before he could stop them. 'Do you know who's next on Judd's hit list, Dad? Iris, that's who. Iris told me he's offered her singing lessons in Los Angeles, with Pia Jordan, no less. And she's dying to go but she doesn't want to let you down.' Shay's lip curled contemptuously, not because he blamed Iris for wanting to please their father but because he knew he wanted the very same thing and he hated himself for it.

'Pia Jordan? Los Angeles?' Lochlin gaped, his head reeling. 'Oh my God . . . Judd is going after Iris.'

Shay sat down again. Suddenly, he felt guilty for yelling the news out so brutally. Seeing the blood drain from his father's face, he knew it had been a huge shock.

Lochlin was barely aware of Shay's presence. Clutching the edge of the desk, he grappled with the realisation that Judd wasn't just back to take Tavvy away from him; he was going after his children too. Lochlin drained his Scotch, his knuckles white with tension.

'I just thought you should know,' Shay mumbled.

Lochlin nodded, feeling dreadful as he admitted the truth to himself. He *was* pushing his family away. He had been so desperate to protect Iris, he was stifling her talent. He was so proud of her yet he wouldn't let her be free to pursue her career. And what about Shay? Lochlin stared at his son. Shay was twenty-four years old but Lochlin couldn't help thinking of him as a young boy even though in many ways he was mature for his age. Deep down, though, he knew Shay could be a brilliant asset to the business – if he took the job seriously.

Maybe he should just offer Shay a job, Lochlin thought. If it didn't work out, then fine, but perhaps Shay deserved a chance . . .

Shay stood up. 'What are you going to do about Iris?' he asked in a quiet voice.

Lochlin let out a shuddering breath. 'I want to say yes, I want her to have this opportunity but it feels . . . if I agree, it feels as though Judd is winning.'

'Fucking hell, Dad!' Shay roared in frustration. 'Can't you just forget about this thing with Judd Harrington and think about Iris? It's not about winning or losing, it's about what's best for her!'

Lochlin jumped up. 'Don't tell me how to do my job, Shay. I'm more than fucking qualified to decide what's right for Iris from a business point of view, and as her father. I'm sick and tired of you telling me what to do!' He spoke without thinking. 'You'll never work at Shamrock, not while I have breath in my body.'

Shay turned white. Staggering back, he put a trembling hand to the door and felt for it blindly. With as much dignity as he could muster, he slipped out of the room. Dashing a hand across his eyes to brush his angry tears away before anyone could see them, he realised Erica had heard most of the horrible row. He squeezed her shoulder, giving her one of his heartbreaking smiles.

'Sorry you had to hear that, darling,' he said in a tight voice. 'Families, eh?' His dark eyelashes grazed his cheekbones momentarily before pride forced his head up high. 'Looks like we're not going to be working together after all, angel. But don't worry, our pact still stands. Loyalty means something to me, even if it doesn't mean anything to my father.' With that, he was gone.

Erica jumped out of her chair and uncharacteristically barged into Lochlin's office. About to blast him, she found him with his head in his hands, tears dropping on to the papers on his desk.

'What have you done?' she asked him, aghast.

Lochlin met her gaze. 'Lost him,' he mumbled incoherently.

'I've lost him.' Judd had only been back five minutes and already he was destroying everything Lochlin cared about. And the most crushing thing of all was that Lochlin was making it easy for him.

Judd contemplated Charlie contemptuously. 'So you really think exploding guitars and dancing girls are what you need to get you back out into the spotlight?'

Charlie, wearing a diamanté-studded black shirt and a pair of obscenely tight jeans that left nothing to the imagination nodded in confusion. 'Don't you think so?'

'No. I do not.' Judd tapped his gold pen on the desk. 'I think it sounds incredibly expensive and, frankly, like a bad copy of a Kiss concert from the seventies.'

Darcy inclined her head in agreement. Charlie went bright red, looking for all the world as if someone had let the air out of his tyres. She felt slightly sorry for him; Charlie clearly thought his new contract meant he would have a glittering stage comeback but she knew all too well that Judd had nothing of the sort in mind.

'I don't think gimmicks are the way to go,' Judd was saying, impatiently tossing his pen on to the enormous glass-topped desk and drumming his fingers instead. God, he was bored! Charlie was clearly past it and he didn't have a single original idea about how he should be marketed or how best to promote himself. Frowning at Charlie's bleached-blond hair and navy eyeliner, Judd was half tempted to rip up Charlie's contract and pay him off; he could do without limping puppies that would cost more than they would make. But then signing Charlie had never been about an appreciation of his talent. Signing Charlie had been about swiping an artist – and a so-called loyal friend – from under Shamrock and, more to the point, Lochlin Maguire's nose.

By Judd's side, Darcy crossed her legs under the glass table. She was wearing an exceptionally short skirt and no underwear, for Judd's benefit later. She fixed her cool gaze on Charlie.

'We think album sales are your strength. That and your strong fan base.'

Charlie looked vaguely mollified and wiped his sweating brow with a scarlet handkerchief. As long as they didn't suggest another greatest hits album, he was prepared to be open-minded.

'To that effect, we're thinking of another greatest hits album,' Darcy said without enthusiasm.

Charlie's heart sank.

'Exactly,' Judd said pompously, as if he'd offered Charlie the Holy Grail. 'Repackaged, naturally, with a much younger vibe and some funky new graphics. Maybe with a few remixes thrown in as well, who knows? Something fresh but still with plenty of the old Charlie Valentine for all those devoted fans.' He shot his cuffs. He had shown Charlie his best offer; he was bottom of Judd's list of artists and, frankly, he should be delighted with the suggestion. Besides, Charlie was hardly likely to go back to Lochlin, tail between his legs, was he?

Charlie realised he'd made a terrible mistake. Lochlin had been unforthcoming with ideas but he hadn't once suggested something as ridiculous as another greatest hits album. Funky new graphics? A younger vibe? If he wasn't already, Charlie would be a veritable laughing stock by the time Judd had finished with him.

'Er . . . are you really sure it's the best idea?' he ventured. 'I'm not sure that's right for the current market . . .'

'It's the best I can give you,' Judd shot back nastily.

Darcy felt a modicum of sympathy for Charlie. Of course another greatest hits album was a bad idea! It would pretty much sound the death knell for Charlie's career but Darcy knew Judd didn't give a shit about that. She glanced at him, feeling the familiar flip-flop of desire in her knickers. He had such a strange sexual power over her – it was as if he knew the sex was so mind-blowing, she couldn't stay away from him, even if she wanted to.

Darcy shivered. She couldn't wait for Charlie to leave. Knowing Judd as well as she did – sexually, at any rate – she knew damn well her skirt would be up around her hips seconds after Charlie's departure and his insistent fingers would soon be expertly probing her G-spot. Darcy also knew she would find herself repulsed and turned on in equal measure by the experience but, like a junkie craving a fix, Darcy also knew she would be back for more.

As if he could read her mind, Judd threw a red-hot look in her direction and twirled his gold pen between his fingers, somehow managing to make the gesture seem suggestive. 'I think we're done here, don't you?' he said, not even looking at Charlie.

Feeling as if he'd been summarily dismissed from the headmaster's office, Charlie made his exit with as much dignity as he could in his tight spangly jeans.

Judd swung his chair round to face Darcy, already unzipping his Savile Row trousers.

Darcy squirmed with anticipation and, staying where she was, opened her legs. Underneath the glass table, Judd could see everything. They both jumped with shock as someone with long red hair burst into the office.

A vexed Heidi rushed in after her, her cheeks bright pink.

Darcy hastily snapped her legs together.

'I'm so sorry, Mr Harrington, I tried to stop her but she wouldn't take no for an answer . . .'

Judd zipped up his trousers and straightened his yellow tie. 'No need to apologise, Heidi.' He stared at the intruder, intrigued to know why she was so desperate to see him. A wannabe pop star, perhaps? There had been several hundred of them bombarding the offices since the news had broken about the Jett Record Corporation. Girls and boys of all different ages had arrived in their hordes, brandishing naff head shots and tinny demo CDs. This one had managed to get past security downstairs, as well as risking her life by stalking past his appointed Doberman Heidi, Judd thought, impressed. Not even Darcy had managed to do that.

The girl stood in front of him arrogantly, her long red hair over one shoulder, her hands on her hips. She was in her early twenties,

Judd guessed, and she wore a fitted black leather jacket over a sexy, low-cut T-shirt which showed off the provocative tilt of her breasts. Her eyes were blue, almost unnaturally so.

'I'm Savannah,' she said by way of introduction. Her New York twang was unexpected.

'And what can I do for you, Savannah?' he inquired, wondering why he wasn't more put out at her audacity. As it was, he couldn't help admiring her for being so bolshie and he couldn't shake off the feeling he'd seen her somewhere before. Seconds later, the girl achieved something few people had ever managed in Judd's life before. She left him utterly speechless.

'I don't know. What *can* you do for me?' she said, taking a seat without being offered one. '*Daddy*,' she added with an impish smile.

Chapter Seven

Judd swallowed. A nerve flickered in his jaw. Finally, he stroked his chin, trying hard to get a handle on the situation.

There was silence in the room as all three of them stared at Savannah, the only sound Judd's high-tech clock ticking mechanically in the background.

Darcy scrutinised the girl. She was sure someone like Judd, with his money, was a prime target for this sort of stunt. But . . . the red hair, the brilliant blue eyes, the flash of arrogance in the withering stare – the resemblance to Judd was uncanny. This *had* to be his daughter. Darcy glanced at Judd to gauge his reaction but his blank expression told her nothing. If he was jolted by Savannah's arrival, he was hiding it well.

'Pleased to see me?' Savannah asked Judd, her careless tone at odds with the fingers clawing restlessly at her jeans.

'Everyone out!' Judd barked. Heidi scarpered, shutting the door behind her soundlessly. Darcy stayed put.

'I mean it,' Judd snarled at Darcy. He gave her a dangerous glare. 'Get out.'

Incensed, she yanked her skirt down and stormed out of the room.

Savannah gave Judd a good-natured grin. 'Well, I'm guessing that's not your wife. Wives tend to wear underwear.'

Judd wasn't amused. 'Do you expect me to just take you at your word? How the hell do I know for sure you're my daughter?'

'Aside from the glaringly obvious physical resemblance?' Savannah's tone was sarcastic. She pulled some paperwork out of her pocket, plus a selection of photographs of both Judd and her mother. 'But feel free to do a DNA test, I'm happy to oblige.'

'Candi Summers,' Judd murmured, transported back some twenty-odd years to New York. He'd been investing in another business with Kitty's money – a lucrative strip club, as a matter of fact, and Candi had been working in a nearby bar as a singer. He stared at the photograph of Candi, her blond hair teased into big, *Dynasty*-style waves and the diamantés on her outfit looking as tired and life-weary as she did.

Glancing back at Savannah, Judd could see why he thought he recognised her; aside from the red hair and blue eyes, Savannah had the same nose and cheeks as her mother and the same build – narrow shoulders and long legs.

Judd smirked, his mind wandering back over the years. That's right, Kitty had been giving him the cold shoulder over some of his affairs and in retaliation he had spent as much time as possible in New York in the warm arms of a stripper. His fingers tightened on the photograph as he recalled how he had returned from one trip to find Kitty's bags packed in the hallway. The silly bitch thought she could leave him but he had soon beaten that idea out of her.

'How is Candi?' he inquired. His tone was polite but he was surprised to find he was genuinely interested. He had always been fond of Candi. What she couldn't do with her tongue . . .

'She's dead.' Savannah studied him. My father, she thought in wonder, regarding him with what she hoped was cool detachment. Secretly, she was rather impressed by his domineering presence and egotistical attitude but she'd rather die than admit it. The way he'd dismissed his PA and his mistress on her arrival had been nothing short of masterful. This was clearly a man who was used to being in charge.

For his part, Judd was studying Savannah just as closely. He had always longed for a daughter and she was his all right. He could see himself in her physical appearance and in her attitude. Like him, she was brazen, self-confident and, he suspected, in her own way ruthless. He could see it in her eyes; the direct gaze she turned on him was both aloof and calculating.

'How much?' he asked her softly, his piercing blue eyes fixed on Savannah's identical ones.

'What?'

'How much?' he repeated. 'Don't play dumb, name your price.' He raised his red eyebrows at her, wondering if he was actually going to need to wave his chequebook in her face. 'You're here to blackmail me, right?'

'No.' Savannah wriggled uncomfortably in her chair. 'At least, I do want something but it's not a pay-off.'

Judd was unnerved. Surely she wanted money – what the hell was she doing here otherwise?

'Firstly, I . . . I want to be part of the family,' she told him, surprising herself. Where had *that* come from!? It hadn't even entered her head that she wanted to cosy up with the rest of the Harringtons – at least, not until she'd read up about her half-brothers. She knew there were three of them, but that was it.

Judd laced his fingers together, his mind racing. What did Savannah think he was going to do, welcome her with open arms and let her move into Brockett Hall with him, Kitty and the rest of them?

Suddenly, the idea appealed to Judd's twisted sense of humour. Kitty would spit with rage that he had dared to bring his bastard daughter into the house and Sebastian's nose would be firmly pushed out of joint. He didn't care about Elliot. Wondering what she she wanted, Judd watched as Savannah's eyes slid to one of the signed photographs on the wall.

'You want a career in the music business,' he realised with interest. He assessed her. She undoubtedly had something; her long red hair was unusual and she had arresting features. Her figure was slender and gym-toned – she had the lithe stance of a dancer, he thought, hoping Savannah hadn't followed her mother into a lap-dancing career. He didn't care that Candi had flashed her tits for a living but no daughter of his was going to strip in front of pervy old men.

Savannah stared back at him, daring him to laugh at her.

'Sing,' he demanded.

'What?'

Judd pointed to a spot by the door. 'Go on. Sing, dance, whatever it is you do. You didn't think you could waive the audition stage just because we're related, did you?' He raised his eyebrows mockingly.

Savannah got to her feet shakily. Fluffing out her red hair self-consciously, she closed her eyes, imagining she was back in New York at an audition.

Opening her mouth, Savannah sang Britney's latest hit, pitch perfect but with her own take on the song. She did a dance she'd choreographed herself, complete with sexy gyrations and some obligatory hair flipping.

Judd considered his daughter. Her voice was unremarkable but she could dance, that was for sure. And with her extraordinary looks and toned figure, she was memorable, if nothing else. She had star quality – not in the way Iris Maguire had it, but there was something to work with.

'You could be good,' Judd allowed.

'I *am* good,' Savannah threw back haughtily.

Judd felt an unexpected swell of pride. God, but she reminded him of himself! 'You could be,' he corrected her in a sharp voice, 'with the right training and a good marketing team behind you. Right now, you're nothing more than a raw talent that needs some serious work.'

'But I'm talented, right?' Savannah grinned and stepped towards him. 'You just said so.'

His mouth twitched. 'I did.'

'So you'll take me on? As a recording artist, I mean?' Savannah could barely breathe. After all the years she had spent traipsing to auditions all over New York, securing small jobs but nothing of any note, was she finally going to be given her golden ticket by the father she never knew she had?

Judd nodded. 'Yes.'

'Oh my *God*!' Savannah let out a shriek and without even knowing she was going to do it, threw herself into Judd's arms. Drawing back from him apologetically, she was stunned to see him giving her a wolfish grin.

Realising Savannah could be useful to him in many different ways, Judd congratulated himself on impregnating Candi all those years ago. Not only was it the perfect opportunity to show Kitty who was boss once more and push his sons' noses out of joint, Savannah had enough raw talent to put Judd firmly on the musical map, as it were.

'Welcome to the family,' he announced grandly, holding his arms out to her.

A few days later, the weather still hadn't cleared so, abandoning all hope of sunning herself on the veranda, Tavvy headed to the cosy music room at the back of the house. It overlooked her favourite patch of the overgrown garden. With all the rain, glittering spider's webs sat intricately laced across a rather rickety-looking arbour and the long grass was bent sideways from the downpour.

If one could predict one thing about English weather, Tavvy thought gloomily as she wrapped one of Lochlin's chunky cream cardigans more tightly around her body, it was that it was tediously predictable. Still, with the house to herself and most of the house-work done, she decided she deserved a sneaky half hour at the piano to try out the tune she'd written recently. Just to see what it sounded like.

To her surprise, Tavvy found Shay sprawled across an overstuffed velvet sofa. Wearing a white shirt and a pair of grey jeans, Shay had his head buried in the latest copy of *Music Mode* and his hand halfway down a tube of Pringles.

'Hey.' Tavvy tweaked the top of his magazine. 'Day off?'

Shay looked cagey. 'I'm throwing my first ever sickie.'

'I see.' Tavvy wondered if Shay's odd behaviour had anything to do with the foul mood Lochlin had been in for the past week. They had both been avoiding each other like the plague and neither of them was talking about the problem, whatever it was.

Lochlin and Shay were so *alike*, she sighed to herself in exasperation, wishing she could crash their heads together. Headstrong and stubborn, they always backed themselves so far into a corner they only had misplaced pride for company.

Unable to bear seeing Shay looking so miserable, Tavvy sighed. 'What's in this month's *Music Mode*?'

Shay lethargically flipped a page. 'A big feature on Melody Gardot, this girl everyone is talking about. Incredible voice – she's changing the face of jazz music.'

Tavvy nodded. 'A wonderful songwriter.' She was pleased Shay had such an in-depth understanding of music. He had inherited his love of jazz from his grandfather Niall, who had adored it, spending years collecting originals on vinyl. Shay treasured the records that had been left to him, refusing to let anyone else touch them. Noticing the violet shadows under his eyes, Tavvy wondered if she could coax her son out of his depression by letting him in on her secret. More to the point, she was genuinely interested in his opinion.

'Hey, if I tell you something, will you promise not to breathe a word of it to anyone?'

Intrigued, Shay put his magazine down and nodded.

'I've been writing a song recently.' Tavvy registered Shay's astonishment. 'I know, crazy, isn't it? I haven't done it for years but this song suddenly came to me and it's been niggling at me like a toothache.' She sat down at the piano and ran her fingers across the keys expertly. The Steinway had been a gift from Lochlin and its tone was so exquisite, it was almost impossible to play badly. 'I gave in and put it down on paper. It'll never be recorded, obviously, but I can't help thinking it's rather good.'

Shay raised his eyebrows. 'Wow. Does Dad know about this?'

Tavvy shook her head, her tawny hair falling forward as she began to play. 'You know how he feels about me and music – or rather, the life I was leading when I was involved with music. This is just a one-off.' At least, she hoped it was a one-off; she didn't have time to stare dreamily into space and toy with lyrics.

Feeling a shiver down his spine, Shay listened to the song; it was good . . . really good.

'It's called "Irresistible",' Tavvy explained. 'It's sort of a follow-up to "Obsession", you see. It's about being totally in love with someone . . . the wrong person, even, but it's so intoxicating, you can't stay away.' She hummed along to the music, throwing in some of the lyrics she'd started to write. '*Irresistible*,' she sang in her distinctive, husky tones.

> *I can't bear to be apart . . . I can't eat, I can't sleep,*
> *Don't wanna be without you,*
> *No, I can't bear to be without you . . . 'cos you're just so irresistible . . .*

Shay felt his mood plummet even further. The lyrics reminded him of Saskia's words at the party and on top of everything else that had happened, the thought that he'd never been in love was suddenly unbearable. Angrily, he got up to leave.

Tavvy stopped playing. 'Shay, what's wrong? Have you and Dad had a fight?'

'You could say that.' He glanced at his mother. He'd already spoken to Iris who had begged him to discuss it with their mother but, until now, Shay had refused.

'Dad told me he doesn't want me working at Shamrock,' he said flatly. 'Ever.'

'What?' Tavvy blinked at him. 'Lochlin has been talking about you working at Shamrock for years, he has big plans for you to take over from him one day.'

Shay grimaced. 'One day? I want to work there now, Mum, not in ten years' time when Dad's finally had enough!' He threw his magazine down. 'It doesn't matter, anyway. We had a row about Judd Harrington and Iris's singing lessons and he told me the only way I'd ever work at Shamrock was over his dead body.'

Tavvy gasped. Horrified, she realised Shay had borne the brunt of Lochlin's wrath towards his arch enemy.

'Well, at least he knows about the offer now.'

'Great.' Shay looked wounded. 'I got the bloody blame for it!'

'I know it seems that way but your father will calm down. You know what he's like when he loses his temper.' Tavvy squeezed Shay's hand, wishing her family weren't such complicated souls. 'Leave it with me. I'll speak to him, all right? God, you're both so hot-headed!'

Shay shrugged. 'Don't bother speaking to him.' He meant it. 'This is the kick up the arse I've been needing, to be honest. All I have to do now is figure out what the hell I'm going to do with my life.'

Tavvy felt anxious. Knowing how obstinate Shay and Lochlin both were, she couldn't help thinking this rift between them wouldn't be resolved overnight.

'Are you coming to Caitie's recital?' she asked, doing her best to smooth the waters. Guiltily, she remembered Caitie's costume, a complicated construction she'd designed herself, with a boned bodice and a skirt of real leaves. It was currently lying in a heap on the spare room bed, out of the way of Nutmeg and Mickey's clumsy paws but in hundreds of different pieces that needed sewing together.

Shay eyed Tavvy warily. 'Is Dad going to be there?'

Her fingers twisted uneasily in her lap. 'Er . . . I think so.'

'Then count me out.' Shay shot her a crooked smile. 'I've heard Caitie do that Titania speech fifty times already and I'd hate to spoil her big moment by moping around and being a miserable bastard.'

It was about time he made his own mark as a Maguire, without his father or Shamrock to fall back on, Shay thought as he left the room, leaving a worried Tavvy staring after him.

Listening to the rain thundering down outside, Kitty stood in front of Mrs Meaden's astonishing array of homemade preserves. Absent-mindedly, she picked up a jar of raspberry jam as she came to the conclusion that Judd had found himself another mistress. The most likely candidate was Darcy Middleton, the latest addition to the Jett team; Darcy was an attractive, confident-looking girl in her early thirties, from what Kitty could remember from the Valentines' Ball. Fiercely intelligent and as sexy as hell, Darcy was Judd's type in a nutshell.

'Can I help you?' Mrs Meaden asked excitedly. She'd been dying to get a proper look at her American neighbour.

'Oh, yes, please,' Kitty said, forcing herself to smile. 'My son Elliot really misses his grape jelly but I'm not sure what might taste similar over here.'

Mrs Meaden discreetly gave Kitty a sideways glance. Aside from the hair which was a bit bouffant, Kitty Harrington was a sweet-looking lady in her late forties with a trim little figure. Her grey eyes were full of sadness but Mrs Meaden wasn't surprised. Kitty looked far too nice to be married to Judd Harrington, the dangerous bastard.

'I'd suggest my damson jam,' she said, passing Kitty a large jar of her bestselling preserve. 'If I say so myself, it has a lovely plummy flavour and a spoonful of this brings a boring old crumpet or muffin to life in a jiffy.'

'Bloody good choice,' said a deep voice. 'I smother my crumpets with it every Sunday.'

Kitty swung round to find a man standing behind her wearing a pair of baggy jeans and a navy fisherman's jumper that was unravelling at the neck. His shaggy golden hair was damp and dishevelled from the rain but his caramel-brown eyes were friendly and engaging.

'Er . . . I'm Kitty Harrington,' Kitty said politely, extending a hand. 'We've just moved here from the States . . . my son really misses his home comforts.'

'Don't we all,' the man said warmly. 'I'm . . .' About to introduce himself, he glanced down at his clothes. 'Gosh, look at me! I don't usually look like this. I forgot to pick up my dry-cleaning so these were the only clothes I could find. Lovely accent, by the way. I'm guessing you're from Boston originally.'

Kitty nodded. She couldn't help thinking the man, whoever he was, looked rather handsome in his scruffy clothes. Admittedly, the jeans were torn at the bottom and the jumper had a splodge of something that looked suspiciously like tomato ketchup down the front of it but with his snub nose and wide mouth, he was charming and friendly. As he hastily raked his fingers through his hair, she caught a waft of cigar smoke and she breathed it in as he took a distinctive red box out of his pocket.

'What do you think? Will she like them?' he asked, discreetly showing the contents to Mrs Meaden, who gasped in delight.

'Diamond earrings from Cartier!' She tutted. 'She doesn't deserve you, that girl.'

He laughed. 'Of course she does. I've been working like mad recently and neglecting her shamefully. I'm going to take her to Barbados to make up for being such a terrible husband.'

'Hardly!' Mrs Meaden scoffed.

'Oh great, you've got some of my favourite wine in.' He reached past Kitty to look at a bottle. 'This is perfect with steak – if you like red wine, that is. One of those home comforts we were talking about.' He gave Kitty a wide smile. 'Put me down for a case, would you, Olive darling?'

Mrs Meaden smiled prettily then rearranged her features in case anyone saw.

'You miss home, then,' the man said to Kitty, feeling around in his pockets for some cash. 'Bugger, no wallet.'

She started. No one had actually asked her if she missed America since she'd arrived. 'Sometimes,' she said. Seeing his raised eyebrows, she smiled. 'All right, I miss it quite a bit.'

'I'm not surprised. What do you miss?'

'Oh, predictable things like the sunshine, I guess . . . and my friends.' Her expression became sober. 'And my son, Ace. I really miss him.' To her horror, her eyes filled with tears.

He immediately put his arm round her. 'Gosh, what an idiot. I've completely put my foot in it.'

'No, no.' Kitty wanted the ground to open up and swallow her. She breathed in his cigar smoke and spicy cologne scent, wondering when anyone but her younger sons had last been so affectionate towards her. And they said the British were reserved! 'It was very sweet of you to ask me. No one else has asked me how I'm feeling being so far away from home.'

He squeezed her shoulder kindly. 'It's horrible, isn't it? You feel like such a fish out of water.' Seeing her face, he explained. 'I used to work abroad when I was younger, trying to further my career and all that, but I just found myself missing fish and chips and Marmite.' He laughed. 'Pathetic but true. Look, I've got to dash, but it was lovely to meet you. And if you ever feel low again, just give me a call and come over to Foxton Manor for a good old English cuppa.'

'I-I will. Thank you.' Kitty wiped her eyes. 'Sorry for soaking your shoulder.'

'I'll live. And what's a wet shoulder between friends?' There was a twinkle in his eye. 'Don't forget my offer . . . very much underestimated in your country, the cup of tea.' He waved at Mrs Meaden. 'I'll settle my account at the weekend, darling. Bye!'

With that, he was gone.

Kitty stared after him. 'I didn't even catch his name. Wait, Foxton Manor. That means he's . . .'

'Lexi Beaument's husband,' Mrs Meaden finished wryly. 'Leo.'

Kitty was stunned. 'But he's so . . . and she's so . . .'

'I know exactly what you mean.' Mrs Meaden pursed her lips.

'Lexi's a lazy so-and-so, in my opinion. Leo works so hard because he knows she likes her earrings and her holidays, and all she does is swan around in mini skirts.'

Kitty wondered why she felt so disappointed. Lexi had been very friendly towards her but she couldn't help thinking Leo wasn't the kind of man to keep Lexi's attention for too long. He was handsome and obviously caring but Lexi liked glitz and glamour and excitement. Kitty hoped she'd bump into him again, or she could always go for that cup of tea Leo had promised her. Suddenly feeling upbeat for the first time in weeks, Kitty purchased the damson jam and left the shop.

Across the fields, dressed in a startingly loud pair of Hawaiian shorts and a black vest, Charlie was sulkily pouring himself a gin and tonic. 'I mean, another greatest hits album, Suse! Can you bloody believe it?'

Susannah sighed and set aside the accounts for Valentine, her make-up brand, and prepared to give Charlie her undivided attention. Reclining on a towel by their indoor jacuzzi tub and heated swimming pool, Susannah could almost believe she was in the Bahamas. Almost. She watched her husband slip into the jacuzzi wearing an oversized diamond crucifix.

'Jesus, it's hot!'

Susannah laughed and sipped her gin and tonic. 'It's meant to be warm, Chas, like a bath.'

Charlie frowned and hoped the chlorine didn't turn his hair green.

'Right, so this greatest hits album. I guess it's a shame you don't get to record any new material,' she said carefully, 'but you have so many fans who will still rush out and buy this album, I don't think it will hurt your sales or your profile. Particularly if the record company are planning to freshen up some of the tracks.'

'Hmmmm.' Charlie looked sceptical.

It was obvious to Susannah that Jett weren't putting any serious budget behind Charlie's relaunch; they were simply churning out the same tunes with a slightly different look. Susannah stirred her G&T with her finger. She wished Charlie had held on for a bit longer with Lochlin instead of rushing to sign a contract with Jett. Contrary to what Charlie thought, Susannah was sure Lochlin hadn't given up on him; he was just waiting for the right time. And probably hoping Charlie might get himself back in the studio to get down to some proper songwriting.

Charlie swiped some bubbles in the air. 'Even that Darcy Middleton bird looked as though she thought the greatest hits album idea was crap.'

'Chas, do you think Judd is shagging Darcy?' Kitty had mentioned Judd's new sidekick at work as a possible mistress and Susannah had a feeling Kitty's feminine intuition was right on the nose.

'Without a shadow of a doubt,' Charlie replied immediately. 'She's hot, that girl, but I wouldn't trust her as far as I could throw her.'

'She's supposed to be superb at her job.'

Charlie ran a wet hand through his hair before remembering the chlorine. 'Can't be that good, she doesn't stand up to Harrington one bit. Mind you, if I was in her shoes, I wouldn't rock the boat either.' He drained his gin and tonic.

Susannah glanced at her accounts again. 'And what about all the rumours about Judd and Lochlin? I haven't a clue what went on, it was all so long ago.'

'I wouldn't put anything past Judd.' Charlie shrugged. 'I think that man's capable of anything.' He looked glum. 'Do you think Lochlin will ever forgive me?'

'I'm certain of it. Just give him time.' Deep down, Susannah wasn't sure. If Judd Harrington really was Lochlin's enemy, Lochlin would see it as the height of disloyalty for Charlie to jump ship.

'I feel like such a shit,' Charlie said, heaving himself out of the tub. He threw a towel over his shoulder moodily. 'I'm off to play my guitar.'

Looking up, Susannah caught sight of the twins wobbling out on five-inch heels, their blond hair in pigtails. Wearing bright red swimsuits with legs cut higher than the ones on *Baywatch*, they'd both slapped on so much fake tan they were positively orange.

Seeing their disgruntled faces, Susannah took off her sunglasses. 'What's the matter?'

'We don't want to go to the recital,' Skye said petulantly, slamming a glass of juice down.

'We really don't,' Abby added, playing with a bleached blond pigtail.

'Why not? Is it because Caitie Maguire is heading the bill?'

Skye looked injured. 'Christ, whose side are you on, Mummy? I thought you'd understand how upset we are about missing out. *Again*.'

Susannah hid a smile. 'Sorry. Of course I understand. But there'll be other opportunities. Titania isn't the only part in the world.'

Abby stuck her bottom lip out. 'Hugo, our drama teacher, said we looked too "knowing" to play Titania.'

'You do look rather . . . grown up for your ages,' Susannah replied diplomatically. She tugged one of Skye's pigtails. 'But you're just as talented as Caitie Maguire. You just need the right parts, that's all.'

Skye's eyes glazed over. 'I'm going to play Juliet in the summer play this year. I don't care what Hugo says, that part is mine.'

'Or mine.' Abby frowned.

Susannah grinned and went back to her accounts, her eyes widening with delight when she finally clocked the figures. 'Oh my God, Valentine made a two-million-pound profit last year!' she squealed.

'Is that good?' Abby asked, bored.

'It's *very* good,' Susannah told her, getting to her feet. 'This calls for a celebration. We must have champagne!'

'We can't drink, Mummy,' Skye called out slyly. 'We're underage, remember?'

'Oh, sod that!' Susannah said, tearing the foil off a bottle of Krug. She gave them a pointed glance. 'And if you think I don't know you two drink, you're very much mistaken.'

The twins giggled and held up their glasses.

On her way to Caitie's recital, Iris decided to find Shay and convince him to come along. She peered out of the window at the summer house and seeing faint candlelight inside, headed towards it. The summer house was a quaint construction built from beech wood, covered with rambling roses and topped by an unusual glass roof. Piled with colourful stripy cushions from Morocco and full of travel books and tea glasses in jewel-like colours, Iris knew it was one of Shay's favourite places to slink off to when he needed to lick his wounds.

'Knew I'd find you here,' she said, poking her head inside and waving a waft of cigarette smoke out of her face. 'God, it's like a nightclub in here!'

Shay gave her a brief smile. 'Glass of red?' he offered, holding up a bottle. 'Or rather, a swig of red because I forgot to bring the glasses.'

Iris flung herself on to the cushions and took the bottle from him. 'Still pissed off with Dad?'

Shay blew smoke towards the open doorway. 'We're not speaking, if that's what you mean.'

'I'm sure he didn't mean it about not working at Shamrock,' she told him gently. 'He was just angry – you know how he goes off on one. You do exactly the same.'

Shooting her a furious look, Shay relented. 'I suppose. It's just . . . I know I'm my own worst enemy but I thought Dad, at least, would have faith in me.'

Iris handed the bottle back. 'You feel as though you've got something to prove. I know *that* feeling.' She sighed. 'He's an amazing father and I love him to pieces but he's so over-protective. Of both of us.'

Shay sat up, stabbing the air with his cigarette. 'Judd Harrington arriving has changed everything. Dad bangs on about family loyalty and we've always bought into it, but now it feels as if he doesn't even trust us enough to tell us what the hell is going on with this feud.' He drank from the wine bottle again. 'Fucking hell, why do we want his approval so badly?'

Iris smiled. 'There are worse crimes. Now, can I convince you to come to Caitie's recital?'

Shay's eyes flickered to the floor. 'I don't think so. Is she going to hate me for ever?'

'Knowing Caitie, I very much doubt it.'

'Good. I don't want to spoil her big moment by causing a scene and rowing with Dad but I think it could happen if we're in the same room right now.' He nodded up at the glass ceiling. 'Quick game of "Rude Stars" before you go?'

Knowing Shay didn't want to be left alone just yet, Iris held her hand out for the wine bottle. 'Oh, all right. But you always win, your mind is much smuttier than mine.'

'How dare you. Now *that*,' Shay said, shooting her a grateful smile before pointing up at the stars, 'is most definitely the well-known star formation Scrotum . . .'

Feeling the chilly night air on her face as she stood on the makeshift stage, Caitie shivered and surveyed her audience as she said her lines.

> *Set your heart at rest,*
> *The fairy land buys not the child of me.*
> *His mother was a votaress of my order:*
> *And, in the spiced Indian air, by night . . .*

She was displaying admirable poise considering she had spent the day before throwing up and watching reruns of Kate Winslet in *Sense and Sensibility*. On stage in the middle of the woods near Pembleton, Caitie was mesmerising her audience, her drama teacher Hugo proudly standing by.

'Isn't she wonderful?' Tavvy whispered to Lochlin, snuggling up to him on the bench. She knew she was biased but Caitie really was talented.

Dressed in a beautiful pale green dress with a boned corset and a skirt made of real leaves and with cheeks streaked with silver glitter, Caitie looked totally believable as the Queen of the Fairies. She made the most of her lines without milking them, knowing exactly when to pare back and when to inject emotion.

Tavvy examined her scratched fingers. 'At least the costume looks good. I was up all night stitching those bloody leaves on one at a time.'

'She looks grand,' Lochlin said, distractedly.

Tavvy glanced at him, feeling apprehensive. She still hadn't spoken to Lochlin about Shay or about the situation with Iris and it was eating away at her. She took Lochlin's hand, about to tell him everything when Iris slipped into the seat next to her, looking flushed.

'I was watching from the back,' Iris whispered truthfully. 'I rushed down as the lights dimmed.'

'*And for her sake I will not part with him*,' Caitie finished in a soft voice. When the applause had died down, she slipped off the stage towards her parents and Iris. 'Was I all right? I can't even remember saying the words or anything.' She looked stricken. 'Did I mess up?'

Iris hugged her. 'You were brilliant! Not a shred of nerves. I'm so jealous.'

'Really? Wow, thanks.' Caitie looked relieved. 'Hang on, where's Shay?' She frowned. 'A few weeks back he promised me he'd come tonight but he's been so moody lately, I don't know what's got into him.'

'He said to say sorry,' Iris said quickly. 'He had some urgent stuff to do.' She avoided her father's bloodshot eyes but Caitie didn't notice the undercurrent.

Catching sight of a flash of blond hair at the edge of the woods, Caitie clutched her chest in excitement. Was it Elliot? Had he really come to see her? Feeling her heart lurch, Caitie realised it was indeed Elliot lurking behind a tree and her mind ran away with itself. He had to fancy her, he had to! Why else would he be here? As Iris went to get some drinks, Caitie grabbed her moment and shot to Elliot's side.

Feeling equally opportunistic, Tavvy didn't waste any time. 'Lochlin, I have to speak to you.'

'What about, darlin'? I'm so tired, I just want to go to bed and sleep for ever.'

'I know. It's just . . . Shay told me about your argument.' She stroked his face. 'Why didn't you say anything?'

Lochlin looked shocked. 'I was going to but it was so terrible. I lost my temper . . . told him I didn't want him to work at Shamrock, ever.' He clutched his dark hair. 'I didn't mean it, of course I didn't. But he was going on about Charlie and then he dropped a bombshell about Iris and singing lessons.'

Tavvy chewed her lip. 'About that . . .'

Lochlin gaped at her. 'You *knew*?'

Quickly, she explained about the confrontation with Iris. 'It's tearing her apart, Lochlin. She wants to go but she doesn't want to let you down. She wasn't even going to tell you Judd had made the offer because she knew it would hurt you.' She linked her fingers through his. 'You know she'd never sign a deal with anyone else but Shamrock.'

Lochlin groaned. 'I feel like shite. I want her to go because it's such a great opportunity but Judd arranged it – *Judd*, Tavvy.' He rubbed his stubbly chin. 'But if this is a chance of a lifetime for Iris, we should let her go, shouldn't we?'

Tavvy felt a spark of hope. 'Look, I had this idea. You remember my friend Maria, the one I used to live with when I was performing? Well, she has a daughter, Luisa, who lives in Los Angeles.'

'So what?' Lochlin looked impatient.

'She could be Iris's chaperone,' Tavvy announced happily. 'Luisa is twenty-seven now and she has her own apartment. I called Maria and she said Luisa would be the perfect chaperone for Iris.' Realising she was talking as if the decision had already been made, Tavvy faltered, lifting her amber eyes to Lochlin imploringly. 'What do you think?'

Lochlin considered the idea gravely. Since his horrible row with Shay, he'd done nothing but think about the dreadful things they'd said to each other. And as for Iris, Lochlin hadn't been lying to Tavvy when he said he'd thought about Judd's offer from a million different angles and he couldn't for the life of him see how it would be harmful to Iris. Knowing Judd as he did, Lochlin felt instinctively there must be a catch somewhere but if there was, he hadn't been able to figure it out. Seeing Iris approaching, Lochlin made a decision.

'You should go to LA,' he told her before he changed his mind.

'What?' Iris gawked at him, her heart in her mouth.

Tavvy nodded, smiling.

'Have those singing lessons and come straight back so you can sign a contract with Shamrock.' Lochlin's voice was gruff.

'Oh my God.' Iris's amber eyes filled with tears and she gazed at him beseechingly. 'Don't say it if you don't mean it, Dad, please . . .'

'I mean it,' Lochlin said, pulling her into his arms.

Iris wound her arms around his neck. 'Thank you, thank you, thank you,' she repeated disbelievingly. 'I can't believe this is happening.'

'I can't believe you're going to be leaving us.' Tavvy burst into noisy tears. 'We'll miss you so much. But you deserve it, you really do.'

Iris looked worried. 'But what about this thing with Judd? The feud?'

Lochlin brushed her tears away with his thumb. 'Forget about that. Just go and grab this opportunity with both hands, my darlin'.'

Caitie, buoyed up from her chat with Elliot, bounded over. 'What's going on? Why are you all crying, you big babies?'

'Iris is going to Los Angeles,' Tavvy told her.

Caitie whooped. 'I'm so jealous, I could die,' she declared. 'Oh Iris, you're going to be a bloody pop star at last!' She called Jas over. 'Jas, Iris is going to America!'

Almost deafened by the shrieking women around him, Lochlin took Iris to one side. 'Are you sure you can handle this?'

She nodded, her eyes shining with gratitude. 'I really think I can, Dad. I won't let you down, I promise.'

'I know you won't.' He tucked a lock of her tawny-blond hair behind her ear and cupped her face in his hands. 'I just have one condition.'

Iris panicked but she nodded.

'Firstly, you won't have anything to do with Judd or his family, will you?' Lochlin's eyes let Iris know how serious he was. 'I haven't forgiven him for the things he's done and he's a very dangerous man, you have to understand that.'

Iris wished she knew what was going on. 'You needn't worry, Dad.' She had no intention of getting involved with any of the Harrington clan.

Lochlin carried on. 'Secondly, do not, under any circumstances, sign a contract with the Jett Record Corporation. Do you understand me? Never.'

'As if!' Iris kissed him. 'You can trust me, I promise. Now, can we go and celebrate?'

As she skipped off, Lochlin hoped to God he'd made the right decision. He reminded himself that he trusted his daughter with his life and he knew she meant every word she'd just said. So why the hell was he suddenly filled with such foreboding?

Chapter Eight

Feeling one last, intensely delicious shudder go through her body, Darcy flung herself face down into a pile of pillows.

'Better?' Judd purred, trailing a finger down the length of her spine.

'Marginally,' Darcy allowed, turning her face away from him. Feeling his knuckles kneading the taut muscles in her shoulders, she afforded herself a small smile. After he had callously dismissed her from his office the day Savannah had arrived, Darcy had been steadfastly and coldly holding Judd at arm's length. Her skirts had become shorter, her necklines more provocative but she would not allow him to lay a single finger on her until he apologised. It might seem childish but to Darcy it was the principle of the thing. There was no way she was going to let Judd think he could treat her so shabbily in front of his daughter – or his staff – because, in her experience, allowing that level of disrespect to go by unchecked could only put her at a disadvantage in the long run.

It had worked. Judd had been charm itself, taking her out for a sumptuous dinner in a small but lavish restaurant in Mayfair, then a night in a roof suite at the Dorchester. Darcy had barely had time to admire the modern four-poster bed and the heated marble floor in the bathroom before Judd had peeled her clothes off, licked her in some very rude places before hurling her on to the bed for a marathon sex session.

Darcy turned to face him, wondering at the butch expanse of his shoulders. Judd was so tightly packed with muscle, he resembled a Roman gladiator.

'What did you think of Savannah?' Judd said, reaching out to cup a creamy breast.

Darcy took a moment to consider her answer, finding it difficult to concentrate. In all honesty, Savannah had seemed like an over-confident brat, swaggering in and tossing her red hair all over the place. However, Judd clearly seemed to think his new daughter was a chip off the old block so Darcy thought it prudent to refrain from brutal frankness.

'Smart, sassy and ambitious,' she replied, picking three flattering adjectives.

Judd nodded approvingly, licking his finger and circling Darcy's candy-pink nipple. 'Isn't she? I can't wait for her to meet the family.'

'Yes, but you can't just roll up with her one day and say here's my illegitimate daughter, she's moving in with us,' Darcy snorted, propping herself up on her elbow. Seeing the look in Judd's blue eyes, she almost gasped. 'Oh my God, you're not serious! What the hell is Kitty going to say?'

'I couldn't care less.' His mouth twisted heartlessly. 'She's going to have to deal with it – they all are. Savannah is part of the family now and they'd better fucking well accept that. I don't actually think any of them would dare to say a word about it.'

Darcy pushed her cinnamon-brown hair out of her eyes and said nothing. Judd really was the limit. What sort of man took his bastard daughter home out of the blue and expected his family to just suck it up?

'Sebastian will go mad but what about your other son, Ace, is it? How will he react?'

Judd smirked. 'He'll probably shake my hand and congratulate me. He's much the same as I was at his age, a playboy with hundreds of women on speed dial.'

Judd snatched the sheet away from Darcy and tied it round his waist like a makeshift toga. 'What did you think of my plans for Savannah at Jett?'

Darcy casually flung her arms above her head and tilted one leg until she looked like a slender nude in a painting. 'I thought they were excellent,' she lied, knowing it was more than her life was worth to slag Savannah off to Judd. Privately, Darcy thought Judd was mad to believe Savannah could be a huge singing sensation. Savannah would be better off pursuing a career as a dancer or a TV presenter, because her voice wasn't special enough to stand out from the crowd.

Judd poured himself a Scotch without offering her one. 'Glad to hear it because you're in charge of her while I'm out of the country. Her career, that is.'

'When will you be out of the country?' Darcy frowned. She couldn't shake off the niggling feeling that her relationship with Judd was leading her to compromise herself in some way.

Judd threw the drink down his throat and poured himself another. 'I'm off to Los Angeles in a few days' time, to see Ace.' He leered at her naked body. 'What do you know about Shay Maguire?'

'Lochlin's son?' Darcy thought about the Valentines' Ball. Having met Lochlin, she'd had no trouble working out that the moody, dark-haired boy with the shamrock-green eyes and the devastating cheekbones was his son. Their eyes had met across the crowded dance floor – cheesy but it had also been the most electric moment. Darcy shivered at the memory. She gave a non-committal shrug. 'Not much. Why?'

'I want him ruined,' Judd stated, slamming his glass down on to a beautiful walnut table. 'Destroying Lochlin isn't enough. I want all of them – the entire family – brought to their knees.'

Darcy refrained from rolling her eyes. This vendetta of Judd's sounded so dramatic. 'Why don't you leave Shay Maguire to me?' she offered casually.

'What do you have in mind?'

'I have no idea,' she said carelessly, staring up at the ceiling. At the thought of seeing Shay again, Darcy stretched her limbs seductively, though the gesture was subconscious .

Judd dropped the sheet and climbed back on to the bed. 'All right,' he said, pushing his face close to hers until her hazel eyes snapped open again. 'You can have the Maguire boy but,' he grabbed her chin with his hand, his fingers digging into her soft flesh, 'don't you fucking dare fall for him,' he warned her, his expression so unforgiving, Darcy almost quailed. Wishing she could disappear into the plush mattress of the four-poster, she just about managed to shake her head, her chin still in Judd's vice-like grip.

'I-I won't.'

'Good. Because if you do, you'll regret it.'

Darcy nodded, suddenly afraid. Gasping as he flipped her over on to her front, she wondered if she should just grab her things and get the hell out of there.

Judd ran his hand over the delectable curve of Darcy's bottom. One of the things he liked most about her was that she mistakenly thought she was in charge. The lavish dinner, this roof-top suite were simply a means to an end for him. A few words and a handful of cash were no skin off his nose. Darcy was useful to Judd right now; he needed someone to run Jett while he was absent because he didn't trust anyone else; in particular, Sebastian, the useless idiot.

Stroking the nape of Darcy's neck with infinite care, Judd caressed her creamy shoulders before slowly winding her long dark hair around his fist. It was time for the next part of his plan. Lochlin had agreed to let Iris go to Los Angeles, the trusting fool, clearly believing Iris could come to no harm. But he was sadly mistaken, Judd thought, pulling Darcy's head round so he could crush his lips to hers. If everything went according to plan, in a few months' time, Lochlin was going to wish he'd never agreed to let beautiful young Iris out of his sight. Triumphantly, Judd covered Darcy's body with his.

'Blimey,' Shay said, putting his arm around Caitie's shoulders as they heard the taxi pulling away. 'I can't believe Iris has actually gone.'

Tavvy and Lochlin stood beside them and Tavvy had tears streaming down her cheeks. 'I miss her already,' she wailed, feeling foolish.

Caitie sniffed into Shay's sleeve. 'We won't hear her singing around the house any more.'

Shay slapped Caitie's arm away from his sleeve. 'Iris hasn't died, she's gone to LA for a few months. And will you stop wiping snot all over my jumper?'

'*You* sing around the house too,' Lochlin commented, reaching out and tugging one of Caitie's curls. He smiled. 'Not as well as Iris but it's better than nothing.'

Knowing she was going to miss Iris more than she could say, Caitie brightened at the sight of a text message from Elliot. She sidled off to read it in private.

'I'm glad Iris has gone to LA,' Shay commented. 'I mean, for her sake. It's such a brilliant opportunity and it's about time her singing career took off.'

Meeting his son's eyes, Lochlin was devastated when Shay looked back coldly before shoving his hands in his pockets and glancing in the other direction. Lochlin had mistakenly thought the dust would settle after a few weeks and that both of them would climb down and apologise. How wrong he'd been. Shay had been moody and withdrawn ever since, acting as if he had the weight of the world on his shoulders.

Witnessing the exchange, Tavvy felt on the verge of hysteria. She wanted to scream at them to stop being such idiots but she knew interfering would only make things worse.

Lochlin took his glasses off, feeling immeasurably tired. So far, Jett had stolen seven acts he'd had his eye on before he'd had a chance to cobble a deal together. If that wasn't bad enough, three of his key staff, including his most reliable friend and A&R rep, had abruptly handed in their notice, claiming not to have jobs to go to. Lochlin was convinced they were already on Jett's payroll and, as a result, he no longer trusted anyone. If only Shay was by his side, learning the business and acting as his adviser, Lochlin knew he'd feel stronger. How stupid he'd been, rejecting Shay like that.

Feeling a sudden stabbing pain in his chest, Lochlin gasped and shakily held on to the wall. He'd had a few of these incidences recently, nothing serious, just a shortness of breath and some brief pains. He was sure it was just stress.

'Lochlin?' Tavvy grasped his arm, her amber eyes clouding over with distress. 'Are you all right?'

'I'm fine, darlin', fine.' Lochlin steadied himself. He gasped as another pain seared across his chest.

Shay held a hand out to him. He'd never seen his father like this before; his pallor was grey and there were exhausted bags under his eyes; he looked as if he had aged ten years in the last couple of weeks. Not only that, for the first time in his life, Shay thought his father seemed frail.

'Jaysus, I'm fine, do you hear me?'

'We're just worried—' Shay started.

'Fucking hell, leave me alone, can't you?' Lochlin exploded. 'All of you. I'm fine and I don't need you lot treating me like some *fucking* geriatric.' Pushing past them, he headed back inside his home office.

That's *it*, Shay thought furiously, stalking out to the summer house, in spite of the chill in the air. That's the last time he was ever going to even attempt a reconciliation with his father. As far as Shay was concerned, his father could damn well manage on his own.

Left standing alone, Tavvy felt distraught. What the hell was happening to her family? It seemed as if everything was falling apart and suddenly she felt afraid for Iris.

Leo watched Lexi sliding into the red Lotus Elise he'd bought her for Christmas, and wondered where she was going. She'd told him she was off to meet some old modelling pal who had boyfriend troubles but since when did she wear her sexy backless Dior dress and spike heels to meet a girlfriend?

Leo sucked apprehensively on his cigar. Lexi had barely glanced at the diamond earrings he'd bought her and she'd only shown a flicker of interest when he mentioned he'd booked the Sandy Lane Hotel in Barbados. Leo ran a hand through his dishevelled blond hair, wishing his gut wasn't telling him Lexi was having an affair. When he'd first met Lexi years ago at a dinner party, he'd been hit with an overwhelming urge to protect her. Ruthless in business but soft-hearted when it came to women, Leo had fallen for Lexi, hard. Hearing her saying that photographers had told her she was too fat and not pretty enough during her modelling days, Leo had told her he would take care of her for the rest of his life. Despite warnings from his friends and family, Leo and Lexi had married a few months later.

Leo crushed his cigar in an ashtray. He'd worked too hard, given too much of himself to lose Lexi.

But now, gazing out of the window at his empty driveway, he wondered if it had all been worth it. Perhaps Lexi *was* with him for his money, after all; perhaps the unimaginable was actually the truth and he'd been too blind to see it before now. Leo paused, thinking about Kitty Harrington, the nice woman he'd met in the village shop the other day. Perhaps she was *too* nice, Leo thought wryly. Perhaps *he* was. Because it always seemed to be people like him and Kitty Harrington who got shat on.

Leo poured himself a glass of wine. He supposed there was nothing he could do but wait and hope Lexi was being faithful to him.

Lexi forgot all about Leo as she punched the details of the hotel into her satnav. All she could think about was Sebastian's millions . . . or rather, *billions*. She glanced at her reflection in her rear-view mirror, sure she was going to knock his socks off. After slathering herself in Laura Mercier Chocolate Truffle soufflé, she had put in some new contact lenses which made her eyes look even greener and, beneath the devastatingly gorgeous Dior dress, she was wearing the sluttiest red underwear known to man.

Jumping two red lights to get to the hotel on time, Lexi parked her car at the front. Having received a text from Sebastian en route telling her to meet him by his Porsche out back, she teetered across the car park. Sebastian beckoned for her to get in.

'Can we go into the hotel now?' she said, hoping she hadn't shut her Dior dress in the car door.

'No.' Sebastian gave her an appraising glance.

Ignoring his vivid hair, Lexi reminded herself of his inheritance. 'Why not?'

'Because I can't afford to have the name of this hotel showing up on my credit card bill,' he said smoothly. 'Martha might see it and try to divorce me so we're going to have to stay in here.' Seeing her look of horror, he played his trump card. 'Do you know how much I'm worth, Lexi?'

Lexi cast her eyes down and surveyed the glittering lights on the dashboard of the Porsche. She bloody well wished he'd tell her because then she could decide whether shagging him in the bucket seat of his car was worth her while or not.

Sebastian glanced at Lexi's long bronzed legs, one of which was clearly visible through the slit in her skirt; the calf shapely, the thigh slender. His groin throbbed with lust and Sebastian was out for what he could get. 'I'm fucking *loaded*, if you must know. I've got more money than you can possibly imagine.'

Catching sight of his Rolex, Lexi chewed on her lip gloss. Talk about an anti-climax! This was not the sexy, romantic evening she'd pictured and Sebastian was hardly her ideal man as it was. But Lexi didn't care about Martha or credit card statements; she *wanted* Sebastian to get found out, she wanted him to divorce his wife and marry her so she could really live the life she thought she deserved. Leo was one of the greatest guys she had ever met but they had little in common and she wanted more glamour and more excitement. It was a case of yachts versus cars . . . and diamond rings that weighed her hand down rather than discreet stud earrings. Just as Leo had suddenly become more attractive when she found out he was a self-made millionaire, Sebastian, with his trust fund and rich daddy, seemed like a sex god.

Glancing at him, Lexi realised he didn't have a good enough reason to walk away from his marriage – yet. Hitching her Dior skirt up around her waist, she loosened the neck of the dress and allowed it to fall away, revealing her perfectly spherical boobs. Seeing desire sparkling in Sebastian's pale blue eyes, she straddled him in her four-inch heels and tried not to set the horn of the Porsche off with her bottom.

Ridiculously turned on, Sebastian started reciting the names of the American presidents so he didn't disgrace himself and come in his pants.

Watching his lips moving, Lexi hoped to God this was going to be worth it. Sinking her manicured fingertips into Sebastian's bright red hair, she put any thoughts of ginger pubes out of her head and lowered herself on to his lap.

'Ace! Wake up, it's your father!' Jerry hissed, jiggling Ace's tanned shoulder. Feeling severely hung over, the sight of the pneumatic blonde sprawled across Ace's navy silk sheets was making Jerry's stomach lurch. Looking as though she was sleeping on two water floats, the girl's legs were spread so wide, a gynaecologist might have baulked at the view.

'Ace . . . wake *up*, for fuck's sake!' Jerry waved the phone at him. 'He's called three times already and he sounds seriously *pissed*.'

Bleary-eyed from a heap of cocaine and far too much sex, Ace groaned. Running a hand through his dishevelled mahogany hair, he gingerly sat up and struggled to peel his eyes open. Coming face to face with Jerry's bulging white Calvins, he took the phone with shaky hands.

'Hi, Dad,' he croaked. The naked blonde rolled over and squawked in protest but ignoring the gargantuan water buoys prodding him in the back, Ace focused his attention on the phone call. 'Yes, of course, I'll be there. What time?' He rolled his sexy grey eyes in Jerry's direction. 'See you there in an— Christ! He just hung up on me!'

'Everything all right?'

'Haven't a clue. Dad says he's in LA and he wants to meet for a drink. Said he has some business to discuss.' Ace yawned, revealing white teeth and a furry tongue.

Jerry watched Ace's tanned muscles rippling as he flipped the sheet back and emerged, naked, from the bed. Toffee-brown from all the nude sunbathing he did, Ace stretched, sporting a mammoth hard-on. 'God, my father's a sadist. He knows I'm never up before midday unless we have a race.'

'At least you'll have good news to tell him,' Jerry said, knocking back a glass of flat Cristal to take the edge off the dryness in his mouth.

Ace lit a cigarette and grimaced. 'Even my father can't argue with first place, surely?'

Winning at the Las Vegas NASCAR track had been a day to remember. It had been achieved in a blaze of glory and Ace could recall every single second of the race. He'd been so fired up, so focused. He and Jerry had celebrated as they always did after a good race, with a huge party in the Palms Hotel and a crowd of nubile models. The party had continued back in LA at a local bar before a group of them had traipsed back to the Bel Air apartment.

'Fourth place for me,' Jerry lamented, rolling his eyes. 'Am I destined to live in your shadow, buddy?'

'Don't be daft,' Ace retorted, the cigarette hanging out of his mouth as he wrestled with the balcony door. He caught sight of a huge box in the corner of the room, emblazoned with a snarling black wolf's head against a white background. 'Is that another box of Jett merchandise?'

Jerry nodded. 'Your father sent it. He's had your uniform customised too. Look.' He held up a pristine racing suit bedecked in Jett Record Corporation sponsorship badges. 'You're gonna look like such a pimp.'

'Fuck.' Once outside, Ace gulped down some hazy Los Angeles air and did a double take at the kidney-shaped pool below. 'Who *are* all these people?' he asked in bewilderment. About twenty prostrate bodies were dotted around the poolside, with one girl asleep on an inflatable lilo in the pool. Seeing her silver nipple tassels and a tattoo of the American flag on her shaved privates, Ace went off in fits of giggles. Now that's what he called patriotic.

Back inside, Ace jerked his head in the direction of the blonde in the bed. 'Christ, what's her name, Jerry? They always wake up and expect me to remember and you know I can't cope with such formalities.' He screwed his nose up humorously as he scrabbled around in his memory bank. 'The only name I can ever remember is Allegra. Do you think that's why she keeps coming back?'

'No, it's because she's a crazed stalker who wants you locked up in a dungeon so she can have you all to herself.' Jerry massaged his pounding forehead and glanced at the girl in the bed. 'That's Tiffany. Think of *Breakfast at Tiffany's* – you like that film.'

Giving him a grateful thumbs-up, Ace padded into the bathroom and turned on the power shower. Water thundered against the glass doors as it shot out of jets in the walls and out of the monsoon shower head.

'Hey, when I'm done with my father, shall we go and get some lunch?' Ace called from the shower. 'We can go to that place off Sunset you love so much.'

As Ace sang in the shower, endearingly off key as usual, a female voice from the other room seductively called out to Jerry.

Jerry sighed and decided he might as well go back to bed. After all, like Ace, he had a reputation to uphold.

* * *

'He's here,' Jas told Caitie, almost as pleased as her friend. 'He must be here because of you. Go on, go and say hello.' She gave Caitie a gentle shove, shyly thinking how handsome Elliot looked with his faint tan and broad shoulders.

Abandoning her copy of the play, Caitie dashed to Elliot's side, forgetting to act cool. Wearing a pair of dark jeans and a grey jumper, he kept pushing his floppy blond hair out of his eyes as if he was nervous.

'Wow. You defied your father, then?'

Elliot smiled. 'Actually, my father isn't likely to turn up here. He flew out to Los Angeles this morning to see my brother, Ace.' Running his eyes over her, he decided Caitie looked exceptionally cute in a cut-off skirt and leggings and an emerald-green cashmere jumper that brought out the colour of her eyes. He thought his friends in LA would fancy her like crazy and would probably be winding him up about the fact he hadn't asked her out yet.

'I'm so pleased you're here,' Caitie told him, meaning it. Even though she knew her father would go nuts if he found out she was fraternising with the enemy, she couldn't help feeling deliriously happy.

Elliot grinned at her and glanced around the hall, which thankfully, was nowhere near Brockett Hall. It boasted high, vaulted ceilings, a huge stage at one end and stained-glass windows which threw out insanely dramatic light. Wondering if he had the courage to ask Caitie out, Elliot was almost knocked sideways by the arrival of the drama teacher.

'As I live and breathe, Romeo Montague in real life form.' Hugo took Elliot's hand delightedly, his eyes shining behind his geek-chic glasses. In his late twenties, Hugo had cropped blond hair like a figure from a Michelangelo painting, expressive brown eyes and a cupid's-bow most women would envy.

Elliot felt absurdly flattered but slightly terrified. Surely he'd need to audition first?

Caitie beamed. She knew she was right about Elliot being

perfect for the part of Romeo! 'There's just one *teeny* little thing you need to know about,' she told Hugo, holding her finger and thumb up to indicate just how trifling a thing it was.

Hugo's puppy-dog eyes had turned to liquid chocolate as he drank Elliot in.

'There's no one else to play Romeo,' he said, staring at Elliot. 'So I hope it's nothing serious.'

'Er . . . he's American.' Caitie winced, peeking through her fingers to judge Hugo's reaction. 'But he can do an English accent – I can teach him.'

Hugo gulped. 'I hope so. Because nothing can stop you playing Romeo, young man. Nothing.'

'I'll . . . er . . . I'll do my best. And . . . thanks.' Elliot refrained from mentioning that the last time he'd attempted an English accent, it had made Ace fall about laughing.

Caitie's heart swelled at the thought of spending lots of time with Elliot, rehearsing their lines. If she *got* the part of Juliet, that is. Rehearsals were in a few weeks' time and she was going to spend every spare moment she had perfecting her delivery.

'Hey, I found something out about my father,' Elliot said after Hugo had stalked away. 'I don't know if it means anything but he left here around twenty-five years ago to move to the States. Quite abruptly, my mom said. She also warned me against delving too deep as she thought my dad would be really angry about it.'

Caitie looked thrilled. 'That has to mean something!'

'Oh, and my grandparents left just before he did,' Elliot added. 'They're dead now and I never met them. Whatever happened was bad enough that my dad never spoke to them again. My mom said he'd mentioned them when they first met but refused to say why he hated them so much.'

'*Really*.' Caitie pulled Jas into their secretive circle. 'Jas, this is *so* exciting! I'll do some digging at my end too but I won't be able to ask my parents. I swear there's a story here – there always is when no one wants to talk about it, don't you think?'

Elliot shrugged. He wasn't as bothered about delving into the past as Caitie but if it was that important to her, he would do his best to find out what had happened. Biting her lip, Jas looked at her best friend anxiously. Whatever it was had been buried for a reason and Jas couldn't help thinking Caitie was digging up something that was best left alone. But once Caitie had an idea in her head, there was no stopping her. Jas gave Elliot a watery smile and hoped to God the family secret wasn't anything dangerous.

Nearby and out of sight behind a screen, Skye and Abby Valentine had been listening avidly to Caitie and Elliot, their heavily kohled eyes popping. Ever since Skye had made a play for Iris's boyfriend Ollie at the Valentines' Ball, Caitie had steadfastly ignored both of the twins and Skye didn't like it one bit. Caitie was extremely popular and her disdain meant being shunned from tons of parties.

'I've worked out how to get back at Caitie for ignoring us,' she said.

Abby looked doubtful. 'What do you suggest, Mozart?'

'It's Einstein, you dumb arse, not Mozart,' Skye told her crossly. God, her twin was stupid! 'I'm going to try out for the part of Juliet.'

Abby gasped. '*You?*'

Skye looked affronted. 'Caitie wants Elliot and now he's Romeo. So I need to be Juliet, right? In the play and in real life.' She smiled evilly. 'I'm not sure it was Shakespeare but as someone once said, "All's fair in love and war." '

Abby almost fell over. Stealing Elliot away from Caitie was one thing but being picked to play Juliet over her, surely that was impossible? Caitie was the best actress for miles around.

Peering round the screen and seeing the way Elliot was gazing at Caitie, Abby thought Skye would be lucky if she got as far as holding Elliot's hand, let alone anything else.

* * *

Ace rolled up late to the rooftop bar his father had invited him to in West Hollywood. Wearing his trademark Ray-Bans with his wet auburn hair slicked back from his face, Ace looked like a film star.

He moved smoothly through the crowded tables, waving to a few people he knew and managing to catch the eye of several striking women before he reached Judd's table.

'Great to see you, Dad,' Ace said, sliding into the chair next to him and taking off his shades.

'Luckily for you, I've been enjoying the view,' Judd replied curtly. 'And I think you mean, "Sorry I'm late".'

Feeling his good mood plummet, Ace ordered himself a Scotch on the rocks from a salivating waitress, not even noticing her flirtatious smile. His head was still throbbing from last night's excesses but, judging from his father's hostile manner, Ace was going to need some serious alcohol to get through their meeting.

Judd stared at a brunette at the bar with fantastic breasts and lips like softly plumped pillows. 'So, first place in Vegas,' he commented, not taking his eyes off the brunette.

Ace nodded. 'It was awesome. It's such a cool track and I was determined to prove I could do it.' He lifted his chin defiantly.

Judd's cold blue eyes connected with Ace's as he sipped his drink. 'Good for you. Just make sure you keep it up.'

Ace suppressed a sigh and rubbed his hair to dry it off in the sun. Somehow, whatever he did, his father never seemed proud of him; the words 'well done' were not in his vocabulary.

Knowing his father detested small talk, Ace got straight to the point. 'So, what did you want to talk to me about?'

Judd removed his wallet from his pocket. 'Firstly, I have some news. The rest of the family don't know yet, so you're privileged.' He tossed a photograph across the table.

Ace picked it up curiously, looking at the red-headed girl. She had to be about twenty years old and she had a stubborn mouth and an arrogant chin. She was also the spit of his father. His mouth dropped open.

'That's right, she's my daughter.' Judd preened. 'Savannah is your half-sister.'

'Fuck!' Whatever he'd been expecting, this was shocking to say the least. Ace was stunned. 'Well, that's an advert for condoms if ever I saw one. I can't think of anything more hideous than someone turning up in twenty years' time wanting to play happy families.'

Judd's expression was chilly. 'Actually, I'm delighted Savannah is joining our family. I've always wanted a daughter.'

Feeling nauseous, Ace motioned to the waitress for another round of drinks. He wasn't sure his mother was going to be overjoyed about Savannah's existence. Older than Elliot, Savannah was clearly the result of one of his father's many affairs. Ace's stomach tightened at the thought of his mother hearing the news.

He stared at his father, wondering if he was some kind of sociopath. He also made a mental note to send Elliot a text later. Someone over in England needed to be warned about this bombshell; otherwise, the fallout was going to be catastrophic.

Judd carried on, not noticing Ace's scrutiny. 'I've also given her a recording contract at Jett. Savannah's very talented, a really special girl.'

Hearing the pride in his voice, Ace felt an absurd stab of jealousy over his father's illegitimate offspring but quickly told himself to grow up. Savannah might be flavour of the month right now, but if Ace knew his father, she wouldn't be for long because she was only human and that meant she was going to do something wrong sooner or later. And then Savannah would be just like the rest of them; trying desperately hard to please Judd and barely understanding why she had fallen short of expectation.

Ace held his tongue as Judd tersely pushed another photograph across the table.

'And this is Iris Maguire,' Judd said. 'She's the daughter of someone I used to know a long time ago – Lochlin Maguire. He owns a record label which is the main reason I've set up Jett. She's a world-class singer and she's in LA at the moment, working with Pia Jordan.'

Ace glanced at the photograph and rubbed his chin. Iris Maguire was absolutely gorgeous. She had long, tawny-blond hair and mesmerising amber eyes. Her body was slender, her dress sense bohemian. Ace shrugged and pushed the photograph back across the table.

'She's even more beautiful in person, I can assure you,' Judd informed him, much to Ace's bewilderment. 'She's a rough diamond, in dire need of a makeover, but she's got star quality like you wouldn't believe.'

'What does this have to do with me?' Ace asked impatiently. He glanced at his watch, wondering if he was going to be late for lunch with Jerry.

'I want you to seduce her,' Judd murmured softly.

'What?' Ace burst out laughing. His father couldn't be serious. 'Are you pimping me out?' he added humorously, sure he must have misunderstood.

'If you want to see it that way.' Judd's face was stony.

Ace was flabbergasted.

'I can't imagine it will be that much of a hardship for you. She's breathtaking.' Like her mother, Judd thought, feeling a pang in his heart like a poison-tipped dagger. He couldn't bear thinking about Tavvy at the moment; she seemed so far away and not just in miles. Judd took no notice of Ace's staggered expression. 'Pia has tickets to the Toyota Pro/Celebrity race. You need to "accidentally" bump into Iris.' He threw his neat Scotch back without flinching. 'Iris's father will have warned her to stay away from the Harringtons. Let's just say there's no love lost between our two families.' Judd wasn't prepared to say any more than that at this stage.

Ace wished Jerry was here to witness this conversation; he'd never believe him otherwise. He wondered idly if he could get his father sectioned. He wasn't just a sociopath; he needed serious help.

'So you will need to use your not inconsiderable powers of seduction to win her over,' Judd continued gravely. 'Do whatever you have to do and I don't care what it costs.' He tossed a black credit card across the table. 'That's a Centurion Card, so you can spend to your heart's content. The Monte Carlo apartment is at your disposal and I will sanction anything you need to make this happen. Your main problem will be convincing Iris that your motives are pure and the fact that you are a Harrington is simply a coincidence.'

Ace picked the credit card up and turned it over in his hands. 'All this, just so I can seduce this girl Iris Maguire?'

'Well, there's a bit more to it.' Judd leant forward. 'I don't just want you to sleep with her, I want you to get her to fall in love with you.'

Ace scoffed. 'I'm good, Dad, but I'm not *that* good. And what about Allegra?'

'What *about* Allegra?' Judd's lip curled. 'You weren't late because of her this morning, were you? No, I didn't think so. And while we're on that subject, all other women are off the agenda, Ace. No Allegra, no NASCAR groupies. It's Iris Maguire and no one else until I say otherwise.'

Ace started laughing in disbelief. Now he knew his father had lost it. He hadn't been monogamous since his first girlfriend had cheated on him at the age of ten, which was when he'd made a pact with himself never to put all his eggs in one basket again.

'I mean it,' Judd informed him. 'If you slip up, even once, I'm pulling all your NASCAR sponsorship and the money I put into your team.'

Ace stopped laughing.

'Seriously, you'll be out of that flashy bachelor pad before you can say monsoon shower.' Judd hoped he was making himself clear. 'And your relationship with Iris Maguire ends when I say so, do you understand? Make her fall in love with you and when I give you the nod, it's over.'

Ace swallowed. What the hell was this all about? Could his father really have such a vendetta going with this Lochlin Maguire that pimping out his own son to seduce Lochlin's daughter seemed sane to him? Ace thought it sounded rather like a twisted game of chess with members of the Maguire family and the Harrington family as hapless pawns, and his father presiding over them all like a demented adjudicator.

Ace wondered if his career as a racing driver was really worth doing something as low as this. Then, as he saw the formidable look in his father's eyes, he wondered, alarmed, if he had any choice in the matter, regardless of what was at stake.

Judd stood up. 'Another thing. I want Iris to sign to Jett Records. That could be tricky because she promised her father she would only ever sign to Shamrock.' He smiled wickedly. 'But if anyone can pull it off, you can.'

'Get her signed to your record label as well.' Ace tossed the credit card on to the table incredulously. 'Marvellous. Should be easy, Dad.'

'Oh, and one last thing.' Judd patted his son's shoulder without an ounce of affection. 'Fall in love with a Maguire and you won't need to worry about your racing career ever again because you won't have one. Not because I'll pull your sponsorship but because I'll personally break both of your legs. Got it?'

Ace watched his father stride out of the bar, his mouth hanging open in shock. Within seconds, the waitress with the waist-length black hair had slipped into Judd's seat. 'Fancy a drink later?' she flirted. 'And maybe breakfast tomorrow morning?'

Ace slowly put the credit card in his pocket. So this was what it felt like to be a kept man, he thought, his head reeling.

'Well?' said the waitress, her botoxed brow wrinkling fractionally as she contemplated being turned down. Ace Harrington, NASCAR racing driver, and one of the biggest studs around – a dead cert . . . surely?

Ace got to his feet unsteadily. 'Er . . . no, sorry.'

The waitress's hundred-watt smile faltered. 'No? Did you just say no?'

Ace wondered how he could put it politely. 'Apparently, I'm . . . what's the expression? Spoken for.' His mouth twisted bitterly. 'Actually, make that bought and fucking paid for.'

Leaving the waitress mouthing at him like a goldfish, Ace stalked out of the bar.

Chapter Nine

Iris leant over the balcony and grinned as she inhaled. Reeling from the heat, she stared out across Venice Beach, dazzled by the sights. She'd been in Los Angeles for four days. At home at Pembleton, the air was familiar, scented with flowers and invariably infused with rain; here, the air was filled with sunshine and expectation. And Iris couldn't get enough of it.

Luisa's apartment, set in a five-storey block called the Tropical Shade Apartments, was located several streets back from the beachfront itself. Each door was painted in pretty pastel shades and the apartment was tiny, or as Luisa described it, 'Bijou', but it was colourful and homely, bedecked with posters of dance movies, empty record sleeves and shelves full of the glitzy dance trophies Luisa had won over the years.

'Have you managed to get some sleep today?' Luisa asked, bursting into the sitting room like a tornado. Dressed in bright yellow cut-off trackies and a matching yellow vest top, her mocha-coloured skin looked even darker than usual.

Iris shook her head, loving the way Luisa pronounced 'have' as 'haff'. In spite of starting off her early years in Brixton with her mother, Luisa's accent was as thick as Spanish chocolate and her almost-black eyes danced and shone as she spoke.

'No, I'm too excited. I soaked up the sun on the balcony for a bit and then I went down to the cash and carry and bought some Twinkies and ten Hershey bars, just because I could.'

Luisa laughed. 'You're gonna get fat if you eat all those, *querida*.'

'I didn't *eat* them,' Iris replied with a grin. 'I just wanted to *buy* them.'

Luisa rolled her eyes. 'Margaritas?' she offered, going into the compact kitchenette. 'I'm making the ones with mango.'

'Then count me in.' Listening to Luisa expertly pounding tart Mexican limes and mango pulp together, Iris remembered how hostile Luisa had been when she'd first arrived. With a mixture of Mexican blood from her mother, Maria, and a dash of Caribbean from her father – a second-rate keyboard player who'd scarpered back to Tobago as soon as he'd discovered Maria was pregnant – Luisa, with her mop of wiry black ringlets, her smooth mocha skin and eyes like shiny black olives, was unusual looking, to say the least. She was also fiercely independent and in the first couple of days of Iris's arrival, she had bristled with ill-disguised resentment.

It was only when Iris had informed Luisa that she had no intention of getting in her way while she was in LA, adding that she was 'more or less toilet trained', that Luisa had relented and burst into apologetic laughter. Since then they had got on like a house on fire with Luisa showing Iris the sights and introducing her to her lively gang of friends who were all equally charmed by her.

Luisa emerged from the kitchen. 'Here. Go easy, it's what you'd call a belter.' She laughed as Iris choked on the margarita. Iris was one of the most naturally beautiful girls she had ever seen. Granted, she needed a makeover, Luisa thought critically; she was in dire need of some decent make-up and a stylist would love to get her hands on her, but apart from that, the combination of bee-stung lips, the sexy tangle of tawny-blond hair and a fun-loving nature made Iris drop-dead gorgeous. Luisa understood exactly why Iris's parents had insisted on a chaperone; Iris might not be gauche or lacking in social awareness but she was trusting and sweet and far too nice for a hard, cynical music industry that wouldn't think twice about taking advantage of her.

The phone rang and Iris reached out a hand but Luisa shook her head and flung herself on the sofa. 'Probably just my sleazy ex-boyfriend,' she said with narrowed eyes. 'Ignore it.'

But it wasn't. It was Pia Jordan and after announcing herself in clipped tones, she proceeded to tell Iris there had been a change of plan and that instead of starting on Monday morning, her first singing lesson would start in thirty minutes.

'I hope you have a pen because this is the address,' Pia barked, as if she barely had time to talk. She trotted it out like a machine gun. 'Don't be late.' The phone was hung up brusquely.

'What . . . how on earth . . . I'm not r-ready . . .' Iris cursed herself as her stutter came out of nowhere. She hadn't practised, she didn't have her music prepared . . . She stared down at the empty cocktail glass in her hand. 'And I'm pretty much pissed after that drink.'

Luisa glanced at her watch. 'I have a car. It's an old heap but we can get there. If we leave now.' Her dark eyebrows shot up doubtfully. 'Just.'

Iris leapt off the sofa and looked down at her scruffy white shorts and yellow vest top. 'I look such a mess . . .'

'No time to change,' Luisa cried bossily as she grabbed her car keys from the wicker table in the hallway. 'It's boho chic. Grab some flip-flops and your shades and let's go!'

Doubtful Luisa's crappy red Ford Capri would get them there in one piece, Iris clung on for dear life as Luisa zipped past the crowded beachfront, full of half-naked bodies in the teeniest of bikinis and the tightest of Lycra shorts.

'Santa Monica,' Luisa shouted, gesturing towards the distinctive pier as she almost took a hairpin bend on two wheels. Checking the scribbled directions once more, she shot off down a back street and after a while pulled up outside a smart-looking studio with a discreet plaque on the door. Luisa gave Iris a push. 'Go on, I've nearly killed us getting here, don't you make it a wasted trip. I'll be across the street in that coffee shop, all right? Go, *querida*!'

Gulping, Iris headed indoors. Pia Jordan had a fearful

reputation. She was known as the best in the business, with a legendary temper and demanding expectation of her clients. Rubbing her sweaty palms on her white shorts apprehensively, Iris couldn't help wondering what the hell she was doing here. She found a vast studio which was empty apart from a piano and a statuesque black woman.

'You were almost late,' snapped the woman. Wearing a pair of white tailored trousers and a cropped black top that showed off a toned six-pack, Pia had sleek elfin hair that looked as if it had been slicked back with oil and small, intelligent-looking eyes.

'I didn't have a car . . . my friend drove me in this old—'

'Not interested.' Pia snapped her fingers at Iris impatiently. 'We have work to do so let's get started. Warm up then sing.' Thrusting a song sheet at Iris, she waited.

Iris took the sheet, with a thumping heart. After performing a set of perfect scales without any piano accompaniment, she glanced down at the music Pia had given her. It was a song by a well-known soul singer, something Iris had never sung before and which she was sure wouldn't suit her voice. It was out of her natural range and about as challenging as a song could be, the notes rippling from one end of the scale to another.

'Are you . . . a-are you going to p-play the piano?' she stammered, desperately worried about doing the song justice. How many octaves did Pia think she could sing, for heaven's sake?

'Do I look as if I'm going to play the piano?' Pia inquired rudely, her forehead furrowed with irritation. 'I want to hear your voice. I need to know if you can reach the notes without assistance. The piano masks mistakes.' She put her hands on her hips and scrutinised Iris.

That stutter better not make an appearance when she sings, Pia thought unrepentantly, because otherwise, she was sending this lame duck straight back to Judd. Still, she looked incredible, Pia mused. The white shorts and sunshine-yellow top suited Iris's slender figure and the cloud of blond hair was adorable. And as for the face, Pia caught her breath. Considering Iris's face was free of make-up and slightly sweaty, she was still astonishingly beautiful.

On the verge of running out of the studio in utter terror, Iris focused on slowing her breathing down. Fervently, she prayed for her stutter to subside. Pushing aside the thought that her career was in the balance at this very moment, Iris closed her eyes and pretended she was at home in her bedroom. No pressure, she told herself with a silent laugh. It's just my voice and this song. All I have to do is put them together.

She opened her eyes and fixed them on Pia's six-pack because it was a hell of a lot less daunting than meeting her stony gaze. Opening her mouth, Iris started to sing. Her voice was slightly weak at first but, gaining momentum, she realised it wasn't straining half as much as she had expected it to and she only stumbled once as she hit all the tricky notes.

'Again, please,' Pia snapped, her expression unreadable as she leant back against the piano. She was glad she'd mastered the art of disguising her inner thoughts over the years because she wouldn't dream of letting Iris know how elated she was to hear such a rich, husky tone. Pia made Iris sing the song over and over, then she gave her a rock ballad to master before disappearing into her office to take a phone call. It was Judd. They shared an on-off relationship, hooking up whenever he was in LA, but now that he owned a record company, Pia was a professional contact too.

'Hey.' Pia watched Iris through the frosted glass. 'Yep, she got here on time and she's been working her ass off. Am I pleased? I'm crazy fucking happy!' She swelled with pride as she heard Iris pull the difficult note off perfectly and, before she could stop herself, Pia flipped her thumb up in approval. 'She's worked harder than most of my regular clients ever do and she looks like a Goddamned angel. What's not to like?'

As Judd barked orders down the other end of the phone, Pia tuned him out and focused on the contacts she had in the music business. Iris Maguire needed to record something and she needed exposure and Pia had the perfect slot coming up on an awards show. Judd had been keen for Iris to present an award but Pia wanted to push for a song too and she was prepared to call in any favours she needed to in order to achieve it.

Tearing her eyes away from Iris, Pia realised Judd had stopped his characteristically blunt diatribe and she rushed to answer him. 'Yeah, yeah, that all sounds great. You did good sending Iris Maguire to me, Judd. She's gonna be a star all over the fucking world when I've finished with her.' Snapping her phone shut, Pia went back into the studio and in clipped tones sent Iris home so she could make a dozen phone calls to all her contacts.

Shattered, Iris staggered outside, ready to drop. As Luisa quickly brought her car round and picked her up, Iris gratefully sank into the front seat.

'Jesus Christ, the woman's hardcore,' she cried, filling Luisa in as quickly as she could. 'I think Judd called while I was there. Talk about checking up on me.'

'Really? That's just too weird. I do not know if you should trust him, Iris. He sounds like a crazy man.'

As they pulled into the apartment car park, they both stopped talking. Sitting in the middle of the car park, wrapped up with the most enormous red bow, was a brand new silver jeep. It was surrounded by a group of people from the apartments who were reading a note that was attached to the windscreen. Luisa parked the car and they both jumped out excitedly.

'Hey, which one of you is Iris?' called one of the boys Luisa recognised from the floor below hers.

Iris turned scarlet. 'That's me.'

'Then this car is yours.'

'Mine?' Iris glanced at Luisa and shook her head. 'There must be some mistake.'

The boy read the note out loud. 'It says, "Iris, welcome to LA. Car keys in the apartment. Judd." ' He showed it to her, running his eyes over her slim figure appreciatively. 'Who is he? Your sugar daddy or something?'

Iris reread the note, shaking her head in disbelief.

Luisa whistled as she walked around the car. 'Oh my God, Iris. He bought you a car . . . the man bought you a Goddamned car!'

Iris was bewildered. She had no idea why Judd would make such a gesture but she knew she couldn't possibly accept the car. She had an idea that doing so would be tantamount to climbing into bed with the enemy in her father's eyes.

'Move *back*!' Luisa yelled at the crowd of spectators, batting them out of the way. 'We're going to have such a great time in this, Iris! Let's get the keys. Come on!'

Iris ran her hands along the bonnet wonderingly. It was gorgeous, perfect for whizzing round LA. No one had ever bought her such an extravagant present in her life and whilst she appreciated not being spoilt as a child, she couldn't help being utterly bowled over by Judd's generosity.

All the same, it was going back first thing in the morning, Iris told herself firmly. She'd made a promise to her father and she was going to respect it.

'Don't you dare send it back,' Luisa said, reading her mind. '*I'll* keep it if you don't want to. Or just think of it as a loan. We'll use it and give it back later, yes?' She dashed upstairs to get the keys.

Iris tugged the enormous bow off the car. Could she do that? If she sent the car back later, maybe it wasn't the same as accepting it as a proper gift. Swamped with guilt, Iris couldn't help feeling it had been a brilliant day.

'Over my dead body. Got it?'

Like an obstreperous teenager, Savannah pushed the file Darcy had put together back across the desk and folded her arms, shaking her red mane in defiance.

Darcy's eyes narrowed. Since Judd had buggered off to the States to deal with his mysteriously 'urgent' business, she'd been left in charge of Savannah's career at the Jett Record Corporation. Having spent a great deal of time thinking about how to change her image, what sort of music she should record and how the albums should be packaged, Darcy couldn't believe Savannah was being so rude and ungrateful. Didn't she know how many girls would kill to be in her place? Didn't she realise how lucky she was that Judd was ploughing so much money into her career?

Savannah, seated the other side of Darcy's ridiculously butch oak desk, was feeling equally resentful. She had met her father, expecting to be introduced to the rest of the Harrington clan, but he had disappeared back to the States and left her to it. And not only that, he had left her to the mercy of his bolshie mistress who looked as if she would rather be anywhere but dealing with her launch. Dressed in a black silk shirt and a cream pencil skirt, Darcy was the epitome of class and elegance but she had a glint in her hazel eyes that suggested she was no pushover.

'Right.' Darcy flexed her tense neck. She knew Judd would freak out at her if she didn't make some headway with Savannah. Out of all of his children, Savannah was his favourite, at least for the time being. 'What don't you like?'

'I don't like any of it.' Aggressively, Savannah flipped the pages, stabbing her fingers on them. 'I hate the image, I can't stand the look of the CD covers and as for the sort of music you think I should be singing, no way!'

'If you don't go for something edgy, you're going to end up looking like a bad Britney Spears copy with your voice,' Darcy argued, her eyes flashing. 'Only Britney can do Britney. What I have in mind is a rockier image for you – black leather, messy hair, and smoky make-up. A rougher look, something a bit different from the run-of-the-mill, manufactured rubbish that's everywhere out there.'

Savannah stared back at her insolently.

Darcy pushed on. 'I see you on the cover of your CDs looking like the bad girl mothers don't want to see their sons marrying, and the music is what's known in the business as "edgy pop". It doesn't have that manufactured feel and it's harder and cooler than the usual cheesy crap that's usually given to solo artists who can't write their own material.'

Savannah lifted a shoulder jerkily. She could see what Darcy was trying to do and her ideas were probably spot on. She could even grudgingly admit that if Judd had been the one to present her with the same ideas, she would have been wildly excited by them. As it was, she was so pissed off with her father for disappearing as soon as she'd laid eyes on him, nothing would be good enough for her until he came back and paid her a bit of attention.

'The hair's OK,' she conceded, lifting her blue eyes to meet Darcy's.

God, she was like Judd, Darcy thought. That cold, haughty stare, the way the chin jutted out when she was being defiant, the supreme self-confidence . . . Before she could proceed with her plans for Savannah's career, Heidi came in without knocking. Throwing Darcy a frosty scowl, she set down a Starbucks coffee cup next to Savannah.

'A caramel macchiato, as requested, Savannah.'

'Hey, thanks, Heidi.' Savannah took a sip. 'Mmmmm. That's so great.'

'Aren't they? They're my favourite too.' Heidi gave Savannah a warm smile, ignoring Darcy pointedly.

Cheekily, Savannah put the heels of her boots on Darcy's desk. 'Oh, that's so good. It reminds me of home.' Realising Brockett Hall would hopefully now be her home, she corrected herself. 'I mean, it reminds me of New York.'

'You'll have to cut down on those if you want to be a pop star,' Darcy bitched, fuming at Savannah's impertinence. Why the hell should she have to put up with this sort of behaviour? She wasn't sure Judd was worth this kind of stress. And Heidi was so far up Savannah's backside, she could probably clean her teeth for her, Darcy ranted inwardly. Taking a deep, calming breath, she shot her point home. 'Magazines can be very unforgiving if someone in the public eye develops a fat arse, Savannah. Just something to bear in mind.'

Savannah gave her a withering stare. 'I'm not *in* the public eye . . . yet.'

Heidi shook her head reproachfully. 'I think it's really unhealthy to tell a young girl she can't have the odd treat. Are you calling Savannah fat?'

'Yeah, are you?' Savannah demanded in a truculent tone.

Almost at breaking point, Darcy fought hard not to explode. She clenched her fists underneath her desk.

Bored with the conversation, Savannah made a mental note to bad-mouth Darcy like crazy when Judd got back from his trip. She got up. 'I'm done talking to the monkey,' she observed dismissively, enjoying the sight of Darcy's face turning an interesting shade of puce. 'Or should I say, my father's bitch.'

Darcy recoiled as if she'd been slapped. 'Why, you little—'

Savannah waved her hand. 'Next time, I'm talking to the organ grinder. My father should be in charge of my career, not you, so I'm only dealing with *him* from now on.'

Flouncing out, she was swiftly followed by Heidi who couldn't resist giving Darcy a jubilant smile as she left.

Frustrated, Darcy slammed her hand down hard on her desk. When the fuck was Judd coming back to deal with his out-of-control daughter?

Darcy spun her chair round to face the window, feeling tense and unsettled. She kept telling herself it was because she missed Judd but she really didn't think that was the case. Judd was hardly the most attentive man she'd ever been with – far from it. He was demanding and aggressive and he expected her to be at his beck and call, working to his schedule and never once uttering a word of complaint.

Her life wasn't her own any more, Darcy mused. It was as if she'd been consumed by Judd, as if she'd lost herself by being drawn so deeply into his world. She could barely remember who she was before. Judd was a force of nature, everyone said so, but he was far more than that. He was so self-centred, nothing else mattered in his world apart from him and that meant that anyone involved with him had to dance to the same tune. And what about all the work he'd asked her to do recruiting Lochlin's staff?

Darcy stared out across the London skyline. Against her better judgement, she had allowed Judd to convince her that poaching a number of Lochlin's staff members from Shamrock would be a good idea. It had left a bad taste in her mouth, but the job was done. The staff in question had been carefully selected for their skills and, in some cases, their personal situations, the idea being that they would be unable to refuse the huge amounts of money and outlandish bonuses on offer.

Darcy drummed her fingers on the table. Why on earth had she done it? She had always prided herself on playing by the rules when it came to business. She was ruthless and she was ambitious but Darcy had never before compromised herself professionally in her career. Just a few months in Judd's company and she had sullied her integrity and left herself wide open to ruin. If she left Jett – and Judd – now, it would only take a few phone calls to put the word out there that she was unreliable, unprofessional and untrustworthy.

Darcy knew she had no choice; all she could do now was live with her decision. For someone who had always lived her life by the mantra 'no regrets', she was certainly having a few now. Judd was due back from the States shortly and would no doubt want to resurrect their twisted relationship as soon as his feet hit UK soil. Darcy's stomach was churning at the mere thought of it.

And what about Shay Maguire? She still hadn't done anything about him because she couldn't bear the thought of screwing someone else over. However, she knew Judd would be on her case if she left it much longer. Darcy shivered. She was beginning to think Judd would be very frightening if he didn't get his own way.

She had made her bed, professionally and personally, and she had no choice now but to lie in it.

Darcy yanked Savannah's file towards her with gritted teeth and prepared to go back to square one.

Tavvy took a break. She'd been mucking out the stables all evening and Petra was busy rehousing Moccachino, the horse she'd rescued before the Valentines' Ball. She glanced at the old barn, shielding her eyes against the fading sunlight. It was a dilapidated building with half the roof missing and a serious case of mould on one of the internal walls but with a bit of work and an injection of cash it could provide all the extra space they needed and they might even be able to build a cat sanctuary on the side. Perhaps the Midsummer Ball would pay for all the extra work.

Humming yet another new melody that was niggling at her, she almost threw a mound of horse manure all over Lochlin.

'Ooops, sorry!' She laughed. 'You hardly ever venture out here.'

'Jaysus, woman, this stuff's like glue! No wonder I don't come up very often.' Dressed in an immaculate suit with white shirt and a dark green tie, Lochlin wasn't exactly appropriately dressed for traipsing round the stables, whereas he thought Tavvy looked as though she was in her element, trussed up in Caitie's fake fur coat and a pair of welly boots. Her cheeks were pink from the cold and she seemed relaxed and contented. Just for a second, Lochlin envied her. He couldn't remember the last time he had felt chilled out and happy.

Tavvy leant on her spade and contemplated Lochlin. Recently, she had been aware of a growing rift between them and she hated it. It was as if everything had shifted between them since Judd Harrington had come back. Physically, Lochlin was a changed man; he had unsightly bags and his brow was so deeply furrowed, it looked as though someone had driven a tractor across it.

'Noah's Ark is fast becoming a business rather than just a hobby,'

Lochlin commented. 'Maybe I should just retire and work out here with you.'

'That sounds lovely. But somehow I can't see you retiring just yet.'

'No?' He fixed tired green eyes on her. 'I wouldn't be too sure.'

Tavvy frowned. Lochlin didn't sound like himself. And when had he got so *thin*? she wondered Even the collar of his shirt seemed too large.

'Are things that bad at Shamrock?' she asked, concerned.

Lochlin glowered. What could he say? That he no longer trusted anyone in his office, not even Erica? That he suspected everyone was stabbing him in the back or trying to ruin him? Lochlin knew his thoughts made him seem paranoid at best, hysterical at worst.

'Has Charlie been in touch?' Tavvy asked gently, knowing how hurt Lochlin had been over his defection.

Lochlin shook his head. 'Look, as an artist, I can't blame him for going to Jett. They've obviously offered him something I wasn't about to.' His eyes clouded over. 'But as a friend, do I feel let down? Yes, I do. Even Leo seems to be keeping his distance at the moment.' As he said the words, Lochlin knew he was playing down his disillusionment. He, Charlie and Leo had been like the Three Musketeers and, right now, he felt like Athos without Porthos and Aramis to lean on.

Tavvy put down her spade. 'Iris called this morning,' she said.

'She did? How's she doing?' Lochlin's eyes darted to hers anxiously.

'She's having the time of her life,' Tavvy assured him hastily. 'She's working hard and Luisa's looking after her. They're going to some celebrity event apparently, which they're both very excited about – some Toyota thing.' She didn't let on that Iris had been disturbingly evasive on the phone. Tavvy knew her daughter and she was certain Iris was hiding something.

Lochlin let out a relieved breath. 'That's grand. I haven't been able to sleep for worrying about her.'

Tavvy stared at Pembleton, thinking how warm and inviting it looked, its terracotta bricks resembling gingerbread slabs and its romantic, turret-like chimneys sitting proudly on top. As much as she loved her home, Tavvy suddenly wondered if Lochlin felt claustrophobic.

'Why don't we get away?' she suggested out of the blue.

'What? Where?'

Tavvy's mouth curved into a smile. 'I don't know, anywhere. Somewhere in France, perhaps. You, me, a few bottles of good wine and acres of stunning French countryside.' She curled her fingers round his arm. 'It'd be just like the old days.'

For a second, Lochlin almost looked nostalgic. Then the weight of his responsibilities came down heavily on his shoulders again. 'I couldn't possibly take the time off. Not when things are so . . . uncertain.'

Disappointed, Tavvy stared past him. 'Everything is different, isn't it? Since Judd . . . nothing is the same, not even me and you.'

Lochlin's arm tensed beneath hers. 'What do you mean? Don't say that, I can't bear it. I can't bear the thought of him coming between us.'

'Then don't let him,' she begged, turning to face him. 'Whatever Judd does, or tries to do, we need to stick together – you, me, the whole family.'

'I know we do!' Angrily, Lochlin pulled his hands away from hers. 'But how can we when Iris is halfway across the world and Shay might as well be?'

Tavvy recoiled, wondering when his temper had ever been this short. 'You can't blame Judd for the way Shay's behaving.'

Lochlin threw her a hurt glance. 'Oh no, that's all *my* fault, isn't it?'

'I didn't say that,' she protested.

Lochlin put a hand to his chest, feeling it constricting again. Why did he feel as if no one was on his side right now? He didn't think he'd ever felt more alone in his life.

'Lochlin.' Tavvy raised her amber eyes to his, frightened to death by his pallid face. 'We'll be all right, won't we?'

Lochlin looked at her, doing his best to ignore his shortness of breath. 'I don't know. Will we?' With that, he turned and left her standing in the wild grass.

Shocked, Tavvy felt tears streaming down her cheeks.

Christ, if Judd really was back to destroy them all, he was doing a bloody good job of it so far, Tavvy thought, watching Lochlin disappear out of sight.

'You're not seriously thinking of going through with it?'

Jerry, having just heard about Judd's plans for Ace to seduce Iris Maguire, was gobsmacked.

Ace wasn't listening. Hurling his crash helmet to the ground, he raked his fingers through his hair in frustration. 'Fucking hell, I can't drive for *shit* today!' Drenched with sweat, he glared at his car, wishing he could blame it for his abysmal round at the Bristol Motor Speedway in Tennessee.

'This track is so fucking *short*,' Ace complained, knowing that wasn't the reason for his horrendous driving. He detested the Bristol track where speeds tended to be lower but he had never completed such a terrible round here before. Spectators were stacked high in the stalls, rumoured to be over one hundred thousand on a good day, and they were jeering at him. Ace wasn't surprised, he'd driven like a fucking novice.

Unzipping his suit as he and Jerry strode away from the track, Ace scowled. 'I can't believe my father even asked me to do this seduction thing, Jez. He's a fucking maniac.'

'It's immoral,' Jerry stormed.

Ace welcomed Jerry's support, glad he wasn't the only one who thought his father was losing his grip on reality. 'I mean, this chick Iris looks gorgeous and don't get me wrong, most men would rip their right arm off to take her to bed. If I'd met her without knowing any of this, I'd be all over her like a rash.' Ace rubbed a hand over his face, streaking dirt through the sweat. 'But it's not just that. It's signing record deals with Jett, dumping her when my father says so . . .'

Jerry nodded. He couldn't believe Judd had pulled such a stunt. He and Ace had always had a good father-son relationship; not affectionate as such, but mutually beneficial. As far as Jerry could see it, Judd funded Ace's life and Ace lived out Judd's dream zealously. He possessed dazzling, natural talent on the track and being a lover of danger, he took risks fearlessly. Off the track, Ace bedded women with the same supreme confidence and Judd loved that.

'He means it, though,' Ace said grimly, draining a glass of champagne in one gulp. 'If I don't go through with this, he'll take back the sponsorship, the apartment, the lot. It'd be you and me in a tiny condo on the wrong side of town, drinking cheap beer and shopping at K-Mart, Jerry.' His grin faded. 'But that's not the point. It's my career. How on earth would I be able to do it without my father? He funds everything. He's always giving Joe cash to pay for publicity and better equipment.'

Joe Wilson ran their driving team Wilson Racing and it was true, Judd had provided an awful lot of cash to the team over the years. If Ace hadn't been such a phenomenal driver, his team mates would have given him no end of stick for being the rich kid, but as it was, Ace could out-drive all of them. Should Judd pull his funding, however, Joe might not be able to keep the team afloat.

'We could . . . get another sponsor?' Jerry suggested half-heartedly. 'Or we could drive for another team.'

Ace shook his head. 'Not one pays out as much as my father. And what are the odds of us ending up on the same team?'

Jerry was desperate to think of a solution to help Ace. He knew how much driving meant to his best friend – he lived and breathed it, it was who he was. Jerry loved the glamour of his racing career too but, for Ace, it was his life. He rubbed his chiselled chin, deep in thought as Ace received a text message.

Turning pale, Ace held it up to show Jerry. It was from Judd, telling him to steer clear of the party tonight as too many girls would be there.

Jerry gaped at the phone in disbelief. Judd was outrageous.

'Ace Harrington. Well, well, well.'

Ace spun round to find Bree, a stunning twenty-year-old blonde he'd met the year before, standing in front of him. A former Miss Tennessee and a wannabe playmate, she was wearing a minuscule sunshine-yellow dress that made the most of her bronzed thighs and gravity-defying cleavage.

'You never called,' she purred, her green eyes connecting with his as she leant in for a kiss. 'Will I see you later at the party?'

'Sorry, no,' he replied, memories of their erotic coupling rushing vividly into his mind. He kept his hands firmly behind his back and gave her a chaste kiss on the cheek.

'What?' Bree was clearly puzzled. Ace Harrington, legendary playboy, not attending an after-race party? It was unheard of, however terrible his round had been.

Bree's eyes registered her disappointment but she was gracious. 'Well, you know where to find me if you change your mind.' She gave Jerry a searching look but he kept his face impassive, not wanting to betray Ace.

Ace drooled as he watched Bree walk off, her yellow dress so tight across her buttocks, it was obvious to all and sundry that she wasn't wearing any underwear. 'Fucking hell!' he groaned. 'That was one of the hardest things I've ever done.'

Jerry, refusing a calorie-laden canapé because he had a photo shoot for Ralph Lauren in two days' time, grabbed Ace's arm. 'Are you really going to go through with this?' he asked again.

Ace bit his lip. 'I honestly don't think I have any choice, Jerry. It's not just about me, I have to think about Joe and the guys on the team.' He gazed round the hospitality tent longingly. It was teeming with gorgeous girls wearing practically nothing, champagne on tap and delicious food circulating endlessly.

Slamming his champagne glass down with obvious regret, Ace headed for the exit.

Jerry's blue eyes were full of concern as he followed his friend.

'No need for you to leave too, bro,' Ace said lightly, over his shoulder. 'This is the deal I made with my father. No other women. So that means no Bree and no Allegra.' He held his phone up. 'Allegra's been calling me non-stop so I've had to tell her I'm off women for now and concentrating on my racing.' He gave Jerry a rueful grin. 'Hey, knock yourself out and I'll catch up with you in a few days' time, all right? And at the Toyota event I can meet Iris Maguire and get this whole thing up and running.'

Reluctantly, Jerry went back to the party, his gut telling him that Judd's demands could only end badly.

And as Ace headed back to his hotel to take an ice-cold shower, he couldn't help thinking exactly the same thing.

Chapter Ten

Shay ordered another Jack Daniel's and Coke at the bar and turned to face the jazz band who were setting up at the front. It was Friday night after a hellish day at work but despite the cajoling of his best mate Robin at *Music Mode*, he had laughingly turned down offers of pub crawls and piss-ups in the West End. Shay had no desire to wake up naked in a skip on the other side of London or screwing one of the temps on his boss's desk, as Robin often did after a night out.

This had been a bad *week*, Shay thought, nursing his drink morosely, glad he was in his favourite jazz club so that he could kick back and think about everything. Work at *Music Mode* had been uninspiring to say the least recently and since Iris had left for LA, he and his father had barely spoken.

Dad's a stubborn, pig-headed fool, Shay thought, smiling briefly as the band began to play his favourite song, 'Linger In My Arms A Little Longer'. He realised his father had changed since Judd Harrington's arrival but the game-playing seemed so pointless. He sighed and wondered what to do about his future. Shamrock was no longer an option and Shay wasn't sure he cared about anything else.

'Fancy some company? They're playing my favourite song so I thought I'd be brave and ask you if you fancied a drink.'

Shay turned to find an attractive brunette standing next to him at the bar. He was about to politely turn her down when he did a double take.

'You're the girl from the Valentines' Ball!' he blurted out. He flushed, feeling idiotic.

'And you're the *boy* from the Valentines' Ball,' she teased, smiling at him. She perched herself elegantly on the nearest bar stool. 'And as flattering as it is to be described as a girl, I think I'm a little old for that.'

Shay wasn't sure how to respond but seeing her close up, he realised she was definitely a woman, not a girl. She had slight lines around her eyes and mouth and he guessed she might be in her early thirties.

She was stunning, Shay thought, brightening. She had a full mouth and an angular jaw which was softened by a retroussé nose and cool hazel eyes. She wasn't conventionally pretty but she had something, most notably a fantastic figure which, covered by a classy black dress, flared in and out in all the right places, like a burlesque dancer's.

God, she was sexy, Shay thought, feeling like a schoolboy.

'Shall we get a bottle?' she suggested, nodding to the barman to place a bottle of Jack Daniel's on the bar. She turned to Shay. 'When you've had a bad day, only the bottle will do.'

Shay agreed, realising he must look like a moody bastard, drinking alone and moping into his glass. 'Should we drown our sorrows together?'

She knocked her glass against his. 'Definitely.'

'My name's Shay. I don't even know yours . . .' he started, pausing as she covered his hand with hers.

'Let's not bother with names. It makes it more exciting, don't you think?'

Shay smiled, intrigued. 'Fair enough.'

Darcy filled up their glasses, her heart thumping madly in her chest. She felt like a spy in a Bond movie – but far from being a Bond girl, she knew she was one of the baddies.

Darcy turned towards the stage. She still wasn't entirely sure how she was going to do any damage to Shay. She had simply followed him from his office to the jazz club. The only problem was, Darcy couldn't help wishing she was sharing a drink with him under different circumstances. Shay seemed mature but he was young, twenty-five at the most. He was broad-shouldered and heavier-set than she remembered. With his strong jaw and understated confidence, he looked anything but boyish. And those *eyes* . . . wow. As green as shamrocks and sexily intense. When he fixed them on her, she found herself practically twisting with desire on her bar stool.

'You like jazz?' Shay asked her. He was sure he could feel the air between them sizzling with chemistry.

'I love it. I have stacks of original stuff by people like Miles Davis and Louis Armstrong, even some rare live recordings from New Orleans.' Darcy crossed her legs, thinking about Judd's crude sexual advances. She had a feeling Shay would display far more finesse in the bedroom. Glancing at his kissable mouth and movie star cheekbones, she wondered what he'd be like in bed but she pushed the thought away.

Shay was pleasantly surprised to discover someone else with a love of jazz. Most of the women he encountered thought his music taste was dull and old-fashioned but here was a woman whose taste matched his own. They chatted animatedly about music for over an hour, discussing various bands and singers who were just breaking into the scene, pausing only to drink and listen to the jazz band.

Barely noticing how much time had passed, Darcy realised with a jolt that she had no wish to destroy Shay but, remembering the scarily ruthless look in Judd's eyes before he left for Los Angeles, Darcy reminded herself why she was here.

'So. You've had a bad week. What happened?'

'I'm just in a bit of a rut, work-wise.' Shay allowed her to refill his glass. 'I've always wanted to work with my father but that's not going to happen now.' His mouth twisted bitterly. 'I work at *Music Mode* magazine but it's not exactly my life's ambition.'

Darcy feigned surprise. '*Music Mode*? How strange, I know Dev, the editor.' She and Dev had hooked up years ago when she was starting out and Darcy had only broken up with him because he wouldn't stop going on about getting engaged. She and Dev had kept in touch on and off over the years and the realisation that he worked with Shay might just give her a way in. Still, Darcy was finding the thought of trapping Shay harder as the minutes passed.

Drumming his fingers on his thigh in time to the music, Shay couldn't help noticing she had sensational legs. She wore sheer stockings with a seam and on her they looked classy and extremely sexy.

Darcy decided to chance her arm. 'When I knew Dev, he was a total back-stabber,' she lied.

Shay frowned. 'Really? I think Dev's a top bloke, really professional and an all-round nice guy. Perhaps he's changed.' His mouth tightened with faint disapproval.

Darcy took a sip of Jack Daniel's and deliberated. Somehow, she wasn't surprised at Shay's reaction. She took a different tack.

'So he doesn't throw wild parties in the office any more then? Wow, he *must* have changed.'

Shay looked incredulous. 'Antics in the office? Dev? No way!' Hearing her laughing, he realised he wanted to make her laugh again. 'My friend Robin is disgraceful. One night he got so pissed he snorted coke off Dev's desk and had filthy sex on it.'

Darcy's eyes lit up. Bingo! Finally, something she might be able to use. She forced herself to continue, even though all she wanted to do was kiss Shay's sexy mouth and forget Judd existed. He smelt gorgeous – Jo Malone's Pomegranate Noir, if she wasn't mistaken – and it was an effort for her to remember what she was supposed to be doing. 'Hilarious,' she purred, stroking his thigh.

Shay grinned, buoyed up on Whiskey and the intoxicating sound of her laughter. 'He's done worse things than that. Once, he was so cross that Dev hadn't let him interview his favourite band, he hacked into Dev's computer and sent an email to all our competitors, telling them exactly what he thought of them. Dev's never been able to work out who did it.' Realising he was being indiscreet, Shay stopped talking. 'Don't listen to me, I've had too much to drink. Robin's a bit outrageous at times, but he's brilliant at his job and he can't afford to get fired. He was declared bankrupt a few years back.'

Darcy felt her stomach sink. Feverishly, she turned to face the bar again, her mind all over the place.

Shay did the same. He felt some weird connection to this woman but he couldn't put his finger on it. He just knew he didn't want the night to end. Their thighs touching, Shay turned to her. 'Do you want to get out of here?'

Darcy spoke at the same time. 'There's this hotel on the corner . . .'

Throwing some money across the bar, Shay snatched Darcy's hand and led the way out of the club, towards the hotel she'd mentioned. Once inside, Shay quickly booked a room.

Standing beside him with lust pumping through her veins, Darcy wondered when she had ever done something as insane as this in her life before. Sure, she had taken men to hotels, and of course she had had sex with men she barely knew before, but this was Shay Maguire . . . this was the man she was supposed to be destroying. More importantly, she was cheating on her lover, Judd, who was the single most frightening man she had ever met.

Stepping into the lift next to her, Shay couldn't wait. Pulling her into his arms, he kissed her, sliding his hand around the curve of her hip. Darcy leant into him, kissing him back ardently. They barely made it into the dimly lit room before feverishly removing each other's clothes.

Holding his breath, Shay peeled the black dress from Darcy's shoulders, leaving her standing in an elaborate half corset, a tiny thong and sheer hold-up stockings.

'Jesus,' he said, unable to stop himself. Her body was perfect, both slender and curvy, with a waist he could span with his hands. 'You're so fucking sexy,' he murmured into her ear. 'Intelligent *and* beautiful. Lucky me.'

Darcy wound her arms around his neck. She wasn't used to compliments, Judd wouldn't dream of telling her she was beautiful. But it wasn't just that, it was the way Shay held her. His arms were strong and masterful but his touch was tender and practised. She slammed her hand against the stereo, hoping to find some jazz. Instead, one of Charlie Valentine's greatest hits, 'Sexy Girls in Satin', came on and they both burst out laughing.

'My father used to look after Charlie Valentine,' Shay panted, tugging his shirt over his head. Undoing his trousers, he pushed Darcy down on to the bed and ran a hand down her stockinged thigh. 'I told him he should get Charlie to go back into the studio and write some new material.' He jerked his head in the direction of the stereo. 'I mean, like it or hate it, he's talented, right? He just needs an image overhaul.'

Darcy nodded and pushed Shay's trousers down with the toe of her shoe.

'Then he could be launched as a serious artist.' Shay left a trail of hot kisses down her taut stomach, loving the way it quivered beneath his touch, and he slid a stocking down her slender thigh.

Darcy, unhooking her corset and tossing it across the room, just stopped herself from saying she had told Judd the very same thing about Charlie.

'What the fuck am I going on about?' Shay said with a wide grin, suddenly looking his age. 'I'm in bed with the most gorgeous woman I've ever met and I'm talking business.' He leant down and sucked on a perfect pink nipple as she slipped her hands inside his boxer shorts.

'Fuck me,' she whispered, so flattered and turned on, she was literally writhing around beneath him. 'Please . . .'

Shay looked down at her, stunned at how gorgeous she looked with her cinnamon-coloured hair spilling out all over the pillow and her creamy, naked skin glowing from his touch.

'I can't think of anything I'd like to do more,' he breathed, sliding her knickers off with agonising slowness before sinking into her with a pleasurable groan.

Hours later, they lay on their sides entwined, their chests touching and their mouths almost making contact.

'What will you do about work?' she asked him, fascinated by the different shades of green in his eyes.

Shay stroked her hair. 'Fuck knows. I wanted to work for my father but that's not going to happen now.' He told her about the row, astonished that he was discussing his innermost thoughts with her. He was usually so private but for some odd reason, he felt uninhibited with this beautiful stranger.

'Sounds grim,' she said sympathetically. 'You idolise your father, don't you? That's why his rejection hurts so much.'

He was taken aback by her insight. 'I suppose I do idolise him in some ways. I hadn't really thought of it like that.'

She stared past him, her hazel eyes brimming over with emotion. 'I felt that way about my father too so I know what you're talking about.'

'Did he reject you too?'

She raised her pale brown eyebrows, her eyes meeting his. 'In a manner of speaking. He died.' She blinked, hating herself for feeling emotional about something that happened so long ago. 'I've . . . I've never forgiven him, you see. He left me with my mother which was the worst thing he could have done to me. My relationship with my mother is non-existent now.' She averted her eyes. 'I left after my father's funeral and I haven't been back since.'

Shay thought she looked breathtaking without make-up. 'That's a shame. My mother's great but I guess not everyone is that lucky.'

'I guess not.'

Shay moved an inch and kissed her, holding her face in his hand. 'I have no idea why I'm so tired,' he said, falling back against the pillow.

Darcy gave him a wicked smile. 'I have,' she said, trailing her hands down his chest. 'That much sex would knock anyone out.'

'I'll just need five minutes,' he murmured, already drifting off.

Darcy stared down at him, all at once gripped with a sense of loss. Whilst they'd been in this room with their hands all over each other, telling each other intimate secrets and desires, the outside world hadn't existed. Judd hadn't existed. Now, in the cold light of day, as the sun was beginning to drift in through the crack in the curtains, Darcy knew the spell had been broken.

Feeling distraught, she gently extricated herself from Shay's grasp and, without taking her eyes off him, she put her clothes on. What had she been thinking, going to bed with Shay Maguire? Darcy slowly tied her hair up, feeling tears pricking at her eyelids. She knew exactly why she'd done it: because she'd never felt so attracted to someone in her life before. Sex had never felt so meaningful, it had felt so *right* and Darcy had been with enough men to know the difference. It was the way Shay had made her feel, the way he'd managed to make her feel like the most beautiful, intelligent and sexy woman he'd ever laid eyes on.

Darcy shakily put some lipstick on, not sure she had the strength to do what she had set out to do. At the same time, she knew damn well Judd would kill her if she didn't. After all, Shay had provided her with the information she needed and all it would take was one phone call and the deed would be done.

Thinking about Judd, Darcy brought herself up short. What did she think – that she and Shay could disappear off into the sunset together? Judd had the means to ruin her professionally but, worse than that, she was scared stiff of what he might do to her if she walked away from him. She gazed at Shay's heartbreakingly perfect cheekbones, watching the way his dark lashes almost grazed them as he slept.

'Linger in my arms a little longer,' she murmured. Her favourite Louis Armstrong song and, as it turned out, Shay's favourite song too. It was too clichéd for words but it felt absurdly romantic too. Forgive me for what I'm about to do, she told Shay silently.

Not even sure why, Darcy picked up his mobile and punched his number into her phone. She needed to feel a connection with him, however tenuous, because walking out was going to take all the courage she possessed. Seeing eight text messages from Judd checking up on her, Darcy was terrified and she fled from the room, knowing she would spend the rest of her life thinking about Shay and the monumental fuck-up she'd made getting involved with Judd Harrington.

An hour later, Shay woke up, wondering where the hell he was. Putting out a hand, he realised the beautiful stranger had gone and he felt a stab of disappointment. It had been one of the best nights of his life and he still didn't even know her name. Jumping up and pulling his clothes on, he headed down to pay the bill.

'It's been paid,' the receptionist told him, checking her screen.

'What? Shay rubbed his eyes, wishing he could lay his hands on an espresso. 'But I left my credit card details last night.'

The receptionist checked again. 'No, it's definitely been paid. Miss Middleton left this for you as well.' She handed him a small white envelope.

'Miss . . . *Middleton*?' Shay took the envelope, thinking he must have misheard.

'Yes.' The receptionist frowned, wondering if he was high. 'Miss Darcy Middleton, the woman you checked in with. She paid the bill and left you that message.'

Shocked to the core, Shay staggered to a nearby seat and sat down. He couldn't believe it. The woman he had just spent the night with . . . the most incredible night of his life, for the record . . . worked for Judd Harrington. Worse than that, if rumours were to be believed, Darcy was Judd's mistress. Shay swallowed. No wonder Darcy didn't want to 'do names'. No wonder she had disappeared without saying goodbye. Shay slapped his hand against his head, unable to believe what he'd done. He had bedded the mistress of his father's biggest enemy, and it felt very much like he'd fallen head over heels in love with her as well.

Confused, Shay opened the envelope. Scrawled across it was one word. 'Sorry.' He slumped back in the seat. What was she sorry for? Dashing out without a word, he presumed, hoping that was all she was sorry for.

Two days later, Shay realised exactly what Darcy's apology was about. Called into Dev's office at 9 a.m., he was unceremoniously fired. When he asked for an explanation, Dev furiously told him that hacking into his boss's computer came under the banner of 'gross misconduct' and shagging on his desk when high as a kite was just downright unprofessional.

'This is so unlike you,' Dev had said, eying Shay carefully. He was loath to lose such a brilliantly creative employee and he respected Shay enormously. If Darcy hadn't convinced him so forcibly that Shay was the culprit, he wouldn't have believed her in a million years. 'Look, Shay, if you didn't do these things, just say the word and this can all go very differently.'

Staunchly loyal to his best mate Robin, Shay did the honourable thing. He cleared his desk, instructed Robin to keep his mouth shut and left.

Dumping his box of personal effects on the top of the nearest bar he came to, Shay proceeded to get horribly drunk. Not because he'd been sacked but because in spite of what she'd done to him, he couldn't stop thinking about Darcy Middleton. Asking the barman for the bottle and splashing three measures of Scotch into his glass, Shay also knew that it would be a fucking long time before he did.

Wearing a white linen shirt and shorts, Judd was stretched out by the glittering, oval-shaped swimming pool at Brockett Hall with his Armani sunglasses shielding his eyes. Shay Maguire had been taken care of and Judd was delighted that Lochlin's handsome and somewhat cocky son had been put in his place. Darcy had done him proud.

Judd glanced briefly at the swimming pool. It had been drained and relined with tiny, petrol-blue mosaic tiles, leaving a rippling expanse of dark water that shimmered invitingly in the midday sunshine but it looked just the same as it had all those years ago. Abruptly, Judd was hit by memories. New Year's Eve 1984 . . . Christ, was that date going to be indelibly printed on his brain for ever?

Somebody do something, a voice had screamed, but nothing could be done because it was too late; the pale blue water had been disturbed, its tranquil beauty marred by clouds of billowing red like vast crimson jellyfish. Somehow, though, the water had been still, as still as the lifeless body floating face down in it.

Judd averted his eyes. Had he done the right thing coming back here? Brockett Hall was his once more, a Harrington at the helm. A Harrington with a backbone, he sneered to himself, despising his parents all over again. He had shamed them, disgraced the family name, they said, and after they left him to his fate, he had fled to America with one of his posh boarding school friends who had been keen to introduce him to the socialite scene.

'*Ripe with rich debutantes*,' Rupert had snickered and he hadn't been wrong. Fat girls, thin girls, slutty ones, virgins – the place had been teeming with privileged girls in pastel gowns with painfully formal updos. Discovering Kitty Delaware, a shy, slightly plump and extraordinarily rich young woman, Judd had honed in on her like a bee to a honey pot – or rather, like a ruined young man to a naive girl with a trust fund. Using his smooth charm and his English accent, he had wooed Kitty, married her and ingratiated himself with the Delawares, all in the space of a few months. And her family were soon falling over themselves to invest in his business ventures and hand over shares in the family company.

Judd smirked and glanced around the pool. Elliot, wearing a creased scarlet football top, was under a huge oak tree, smothered in sun cream and surreptitiously reading something. He claimed to be playing football for the school every time he disappeared out of the house at strange hours but Judd wasn't convinced.

As for Martha, she was crying behind her sunglasses because Judd had slyly informed her that Sebastian hadn't set foot in the office that day, despite leaving Brockett Hall dressed in a suit with his briefcase in hand first thing. Appearing to be engrossed in the latest Jackie Collins, but holding it upside down, Martha was wearing a striped robe and her feet were so sunburnt, they looked as pink as freshly peeled prawns. She was clearly devastated at the thought of Sebastian being up to no good and Judd had delighted in baiting her all morning.

'W-we didn't know you'd be home today.' Wearing delicate Dior sunglasses and a pink sundress, Kitty handed Judd a glass.

'How very *English* of you,' he commented sarcastically, sipping the Pimm's and enjoying the way Kitty shrank back in his presence. He checked his watch and abruptly headed indoors. Right on time, he found Savannah outside the front door, her finger on the doorbell. Wearing a new white Gucci dress Judd had treated her to at the weekend, which made the most of her wide shoulders whilst finishing in a demure swirl around the knee, she was teetering in some extremely high strappy Gucci sandals and nervously raking her fingers through her titian hair.

'Are they ready for me?' she asked. In spite of herself, Savannah felt nervous. Telling herself the huge moat out front was pretentious, she couldn't help being wildly impressed by it – that and the expanse of marble floor and ostentatious furnishings inside Brockett Hall. It *reeked* of Daddy's millions, Savannah thought gleefully. She squared her shoulders; she was a Harrington and she had every right to be here. Sparing a thought for Kitty, Savannah realised her arrival would be a shock but if Judd was happy to introduce her as his own, she wasn't going to complain.

She followed Judd outside and paused at the edge of the pool. 'Hi, everyone,' she drawled. 'I'm Savannah,' she added.

Martha and Elliot looked up at the sound of an American accent, staring at her curiously. Elliot felt sick. This was what Ace had warned him about – their illegitimate sister. Forbidden from telling his mother, Elliot wished he'd ignored Ace's request and spoken up to save her the humiliation, but he hadn't expected his father to brazenly present Savannah at the house like this.

Judd noticed Savannah's impatient frown. It amused him when she behaved like such a spoilt brat. He wasn't sure why, because he wouldn't stand for it from anyone else.

Kitty got to her feet, her stomach lurching. Surely this child wasn't Judd's new mistress, she thought queasily. Whoever she was, she was sure of herself and beautiful, with a glorious mane of red hair that hung down her back.

'Savannah is my daughter,' Judd informed Kitty, casually sipping his Pimm's. 'I met her mother when I was working in New York some years ago. Twenty-one years ago, to be exact. Candi. I told you about her at the time, I think.'

Kitty almost lost her grip on her glass. Not trusting herself with it, she placed it on the table with a measured movement, her face ashen. Feeling faint, she recalled the affair Judd was referring to. It was the affair he had flaunted so cruelly, Kitty had packed her bags to leave him. She'd been stopped by a stinging backhander from Judd which had crushed both her cheekbone and her spirit irrevocably.

Staring at Savannah, Kitty could see the resemblance in the giveaway red hair, as well as in the aggressive tilt of the chin and the determined look in her bright blue eyes. Blinded by tears, Kitty barely heard what Judd was saying.

'Savannah will, of course, be moving in with us at Brockett Hall,' Judd announced in brisk tones. 'Her things will arrive shortly and I expect you all to make her welcome. This isn't Savannah's fault and her mother is dead so we're her family now.'

Kitty stumbled slightly. 'Do excuse me,' she said politely to Savannah. Shakily, she made her way to the door, only just making it inside before throwing her Pimm's up all over the dining-room floor.

Horrified, Elliot got to his feet.

'Leave her!' Judd barked.

'She's in shock,' Elliot said in a hesitant voice.

'I should imagine so,' Judd agreed, popping his sunglasses back on. 'But she's just going to have to get over it; you all are.'

Savannah frowned. It wasn't quite the reaction she had been expecting. Contrary to Judd's critical description of her, Kitty seemed a sweet and genuine lady, but in her shoes, Savannah would have rather died than give away how devastated she was.

'What's going on?'

Fresh from an energetic bout of sex with Lexi in the somewhat unsavoury toilets of a pub five miles away that had left him with a cat scratch down his back and aching balls, Sebastian joined them, a carefree bounce in his step as he swung his briefcase self-consciously. Lexi had been appalled at the idea of having sex in the pub toilets but he had soon convinced her it was for the best. The gym was out of the question now; Mrs Meaden had almost caught them at it in the steam room and Sebastian had practically dislocated his knee cap when he slipped on the wet floor.

'Where the hell have you been?' Martha screeched, emboldened by several glasses of Pimm's. 'And don't you dare say you've been at work again because I know for a fact you haven't!'

'Fuck off, Martha,' Sebastian snapped curtly, angry at being questioned in front of everyone. 'At least I haven't been sitting on my fat ass all day.'

'Hey!' Savannah stepped forward, her hands on her hips. She couldn't bear bullies. 'Why don't you just back off, you fucking creep! Can't you see she's upset?'

As Martha gaped at Savannah with something close to hero worship, Sebastian narrowed his eyes at her furiously. 'Who the hell are *you*?'

'Your sister,' Savannah shot back with a smirk. 'Well, half-sister, to be more accurate. I've come to live with you. Isn't that nice?'

Judd gave his son a wicked grin, enjoying the look of horror on his face. Spotting a telltale smudge of baby-pink lipstick on his neck, Judd shook his head contemptuously. Christ, couldn't Sebastian even have an affair properly?

'What the fuck!' Sebastian exploded. His face turned the colour of Martha's sunburnt feet and beads of sweat popped out on his forehead. In the space of five minutes – probably the amount of time it had taken his father to sire this . . . this *girl* – Sebastian's inheritance had just been split another way. Livid, he turned on his father. 'You've got to be fucking kidding! You're just going to move your illegitimate brat into Brockett Hall as if she's one of us?'

'She *is* one of us and, frankly, she's worth ten of you,' Judd spat back.

Sebastian gibbered. His father had always wanted a daughter and now he had one. It was bad enough having to compete with Ace, Sebastian thought childishly. Now he had this . . . this impudent girl . . . this *she-devil* to take his father's attention away from him. Martha stared at Savannah, in awe of her confidence. How she wished she could stand up to Sebastian in the way Savannah had!

For her part, Savannah was bored stupid. Her big arrival had been overshadowed by Sebastian, and deciding everyone was being too damn serious, she tore off her Gucci heels. 'I hope no one minds if I make myself at home? I fancy a dip.' Peeling her white dress over her head to reveal a firm body and a pristine white bra and thong, she strolled to the edge of the pool and dived in elegantly. Emerging from the freezing cold water with a shocked whoop, she smoothed back her red hair sleekly.

Judd gave a shout of laughter and clapped as Savannah dived underwater to do a surprisingly good handstand, her slender legs waggling in the air.

'Join me!' she called, spitting water out of her mouth. 'Come on,

I'm not that bad.' She submerged herself again, flipping her bottom up at them all cheekily.

Sebastian sulkily stormed into the house. Martha dashed after him.

'Right.' Judd checked his watch. 'I'm going to the office.'

Elliot looked startled. 'But . . . you can't just tell us about Savannah then leave us to it.'

'Watch me.' Blowing Savannah's feet a kiss, Judd called his driver and left.

Savannah, bursting out of the water and finding the veranda empty apart from Elliot, pulled a mocking face. 'Something I said?' she asked with a glint of humour. She swam over and put her chin on the edge of the pool, looking up at him beguilingly. 'So, your brother is a prize asshole, isn't he? His poor wife.'

Elliot knelt down and handed her a towel. 'You don't know the half of it. Ace is much nicer but he's still in the States so you won't meet him for a while.' He hesitated but felt duty bound to tell his half-sister what she was dealing with. 'Be careful . . . with Dad, I mean. He might be all over you now but if you upset him or let him down, he can turn really nasty. I just thought you should know.'

'Don't you worry about me, honey,' Savannah pulled herself out of the water and wrapped the towel around her wet body, thinking Elliot was really rather nice. 'I can look after myself. I have done for years and no one, and I mean *no one*, treats me like shit.' With that, she turned smartly on her heel and headed indoors, leaving little wet footprints in her wake.

Although he couldn't help thinking Savannah was under-estimating their father, Elliot believed her.

'Right, everyone!' Hugo, resplendent in a white shirt, a navy and white checked tank top and a small navy bow tie, clapped his hands. 'We'll start the auditions for Juliet in a few minutes so if you're planning to try out, please ensure that you have a scene prepared. Now, who's first?'

Caitie nibbled her fingernails. Elliot had just arrived but Jas was late and she needed her best friend's support. But keen to get it over and done with, Caitie was about to step forward when Skye Valentine pushed ahead of her. She was even more taken aback that Skye had removed all of her make-up and had tied her hair back into a girlish ponytail. She'd even toned down her fake tan to a pale ginger glow.

'I'll go first,' she announced, throwing Caitie a defiant look. Wearing flat moccasins and a drab brown dress, Skye walked sedately up the steps to the stage. Taking up her position in the centre, she ignored the small crowd who'd gathered to watch her audition, including Abby, who was at the front, waving supportively.

Hugo was taken aback. 'Er . . . fair enough. Off you go, then.'

Skye took a deep breath as if composing herself before launching into Juliet's famous balcony speech.

'*O Romeo, Romeo, wherefore art thou, Romeo?*' she began in an unnaturally high voice. She delivered the next few lines, grimacing like a constipated horse.

Hugo, struggling not to giggle, almost missed his cue. 'Sorry . . . er . . . "*Shall I hear more, or shall I speak at this?*" '

Skye clutched both hands to her chest and stared at Hugo so intensely, he wanted to run for cover. Labouring over the speech as though she was in an advert for laxatives, she stopped mid-sentence, clasping her hands together in what she assumed was a virginal pose.

Perplexed, Hugo clapped loudly, encouraging everyone to join in. Caitie frowned, wondering why it felt as if all-out war had been declared. Ever since the Valentines' Ball, Skye seemed to have been gunning for her and Caitie couldn't help wondering what she was supposed to have done.

'Who's next?' Hugo asked, giving Caitie a pointed look.

'Go on.' Elliot smiled, giving her a nudge. 'Show us all how it's done.'

Suddenly paralysed with nerves, Caitie faltered. This part meant so much to her but feeling everyone's eyes on her expectantly, she wasn't sure she could pull it off. Jas still hadn't turned up but Caitie couldn't hold off for much longer. Pushing Skye out of her mind, she stepped forward through the throng of people and up on to the stage. Before she could back out, she began, her voice as clear as a bell:

> *Art thou gone so love, Lord, ay husband, friend,*
> *I must hear from thee every day in the hour.*

She climbed the stairs until she was standing above Elliot, truly believing in that moment that she was Juliet. Elliot turned to face her, his brilliant blue eyes lighting up. He held a hand out to her as she continued.

> *For in a minute there are many days,*
> *O by this count I shall be much in years,*
> *Ere I again behold my Romeo.*

Elliot got to his feet and bowed his head. With their eyes locked on to each other, oblivious of everyone else in the room, Caitie and Elliot played out the scene for all they were worth. Their chemistry was electric and Hugo, initially miffed at missing out on the opportunity to whisper sweet nothings to Elliot, was instantly beguiled by their obvious connection. Elliot was pleased with his English accent; he had worked hard on it and it sounded better than he had thought it would.

'*Adieu, adieu,*' he finished softly. Even though it wasn't in the script, he leant in and cupped a hand around Caitie's neck. His heart was thumping in his chest but for some reason he didn't feel scared. He kissed her, nudging at the corners of her mouth, and the kiss went on for ever. Caitie, fully entrenched in the role of Juliet, had never experienced anything more romantic in her life. All her guilt over her father and the family feud evaporated; in Caitie's head, she and Elliot were 'star-cross'd lovers', forbidden from being together but utterly unable to resist one another.

As Caitie let out a blissful sigh, Elliot felt as if he'd been hit by a thunderbolt. For the last few years, he'd worried himself sick he was gay but now he knew for a fact he wasn't. Because he had never felt this way before. He didn't know if it was because he was playing Romeo in the play or if it was just down to Caitie but the kiss had sent sexy tingles from his head to his toes and everywhere in between.

'Wow!' Caitie breathed, feeling exactly the same. 'We are *so* meant to be together.'

Elliot grinned at her and they were both so caught up in the moment, they didn't notice Skye shooting daggers of pure hatred in their direction.

'Oh, bravo!' Hugo yelled, jumping to his feet hysterically. 'That was magic, absolute magic! The English accent was superb – oh, with you two in the lead roles, this is going to be the best production of *Romeo and Juliet* anyone has ever seen!' Seeing Skye's hands clenching with fury, he hurriedly covered his tracks. 'I mean . . . I haven't decided on the roles just yet, of course. But I'm overjoyed, truly overjoyed.'

Caitie and Elliot blinked and came back to earth. Climbing down from the stage, they could barely keep their eyes off each other and only tore their gaze away when Jas rushed over to them.

'I just caught the end of that – it was electric!' She gave Caitie a wink to indicate she'd witnessed the snog.

Caitie grinned then faked a pout. 'Where *were* you? I was lost without my bezzie mate cheering me on.'

Her cheeks pink with excitement, Jas drew them to one side. 'Sorry, I got caught up talking to Mrs Meaden.'

'About what?' Caitie frowned, wondering what could be so important.

'About the past,' Jas told her with a nod. 'And you'll never guess what.'

'What?' Caitie and Elliot were agog.

'She says someone died here years ago.' Jas's eyes were shining with excitement. 'She wouldn't say anything more than that but I got the impression there was something funny about it. That the death might have even been . . . a *murder*.'

Elliot felt a prickle of discomfort. 'Are you saying this has something to do with my father?' He was unnerved enough by Savannah's arrival; he wasn't sure he could cope with anything else.

Jas blushed. 'Well . . . I don't know about that. But it did happen twenty-five years ago so . . .'

Caitie clasped her hands together in excitement. 'It has to be significant, it just has to be! We have to find out more. Who do you think got murdered? Do you think it was covered up or do you think the murderer never got caught?'

Elliot protested. 'I think you're getting a bit carried away, Cait.'

Before she could answer, Skye and Abby had joined them.

'I suppose congratulations are in order,' Skye said with bad grace.

'Yeah, congratulations,' Abby said, giving Caitie an evil look.

Skye fixed her eyes on Elliot and gave him a look that could have stripped paint. 'Do let me know if you fancy coming out for a drink, won't you? I know you'll be busy with *Romeo and Juliet*, but it's all so juvenile, isn't it? Young love and all that.' She batted her eyelashes furiously, allowing her eyes to travel down to Elliot's groin. 'Me, I prefer to get right to the . . . er . . . heart of the matter.'

Abby sniggered.

Elliot turned scarlet. The twins sashayed away, Skye not quite pulling it off in her brown dress and flats.

'Christ,' Elliot murmured. 'I think she just propositioned me.'

'The cow!' Caitie spluttered, unable to believe what she'd just seen.

Jas nodded, feeling sorry for Caitie – and for Elliot, who looked as though he wanted to scrub himself with wire wool. 'She's certainly not backwards in coming forwards, or whatever the phrase is.'

Elliot gave Caitie a reassuring smile. 'Forget about her. We have a play to learn.'

Caitie let out a jerky breath. 'True. And there's this mystery to get to the bottom of.' She tucked her arm through Jas's. 'Now tell me everything Mrs Meaden said. I want to hear it all, word for word.'

Outside, Skye was about to explode. 'Shit. That didn't go how I'd planned. Did you see Elliot's face? He looked as though I was about to rape him or something.'

Abby agreed. 'So, what's plan D?'

Skye restrained herself from giving Abby a hearty slap.

'It's plan B, you silly bitch, and I haven't a clue yet. I just know it needs to be more . . . creative. I'm going to do something *really* bad this time.'

Abby broke into a grin. *Now* her twin was speaking in a language she understood.

Sitting outside a pub in the middle of nowhere, Leo wondered how fate had brought him here. Driving home from work a different way due to roadworks, he had spotted Lexi coming out of a pub dressed like a hooker, followed out by a red-headed man. She had shot off in her car at high speed, her companion heading in the other direction.

Feeling like a second-rate detective, Leo went into the pub. A sleek Boxer lay at the foot of the bar, her jowls resting on her paws. Hearing Leo come in, she lifted soulful brown eyes to his before flopping down again.

'What can I get you?' the pretty girl behind the bar asked. She was wearing a Day-Glo yellow T-shirt with '*I'm Fit*' emblazoned across it and she had stubby fingernails painted with black varnish.

'Er . . . the girl that just left . . . the one in the pink dress. Does she come here often?' Leo felt faintly embarrassed.

The barmaid eyed him sympathetically. 'Are you her husband?'

'Yes. Yes, I am.' He bent down and rubbed the Boxer's sleek head. 'And I'm probably being really stupid but . . .'

The girl motioned for him to carry on stroking the dog, 'You can't stop now; Meg loves a cuddle. Look, that woman . . . your wife . . . she comes in here on her own and buys a drink but then this man turns up.' She paused apologetically. 'Then she wanders off into the toilets and the bloke – Sebastian, I think he's called – joins her.'

Leo felt a pain in his chest. So his suspicions were right; Lexi *was* having an affair. All her absences, the dropped phone calls – he wasn't being irrational and he wasn't being paranoid. Grief-stricken, Leo was nonetheless ashamed when a tear splashed down on to Meg's toffee-coloured coat. He frowned suddenly. Sebastian?

Out of the blue, it came to him. The new family who'd moved into Brockett Hall . . . the Harringtons. Some of them had red hair and if he remembered correctly, one of the sons was called Sebastian. And the Harringtons were loaded. Loaded beyond even Leo's wildest dreams.

Deciding to cancel the romantic dinner at his friend's restaurant, L'Absinthe later that night, Leo thanked the girl and left the pub. Sliding into his car, he slumped over the steering wheel in utter despair.

'This is a-mazing,' shrieked Luisa, thoroughly excited as she leant over to get a good view of the track. Escorted by Pia, she and Iris were watching the Pro/Celebrity race at the Toyota Grand Prix of Long Beach and to their astonishment they were in some of the most sought-after seats, with incredible views all the way up Pine Avenue.

'Nothing but the best for Judd,' Pia commented wryly as she popped a pair of oversized sunglasses on to her dark nose. Wearing black linen trousers and a coral-coloured jacket with a pair of bejewelled flip-flops, Pia looked cool, stylish and almost approachable.

Iris was just glad of the break. Pia's singing schedule was relentless and she had been practising non-stop since their first meeting. Her poor neighbours had heard her rendition of 'Listen' thousands of times and Iris was worried she might lose her voice soon. She had a big performance on Saturday at a local awards show; it wasn't exactly the Brits or the MTV Awards but it was a prestigious, televised event. Every time Iris thought about it, butterflies fluttered around her stomach.

Pia leapt to her feet. 'Jesus, where did those paps come from?'

Iris jumped as a paparazzo appeared in front of her, his camera snapping away. Wearing the standard photographer's uniform – cap pulled down over the eyes and loose clothes and trainers for running – a crowd of paps gathered around them, their camera straps wrapped round their wrists.

'What the hell?' Luisa shrieked.

'Out of the way,' demanded one of the paps. 'You're not Iris Maguire!'

Iris's mouth fell open. 'That's . . . that's me. Why are you taking photos of me?'

'Next big thing in music, we hear,' said another photographer, elbowing the main one out of the way but only getting a shot of Iris's left shoulder and a lock of hair.

Iris went pink and did her best to smile as tons of shots were fired off in her face. When she was able to take her seat again, she was shaking all over.

'Bloody hell. That was mental. Why were they taking photos of me?'

Pia shrugged but inside she was seething. Punishing her for panning a CD of his daughter's average singing, Judd kept pulling stunts like this on her. She was also furious about Judd's plans for Ace to seduce Iris but Pia knew better than to interfere. 'Judd must have arranged it,' she said curtly. 'I guess you'd better get used to it, Iris. You're going to be famous soon.'

Exchanging an excited look with Luisa, Iris was glad she'd made an effort with her appearance that day in a floaty emerald-green silk maxi dress and black beaded flip-flops. Her blond hair was held back from her face with two tiny plaits, which Luisa said should be her trademark style, but Iris was just pleased it kept her hair out of her eyes on a hot day.

Pia proceeded to fill them in about the race, pointing out a Playboy bunny, a former child star millionaire and a very famous actor Luisa had lusted after as a teenager. 'Keanu Reeves won here once and it attracts some really big names. Ten laps round this twisty track . . . it's pretty nerve-wracking stuff, especially racing against pros.'

Luisa gasped as she spotted a well-known racing heartthrob. 'Look, Iris, it's Jerry Hampton! Wow, who's that sex bomb he's with?'

Iris gazed at the man with the dark auburn hair standing next to Jerry Hampton. He was tall and tanned with a lean physique and his hair was just the right shade of reddish-chestnut. She wondered what colour his eyes were and she was taken aback as the man looked straight at her and gave her a cheeky wink before disappearing to get ready for the race.

When it got underway, the noise was deafening; car tyres squealed, commentators' voices boomed out of loudspeakers and there was the odd screech of metal against metal as cars collided and bounced off the boulders. Iris could barely make out the names as the race neared its end and celebrities and professional drivers jostled for position. Buoyed up by the screaming crowd, she found herself jumping up and down with Luisa as they hit the finish line.

'That was so exciting!' Iris stood up. 'Shall I get us some champagne?'

About to tell her off for drinking when she was due to work

later, Pia relented and pointed to a hospitality tent. Iris headed over, her heart sinking as she saw the massive queues, but spotting a tent without one, she made a beeline for it. Wondering why no one else had seen it, Iris was about to duck inside when she was stopped by an official-looking man in a suit.

'That's all right; she's with me.'

Spinning around quickly, Iris lost her footing and fell into someone's arms. She gasped as she felt warm, firm hands catch her around the waist and her chin grazed the rough material of a racing suit. Her nostrils were flooded with the smell of dust, fresh sweat and cigarette smoke. Blushing to the roots of her hair, Iris realised she'd bumped straight into the tall, fit-looking man with dark auburn hair she and Luisa had been admiring earlier.

'That is, if you don't mind coming in with me?' he drawled sexily, raising an eyebrow as he held on to her. His eyes flirted with hers.

Iris swallowed, her knees buckling slightly. Close up, he was even more handsome; even though his dishevelled, mahogany-coloured hair had been flattened by his racing helmet and his face was streaked with sweat, there was no denying how gorgeous he was. She had wondered earlier what colour his eyes might be but she hadn't expected them to be grey, nor had she expected them to be framed by impossibly long dark lashes.

'I . . . I . . .' To her embarrassment, Iris found herself totally tongue-tied. She could feel the rock-hard muscles of his stomach against her body and his hands, still around her waist, seemed to be burning through the thin material of her silk dress.

'Are you feeling faint?' he murmured, grinning down at her. 'It's just that I can feel your heart beating really, really fast. Mind you, this close up, I guess you can feel bits of me you shouldn't be feeling too.'

Iris's mouth twitched. He was sexy but he was obviously also a playboy, used to women falling at his feet. 'No, I'm not feeling faint,' she said, finding her voice at last. 'Just bloody thirsty.'

'Thirsty? Me too. It's *exhausting* driving those fast cars. Let's get a drink.' Ignoring the disapproving look of the official, he possessively took Iris's hand. 'By the way, I love your accent. Only the British can sound cool saying "bloody".'

Ace led Iris through the tent, sure she had no idea who he was, which was exactly how he wanted it. Suddenly, it seemed imperative to get to know her better. Not because of his father's request, just because he wanted to.

God, she was absolutely ravishing, Ace thought, jolted, as they found a free table and helped themselves to champagne. His father was right about one thing: her photograph definitely hadn't done her justice. It was all about the colouring with Iris; the long, tawny-blond hair that hung down her back was unfashionably long but incredibly sexy and her amber eyes, heavily fringed with black mascara, were sleepily sensual. As for those bee-stung lips, glossy, nude and unbelievably kissable – fuck. Ace was crazy for those lips. He was surprised at the way she was making him feel. He hadn't been joking about Iris feeling things she shouldn't have done when she was thrust up against him; he had felt instant chemistry between them and his body had responded hungrily. Pull yourself together, he told himself with mock sternness. He needed to play this carefully, not act like an immature schoolboy who couldn't control his own hard-on.

'Don't let me get drunk because I'll probably flirt with you shamelessly,' Iris said, sipping the champagne. She felt so comfortable and confident with this guy. 'I'm Iris Maguire, by the way.'

Ace laughed. 'Now there's a challenge I won't turn down. Iris. What a lovely name.'

Iris took in her surroundings. Racing drivers with their suits unzipped and their hair sweaty and dishevelled stood around drinking champagne out of the bottle as they celebrated or commiserated. Iris had never been anywhere so glamorous in her life. She was bewildered by the sight of so many semi-clad women with flowing blond hair of every conceivable shade.

'Fans of yours?' she joked as some of them approached Ace, flicking their hair madly.

'Bimbos,' Ace said dismissively. 'Don't be fooled; they're only after me for my bank balance. Or because I race cars for a living.' Startled, he realised how true that was and he wondered why he'd never cared before now.

Meeting his sexy grey eyes over the top of her glass, Iris decided there was more to this man than his money and his job. He was exceptionally good looking but he was also funny and self-deprecating. Iris had no idea why he'd singled her out for attention but having spent five minutes in his company, she could see why he had legions of female fans with his easy, flirtatious banter. That and the way he was making her feel, as though she was the only woman in the room, made him pretty irresistible.

As they chatted about his driving career and her stint in LA, to his amazement Ace found himself having fun. Iris was clued up rather than academic – rather like him, in fact. But the most surprising thing about her was that she made him laugh. And Ace wasn't just chuckling now and again, he was letting out full-bodied belly laughs, the way he did with Jerry.

'And I've discovered I can't dance for *toffee*,' Iris was saying, rolling her eyes. 'I mean, I'm really, really bad. My friend Luisa is a brilliant dancer but even she's had to concede defeat with me.' She glanced at her empty glass of champagne, wondering how many she'd had.

Inexplicably, Ace felt all warm and fuzzy inside. Iris was open and sincere and now that he thought about it, women rarely made him laugh. They tittered prettily at his jokes and in all the right places but they seldom bothered to try and amuse him. Nor would they dream of poking fun at themselves. Fascinated, Ace watched Iris's delectable mouth curve up as she giggled.

'Show me some of your moves,' he begged, his face lighting up. 'Go on, no one's looking.'

'No way!' Iris cringed. 'My dancing is strictly reserved for the privacy of my bedroom.'

He opened his mouth, about to say something suggestive, then changed his mind. But he could see that she'd guessed at the way his mind was working and he gave her a broad smile. 'Hey, come to a party at mine next Saturday and you could have a boogie then.'

Iris shook her head regretfully, flooded with disappointment. 'I'm afraid I can't. I'm performing at an awards ceremony that night.'

'Come afterwards then.' He stared at her. All of a sudden, it seemed ridiculously important for her to come to the party and not just because his father wanted it to happen. 'Our parties don't tend to get going until around midnight, anyway.' Spotting Jerry, he called him over, keen to introduce him to Iris. 'Jerry, come here!'

Shaking off a brunette and a redhead who were clinging to him like limpets, Jerry strolled over, smiling engagingly as he kissed Iris's hand.

'Hello, gorgeous,' he said, not realising who Iris was. 'Where did you spring from?'

'Back off, Jez,' Ace told him good-naturedly, feeling pleased. 'I saw her first. This is Iris Maguire.' He met Jerry's gaze defiantly. 'She can't come to our party on Saturday.'

Jerry's blue eyes flickered. 'Well, it's very nice to meet you, Iris Maguire. And you must come to the party, and bring your friends, especially if they have accents like yours.' He still disagreed with Ace's decision to do his father's dirty work but if he was going ahead with it, Jerry wasn't going to give him grief.

'I'll . . . I'll see what I can do.' Iris got to her feet, belatedly remembering she was supposed to be taking drinks back to Luisa and Pia.

'Stay,' Ace said, grabbing her hand. 'Please.'

She looked into his grey eyes, wondering why it felt as if she was tearing herself away from him. 'I really can't,' she murmured. 'But . . . I wish I could.'

Standing next to them, Jerry was sure he must have turned green and hairy because he had never felt like such a gooseberry in his life. He gave his friend a sideways glance, perplexed by his behaviour. Something about this felt far more meaningful than it should.

'This is my phone number and address,' Ace said, grabbing a pen from a nearby table. He scrawled the information along her arm in his slightly childish hand. 'For the party. Please come and save me from the bimbos.' He gave her a disarming grin. 'It'd be nice to have a conversation with someone other than Jerry.'

Jerry smiled mockingly. 'Charming.'

Iris tore her eyes away from Ace's and left. Outside, she felt dazzled and it was then that she realised something. 'I didn't even get his name!' she exclaimed out loud.

The official on the door cleared his throat. 'That would be Ace Harrington. Playboy extraordinaire . . . his reputation precedes him.' His expression was sour but tinged with envy.

Iris turned pale. Ace Harrington. *Harrington*. What were the odds?

'Where have you been?' Luisa stalked over, her dark eyes flashing. 'We need to go now and I'm gasping for a drink.'

Pia stalked past, tapping her watch. 'You have work to do, Iris. Meet me at the car.'

Iris was shell-shocked and she turned to Luisa. 'I just met Ace Harrington. And he was . . . the most gorgeous man I've ever met.'

Luisa frowned and led her away from the tent. 'Who's he? Not that hunky one? *So* jealous . . . I bet you met Jerry Hampton too.'

'They invited us to a party on Saturday.' Iris nodded. 'Ace *Harrington*, Luisa.'

The penny dropped. 'Ace *Harrington*,' Luisa echoed. 'Someone you should avoid at all costs or your father will disown you.'

'That's right.' Iris let out a shuddering breath. She had never felt more devastated in her life.

Inside the tent, Ace was equally subdued. He had expected Iris to be pretty and pleasant but he hadn't been anticipating an achingly sexy girl who was funny and completely adorable. He wanted to whisk her home to bed, not just so he could peel off her clothes and feast his eyes on her incredible body but so he could keep her all to himself.

Jerry wondered why Ace looked as if he'd been hit by a truck. 'She's stunning,' he commented.

Ace nodded.

'It went well, then?'

Ace nodded again.

Jerry gave him a shove. 'Earth to Ace,' he said sharply. He'd never seen his best friend look so dazed. Granted, his and Iris's chemistry had crackled, but so what?

'I think I'm in love.' Ace gave Jerry a soppy grin. Draining his glass of champagne, he recovered himself and winked at a startled Jerry. 'Only joking! I don't *do* love, remember?' He checked his phone but there was nothing from his father. 'Before Dad sends out a search party, shall we have one more drink?'

Batting off nubile women on the way, he went to the bar, followed by Jerry who was shaking his head and frowning.

Watching them as she sat in an alcove was Allegra, Ace's on/off girlfriend. Not wanting to be seen by Ace, she stormed out of a side entrance, determined to find out why he was refusing to answer her calls. Because if he was being truthful when he said he was 'off women' and focusing on racing, what the hell was he doing making eyes at some girl called Iris Maguire?

Chapter Eleven

Clutching Caitie's gossip magazine, Tavvy knocked on Shay's door breathlessly. 'Let me in. I have to show you something!'

There was a pause. 'I'm kind of busy in here,' came Shay's response.

Tavvy huffed. 'Unless you're doing something unthinkable under the bedsheets, stop being silly and let me in!'

After a few seconds, Shay opened the door, looking sheepish.

'Look!' Tavvy thrust the magazine under his nose. 'It's Iris.'

Shay's eyes widened as he looked at the photograph of Iris wearing a beautiful emerald-green dress with her hair held back by two cute plaits. He read aloud from the piece. 'Sexy new singing sensation Iris Maguire attended the Toyota Pro/Celebrity race in Long Beach, California, with world famous coach Pia Jordan. Watch out for Iris performing soon in Los Angeles . . . details to follow. Wow. That's unbelievable. Judd must have pulled a few strings to make *that* happen.'

Tavvy nodded, her amber eyes full of trepidation. 'And it's good, right? So why do I feel as if he's taken over our lives?'

Shay winced. 'You don't know the half of it, Mum.' Quickly, he told her what had happened with Darcy Middleton. He hadn't spoken to anyone about it yet; he had been too furious with himself and too humiliated to voice it out loud. But in view of what he was about to do, Shay figured he'd better explain himself up front.

Shaking, Tavvy sat down on the bed, barely noticing the neat piles of clothes stacked up on it. 'So . . . she used you for sex then stitched you up at work?'

Shay shrugged. 'That's about the size of it.' His casual tone belied how he was feeling inside. In reality, he was so livid about the way Darcy had treated him, he could barely see straight. There he was, thinking he had just met the woman of his dreams, but Darcy was on Judd's payroll and she had simply been acting on his instructions. She felt nothing for him, that much was obvious. Darcy had missed her calling. She should have been an actress, Shay thought bitterly.

Tavvy blinked. 'So Darcy did this because she's Judd's mistress? You're saying this is all part of some dastardly plan of Judd's to get back at Lochlin?'

'I have no idea.' Shay dragged his fingers through his hair. 'The important thing is that I move on and get my life back on track. Which is what I wanted to talk to you about.'

Tavvy felt angry tears pricking at her eyelids. 'But . . . but this is horrible,' she interrupted. 'This is so like Judd. It proves your father is right to be worried about him, and now we know he's after all of us, not just Lochlin.' She shivered. 'What about Iris out in LA?'

Shay took her by the shoulders. 'You're getting carried away,' he told her gently. He took a deep breath. 'All of this has made me realise I need to stand on my own two feet. Which means I need to get a place of my own.'

Tavvy's head jerked up. 'What? You're leaving Pembleton?'

Shay chewed his lip. 'I have to, Mum. It's about time I took the responsible route.' He met her eyes. 'Dad doesn't want me at Shamrock and now I've lost my job at the magazine. Robin has a room in his house and I'm going to shack up there for a bit because I need to get my head together and make some serious decisions.'

'So make them here, with us,' Tavvy begged. 'Don't be on your own at a time like this! And how will you pay rent now you've lost your job?'

Shay folded his arms defensively. 'I've got some savings, not much but some. Most people my age have their own place by now and I can't keep freeloading for ever. No wonder Dad thinks I'm still a kid.' It wasn't just his father; Darcy had treated him like a stupid little boy too. Shay had been convinced she felt something for him that night; there had been a spark between them, something romantic and sensual, something *real*. Right up until he had walked into reception and found out who Darcy was, Shay had been certain his future lay with her.

Tavvy suddenly caught sight of the stacks of clothes on Shay's bed. 'Oh my God. You really are going.' Tears ran down her cheeks at the thought of Shay not living with them any more. She could fully understand why he felt the need to be mature and she also sensed how bruised Shay's ego was. In spite of her distress, a genius idea came to her. 'You could move into Bluebell Cottage! You could pay rent on it once you've got a job if it's that big a deal to you, or just spend the money doing it up instead.'

About to refuse the offer, Shay thought for a minute. Bluebell Cottage was situated at the edge of the woods in the grounds of Pembleton and it was a dinky, dilapidated property in dire of need of some TLC. 'I could do it up at the weekends, then at least I could have a place of my own, but I'd rather pay rent once I'm up and running. Thanks, Mum, I really appreciate that.'

Tavvy let out a sigh of relief. If Shay moved into Bluebell Cottage, it wouldn't feel quite so much as though he'd left their lives completely.

His salt-and-pepper hair in disarray, Lochlin's broad shoulders appeared in the doorway. 'What's going on?' He yawned, sifting through a handful of post.

'Shay's moving out,' Tavvy said quickly, thinking it might sound better coming from her. 'Into Bluebell Cottage. I said he could live there.'

Shay braced himself, wondering how his father was going to react.

Lochlin looked flabbergasted. 'Moving out? Of Pembleton? Why on earth . . .'

Getting the nod from Shay, Tavvy filled him in, seeing his green eyes cloud over in dismay when he heard about Darcy.

'I'm an idiot,' Shay offered, feeling the need to state the obvious. He bristled every time he thought about his stupidity. Worse than that, whenever he thought about his time in bed with Darcy, he felt sick with lust and he hated himself for it. 'I signed my death warrant with some stupid pillow talk and I only have myself to blame for the mess I'm in.'

Lochlin shook his head, enraged. 'No, no, you don't need to blame yourself, son. This is Judd . . . he's behind this. You didn't even know who Darcy was.' He clenched his fists. 'Listen, we can't let Judd win, we have to do something. I could phone Dev at the magazine and get him to reconsider. We could—'

'No thanks, Dad. I just want to get on with my life.'

Tavvy put her hand on Lochlin's arm. 'Couldn't he come and work at Shamrock?' she asked timidly. 'I know you two have rowed but this isn't the time for any of us to be at war with each other.'

Lochlin hesitated for only the briefest of seconds but Shay saw it and before anything was said, he shook his head decisively. Part of him wanted to forgive and forget but he now realised he and his father could never work together.

Lochlin cursed his hesitation but it hadn't been because he didn't want to retract what he'd said; it was fear of being knocked back by his son. He'd been exactly the same at Shay's age, Lochlin thought wryly. Ferociously headstrong and hell-bent on finding his own way. But for some reason, Shay's rejection of a job at Shamrock, signalled by the curt shake of his head, had stung like hell.

'I need to pack,' Shay said, stuffing his hands in his pockets.

Watching him shoving clothes into a sports bag, Lochlin felt his chest constrict painfully. He couldn't shake off the feeling that he was about to lose everything. It was as though Judd was waiting in the wings like a demonic understudy, ready to swoop in and claim everything as his own. The thought of it was so horrific, Lochlin had to steady himself against the door frame. As he held on, he felt such a severe pain shooting down his arm, it almost took his breath away and before anyone noticed what was happening, Lochlin thrust the post into Tavvy's hand and stumbled away to shut himself in his office.

Tavvy stared after him and left Shay to his packing. She felt petrified at what Judd might be planning to do next. At least Caitie was still living at Pembleton. Seconds later, she felt a shiver go down her spine. Tucked between two envelopes was a flyer for Hugo's summer play. 'Enjoy the romance of *Romeo and Juliet*,' shouted the colourful flyer, giving details about the performance and stating that it would star Caitie Maguire and Elliot Harrington in the lead roles.

Gasping, Tavvy slumped against the wall. She had no idea if Judd was behind the collaboration or not but either way she knew she was going to have to spend the next few months keeping this from Lochlin.

Screwing the leaflet up and shoving it in her pocket, Tavvy let out a jerky breath. When, and how, was this all going to end?

Savannah finished her routine and spun round expectantly.

'Well, what do you think?' Her pale cheeks were flushed from exertion and her long red hair was messy from being flung all over the place. Hands on her hips, she pouted, wondering why Elliot and Martha weren't giving her effusive feedback. Fuming because Judd had told her he was planning to jet off to Los Angeles again, Savannah was desperate for some attention.

Elliot put down his copy of *Romeo and Juliet* and clapped. Nudging Martha who was staring into the distance as if she'd seen a ghost, she joined in half-heartedly.

'You're a very good dancer,' Elliot said truthfully, hoping Savannah wasn't going to ask him to comment on her voice. It wasn't awful but, in all honesty, he couldn't say it was remarkable. And after hearing Iris Maguire at the Valentines' Ball, Elliot thought Savannah fell very short of the mark.

Martha was too engrossed in her thoughts to be able to provide feedback. Counting dates on her fingers, she checked again. No, she was right the first time; her period was two days late. She and Sebastian had barely slept together recently so it was a bit of a miracle but Martha did recall a bout of rather angry sex they'd had the day Savannah had arrived. If she hadn't been ovulating, Martha would have told Sebastian to eff off because she wasn't exactly in the mood after he'd gone AWOL all afternoon and been so loathsome to her. Ranting about his father's 'bastard bratling', his tirade peppered with a number of ugly swear words, it was hardly the most romantic of couplings but Martha was willing to let it go if it meant getting pregnant after all these years.

Maybe that was why she'd put on some weight recently, Martha thought optimistically. It might not be down to biscuits, after all; it might be hormones.

Savannah flopped on to the grass next to Elliot. 'Judd . . . sorry, *Dad* is taking me out for lunch today. He's just kissing my ass because he's going back to the States again and he knows I'm pissed.'

She glanced up at the sky, noting the dark clouds that were descending. The weather was worse here than in New York, she thought moodily. Savannah was surprised to find herself missing her life there but nonetheless she knew she'd never go back. She'd had a few phone calls from her friends but she suspected it was because they were hoping she could put in a good word with Judd at Jett. Well, they could forget it. A few of them had better voices and there was no way Savannah was going to jeopardise her own fortunate position by showing her father something better.

Elliot put his play down. 'Where's Dad taking you for lunch, then?'

She shrugged. 'God knows. Somewhere posh, he said.'

Elliot raised his eyebrows. He couldn't remember the last time his father had taken him out for lunch, let alone to somewhere posh. Not that Elliot blamed Savannah for that; it was hardly her fault she was flavour of the month. That was all down to their father, who lavished her with gifts and praise and made sure everyone in the family knew Savannah was the new favourite. Elliot wondered what Ace would think of the situation and decided he probably wouldn't care. In fact, he would most likely be delighted to have the spotlight taken away from him so he could get on with his life without being judged and criticised.

Elliot studied his half-sister. She was certainly striking with all that glorious russet hair and her athletic, dancer's physique. On the face of it, she was a dead ringer for his father in both looks and personality but Elliot suspected she wasn't half as brash and mouthy underneath it all. There was the way she'd leapt to Martha's defence the day she'd arrived, for starters. Savannah clearly despised bullies, which meant at least she had one redeemable streak.

'Have you met Darcy Middleton, this bitch Dad's sleeping with at the office?' Savannah asked, lying back on the grass. 'She's the biggest pain in the ass.'

Elliot gave her a wry smile. 'Dad doesn't tend to introduce his mistresses to us. We just know they exist.'

Savannah propped herself up on one elbow. 'Kitty's much nicer. I can't believe how lovely she's been to me since I got here. God knows why he likes shagging these predatory bitches when he's got someone like Kitty waiting at home.'

Elliot couldn't agree more. His mother had been utterly destroyed by Savannah's arrival but, typically, she didn't blame Savannah and had even helped her settle in.

Savannah picked up Elliot's book. 'Why are you so obsessed with this play?'

'No reason.' Elliot was deliberately evasive. As much as he liked Savannah, he still wasn't sure he could trust her yet, not when she was hanging out with his father so much.

Abandoning thoughts of a gorgeous nursery decorated in shades of chocolate brown and cream, Martha belatedly joined in the conversation. 'What do you enjoy doing?' she asked Savannah kindly, realising they didn't know her very well. Martha wanted to make an effort to make her feel welcome. 'I mean, what did you do for fun in New York?'

Savannah considered the question. What *had* she done in New York to have fun? She'd gone to bars, had meals out, attended tons of parties. . . . Gazing up at Brockett Hall, she had an idea. She turned to Elliot and Martha. 'Hey, how about we have a party?'

Elliot shook his head. 'You have no idea what Dad would do to us if he found out we'd used his beloved home as a nightclub.'

Martha nodded rapidly, her mousy hair falling into her eyes. 'Seriously, Savannah, it wouldn't be worth it. Judd turns into a maniac if people disrespect him.'

Savannah pouted. So much for her big idea. 'All right,' she said grudgingly. 'No party.' She sighed and decided to pressure her father about her record deal; it was clearly the only fun she was going to have in this gloomy place.

Later, Savannah was sitting in an exclusive restaurant in Mayfair, tucking into lobster thermidor.

'Your first lobster,' Judd commented, watching her forking up rich sauce and meat.

'Hardly,' she returned scornfully. 'This one just costs more than the ones I've had before. Anyway, when are we going to release a record?'

Judd watched her critically, enjoying her direct approach. Savannah really did have a healthy appetite, unusual in a girl her age but he guessed she worked out and danced so much, she didn't particularly need to worry about excess calories. Still, he didn't want her getting fat so he made a mental note to ban dessert from now on. Judd admired the thigh-skimming black dress she was wearing and her red hair hanging loosely around her shoulders. He imagined his credit card had been dented since Savannah's arrival but he didn't care. He liked spoiling her and her flashy taste mirrored his own. At least one member of his family was a chip off the old block, Judd thought grimly. Sebastian seemed ludicrously distracted, no doubt because of the tart he was shagging, but that was no excuse for not having his eye on the ball at work. There were several contracts outstanding for some acts they were signing up and if Sebastian didn't get his finger out, the artists would be out of contract again due to the built-in cooling-off period. Deciding to give Sebastian a rocket up his arse later in the week, Judd thought about Ace. He was just about controllable but he still needed to prove himself. Hopefully the situation with Iris Maguire would be the making of him.

'Well?' Putting her knife and fork down with a clatter, Savannah fixed her piercing blue eyes on her father. She was becoming impatient; he had promised her the world but he had been out of the country for the past few weeks and now she wanted some answers, especially since he was off again shortly.

Judd took a leisurely sip of his ice-cold Sancerre, soaking up the atmosphere of the expensive, well-kept secret of a restaurant he had recently discovered. His daughter might think she had him wrapped around her little finger but in reality no one was capable of pushing him for decisions, not even Savannah. Clothes and shoes were one thing but when it came to his businesses, Judd was always in charge.

However, luckily for Savannah, Judd was in a good mood. Jett was set to make an extortionate amount of money that year if all of the acts he'd acquired did well, and Shamrock, with a paranoid and floundering Lochlin at the helm, was sailing steadily down the shitter.

'I think we should set up an industry evening and invite all the relevant people,' Judd told Savannah abruptly. 'I have a few songs for you to start practising and then I plan to launch you over here, before sending you to the States.' He rejected the dessert menu without asking Savannah and ordered them two black coffees.

'I might have wanted something,' Savannah snapped. She hated it when he bossed her around. He could be such an asshole at times.

Judd sat back in his chair. 'Tough. You need to start thinking about your image. Fatties don't sell records.' He glanced at his Rolex, not bothering to hide his impatience. Oddly, Darcy had taken a few days off and she seemed to think they wouldn't be catching up before he left for LA but he planned to surprise her later on with something kinky.

Judd refocused his attention on Savannah. 'Why didn't you like any of Darcy's ideas?'

'Because she's a bitch,' Savannah retorted. She ignored her black coffee, refusing to be dictated to. 'She said I need an edgier look, but I look better like this. I refuse to end up looking like some fucking Goth with black nails and spooky make-up.' Her mouth curled petulantly.

Judd's eyes gleamed as he thought about punishing Darcy for upsetting his daughter. He took a perverse pleasure in tasking her with something, then decimating her ideas as publicly as possible. Darcy was smart but she was far too high and mighty at times and it gave him no end of pleasure to annihilate her, both in the bedroom and the boardroom. Judd realised Savannah's expression had become surly again as she waited for him to get back to the point. 'I also want to pitch you against another act I have an interest in. She's called Iris Maguire.'

Savannah's eyes widened but she said nothing. She knew all about Iris Maguire because Elliot was secretly friends with her little sister, Caitie. Judging by the discussions about Iris's voice, it could rival the likes of Beyoncé and Mariah Carey so Savannah wasn't entirely sure they were in the same league. She had an inflated opinion of herself and she had enough ambition to power the whole of London in a blackout but she also knew her limitations.

'She's out in LA at the moment having some singing lessons with Pia Jordan.' Judd put his black coffee down, his jaw clenching.

He'd been livid with Pia when she had told him Savannah's voice was average. How dare she question his judgement? Fucking dumb bitch. Pia needed to learn some manners in future. 'Iris has a big performance soon and I think we should set your industry launch up for shortly afterwards. Then I can stir the press up and pitch you both against each other.'

Savannah frowned and hoped her father knew what he was doing. She had a feeling she might come off worse against an artist of Iris's calibre and she wasn't entirely sure she wanted to be drawn into this stupid feud between the Maguires and the Harringtons. She felt more animosity towards her dumb-fuck of a half-brother Sebastian than she did towards Caitie or Iris Maguire.

Judd drained his coffee and stood up. He tossed a pile of notes on the table. 'Pay the bill, will you? I have an appointment.' He stalked out of the restaurant without another word.

Savannah gaped. He had left her sitting there like an idiot in a restaurant, with no way of getting home. What a bastard! She looked up to see a handsome man with short grey hair standing next to the table.

'Here's the money for lunch,' she said, gesturing to it.

He looked highly amused. 'I'm afraid I don't work here,' he said with a smile.

Savannah flushed.

He held out his hand and shook hers briskly. 'Easy mistake to make. I'm actually here to discuss some business with you.'

Savannah picked up her handbag. Even though, close up, the man looked a bit like George Clooney, she wasn't about to entertain some pervert.

He took out a credit card. 'My name is Conrad Lafferty and I can assure you I'm not some kind of sleaze. Please, let me get that.' He discreetly gave his card to a hovering waiter who instantly melted away. Gathering up the cash, Conrad quickly popped it into Savannah's handbag. 'It would be my pleasure to take care of lunch for you.'

Savannah frowned, catching a glimpse of some sparkling cufflinks. Surely they weren't real diamonds?

Conrad studied her, admiring her thick russet hair. 'As corny as it sounds, I couldn't help noticing you from the other side of the restaurant and now that your father has gone, I thought I should come and introduce myself.'

'How do you know he's my father?' She folded her arms, noticing he had the clearest green eyes she'd ever seen.

'Because you're like two peas in a pod,' he answered patiently. 'Now, I have a proposition for you.'

Savannah got to her feet. 'Just because I have lunch with my father doesn't mean I have a thing for old men.'

Conrad smiled disarmingly. 'I'm probably not as old as you think.' He took an embossed card out of his pocket and placed it on the table. 'And as lovely as you are and as delighted as I would be to have you on my arm, my proposition is purely a business one.' He caught her eye.

Savannah sat down again, intrigued, and Conrad took the seat opposite.

His expression remained impassive. 'I run several businesses, most of them in the Far East. You have a very unusual look and I think you could do very well over there. Redheads, genuine redheads, are all the rage at the moment.'

She narrowed her eyes. 'If you're talking about some sick porn fest, think again.'

Conrad looked faintly offended. 'You really do have an attitude, don't you? Which I like, but you need to rein it in slightly. I'm talking about a pop career. That's what you want to be, isn't it? A pop star?'

'How did you know that?' Savannah was perplexed. Who *was* this man?

Conrad stood up. 'I realise you probably want to give your father a chance with your career, but if that doesn't work out, call me. I'm in town for the next couple of months but after that, you're out of luck because I'm heading back to Japan.' He shook her hand again professionally, without a hint of anything untoward.

Savannah couldn't help feeling disappointed.

'Oh, and in case you need a lift back anywhere, I'll leave my limo out front for you. It's very well equipped.' With that, he was gone.

The maître d' appeared. 'Can I help madam with anything else?'

'No, thank you. Is . . . is he for real?' she said, showing him Conrad's card.

'Oh yes, madam. Mr Lafferty is one of our best customers – a very good tipper, if I might say so.' He inclined his head. 'He's also an astute businessman and he has a reputation for being a very fair man.'

'Is he . . . married?'

The maître d' shook his head. 'Divorced. It would take a special woman to tear Mr Lafferty away from his work again.' He gave her a slight bow and left her to it.

Savannah stared at Conrad's card, her appetite whetted. Outside, she found a sleek black limo waiting, with the initials 'LC' discreetly carved into the doors and a driver wearing a smart green uniform. He opened the door and gestured for her to get in.

Without a word, Savannah did so, gasping at the bottles of champagne and the high-tech coffee machine. Leaning back pleasurably, she wondered what the hell a man like Conrad Lafferty wanted with a girl like her.

'Kitty?'

Unable to concentrate and as it was Friday, Leo had knocked off work early. Loath to go home and either find Lexi absent or, worse, at home, meaning he might have to talk to her about her affair, he had driven into Maidenview. He hadn't expected to bump into anyone he knew, especially not Kitty Harrington. Leo couldn't help noticing how miserable she looked and he realised he wasn't the only one who needed cheering up.

Kitty, finding herself in Maidenview for similar reasons, started when she saw him. 'It's Leo, isn't it? How nice to see you again.' Having cried for days after Savannah's arrival, she knew she must look awful.

Leo wondered why Kitty's eyes were so red and bloodshot. 'So, what brings you here?'

Kitty looked away. 'Haven't you heard? It's all over the village that my husband's moved his illegitimate daughter into the house.'

Leo's eyes widened. 'Oh my God. No, I haven't heard anything. I've been a bit . . .' He stopped, not wanting to sound like a martyr in view of Kitty's news. 'Gosh, you must feel horribly betrayed. You say he's moved this girl in?'

'I don't even know how I feel about it, to be honest. Judd has done so many terrible things over the years.' She blushed, trying to figure out why she was telling a perfect stranger intimate details about her marriage. Maybe it had something to do with the sympathetic way he was looking at her or maybe it was just nice to talk to someone who wasn't involved.

'Look, do you fancy a coffee . . . or something stronger?' he asked, thinking Kitty looked very much as if she was in need of a friend.

She gave him a watery smile. 'That's very sweet of you but I'm sure you've got better things to do'.

'I haven't actually.' Leo gestured to a wine bar on the other side of the road. 'I could do with a glass of wine myself.'

Kitty hesitated. Throwing caution to the wind, she decided a drink would do her good and followed Leo into the small, cosy wine bar.

'Shall we have some Chablis?' Leo asked, politely helping Kitty into a free booth.

Kitty nodded and peeled off her mac self-consciously, wishing she'd put on something more exciting than her reliable navy shift dress and flats.

'You're a lawyer, aren't you?' she said. 'Just like my son, Sebastian.'

'Yes, just like your son, Sebastian,' Leo said through gritted teeth. Reminding himself that Kitty most likely knew nothing about Sebastian and Lexi's affair, he relaxed again.

'Do you think there are two types of people in the world?' Kitty asked suddenly. 'The cheaters and the ones who get cheated on? That's how it seems to me. And it always seems that the good guys get the raw end of the deal.'

Leo gulped his wine down. 'I've been thinking that myself lately.' He paused then felt compelled to explain himself. 'Lexi's been having an affair.'

Kitty gaped. 'Oh, Leo! I'm so sorry. I know exactly how you feel. Judd's done this to me so many times.' She bent her head in shame. 'I'm so weak where Judd is concerned, I always have been. It used to be out of love but now . . .' She faltered, not wanting to admit how violent Judd could be or how embarrassed her family would be if she dared to get divorced.

'Would you ever leave him?' Leo asked, interested.

Kitty bit her lip. 'I tried to once but . . . This is the first time in ages that I've really thought about calling it a day with Judd. I . . . I don't know if I have the courage but there really isn't anything left between us any more.'

Leo sighed. 'People warned me about Lexi, you know. Lochlin . . . Charlie . . . my work colleagues. They all told me she was with me for my money but I didn't believe them. Stupidly, I thought she might actually like me for me.'

'And why wouldn't she?' Kitty said, the words coming out before she could stop them. She blushed furiously.

Leo was immensely touched. 'Thank you. And Judd clearly doesn't know a good thing when he sees it either.'

Flustered by his comment, Kitty got up. 'Thank you for the wine. I really need to get back now.'

Leo gave her a warm hug and a kiss on the cheek. She smelt of rose perfume and her cheeks were soft and free of make-up, unlike Lexi's, which were always smothered in foundation.

Watching Kitty leave, Leo had the strangest feeling that if he wasn't so broken up over Lexi's affair, he might have found himself falling a tiny bit in love with Kitty Harrington.

Darcy was tucked up in bed at home, skimming through some music reviews on the internet. She'd decided to take some long overdue holiday, but the truth of it was, she needed a break from Judd. He was so intense and he had started to demand sex in the office, twisting her into outlandish positions and doing his best to degrade her.

Darcy pushed away the uneasy feeling she got every time she thought about sex with Judd these days and focused on her laptop. With her cinnamon-coloured hair twisted up in a loose bun, for once she was relaxing, wearing a cream cashmere cardigan and some matching socks she'd treated herself to.

Darcy studied the reviews. A few of the groups Judd had taken on were doing really well – a girl band called Stiletto Heels had performed at several venues over the past few months, including GAY, and the industry were raving about their kitsch style and their slick live performances. They had a single coming out in June and Darcy was sure it was going to be a top ten hit, especially with the idea she'd had for a saucy video, which involved the group prancing around in their underwear, stiletto heels and not much else.

Darcy clicked on to another website. A ten-year-old boy with a voice like a young Michael Jackson was in the studio recording an album at the moment – a mixture of age-appropriate covers, as well as a number of new tracks, one of which she was sure had Christmas number one stamped all over it. It was strong enough to challenge a possible reality TV show winner but it all depended on whether Judd took her advice and held off releasing the album until November. The blue rinse brigade would love little Aidan with his puppy-dog eyes and his soulful voice and it made perfect sense to capitalise on this with a festive release.

Not that Judd took much notice of her advice, Darcy thought bitterly. Sometimes she wondered why he'd hired her. Mistakenly she'd thought it was because he valued her industry knowledge and because they had a connection of sorts. Now, it felt very much as if Judd had snapped her up to stop her accepting a role with Lochlin at Shamrock.

Darcy pushed her laptop to one side. The first time she'd met Judd, she'd felt a genuine spark between them. He was sexy and dynamic and he had blown her away with his charm and his smooth patter. The combination of his arrogant plans to take the music world by storm and his bold, erotic advances had won her over, and she had even thought Judd might be the one man who could 'tame' her. Now Darcy realised she didn't *want* to be tamed. Professionally, she wanted to be taken seriously, and in a relationship, she wanted to be respected.

Darcy swallowed and remembered the night with Shay Maguire. She'd never felt so adored and respected in all her life. The tender way he had held her, the erotic way he had made her body respond to his touch . . .

She shuddered, reliving the night she'd spent with him even though it tore her apart. Shay couldn't be more different from Judd. Judd just wanted to use her; Darcy knew that now. He expected her to be at his beck and call sexually, and he used her for anything he didn't fancy doing himself at Jett. Which didn't mean he accepted her decisions or proposals, it simply meant she did all the donkey work while Judd swooped in at the end and changed everything he wasn't happy with.

Like Savannah, for example. He had thrown Darcy in at the deep end while he jetted off to Los Angeles and, over the phone, he had been less than sympathetic, disregarding most of her ideas for ones Savannah had come up with, or choosing his own instead. But being a born risk-taker didn't make Judd a music business expert, and sometimes he really didn't know what he was talking about. The way he wanted Savannah represented was an example of one of his reckless decisions which, in Darcy's experience, was doomed to failure.

She chewed her fingernail. But who could tell Judd he was in the wrong? She had attempted to do so once and she had been silenced with a barked 'Fuck you' and the dull sound of a disconnected phone. Shocked by his rudeness, Darcy felt trapped by her situation but she had no idea how to extricate herself from Judd's evil grasp. And knowing his penchant for revenge, she also knew for a fact he wouldn't let her escape easily.

She froze as she heard her front door slam. Only one person had a key to her flat.

Seconds later, Judd strolled in.

'Pleased to see me?' he drawled, his bright blue eyes running up and down her body.

Darcy had never been less pleased to see him. She whipped her hair out of the messy bun it was in. 'I-I wasn't expecting you,' she stammered. She kicked her socks off under the bedclothes, wishing desperately that she'd gone out earlier. 'I thought you were going back to LA.'

'I am but not until later.' He held up a scary-looking contraption made of black leather and metal clips. 'A little present from my travels I've been dying to try out on you,' he added, giving her a revolting smirk.

Darcy's stomach turned and she felt herself tremble all over.

'Good work with the Maguire boy,' he commented, undoing his tie with exaggeratedly slow movements. 'I'm impressed.'

Darcy flinched, knowing there would be more. Judd never paid her compliments and he had a look in his eyes she recognised; it was verging on malevolent and it signalled danger.

'But I'm not happy with you upsetting Savannah,' he added softly, removing his jacket and flexing his shoulders deliberately. 'She says you tried to turn her into some sort of Goth.'

'I did not!' Darcy protested. 'I simply suggested an edgier image, that's all. Savannah rejected every single one of my ideas on purpose. If *you'd* said them to her, she would have been all for it.'

Judd narrowed his eyes. 'That sounds very much as if you're calling my daughter a liar. Is that what you're doing?'

Darcy's jaw tensed. 'Of course I'm not. I'm just saying . . .' Her voice faded away as she realised it was pointless arguing with Judd. He never gave in and he always thought he was right. Challenging him further could only cause trouble.

'I think you have some serious making up to do, don't you?' Judd asked her quietly, towering over the bed.

Darcy swallowed. Hating herself for being so weak, she cast her hazel eyes down and nodded. Watching him remove his clothes clinically before picking up the weird sex toy he'd brought round, she gritted her teeth. One way or another, she was getting the hell away from Judd. She didn't care how she did it, but as soon as humanly possible, she had to break free from him.

The problem was, Darcy thought, as Judd blocked out the light with his broad shoulders and crawled across the bed towards her, it felt as if they were forever connected to each other by this depraved game they were playing. And Darcy was acutely aware that in a game, the pupil could just as easily become the prey.

Hating herself and doing her best to put Shay's gorgeous, shamrock-green eyes out of her mind, Darcy allowed Judd to swoop down on her.

Chapter Twelve

Standing at the edge of the stage at an upmarket venue in Los Angeles, Iris was wondering if she could somehow get out of her performance. Trembling like a leaf, she took a peek through the curtains and almost passed out when she saw how many people were walking in and taking seats.

Iris gulped. Why did she put herself through this? She loved singing but performing in front of so many people caused her serious anxiety. Reminding herself this was something she'd wanted since she was a little girl, Iris also gave herself a telling-off. She was so lucky; most girls would kill to be in her place right now.

'How are you feeling?' Pia asked, joining her. Wearing a chocolate-brown dress that matched her skin tone perfectly, her short, elfin hair had been coaxed into soft peaks instead of being slicked back like a dominatrix.

'Sick,' Iris admitted, teetering on the cream Chloe heels with ankle straps Pia had convinced her to wear.

'You don't look it,' Pia said, giving her a once-over. Iris looked stunning; her limbs were honey-gold and her tawny-blond hair, which was loose apart from the two small plaits she had looped round her crown, had lightened a few shades in the sun. She was wearing a daringly short cream sheath dress which showed off her slender frame and narrow waist. It had a diaphanous silk kimono over the top which gave it an air of class, stopping several demure inches above the knee.

Iris was wringing her hands. 'I don't know if I'm ready for the big notes,' she fretted, her knees buckling as she thought she heard her name being announced.

'You're not on yet,' Pia reassured her, hoping Iris was going to be able to hold it together. She took Iris's hands in hers. 'You are more than ready.' Her dark eyes were stern but compassionate. 'You have no need to be nervous. You have practised this to perfection and you can handle the notes with ease.'

'Really? Can I? That top note is so tough . . . imagine if I croak . . .'

'You won't.' Pia shook her head confidently. 'And if I've been tough on you over the weeks, it's because you are one of the most talented people I have ever worked with.'

Iris's mouth fell open in shock. Pia hadn't paid her a compliment once during their singing lessons; Iris had learnt to judge her reaction from the furrow in Pia's brow. If it was visible, it meant she hadn't hit the note or interpreted the music properly; if it wasn't, Iris knew she had done something right.

Iris tried to calm her breathing and, randomly, she wondered what Ace Harrington was doing tonight. Since meeting him at the Toyota Pro/Celebrity race, she hadn't been able to get him out of her head. Finding herself drifting off and thinking about his sexy grey eyes, Iris had firmly reminded herself that he was a Harrington and therefore forbidden fruit. But somehow that made him all the more attractive.

'And you're on.' Pia smiled, giving her a shove.

Without giving herself time to think, Iris stepped out on to the stage, almost blinded by the harsh lights. Making it to the microphone stand without incident, she held on to it for dear life, shaking all over. She could barely see the audience but she could make out tables and chairs and the odd face she didn't recognise. Luisa was out there somewhere but Iris had told her to stay out of sight in case she put her off with all her raucous cheering.

For a second, Iris froze. She was on a huge stage, so large, she felt dwarfed by it. There were hundreds, maybe thousands of people sitting there expectantly, waiting to hear her sing. Instead of a backing CD, she had her own live band on stage with her, piano, guitars and drums at the ready. She felt her knees knocking together but she reminded herself that this was a chance of a lifetime.

Hearing the intro to 'Listen', Iris focused her mind, closing her eyes and trying to remember everything Pia had taught her. She opened her mouth and sang. The first few notes were tentative but they grew stronger with each line. Touched by the outburst of applause that greeted her voice, Iris lost herself in the song, remembering to breathe as she slowly crept up to the higher notes, allowing her natural, throaty tone to play out at the lower end. When it came to the huge note in the song, she gave it everything and held it until the music petered out.

Breathlessly, Iris opened her eyes, almost deafened by the crashing sound of hands clapping and feet stomping on the floor. Completely overwhelmed, she mumbled, 'Th-thanks,' into the microphone and dashed off the stage, forgetting she was due to sing another song straight afterwards. Iris's cheeks were scarlet as she was propelled out again by Pia.

'F-forgive me,' she begged the audience, with a shy smile. 'I've never sung in front of so many people before. I got a bit nervous but if it's all right with you, I'll sing something else.'

Wildly encouraged by the loud cheers that greeted her comment, Iris removed the microphone from the stand and nodded to the band who began to play the intro to the new song. 'This is a track by an unknown writer . . . I really hope you like it.'

Sitting in the audience, Judd was impressed. It was obvious to anyone that Iris had been nervous but she had proved herself to be professional as well as hugely talented. Moreover, she had charmed the entire audience with her refreshingly open manner.

It didn't hurt that she looked a million dollars, either, Judd thought approvingly, deciding Pia and the stylists had done a good job with Iris's image. He still hadn't forgiven Pia for her scathing criticism of Savannah's voice but at least she had held up her end of the bargain as far as Iris was concerned.

Encouraged by the fantastic response to her first song, Iris moved around the stage during her second song, enjoying connecting with the audience as they clapped in time to the music. Her nerves disappeared and she threw herself into the performance, determined to enjoy every second and prove that she belonged up on this vast stage.

Sitting at the back with Jerry and blissfully unaware that his father was also in the audience, Ace was blown away. His father had told him Iris was talented but he had no idea she had a voice like that. She could easily hold her own in the charts with all the divas out there. Ace was no expert but Iris's voice had a beautiful, throaty tone that set her apart from everyone else. The second song was catchy and the crowd were really getting into it and Iris had relaxed and she was smiling and waving at people. It seemed as if everyone in the audience had fallen in love with Iris and, looking at her, commanding the stage like a pro, Ace didn't blame them.

What a voice, he thought. What a face, what a body and what a voice. He was used to viewing women as disposable fun, but he saw Iris differently. When they'd met, he'd found her easy to talk to and funny in that self-deprecating way British people often had but there was something so exciting about her as well.

Ace let out a shaky breath. Was he really going to go ahead with this ridiculous seduction plan? He still couldn't believe his father had asked him to do it – he had even sent him tickets to this event to make sure they met up again. The astonishing thing was, Ace had already made sure he had tickets to the concert before the ones from his father had arrived because he couldn't wait any longer to see Iris again, regardless of what he'd been asked to do.

As Iris skipped off the stage, Ace leapt to his feet and roared at the top of his voice. Everyone else did the same, screaming and yelling, demanding an encore. Iris ran out again to graciously accept the applause but informed them there wasn't enough time for her to sing again. The audience groaned with disappointment and booed at not being able to see more of Iris. Pia joined Iris on stage and breathlessly told the audience when they could hear Iris singing live again. She held up a demo CD which she announced would be played on the radio shortly as well and they both laughingly took a bow before disappearing backstage.

Ace nudged Jerry who looked suspiciously like he'd been moved to tears by Iris's voice. 'Aw, you're such a softie, Jez. She is amazing, though, isn't she?'

Jerry dabbed at his eyes. Ace had talked about Iris non-stop since the Toyota Pro/Celebrity race and he had been on top form on the racing circuit ever since, clocking up several wins, seemingly invigorated. Ace's sparkling wit, absent since Judd's initial request, had made a welcome return after he and Iris had met. He was also abstaining from sex with admirable self-restraint, although Jerry wasn't sure Ace was actually that bothered about missing out with other women.

'I'm going backstage,' Ace said, disappearing into the crowds. He had the strangest feeling he was about to start something he might not have the power to stop. Calling over his shoulder, he said, 'Go back to the apartment and get ready for the party, Jez. I'm gonna get Iris to come . . . whatever it takes.'

Jerry nodded and, trying to push down the feeling of trepidation in his gut, he left.

Sweet-talking an official at the entrance, Ace made his way down to Iris's dressing room. She was surrounded by industry reps who were thrusting their business cards into her hands, in spite of her polite protests that she really couldn't commit to anything until she'd been signed up to a deal by her father at Shamrock. Stylists and hairdressers were offering their services for free and on her make-up table sat several gift bags, overflowing with goodies.

Bewildered by all the attention, Iris realised she'd just been asked to model lingerie for two different companies, as well as posing for five magazine shoots in return for glowing reviews and exclusive interviews. Catching sight of Ace on the other side of the throng of noisy music reps, her eyes lit up. Breaking into a huge smile, she forgot that she wasn't supposed to see Ace ever again, let alone speak to him, and gave him a shy wave, wondering what he was doing there.

Mouthing 'Hi', Ace grinned at her.

Pia, acting as Iris's temporary manager, held back the music aficionados with a firm hand, curtly dismissing the ones she felt weren't right for Iris and smoothly sucking up to the ones that were. Receiving a phone call that left her pale beneath her mocha skin, Pia glared at Ace and reminded Iris that she was due at the studio for more practice the next day. Making a swift exit, Pia went in search of Judd at his request, wondering apprehensively how he might make her pay for daring to slag off his new-found daughter.

Managing to slip away from the crowd, Iris found her way to Ace's side. 'I can't believe you're here!'

'You were incredible up there,' he stammered, poleaxed by her beauty. Close up, he could see she was wearing shimmery eye make-up and her amber eyes looked huge with all the smoky greys and silvers outlining them. All of a sudden, Ace felt wrong-footed. For the first time in his life, he was tongue-tied. He had no idea what to say or how to handle the moment and he was baffled. He had chatted up more women than he cared to remember, so why was he suddenly acting like an idiotic novice?

'Really?' Iris was delighted to see him, more than she could say. 'I was so nervous . . . I can't believe I held that note.'

'It was . . . you were . . .' Ace stopped and took her hand. 'God, this is going to sound so stupid but it feels as if it's been ages since I saw you. Too long.'

Iris nodded. 'I know.' She did. She felt exactly the same way and even though she knew she wasn't supposed to talk to him, she couldn't help feeling thrilled to see him. 'We can't . . . I'm not supposed to talk to you . . .' she began haltingly.

'What?' Ace held on to her fingers. 'Why on earth not?'

'The feud . . . you must know about it. Between our two families?'

'Oh that!' Ace dismissed it with a wave of his hand. Judd had instructed him to admit that he knew about it if it came up because it would seem odd if he didn't but he should downplay it. Hesitating, he ploughed ahead, trying to sound as laid back as he could, not because he'd been told to but because he thought Iris might run a mile if he didn't reassure her it was all nothing.

'My father said something about some issue he has with your father but who cares? That has nothing to do with us. It's just some stupid row they had years ago or something. It's all a bit juvenile, if you ask me.'

Averting his eyes, Ace wished more than anything that he'd bumped into Iris by accident. If fate had thrown them together, he wouldn't be feeling so guilty about lying to her about the family feud. Iris was innocent in all this and she didn't deserve to be screwed over. If he wasn't so attracted to her, he would walk away right now and bugger the consequences with his father.

The trouble was, Iris was under his skin, he thought desperately, feeling her fingers slip between his. She captivated him on every level, intellectually, sexually, emotionally. And now that he had heard her sing . . . there was nothing Ace found more of a turn-on than natural talent; that husky, throaty voice of hers would haunt him in his sleep.

Ace reached out and touched a tendril of Iris's blond hair. Whatever his father had asked him to do didn't matter any more, he wanted to know more about her, what she liked to eat, what made her laugh, what turned her on . . .

'You know about the feud?' Iris said, confused. She thought that if he had known about it, Ace would have kept well away from her. She didn't dare to hope that maybe, like her, he felt the irresistible pull of attraction between them.

Ace shrugged. 'It's not about us, is it?' He wanted to believe it so his words rang true.

Iris hesitated. He was wearing a dark suit with a pristine white shirt and no tie and, unlike last time, his dark auburn hair was clean and slicked back. In the dim light, his tan seemed even darker and his grey eyes watched her as her eyes roamed over him.

'All right, maybe our fathers wouldn't like us talking,' he said softly, seeing that Iris was torn. 'But I really like you. I'm just inviting you to a party, nothing more. Who cares about some row from years ago? This is about you and me.'

Iris gazed at Ace's mouth, wanting nothing more than to feel his mouth on hers. Deep down, she felt an intense loyalty to her father; she had promised him she would stay away from the Harringtons. But this was different. Ace might be a Harrington, but he was nothing like his father.

Ace could see Iris was agonising over the decision. Suddenly it was important to know if Iris really did want to spend time with him.

'Look, I'd really like you to come but I understand if you feel you should stay away from me. Well, I don't, but I respect your decision if that's what you want.'

Iris faltered. She knew she should stay away from him. Ace was a temptation she should avoid at all costs because it could hurt too many people if she didn't. But what if she ignored the way she was feeling and regretted it for the rest of her life?

Bending his head, Ace kissed her, pressing his mouth against hers softly. Planning to give her a short, sweet kiss before leaving, he forgot all his good intentions and gave in to his desires. She tasted like honey, sweet and desirable. Feeling her leaning into him, Ace drew her close and slid his hands around her slender waist. Winding his hot tongue around hers, he groaned as he felt her hands in his hair.

Forgetting her own resolve to keep her distance, Iris pulled him down on to her harder, feeling his honed body against hers. Her head was spinning; her mind was telling her no but her body was screaming yes, her senses alert and twitching with life. Pushing her back against the wall, Ace pinned her hands down, moulding his body to hers. He was much taller than her but somehow their height difference worked. Ace sank his hands into Iris's hair, breathing in the fresh, floral scent that came from it.

I've kissed thousands of women before, he told himself breathlessly. This is nothing special . . . *she* is nothing special. She's just another girl. His father's face swam in front of his eyes momentarily but Ace doggedly made it disappear. In that moment, he had to believe seducing Iris was *his* idea, not some warped little mission he'd been sent on by his father. He genuinely wanted her.

'Wait . . . stop,' Iris panted, pulling herself away from him. 'We can't do this . . . my father would kill me if he knew I was doing this.'

Ace gazed down at her, tracing her sleepy amber eyes with his finger. Her bee-stung lips were bruised from the onslaught and she was flushed with lust. 'I don't care,' he told her in a thick voice. Somehow the fact that Iris cared so much about her father made him fall for her even more. 'It's their fight, not ours.'

Iris licked her lips, tasting Ace and hoping to God he would take her home and do incredible things to her. He was so sexy, she didn't know how the hell she was supposed to resist him.

Ace reluctantly untangled his hand from Iris's hair. Uncharacteristically, he was lost for words and he felt his heart crashing in his chest as they drew back from each other.

Iris felt bereft without his hands on her. What was happening to her? It was just a kiss! So why on earth did she feel as if she had known him for ever?

Ace raised agonised eyes to hers. 'You're right, we shouldn't do this, not if you're going to feel bad about your dad.' Even though his father was going to kill him, Ace knew he couldn't go through with this, not when Iris was so racked with guilt. He gave her another slow kiss. 'Shit, sorry. Look, I'm going.' He stepped away from her, needing to put some physical distance between them before he threw her against the wall and disgraced himself. 'I really want you to come to the party but I understand if you can't.' He gave her a rueful smile. 'I mean, I'll hate it, but if that's what you decide. But . . . I'll probably always be waiting for you, if you know what I mean.'

With that, Ace left before he changed his mind.

Iris stared after him, wanting to call him back. She was so upset she didn't even notice Luisa sidling up next to her.

'Oh my God, you were amazing!' she shrieked, her dark curls bouncing as she hugged Iris. 'Were you nervous? You didn't look it . . . well, maybe at the start but who cares . . . and that note at the end . . . wow!' She stopped, realising Iris wasn't even listening. 'What's wrong?'

Iris touched her mouth where Ace's lips had been. 'Ace was here . . . he wants us to go to that party.'

Luisa rolled her eyes. 'Don't tell me, you said no because of this stupid family feud. Seriously, Iris, your life is your life and you can't always live it for your parents.'

Iris nodded slowly. 'You're right. I love my father but this is . . . there's something between us and I know I have to see him again.'

'Tonight?' Luisa said eagerly.

'Tonight.' Iris made a decision and for the first time ever, she threw caution to the wind. Their chemistry was too explosive to ignore. Iris knew if she walked away now, she would spend the rest of her life regretting it.

Luisa knew they needed to move fast before Iris lost her nerve. Selfishly, she wanted to go to the party so she could meet Jerry, but at the same time she could tell how besotted Iris was. Grabbing Iris's hand, she ran to the car park at the back of the building and they jumped into Iris's jeep. Not even bothering to ask for the address as she knew it off by heart, Luisa drove them to the party, gasping as they pulled up outside the stunning glass structure of the Beverly Hills apartment.

Wading through the sea of people, they saw that the apartment was a playboy's dream pad. Black and chrome furniture, dim, moody lighting and a cinema room stacked full of blue movies.

There were pinball machines and video games in each room, three bars and a whole library of *Playboy* manuals in the bathroom.

'Look at the pool!' Luisa cried, pointing at it. 'And what the hell is *that*?' Iris followed her gaze to a vast ice sculpture of a breast. Cheering and whooping, the men were taking turns to suck vodka out of the nipple and Luisa's eyes nearly popped out of her head when she realised the women were doing the same with a gigantic frozen penis.

'There're about five gorgeous women to every man in here,' Iris gulped, taking in the plethora of attractive women. They were draped over every lounger by the pool – redheads, blondes, brunettes; there were several of each, in various stages of undress. Five of them were topless and giggling as they splashed around in the shallow end of the pool, their big wet breasts jiggling. One man tore off his shorts and dive-bombed into the pool and the girls shrieked with laughter and fell on him, much to his delight.

'Cocaine, anyone?' Luisa inquired, gesturing to a mountain of white powder someone had set up on one of the tables. There were silver straws lined up next to it and one girl, who had clearly already indulged, was using one of the straws as a pretend flute, blowing down it crazily.

Iris felt mildly intimidated by her rock and roll surroundings but she carried on looking around for Ace. She couldn't find him anywhere and she began to wonder if she might find him in bed with someone, tired of waiting for her. He said he would always be waiting for her but had he meant it? Was Ace one of those men who just said romantic things and then did whatever the hell he liked? He had a terrible reputation with women, after all. Iris strengthened her resolve; until she found evidence to the contrary, she would take him at face value.

'There's Jerry!' Luisa shouted, making Jerry jump out of his skin. Giving her a broad grin, he beckoned her over, patting his lap. Overjoyed, Luisa skipped over and wriggled on to Jerry's lap like a child. Her arms looped around his neck; she giggled and motioned for Iris to find Ace.

Iris headed back indoors and her heart leapt when she found him alone, ensconced at a glossy-looking bar in his lounge, which had mirrored walls, bar stools that looked like pieces of modern architecture and black leather sofas. His jacket was flung over one of the funky bar stools, his white shirt undone at the neck. He was downing tequila shots morosely. He didn't even notice she was there at first but catching sight of her in the mirror behind the bar, he immediately spun round. Saying nothing, he took her hand and pulled her closer. Burying his mouth in her palm, he kissed it, his tongue circling the skin languorously.

Iris let out a small moan. She didn't know if she was ready for this; she felt overwhelmed by her feelings. She knew she wanted Ace and she wasn't about to back out now but she felt so giddy and out of control. Iris allowed him to lead her up a flight of floating metal stairs to the second floor, wobbling on her Chloe heels as she realised how nervous she was.

Pausing outside his bedroom, Ace abruptly turned the other way and led her to one of the spare rooms. His bed had far too many notches on it; he didn't want to be disturbed by the ghosts of bimbos past when he was with Iris.

Inside the spare bedroom, Ace locked the door. 'Just a precaution. When Jez and I have parties . . . these rooms can get a bit crowded. We don't want an orgy bursting in and joining us.'

Iris ran a shaky hand over the slithery aubergine bedspread. 'Silk sheets . . . they must be hell to clean.'

Ace shrugged. 'I wouldn't know. I'm a spoilt little playboy, as you know. Jerry deals with all that stuff.' He raised an eyebrow. 'Wow, come to think of it, Jerry's very domesticated. I'll never need a wife while he's around.'

Iris wandered over to the window, her heart beating progressively faster. She watched people dive-bombing into the swimming pool naked, muted shouts of laughter accompanying the pounding music. Luisa, using a palm tree as a makeshift lap-dancer's pole, was showing Jerry some impressive dance moves and he was clapping wildly and tossing fifty dollar bills at her.

Seeing Ace's reflection in the glass as he moved towards her, Iris stared back at him wordlessly, closing her eyes as he slid his arms around her waist. 'Use Somebody' by the Kings of Leon was playing on the stereo downstairs, a song Iris had always thought was incredibly sexy. Turning round, she leant against him and they swayed, almost dancing. Taking her face in his hands, he sank his tongue into her mouth, their hot breath mingling.

It was such a deliciously sensual prelude to what was about to happen, Ace felt a jolt of desire shoot through him. Gently leading Iris to the bed, she unbuttoned his pristine shirt with trembling fingers and shrugged it off his broad, bronzed shoulders. His chest was smooth and he smelt of aftershave, smoke and tequila. Iris buried her face in his neck, breathing him in.

'You're so smooth . . . do you shave your chest?' She giggled, not sure why she felt the need to break the moment.

He shook his head, grinning. 'Not me. I'm lucky. Jerry's like a baby gorilla but don't tell him I told you that.' Pushing her down on to the bed, he knelt at her feet and gently removed her Chloe sandals. Instead of the suave gesture he was hoping it would be, the sandals had fiddly buckles the size of dimes and, laughing, he finally undid them, throwing them across the room.

'They're C-Chloe,' she said in a shocked voice. Embarrassed that her stutter had emerged at such a moment, she blushed. As he massaged the arch of her aching feet, Iris felt absurdly turned on by the erotic gesture and she let her head fall back, her hair touching the base of her spine. Moving his hands up her calves, Ace kissed them where his hands had been, turning them and moving his head to leave hot imprints on the back of her knees. Quivering, Iris felt Ace progress to her thighs, his fingertips edging the silk kimono away to find the soft, smooth flesh beneath. Kissing her skin, he moved upwards, planting languid kisses on her inner thighs. Feeling his tongue probing at her skin, Iris opened her thighs. Peeling back the second layer of her dress, Ace let out a sexy growl as Iris arched her back and he briefly buried his face against her, inhaling her scent.

Iris tore off the kimono to allow him better access and, lying back on the bed, she bit her bruised bottom lip, reeling with lust as he peeled back the satin sheath that covered her body. Slowly revealing her small, perfectly formed breasts, followed by her flat stomach and, finally, a tiny cream thong, Ace removed the sheath completely and dropped it to the floor.

'Mr Brightside' by the Killers could be heard outside and Ace glanced towards the window, wondering if Jerry was playing cupid with all his favourite songs. Ace sucked Iris's bottom lip, his fingers trailing down her naked skin. Iris bucked, thinking it was the sexiest thing she had ever experienced, until seconds later when she felt as if her insides were about to explode. Lowering his mouth to her pink nipple, Ace licked it, coaxing it to a wet point with his tongue. He moved to the other, giving it his undivided attention as Iris reached down and dipped her hands into his trousers. Ace tore his trousers and boxer shorts off, revealing an all-over, golden tan and a huge erection.

Iris hid a giggle as she remembered '*burros*', Luisa's pet name for well-hung men which meant donkeys. Unable to control himself any longer, Ace pushed her thong to one side and sank himself into her. Iris gasped and within seconds, they were bucking against each other and rolling across the sheets, their bodies locked together as their hips moved in perfect rhythm. Gathering speed, everything became hazy as they thrashed around across the silk sheets, changing positions before coming sharply, almost in unison. They slumped down on to the bed, shattered and dripping with sweat. They looked at each other and burst out laughing.

'Wow.' Ace pushed his hair out of his eyes.

Iris buried her head in his shoulder. It had been amazing but all of a sudden she felt embarrassed at being so wanton.

‘Sorry.’ Ace kissed her with infinite tenderness.

‘What for?’

‘Leaping on you like that.’ He gave her a lazy smile. ‘In my mind, I was going to take it slowly, build up to it, you know?’ He ran a finger down her thigh. ‘But something took over my mind and I couldn’t seem to control myself. I can’t imagine what that was.’

‘Well, I was just as bad.’ Iris ran her fingers down his side, enjoying seeing him wriggling. ‘Ticklish?’

‘Very.’ Ace gave her a stern look. ‘But don’t even try it, I’m an expert tickler. I could have you begging for mercy.’

Iris sighed blissfully and put her arms above her head. ‘So, how come you’re called Ace? I can’t imagine anyone calling their baby that, not unless they knew you were going to become a glamorous racing driver. I don’t know many bin men called Ace, at any rate.’

He laughed, leaning on one elbow. ‘My name’s actually Alistair but my little brother, Elliot, couldn’t say my name properly when he was a kid. He managed “Ace-ter” and everyone thought it was cute so over time it got shortened to Ace. I suppose I should be grateful; if he’d only managed the end bit, I might have ended up as “turd” or something.’ He traced a finger down Iris’s small nose and rubbed his thumb across her lips. ‘What about you? What’s the story with the stutter?’

She turned away. ‘I-I hoped you hadn’t noticed that. God, there I go again.’

‘Hey, it’s adorable.’ Ace meant it. It was an imperfection he found endearing in her; it was a charming blemish that stopped her from being boringly perfect.

Iris stroked his neck. ‘I don’t know when it started . . . it was when I was a kid and I started to get this nervous thing where I would mix my words up. Then I developed this horrendous stutter in the classroom which became something everyone noticed.’

Ace glanced at her. ‘Did you get bullied because of it?’

She shrugged, not wanting to make a big thing of it. ‘Children can be very cruel, as they say. I was all right, I got through it. Other kids had a far worse time than me.'

'I would have stuck up for you if I'd been there,' Ace said fiercely, wondering why he felt the need to protect Iris when she was clearly capable of taking care of herself.

She grinned and stroked his dark hair out of his eyes. 'My hero. Don't worry, my older brother Shay went to the same school and he was always beating people up on my behalf.'

'I like him already. My brother Sebastian wouldn't stick up for me if he was paid to.' He grimaced. 'Have you met him? No? Lucky you. Elliot's an angel but Sebastian's like my father in duplicate, except he's a complete loser as well.' Ace reached for a cigarette. 'What does your brother Shay do?'

'He wants to work for my father at Shamrock but they've had this huge fight.' A shadow crossed her face. 'Last time I spoke to him, he'd lost his job but he wouldn't really say much about it.' She frowned. Shay had been so evasive on the phone; she was sure there was something going on but, uncharacteristically, he didn't want to share it with her.

Remembering what his father had said about Iris signing a deal with Jett, Ace forced himself to bring it up, loathing both himself and his father in equal measure. 'I guess you must have a record deal with Shamrock, then.'

Iris shook her head. 'No, but my father has promised he'll sign me when I get home. He's very over-protective, he hasn't signed me up because he worries about me being taken advantage of.'

Ace swallowed. Wasn't that exactly what he was doing, taking advantage of her? He didn't want to think that, because that's not what it felt like. He glanced down at her beautiful naked body. If he could forget what his father had asked him to do, Ace thought he might be the happiest he'd ever been in his life. Hating himself, he got the question out of the way. 'You could always sign with Jett, you know, my father's record label.' He cringed inwardly but somehow he felt that if he could say the words, his job was done and his debt to his father was paid. He had only said he would 'try' to get her to sign a contract with Jett, not that he would be able to pull it off. 'I mean, if you're worried your father won't sign you.'

Iris shook her head vigorously. 'Never. I would never sign a deal with Jett. That would kill my father. Seriously, I don't think he'd ever be able to forgive me, Ace. Coming out to Los Angeles, letting your father pay for my singing lessons with Pia – that's as far as I'm going to take it. Anything more, well, I don't know what it would do to him.'

Ace looked down at her, his grey eyes full of longing. 'Apart from being with me.'

'Don't . . . don't spoil it.' Iris shut her eyes, pushing the guilt away with difficulty. She didn't want to think about the terrible act of disloyalty she'd committed. Not when it had been so incredible. 'Make me feel like that again,' she whispered, reaching out for him.

Ace didn't need telling twice. Rolling over, he circled her narrow waist with his hands and pulled her closer. He kissed her, winding his hands around her tawny hair possessively.

Outside, Allegra caught her breath as she jumped back into her car. Planting the bug behind the bar had been easy and she was sure no one had spotted her. Well, apart from a crazy girl with a tattoo of Marilyn Monroe on her breast and a coke moustache but Allegra wasn't worried about her. Picking up her binoculars, she trained them on the upper window of Ace's apartment, wondering why he wasn't in his own room.

Still, what did that matter? Allegra lowered the binoculars with shaky hands. How could he? In all the time they'd been together on and off, Ace had never been as passionate or as tender towards her when they'd been in bed. What was so fucking special about Iris Maguire, anyway? She wasn't even that pretty. And she had tiny tits, Allegra thought, jealously.

Tossing the binoculars aside, she shot away in her car.

A few metres away, Judd watched her driving off, perplexed. It seemed he wasn't the only one interested in Ace's liaison with Iris, but he suspected this woman had very different reasons for being so obsessed with Ace's whereabouts. Judd shot his cuffs, feeling deeply smug. So Ace *was* a chip off the old block, after all. He had done exactly what he had been asked to do and, judging by the amount of time he and Iris had spent in the bedroom, Ace had gone above and beyond the call of duty to ensure that Iris was totally and utterly hooked.

Wondering if he should go back and give Pia another sexual punishment she wouldn't forget in a hurry, Judd drove off feeling powerfully turned on.

Hours later, Ace woke up. Groggily, he reached out but the pillow where Iris's head had lain was empty. There was a small dent in it and burying his face in it, Ace inhaled her fresh, sensual smell. He turned over and stared up at the ceiling. What was happening to him? The pillow smelt of Iris and his body was throbbing all over and all he wanted to do was get her back and . . . he stumbled over the unfamiliar phrase . . . make love to her all over again.

Ace sat up. He wanted to say 'fuck' or 'screw' because it would make it easier to distance himself from what had happened, but he knew he couldn't. It had been passionate and it had been dirty but balanced with the tender caresses, the slow, erotic kisses and the murmured laughter, Ace couldn't possibly degrade it. It had been delicious and right and he had felt as if he could live in the moment for ever. Afterwards, he had wrapped himself around her, feeling her naked skin against his and as he had drifted off to sleep, he knew he had a bloody great smile on his face.

Had she left without saying goodbye? Ace wondered. Pulling on his boxer shorts, he padded downstairs, pulling a face at the debris everywhere. There were empty glasses stained with lipstick and overflowing ashtrays on every surface. Random pieces of clothing littered the floors – sopping wet bikini tops, crumpled shorts, jeans with the belts still attached, the odd flip-flop.

Hearing the sound of someone playing the piano, Ace made for the sun room. So-called because it allowed brilliant, morning sunshine to filter through into it, it also housed a stunning Steinway piano that had come with the apartment. Ace couldn't play it and neither could Jerry but they both thought it gave the place class so they left it there. Ace paused by the doorway, leaning against the frame. Iris, wearing a crumpled blue shirt of his, her tawny hair falling over her shoulders, was playing something, her expressive fingers stroking the keys melodiously.

Seeing him, she smiled, playing softly. 'What a beautiful piano.'

Ace watched as the morning sunshine threw a pool of light on to her, lightening her hair and softening her face with a golden glow. 'What are you playing?'

' "Rhapsody in Blue",' she answered. 'Gershwin. It doesn't sound right without the orchestra but it's such a gorgeous piece of music, the piano part still sounds heavenly.'

'Where did you find the music?' he asked, strolling over. Gazing at her, he was confused when he felt his heart swell with emotion. She looked as sexy as hell sitting there in his shirt, her blond hair dappled with light and her tanned, bare feet barely touching the floor, but something about the way her vulnerable mouth was quivering slightly touched his soul.

'It was in the piano stool, didn't you know? This piano has the most unique sound. It's perfectly tuned but it has such a rich tone.' She started playing her mother's song 'Obsession', her fingers rippling over the piano keys.

'Hey, I love this song,' Ace said.

She nodded. 'Me too. I've always had this stupidly romantic thought that if a man ever sang this to me, I'd know he was "the one".' She played the chorus and hummed along. 'And there's something incredible about a guy who's willing to do something silly like that in front of everyone.'

'Won't be me, I'm afraid,' Ace responded lightly. 'I can't sing for toffee.'

Iris's eyes dropped to her fingers and she tried to ignore the sense of crushing disappointment she felt, telling herself she was being ridiculous. She and Ace had only just met, they were hardly soul mates.

He watched her. The blue shirt she wore was unbuttoned and he caught glimpses of her honey-hued breasts as she played. The shirt stopped several inches above the knee, affording him tantalising shots of her slender thighs and Ace was so turned on, he could barely think straight.

Meeting his eyes, Iris's fingers faltered over the piano keys.

'Don't stop,' he whispered, coming round to stand behind her. Putting his hands on her shoulders, he dipped his hands into the shirt and cupped her breasts. Leaning against him, Iris managed a few more notes before her fingers lost coordination and she hit several bum notes. As his fingers squeezed her nipples, her concentration went out of the window and she let her head fall back. Feeling him lifting her up, Iris let out a squeal of protest.

'Not on the Steinway,' she castigated him.

'I'll buy you another one,' he growled as he opened the shirt to feast his eyes on her gorgeous body. She wrapped her long legs around him and drew him closer and as the piano keys gently plinked beneath them, they totally lost track of time. And even though it cost Ace a new Steinway, he couldn't have cared less.

Kitty gulped as Susannah Valentine swiftly barked orders at her hair stylist. She had been in two minds about coming to Susannah's girly night but with Judd still in LA, Kitty felt like throwing caution to the wind so she'd slipped out of Brockett Hall and over to the Valentines' Gothic mansion before she had a chance to change her mind.

'I'm thinking something with layers,' Susannah was saying thoughtfully. 'Kitty needs an easy to manage style which has tons of "wow" factor.'

Elise, Susannah's personal hair stylist, ran expert fingers through

Kitty's blond bobbed hair. 'I agree. And a colour change – lighter, with some golden streaks.' She started mixing colours.

'I can't thank you enough for doing this,' Kitty told Susannah gratefully, eyeing up her friend's outfit: grey skinny jeans, worn with a black T-shirt with a diamanté skull. Kitty wished she could get away with such a trendy outfit but knew she couldn't. 'This is just what I needed.'

Susannah examined her dark eyebrows in the mirror. 'What, a weekend in a madhouse?'

Kitty smiled. It wasn't exactly a madhouse at Susannah and Charlie's Gothic mansion but it was definitely an experience. Cats and dogs ran around freely and she'd even had to navigate the odd pile of dog poo. There was a parrot and a cockatoo in the kitchen and there seemed to be music blaring out from various different rooms; in short, it was loud, slightly eccentric, but strangely welcoming.

Charlie was ensconced in what Susannah called his 'playroom', which was basically a boy's pad complete with an enormous flat-screen TV, a group of black leather chairs with games consoles built into them and several pinball machines. Rock music pounded out of the room, almost drowning out the tasteful Michael Bublé CD Susannah had put on.

'This place looks amazing,' Kitty commented, glancing around Susannah's lavish ballroom. Hundreds of vast Jo Malone candles had been dotted around the room, giving it a cosy feel, and several stations had been set up along one side of the room. As well as the hairdressing area, there were five nail tables with waiting manicurists dressed in black kimono-style uniforms, a sectioned-off massage area, a team of facial specialists and several representatives from Susannah's make-up line Valentine, who had set up a counter big enough to take over Selfridges in the corner.

'God, look at Mrs Meaden,' Susannah whispered, watching as a poor beauty assistant wrestled heroically with the old lady's corns. 'Now, while your hair is covered in these silver things, I'm going to do your make-up for you.' She blended foundation on the back of her hand with a brush, glad she had asked Kitty over. Her face was pale, in spite of the glowing candlelight, and Susannah knew her new friend must be suffering after Savannah's arrival. Applying some foundation gently, she asked Kitty, with equal care, how she was holding up.

'Actually, I'm feeling pretty good,' Kitty answered, surprised to find she meant it. Glancing up, she caught sight of a line of half-naked men who were beginning to circulate with a selection of mouth-watering canapés and cupcakes. She accepted a glass of pink champagne from a strapping waiter, colouring with embarrassment.

'Good for you,' Susannah said, grabbing the new miracle under-the-eye concealer the brand had been developing and applying a thin layer. 'I can't imagine how you're still smiling after what you've been through.' Frankly, she didn't know how Kitty found the strength to deal with Judd and his shocking antics. Susannah wouldn't have a clue how to react if Charlie brought an illegitimate child home and gave them the spare bedroom. Putting up with affairs was one thing but Susannah wasn't sure she would be able to stomach an insult like that.

Kitty allowed Susannah to make her eyes up in smoky plums and pinks. 'My marriage to Judd has been difficult for a long time.' She paused. 'I think I knew I didn't love him any more, not the way I used to. It's just . . . divorce isn't the done thing in my family. But this is different.'

'Why?' Susannah picked up some blusher and frowned at Kitty.

'It was Judd's attitude, you see,' Kitty explained. 'The way he just expected me to accept Savannah without a word of complaint. It just shows how little he thinks of me.'

'Bastard,' Susannah agreed vehemently.

Kitty didn't want to talk about Judd any more. 'Who's that?' she asked, pointing out a glamorous woman in a long, lemon-yellow dress and gladiator-style sandals. She had the most glorious mane of tawny-blond hair and she looked vaguely familiar to Kitty but she couldn't place her.

Susannah bit her lip. She hadn't been sure if getting Kitty and Tavvy in the same room was a good idea but she figured they couldn't avoid each other for ever. Besides, Kitty was incredibly sweet and Tavvy was hardly the kind to make a scene.

'That's . . . Tavvy Maguire,' she said eventually, beckoning Tavvy over.

Not meaning to be rude, Kitty found herself staring hard. 'It's . . . it's you,' she marvelled, flustered. 'I wondered if you actually existed.'

Tavvy gave her a polite but uncomprehending smile. 'I'm afraid I don't . . .' Hearing Kitty's American accent, she felt a strand of anxiety weaving its way across her chest. Was this Judd's wife?

'You're the woman from Judd's photograph,' Kitty said, astonished to see the living embodiment in front of her eyes. She had imagined the photograph had been of someone Judd had been seeing in the States, she had had no idea it was someone in England. A horrible germ of an idea crept into her head and joined up with one she'd forgotten and all of a sudden Kitty began to feel rather sick.

Seeing there were things for them to discuss, Susannah tactfully left them to it.

Tavvy's normally creamy complexion had turned ghostly white. 'You're Judd's wife,' she stated. She wanted to apologise but she wasn't sure what for; to Kitty for being married to Judd or for her past with him?

Kitty drained her glass of pink champagne in one gulp. Tavvy Maguire was the girl . . . the *woman*, in the photograph. Judd never kept photographs and he certainly didn't carry them around with him to the point where they became crumpled and dog-eared – except for the one of Tavvy, and that spoke volumes. Lochlin Maguire . . . Tavvy Maguire . . . the feud between the two families

. . . these were the reasons Judd had uprooted them all to move back to England, Kitty was sure of it. Staring at Tavvy, Kitty wondered why it didn't hurt now that she was faced with the one woman Judd seemed capable of loving.

Sensing Tavvy's discomfort, Kitty tried to put her at ease. 'Hey, there's no need for us not to be friends, is there? Judd has this photograph of you . . . from a long time ago, I guess. I don't know what went on in the past, but I'm sure there must be history between you and Judd, and our families.'

Tavvy nodded, feeling desperately sorry for Kitty. She was just another innocent pawn in one of Judd's ridiculous games; she didn't deserve this. 'I'll tell you about it . . . one day. But for now, maybe we should just get to know one another. I mean, if you'd like to. Lochlin, my husband, is keen for our families to steer clear of each other but it's not your fault you're caught up in all of this.'

Kitty nodded; she wanted to befriend Tavvy. Tavvy took a seat next to her and once the awkwardness was out of the way, they found themselves chatting like old friends.

Kitty told Tavvy how isolated she felt after leaving her friends behind. 'I really want to find myself a hobby, but I haven't a clue what goes on around here.'

Tavvy pulled a face. 'Not much, not unless you fancy playing poker with Mrs Meaden or going on rambles with the older men in the village.' She sighed. 'I'm afraid Meadowbank isn't exactly buzzing with excitement and intrigue.' The last time it had been was when Judd was last here, Tavvy thought with a stab of bitterness, before pushing the thought aside. 'I have this charity, Noah's Ark. I started it years ago, with some money from one of the songs I wrote. Animals have always been a passion of mine.'

'Oh, me too! I always wanted a dog when we lived in LA but Judd wouldn't hear of it.' Kitty looked wistful. 'That's one thing I love about living in England, all the animals – the cows in the fields and the fact that everyone has cats and dogs.' She smiled. 'Still, I can't imagine Judd welcoming a dog into Brockett Hall.

Just imagine, it'd be peeing up his Georgian furniture and paddling in the swimming pool – disastrous.'

At the mention of the pool, Tavvy started. She recovered herself. 'Noah's Ark has become quite unmanageable recently. We've taken in so many horses we need to build another set of stables but it's extra hands we need. As it's a charity, we don't pay anyone for the work they do but few people are interested in volunteer work.'

Before she could stop herself, Kitty had offered her services. 'I don't mind working for free.' She saw Tavvy's expression. 'Oh, I guess the idea of a Harrington working with you is probably unthinkable.' She shook her head. 'Don't worry, I understand. Judd's warned all of us away from your family too. I shouldn't have said anything.'

Tavvy drank some champagne, her mind turning over the idea rapidly. It was perfect in so many ways. Kitty had time on her hands and she was willing to help out for nothing. It would give her something to do, something to feel passionate about, and it would allow Tavvy the time to develop the plans for the barn overhaul. But what about Lochlin? He would go absolutely nuts if he knew Kitty Harrington was working at the house. But . . . did he need to know?

Tavvy nibbled her fingernails guiltily. She seemed to be hiding more and more from Lochlin as the weeks passed – her song-writing, Caitie appearing in the play with Elliot, and now she was thinking of hiring Judd's wife to help out with her charity! She and Lochlin were meandering apart like two bits of floating driftwood. They used to share everything; it felt alien not to talk openly about things. Sadly, Tavvy acknowledged that Lochlin just didn't seem to trust her any more.

'Why don't you come over and have a look at what we're doing?' she suggested. 'Then you can see if you'd like to be involved.' Tavvy felt terribly disloyal to Lochlin but she figured she'd worry about it if Kitty took the offer up. Used to the LA sunshine, Kitty probably found the idea of stomping around in horse manure in torrential rain incredibly romantic but the reality would most likely see her fleeing back to Brockett Hall to warm up by the fire.

'That sounds absolutely wonderful,' Kitty replied immediately, flushing with pleasure. She chinked her glass against Tavvy's, suddenly feeling free. Wow, I really must have fallen out of love with Judd, she realised, feeling the hurt seeping away. When she had least expected it, life had suddenly taken a turn for the better.

As Kitty had gone out for the evening and Martha had mentioned going into a local town for a special shopping event, Savannah was expecting a quiet evening in, watching reruns of *Sex in the City* in her bedroom. Especially since Sebastian had hit the drinks cabinet like a seasoned pro after dinner, shutting himself in his and Martha's bedroom with a bottle of Judd's exceptionally expensive malt.

Carrying a glass of wine and a packet of Doritos upstairs, Savannah shot a portrait of Judd a mutinous glare on the way.

As she settled down to series two of *Sex in the City*, she was taken aback to hear sounds of a very carnal nature coming from Martha and Sebastian's bedroom across the landing. Abandoning the TV (not even Carrie and Big could distract her from the thought of Sebastian at it), Savannah headed downstairs with a shudder. Wondering how Martha could bear the arrogant bastard pawing at her, she reminded herself that Martha would probably do anything to have a baby and made a mental note to herself to avoid ending up with a man with a God complex.

Making for the kitchen, Savannah was confused when Martha burst through the front door.

'But you're . . .' Savannah stared at her dumbly, wondering how Martha could be upstairs and downstairs at the same time. As the realisation that Sebastian was in bed with someone other than his wife dawned on her, Savannah also noticed that Martha was in a dreadful state. Her cheeks streaming with tears, her eyes red from crying, she dashed into the toilet. About to go after her, Savannah heard a hesitant foot on the stairs. Looking up, she saw a girl with big boobs and shining brown hair coming down them. Wearing a PVC mac with spike heels, it was obvious she was naked beneath it.

'Who the fuck are you?' Savannah demanded in a low voice, thankful Martha hadn't witnessed this *whore* guiltily tiptoeing down the stairs. 'However much he paid for you, it was *way* too much.'

The girl flushed. 'How bloody rude! He didn't pay for me, I'm his girlfriend.'

Savannah's lip curled, stunned that Sebastian had risked shagging his mistress in his own bed. 'His girlfriend? Really? He hasn't mentioned you.'

'My name is Lexi Beaument,' Lexi said primly, feeling affronted. She had been sleeping with Sebastian for months now; how dare this girl speak to her like this?

'Get out, Lexi Beaument,' Savannah hissed, shoving her towards the door. 'You should be ashamed of yourself. He has a wife, you know.'

Lexi almost tripped over in her high heels. She was about to say something but her comment was cut short by Savannah slamming the door in her face.

The *shit*, Savannah steamed, wishing she'd whipped the PVC mac off Lexi and sent her out in her underwear. Hearing Martha crying her heart out in the downstairs bathroom, Savannah put her fury aside and went to comfort her.

'Leave me alone,' Martha shrieked hysterically as Savannah tapped on the door.

'Let me in,' Savannah coaxed, knowing Martha needed someone to talk to. Seeing the door open a crack, she went in. She found Martha sitting on the toilet seat with her head in her hands, piles of shredded toilet paper on the floor in front of her. Savannah knelt down and lifted Martha's chin. 'What's happened?'

'I got my . . . my . . .' Martha was so distressed she couldn't even string a sentence together.

Seeing a packet of open Tampax by the sink, Savannah sighed. 'You thought you were pregnant,' she realised with a flood of compassion.

Martha nodded, snorting into her tissues. 'I thought it was finally happening . . . I was late and I did a test . . . it was positive, Sav! I even told Sebastian I thought I was pregnant the other day. But I was out and I went to the loo and there it was. And I'm going to have to tell Sebastian but he has golf tomorrow morning with all his work friends and he'd go crazy if he saw how upset I was.' Her eyes were red from crying and she had mascara all over her face. 'I j-just want a baby. Is that too much to ask?' She burst into tears again, overcome with grief.

Tenderly, Savannah cleaned up her face with dampened tissues. She wasn't sure where this motherly instinct had come from but there was something about Martha that hit a nerve in her. Maybe she reminded her of her mother; like Candi, Martha was weak and vulnerable but instead of feeling impatient and contemptuous, the way she had with her mother, Savannah felt compelled to nurture Martha. And the thought of Sebastian shagging around and Lexi creeping out in her hooker get-up was making Savannah feel even more protective.

Gratefully, Martha allowed Savannah to clean her up like a child. 'I-I thought you were a right bitch when you arrived but you're not at all.' She gulped, giving Savannah a watery smile.

'Don't tell anyone.' Savannah winked. 'I prefer it if people think I'm evil. Self-preservation,' she added by way of explanation, standing up.

'How can I tell Sebastian?' Martha whimpered. 'He already thinks I'm a failure.'

Savannah's mouth tightened. 'Don't bother tonight. In fact, I'd sleep in the spare room, if I were you. He's been at the malt.'

Martha nodded. 'All right. Th-thanks. You're such a good friend to me.'

Savannah brushed off the compliment, unused to praise. 'Forget it. And don't worry about Sebastian. I'm sure he'll be nicer to you in the future.' Especially if he knows someone knows what he's up to, she thought, an idea coming to her. 'He's playing golf tomorrow, you say?' she asked Martha casually. 'First thing? Great, that means we can have a proper chat in the morning and work out how to tell him about all this. Listen, you clean up and I'll make us some coffee. Back in a minute.' Slipping out, Savannah grabbed something from Judd's office and ran up the stairs two at a time.

Opening the door to Sebastian and Martha's bedroom, she found Sebastian spread-eagled face down on the bed and the bottle of malt empty on the bedside table. As she'd hoped, he had passed out from all the booze and sex. Standing over his naked white body with distaste, Savannah was so revolted, she had half a mind to do something more drastic. Remembering Martha was married to the disloyal bastard and wanted a baby with him, she took out the pen she'd swiped from Judd's office and leant over Sebastian's exposed neck.

Running back downstairs, she put some coffee on just as Martha emerged from the bathroom. 'Feeling better?' she asked brightly.

Martha nodded. 'Do you really think Sebastian will be nicer to me when he finds out?'

'I think he'll be more understanding about a lot of things,' Savannah murmured, taking out some coffee mugs. Or at the very least, when one of his colleagues snickered and pointed out that the c-word had been deeply scored into his neck in marker pen, Sebastian would know someone was on to him – and that it was her. And unless he wanted his affair with Lexi made public, he'd better start treating Martha with a bit of respect, Savannah thought grimly, handing Martha a mug of coffee. It was about time someone looked out for the Marthas of this world and showed the bullies they weren't invincible – and that included her father Judd.

But it was going to take a lot more than marker pen to pull the rug out from under *him*, Savannah thought gravely.

* * *

Shay glanced around Bluebell Cottage approvingly. At least it looked clean and tidy, he decided. It had taken longer than he'd thought it would and he'd already blown up one vacuum cleaner with all the dust. The cottage hadn't been occupied for about twenty years or more, not since Uncle Seamus had been around, but Tavvy usually made a monthly visit to give it a quick clean. However, since Noah's Ark had become a full-time role, the visits had dwindled and the cottage had an air of neglect about it.

Shay wasn't particularly into home furnishings nor had he ever given shades much thought, but his mother had dropped off some cushions and curtains. Spending most of his time in the kitchen, this room looked the most lived in; his Gordon Ramsay and Jamie Oliver cookbooks were stacked on a tiny corner shelf and his Global knives were carefully stashed in a drawer. Apart from a few saucepans, Shay figured that was all he needed.

Well, that and a new job, he thought, setting his laptop up in the tiny dining room he had allocated as a home office. Using the small oak table for a desk, he had his laptop, his mobile phone, a printer and his iPod and docking station. Everything he needed to get going. The only question was, what should he do?

Lighting a cigarette, Shay stared out of the window and thought about his work experience. He had worked in several record companies on and off, as well as working at *Music Mode* magazine for nearly two years. His official role had been to arrange and conduct interviews with bands and write them up but, unofficially, he took time out of his personal schedule to scout around local clubs in London and across the country to discover new talent. If he did, he would interview them and write an article about them to give them a promotional boost.

On top of that, he would meticulously follow the careers of bands he admired and he had always shown an interest in everything Shamrock were involved in, down to the marketing, the promotion and the sales. His father might not think he'd paid attention when he'd been discussing gross profit, budgets and projected sales in the evenings but Shay had hung on every word over the years, building an encyclopaedic knowledge of the music business and of record labels in particular.

I should be a consultant, Shay realised. Just like Darcy Middleton, he thought coldly as he called up his CV. Darcy might be older than him but his knowledge of music and the industry itself was superb and there was something vaguely satisfying about pitching himself against Darcy professionally. Shay hardly thought they'd be up against each other for jobs as Darcy was firmly bedded down at Jett, but he liked the idea of them being in the same arena.

Shay was doing his best not to think about Darcy but every so often, when he was least expecting it, her creamy skin and clear hazel eyes would pop into his head. Most of the time he could push the image of her away but sometimes he drifted off and thought about the night they had spent together. It had been raw and passionate and Shay knew Darcy was unlike any woman he'd ever met before. And having met several women since, he also knew deep down that he was never going to meet anyone like her again.

Forcing himself to focus, Shay worked on his CV for a few hours. Putting modesty to one side, he made the most of his achievements and posted them at the top as eye-catching bullet points.

Before he had a chance to change his mind, Shay confidently fired off a punchy email with his CV attached to a number of directors at various record companies. He wandered off to make a cup of black coffee and by the time he came back, despite the late hour, he already had two emails back, asking him to come in for a chat.

Shay broke into a smile. And Judd and Darcy thought they'd destroyed him, he thought jubilantly. On the contrary, he was just getting started.

Chapter Thirteen

Stretched out on stripy cushions in the summer house with Elliot, Caitie was feeling blissfully happy. Since Shay had moved out, she'd bagged the summer house as her own little hideaway to meet up with Elliot for their *Romeo and Juliet* rehearsals. The just-blooming rambling roses outside were filling the air with fragrance and, inside, the summer house looked magical with jewel-like shades of light bouncing off the walls from the gold, amethyst and lapis lazuli tea glasses.

Jas had joined them to help out as prompt but she was currently leafing through a pile of dusty old photographs of Lochlin and Tavvy, her sheet of shiny brown hair splayed out on one of the colourful pillows.

'So how do you think I should play the scene with the nurse?' Caitie asked, deep in thought. Wearing a pair of boyfriend jeans and a long purple T-shirt, she was flipping through the pages of the play with short purple fingernails. 'You're playing her, Jas, what do you think?'

Jas burst out laughing. 'Sorry, I just found this photo of your dad – he's practically got a mullet!'

Elliot took it from her and smiled at the sight of Lochlin with big hair and an even bigger grin as he hugged Tavvy. From what he'd seen, Lochlin was fairly stern looking these days so it was nice to see him looking more relaxed. Elliot sifted through the photographs, thinking how happy Lochlin and Tavvy appeared together. His parents had never looked this blissful, in person or on celluloid.

'Christ, what *do* they look like?' Caitie said, mortified as she pulled out another photograph. 'Mind you, that dress has come back into fashion now,' she added, pointing at the zips and shoulder pads. 'In fact, I'm sure my mum wore that the other day.'

'She's awesome,' Elliot commented, thinking Caitie looked cute with her dark curls in two plaits.

'Isn't she?' Jas agreed. 'I love my mum to pieces but she's more of your headscarf and Barbour type. She couldn't wear a dress like that in a million years.'

'Neither could mine. I don't think she wore anything like this in the eighties,' Elliot said with a grin.

Their eyes met in understanding.

'I bet your mums can cook,' Caitie said, feeling the need to join in. 'Mine might be glamorous but she can't even work the Aga. Since Shay moved out, I've been living on toast and pot noodles.'

'You could always learn,' Elliot suggested mildly. 'Acting and cooking aren't mutually exclusive, you know. Johnny Depp probably cooks up a mean coq au vin.'

Smiling at Elliot, Caitie knew she was head over heels in love. Elliot clearly didn't know how gorgeous he was but with his floppy blond hair and perfect profile, he had the enigmatic appeal of James Dean or some equally cool film star. I'm so lucky, Caitie thought to herself, barely able to believe they were boyfriend and girlfriend.

Since their kiss, Caitie had thought of nothing else, often drifting off into a dreamy daze as she relived the moment. It had been gloriously sweet and tender, exactly as she had hoped it would be, and in any other scenario, she would have been desperate for another. Being somewhat of a method actor, Caitie was now fully entrenched in the role of Juliet and her heart swelled with the romance of their forbidden love. As she leant over to give him a kiss, Jas turned away and rummaged through the photographs, feeling like a spare part.

'Sorry, Jas, you can look back now!' Caitie apologised. She jumped as Jas sat up suddenly. 'Christ, are you all right?'

Jas nodded. 'How many years did you say it was since your father was last in England, Elliot?'

Elliot shrugged. 'I can't really remember. Well, let's see . . . he was here with my mother when Ace was born but only briefly. So, before that, maybe twenty-five years, something like that?' He looked at her curiously. 'Why do you ask?'

'I think I might just have found something,' Jas whispered in an awed voice. She held up a photograph of a man who looked an awful lot like Lochlin but his black hair was styled into a full-on mullet and he was wearing a 'Frankie Says Relax' T-shirt. 'This isn't your dad, is it, Cait?'

Caitie took it and shook her head. 'No, that's Uncle Seamus. Shay is named after him. He died years ago.'

'How many years ago?'

Caitie looked up at Jas's grave tone. 'Ten, twenty, I don't know. Why?'

Jas tapped the photograph. 'I just remember you saying he died and no one talks about it. Ever. And this is the last photograph I can find of him, unless you know of any others.'

Caitie shook her head, feeling a spark of excitement. Jas was on to something, she knew it.

'So . . . if this is the last photograph, that could mean your Uncle Seamus died around twenty-five years ago.' Jas glanced at Elliot contritely. 'And I just thought if your dad left England around the same time . . .'

'So?' Elliot sat up straight. 'What are you saying, Jas? That my father killed Caitie's uncle Seamus?' He slammed down his copy of *Romeo and Juliet*. 'Aren't we all getting a bit carried away here?' As much as he detested his father, he refused to believe he was guilty of murder.

Oblivious of Elliot's discomfort, Caitie's mind was working overtime now. 'Let me think. Right . . . my Irish grandparents used to live here and then Nana died and Grampy went back to Dublin with my aunts, leaving Dad to run Shamrock. Mum and Dad had just got married but my grandparents were over the moon about that so it can't have anything to do with the wedding.'

Elliot glared at her. 'I don't think it has anything to do with anything,' he said tightly. 'My father is a first-class bastard but he's not a murderer, I'm sure of that.'

Caitie's brows knitted together. 'But we need to find out the truth, don't we?'

Elliot stared at his hands, his expression dark. 'I don't know. Do we?'

'Oooh, I've just remembered something else!' Caitie said, jumping to her feet. 'Mum and Dad hate New Year's Eve. They say they always have done but I've seen photos of them at parties. At least, parties in the early eighties, but nothing after that.' Her cheeks were flushed. 'We're getting closer, I can feel it! I'm going to find those other photos.' Climbing over Jas, Caitie shot out of the summer house.

'But what about *Romeo and Juliet*?' Elliot protested, wondering why Caitie was so hell-bent on pursuing this.

Jas bit her lip. 'Sorry, Elliot, this is all my fault. If I hadn't mentioned a murder and gone on about Caitie's Uncle Seamus . . .'

'It's not your fault. I'm probably just being paranoid.' Elliot lifted his grey eyes to Jas's. 'Perhaps I'm just scared of what we might find if we dig too deep.'

Jas nodded. 'I know what you mean. Trouble is, now Caitie has started . . .'

Elliot sighed. 'I know, I know. She's like a dog with a bone when she wants to be. I've realised that.' He grinned. He was besotted with Caitie but he couldn't help worrying about what they might discover. If it *was* something bad, would she feel the same way about him? Elliot held up his copy of the play. 'I only wish Caitie would forget about this mystery and concentrate on rehearsing these lines with me. She might know them off by heart but I definitely don't.'

Jas grabbed Caitie's copy. 'I'll be Juliet. Until Caitie gets back, I mean,' she added hurriedly, in case her comment sounded forward.

'Great, thanks.' Relieved, Elliot settled down against the cushions. 'How about starting from the scene where Romeo speaks to Mercutio . . .'

Looking up with a frown, Lochlin saw that Leo had come to visit him. Pleased to see his old friend but irritated at his poor timing, Lochlin put down the latest figures he'd been scrutinising with a sigh and motioned for Leo to come in.

'Sorry to barge in like this,' Leo said with a slight smile. He looked thoroughly washed out and his blond hair was all over the place. 'I just wondered if you wanted to pop out for lunch.'

'I'm too busy.' Taking off his black-rimmed glasses, Lochlin wondered when his shoulders had ever been this tense. He flexed them wearily. 'Sorry. I wish I could, but I don't have time for lunch these days.'

'I can see that,' Leo said, gesturing to Lochlin's disappearing frame. 'You look as though you need a good steak.'

Lochlin rubbed his eyes. 'Did you hear about Shay moving into Bluebell Cottage?' He pushed his paperwork aside without realising he'd sent it flying off his desk.

Leo nodded and picked up the papers. 'Isn't it good news about Shay having a new job?' he commented cautiously. 'I mean, after him getting fired and everything.' He pushed his hair out of his eyes, wishing he didn't feel so terrible about Lexi. But he was here for Lochlin, not to spill his own heartache out. 'Look, maybe it will do Shay good. He'll have to knuckle down professionally and that has to be positive.'

'He's so pig-headed,' Lochlin ranted. 'I was just about to offer him a job at Shamrock but he was determined to go off and do his own thing.'

'So let him,' Leo chided softly. 'I'm sure Shay would like nothing better than to work side by side with you at Shamrock but until that's right for both of you, just let him get on with it.' He changed tack. 'And how are things at Shamrock?'

Lochlin slammed his hand down on the desk. 'I guess you've heard the rumours so why fucking bother asking?'

Leo winced. He wished he could help his friend but he could see Lochlin was in self-destruct mode. No wonder he had pushed Shay away; Lochlin clearly wanted to pull himself out of this mess, even if it killed him. But Leo was nothing if not loyal and determined. 'Can I help at all? My shit-hot legal team could look at contracts for you. There might be something we can salvage with the artists who've defected to Jett. They might be in breach of their contracts. Or perhaps there might be loopholes at Jett.'

'Fuck them,' Lochlin snarled unexpectedly. 'I don't want them here, not after they've all stabbed me in the bloody back. Judd's welcome to them, the little traitors.' Staring at Leo suspiciously, Lochlin was filled with mistrust. Stressed out and exhausted, out of the blue, he completely lost it. 'Who sent you? Was it Tavvy? God, all of you think I'm past it, don't you? You think I'm sitting here falling apart just because Judd fucking Harrington is back!'

'Of course not, no one thinks that . . .'

Lochlin leapt to his feet. 'I just wish everyone would leave me the fuck alone!' he roared, losing control. 'I'm not past it and I can handle whatever that fucker Harrington throws at me, got it?'

'Got it.' Leo stood up, wishing he'd never come. 'Listen, this was a mistake. You're busy, I can see that.'

'Wait.' Lochlin stopped him before he got to the door. 'Why are you looking so fucking sorry for yourself?' He guessed Leo looked hangdog because his attempt to save the day had failed.

'Me?' Leo gave his friend a sad smile as he headed to the door. 'Well, since you asked, Lexi's been having an affair behind my back. But seeing as I was the only one who thought my marriage would last, it's all a bit of a cliché, really.' He gave Lochlin a regretful look. 'Maybe when this has all blown over, we'll go out for that steak, eh?'

As he shut the door quietly behind him, Lochlin gasped. Poor Leo! God, what an awful friend he was, screaming at Leo, just because he'd offered him help. Leo was the most genuine and trustworthy friend Lochlin had; how could he have treated him like that? Lochlin knew how devastated Leo must feel about Lexi's betrayal; whatever they had all said about her, Leo had genuinely believed their love affair was genuine.

Lochlin slumped down in his chair, suffused with guilt. It seemed he wasn't a fat lot of use to anyone at the moment. Why couldn't he just open up to someone instead of kicking everyone away from him when he needed them most? Lochlin stared blindly at the family portrait on the wall, thinking he had never felt more alone in his life. Shamrock was disintegrating in front of his very eyes and he was alienating his friends and family – Tavvy, in particular – with his foul temper and paranoid mood swings.

Lochlin spun his chair away from his desk and stared out of the window at the view of Kensington. His marriage was on shaky ground right now but as much as he wanted to confide in Tavvy, part of him didn't want to worry her. What could he say? That Shamrock was falling apart because he, Lochlin, could no longer take the pressure now that Judd was back? No. For now, Lochlin felt it was better to keep things to himself, even it if meant shutting himself off from the people he cared about.

Leaning forward, Lochlin reread the latest press release about Jett's shares going sky high. Doing his best to ignore the suffocating pain in his chest he'd had for weeks now, he poured himself a vast Scotch and wished everything would just go away.

Savannah stood at the edge of the stage, savouring her big moment finally. Dressed to kill in a bright red cat suit with spike-heeled black boots, she couldn't wait to show everyone what she could do. She gave a self-satisfied smile. Her father might have helped her with all his contacts in the record business, but Savannah was a firm believer that you created your own luck and she was absolutely sure it was because she had pursued this dream relentlessly that she was standing here right now.

'Are you sure you won't reconsider about the lip-synching?' Darcy asked in a tired voice.

'No way.' Savannah glanced at Darcy, shocked by her appearance. The vibrant red lipstick she always wore was absent, making her seem pale and wan, and her usually glossy dark hair was tied up in a severe bun. Savannah had no idea when Darcy had lost so much weight but the tight black dress she was wearing highlighted her fragile limbs and hollow cheeks.

Darcy shrugged as if she really couldn't care less. 'Fair enough. Your choice.'

Savannah frowned. Darcy had always been so committed to her launch night; she had worked tirelessly on every aspect of the performance from the lighting to the order of the tracks. Even though Savannah had ignored all Darcy's advice with regard to her image, she had been secretly impressed with the meticulous planning Darcy had put into the event. The fact that Darcy now looked as if she'd rather be anywhere else but here was astonishing. Savannah wondered whether she might be ill but, noticing a purple bruise on Darcy's shoulder, she wondered if her mood was due to something else entirely.

'You're on in a minute,' Darcy snapped, yanking her dress up to cover the bruise. She was barely holding it together and knew she had to appear confident and professional tonight. It was a crucial night for Savannah and if anything went wrong, Judd would be looking in one direction only. She took a deep breath and turned back to Savannah. 'I hope you've bloody well practised.'

'Of course I've "bloody well" practised,' Savannah retorted, relieved to have the old Darcy back in the room. She flicked her long russet hair over her shoulder, appearing more confident than she felt. 'You don't need to worry about me; I've been ready for this all my life.'

Darcy raised her eyebrows. 'Good. Get out there and put your money where your mouth is then. You're on.' She gave Savannah a shove and consulted her checklist to make sure everything was running like clockwork.

Feeling a buzz of anticipation, Savannah headed out on to the stage area, glad the curtains were down for now. Her stomach was doing somersaults. Taking up her position, she turned her back to the curtains, sticking her butt out. The cat suit had a low back and fitted like a second skin, so it made for a dynamic first view. Her song 'Kiss Me Like You Mean It' was a catchy Kylie-esque track that was sure to impress all the big cheeses from the music press.

As she waited for the backing track to start, Savannah couldn't help drifting off into a daydream about the future. If she managed to pull this off, she was going to be a big name in the pop world. Her old friends in New York would be seeing her on billboards and she would be courted by the press. Savannah was so engrossed in lapping up her moment of glory she committed the cardinal sin of missing her intro and as the music kicked in, she struggled to find her place.

Horrified, she skipped a line of the song and changed the beginning of her dance routine. Intending to open with a complicated handstand-into-splits-flip-over combination, she was forced to do a lame twirl which sent her the wrong direction across the stage and left her dazed about her next move. Making a monumental effort to regain her composure, Savannah threw in a couple of extra dance moves to compensate, doing her best to keep singing at the same time.

'*Kiss me like you mean it*,' she shrieked, throwing herself around energetically. Seeing a sea of faces staring at her blankly, Savannah slowly became aware that her voice sounded absolutely terrible. Her key was flat, her tone was non-existent and as for breathing in the right places . . .

'*I'm the girl you wanna be with*,' she sang desperately, flipping around quickly to mask a horrible bum note, '*so you need to kiss me, kiss me like you mean it, yeah . . .*'

Catching sight of Judd standing at the front of the crowd, Savannah was taken aback to see his hostile look, his arms crossed in obvious disapproval. Falling hideously off the final note, Savannah struck her pose and willed the lights to dim. As soon as they'd been extinguished on stage, Savannah scurried off. The crowd of industry reps were too polite to boo but the applause was subdued to say the least and it was clear that they weren't impressed.

'Shit!' Savannah screamed, cursing herself for fucking up her big moment. She had waited all her life for this! What the hell had she been doing, missing her cue like that? She kicked a speaker in frustration, yelping in pain when she remembered her boots were made from stretch satin, not leather. Catching sight of Darcy hovering nearby, Savannah's heart sank.

'Go on, tell me how fucking terrible I was,' she spat defensively, hating the thought that Darcy had probably been right about her image, the lip-synching and a whole lot more.

Darcy shook her head, her eyes distracted. 'You weren't terrible,' she said, taking the wind out of Savannah's sails. 'You just looked a little amateur. But it's nothing that can't be fixed, all right?' She studied Savannah, looking switched on for the first time that evening. 'You think you're the most confident person around but when you get nervous, you forget your words and you concentrate on your dancing.' Darcy visibly pulled herself together and her tone became more brisk. 'Look, you're going to have to chalk it up to experience. Go out there again and be word perfect next time.'

Looking incredulous, Savannah's red eyebrows shot up. 'Go out again?' she said. She shook her head vehemently. 'No fucking way.'

'You have no choice,' Darcy replied flatly. 'You already look unprofessional, a no-show for your second performance would seal your fate and you can kiss your pop career goodbye. You just need to learn from your mistakes and do a few things differently this time, that's all.'

Savannah's shoulders slumped with dejection. Her over-confidence had died with her on stage. Everything she had dreamt of could be about to evaporate into thin air if she couldn't find the courage to start all over again.

Feeling deflated, Savannah lifted her eyes to Darcy's, wishing she'd listened to her in the first place rather than thinking she knew best. And listening to her father, Savannah thought accusingly. What the hell did he know about the music business? He had backed her all the way, applauding every stupid decision she'd made and doing his best to discredit Darcy in the process, as if that was all that mattered. Not for the first time, Savannah began to wonder if her father really did have her best interests at heart.

'Seriously, Darcy, what can I do?' she pleaded. 'I'm sorry I've been such a bitch. I'm listening to you now, I promise. This . . . this means everything to me.'

Darcy mechanically listed her thoughts. 'Forget that cheesy dance number you were planning to do next and sing the ballad. I know you hate it but you've practised it enough and at least it will show them you can sing. You need to be taken seriously. This image isn't right for you and the most important thing is your voice and your personality.' She gave Savannah a brief smile. 'You have personality in abundance, make it work for you.'

Savannah was lost for words. Darcy had never been nice to her – or maybe she had and she'd been too busy mouthing off at her, Savannah thought uncomfortably.

'But . . . but what about all those industry reps out there? Won't they think I'm a complete loser? They savage people on your reality shows over here, and they sing like fucking professionals on live TV.'

'All you can do is try,' Darcy fired back. 'And remember who your daddy is, Savannah. Judd's methods might be questionable but worst-case scenario, I'm sure he can get you out of this mess. The sort of money he has moves mountains. Getting a few magazine editors to forgive one bad performance will be child's play for him, so really, I don't think you have anything to worry about.' Darcy stopped, suddenly realising how much she loathed Judd.

Savannah swallowed. She didn't want her father to bail her out, she wanted to win over the music reps without his intervention.

Savannah glanced down at her shiny cat suit and slutty boots. Suddenly, she felt faintly ridiculous, like a cheap Britney Spears rip-off. She could have been wearing the sophisticated black jeans and leather Darcy had suggested. Why hadn't she listened to her advice? Savannah cursed herself for being so stubborn and immature.

About to apologise to Darcy for her bratty behaviour, Savannah was cut off by the arrival of a furious Judd.

'What the fuck was *that*?' he snarled, his purple face clashing with his bright red hair.

'I'm sorry,' she started. 'I was so excited to be up there, I missed my cue and I—'

'Too fucking right you missed your cue,' Judd hollered in her face, only just about stopping himself from shaking some sense into her. 'Your voice sounded like hell and your dancing was even worse. You looked like a fucking elephant out there, galloping around and doing the bloody splits.'

Savannah turned pale but she lifted her chin bravely. 'I said I was sorry—'

'Sorry won't cut it with all of those industry reps out there,' he growled, clenching his fists as he paced backwards and forwards. 'Do you know how fucking stupid you've just made me look? I've spent weeks, not to mention thousands of pounds, laying the groundwork for tonight and you sing like a fucking second-rate stripper.' His mouth twisted maliciously. 'I wonder why that might be.'

Sucking her breath in, Savannah met her father's eyes straight on. 'Are you saying I sing like my mother?' Her voice was dangerously quiet. She didn't think she'd ever hated someone so much in her life before. She felt desperately let down.

Judd stared back at her, his sapphire-blue eyes boring into hers. 'If you like.'

'Well, fuck you!' she bawled, uncharacteristically bursting into tears. Rivulets of black mascara streamed down her cheeks and her face became red and blotchy. 'How do you think I feel, fucking up my big opportunity? And what sort of fucking father are you? All you care about is the money you've spent and how stupid *you* look.' She paused, fighting for breath.

Judd grabbed her wrist. 'Remember who you're talking to,' he snarled.

'How could I possibly forget? You remind me all the fucking time.' Savannah ripped her arm free, rubbing her red skin. She would never forgive him for this, not ever. 'You're a fucking asshole and I wish I'd never met you!' She ran away, sobbing.

Darcy stared after Savannah. How could Judd crush her like that? She was a royal pain in the arse, that was for sure, but she didn't deserve to be treated as if she was a total failure. Plenty of headline acts had a bad performance and managed to survive.

'And *you*,' Judd hissed at her. 'This is *your* fault. I put you in charge of Savannah's career when I went to America and when I got back, you two were at loggerheads like a couple of fucking children. How could you let her go out there before she was ready?'

Darcy bit down so hard on her lip, blood gushed into her mouth. About to blast him with expletives, she blanched at the hateful glint in Judd's eye. She had always thought of herself as a strong, successful woman who knew her own mind. But over the months, Judd had ground her down. Professionally, he undermined her whenever he could, and he delighted in humiliating her in the bedroom. Darcy couldn't believe she had ever been attracted to the man.

She stalked away from him, desperate for some air. Bumping

into Heidi, she made a snap decision. 'There's an outfit in the back of my car for Savannah, black jeans and a few rock chick tops. Would you mind getting them for me?' She handed over a bunch of keys. 'I think Savannah could do with a change of image if she's got any hope of impressing that baying pack of wolves out there.'

About to tell her where to stuff her request, Heidi changed her mind as she saw Darcy's ravaged face.

She nodded. 'I'll get the clothes. Is she going to sing that ballad you suggested?'

Darcy shrugged. 'I hope so. Then she's got that vampy number to follow up with and if she pulls both of those off, she might have a chance.' She gave Heidi a nod of thanks. She realised now how pointless it was alienating women like Heidi. It wasn't big and it wasn't clever; all it did was leave her feeling lonely and left out of everything.

Joining the crowd of industry reps, Darcy saw how unimpressed they really were.

'Was that a joke?' asked an editor from one of the most prestigious music magazines in the country. 'I was told this girl was comparable to that brilliant kid, Iris Maguire, but that's just laughable.'

'It really isn't a joke,' Darcy assured him, 'but I can quite understand why you might have thought that. Just give Savannah a chance. She'll prove you wrong with her next performance, I promise you.'

The editor pursed his lips. 'She'd better. Otherwise I'm leaving and I'm sure I won't be the only one.'

Darcy tirelessly worked the room, doing some serious damage limitation. She couldn't give a shit about Judd but she cared about Jett, and Savannah deserved a second chance.

'Can I interest you in some champagne?' she said to a man's broad back. Her voice died in her throat when he turned to face her.

'Hello, Shay,' she mumbled, noticing that his dark hair was

shorter and sexier than when she had last seen him but his green eyes, framed by those impossibly long, sooty lashes, were just how she remembered them. Bringing herself back to reality, Darcy realised resentment was radiating out of him, enveloping her in a cloak of bitterness so acrid, she could almost taste it.

'Oh, you remember my name, do you?' he shot back sarcastically. 'Wow, I'm flattered.'

Shay was taken aback at how thin she was; her collarbones were protruding like coat hangers. What had happened to her? Is this what her relationship with Judd had done to her? Thinking about Judd's freckled hands pawing at her gorgeous body, his hips grinding at her like a depraved dog, Shay wondered how she could bear his cruel mouth on hers. Against his better judgement and overcome with sympathy for her, he had a sudden urge to gather her up in his arms and protect her.

Misreading his expression for pity, Darcy drew on the last bit of strength she had left.

'Of course I remember your name.' Her hazel eyes met his and he was sure he could see guilt there. She caught a waft of his aftershave and the plumy, spicy fragrance transported her straight back to that night in the jazz club. Darcy closed her eyes, determined to ignore the memory.

'Well, thanks for sparing me a thought,' Shay said frostily. 'It must be gutting for you that after all that hard work getting me sacked, I have an even better job now and I've doubled my salary.' He gave her his card. 'Not bad, eh?'

Darcy gulped, glancing down at the card. Stunned, she saw the name of one of the UK's biggest record labels and noticed that Shay was now a consultant, like her. Judging by the sharp suit he was wearing, he wasn't lying about doubling his salary. Darcy stuffed the card in her pocket to hide her shaking hands. She wanted to know everything that had happened to Shay since she'd got him fired, how he'd found his way back from what had happened and how he felt about that night. But she also knew she couldn't possibly ask him. Not noticing Judd standing nearby with his ears straining to hear every word, Darcy forced herself to speak, her tone detached.

'That's . . . that's great. Good for you. So it wasn't such a bad thing that happened after all, was it?'

Shay narrowed his eyes. God, she was a bitch! 'Professionally speaking, no. But I wish more than anything that I'd never set eyes on you.'

Darcy recoiled but she held her head high. 'That's not very nice,' she managed, feeling dead inside. 'I thought we had a good time.' The words sounded cold and unfeeling but she couldn't let him see how much his presence had jolted her. If she did, Darcy knew she would completely unravel.

'God, you're a piece of work,' Shay snapped. 'But you're a fucking good actress, has anyone told you that? That night in bed, you actually had me convinced there was something between us.' He let out an embittered laugh. 'But now I can see you're just Judd's little puppet, there to do his bidding, even if it means screwing the enemy.' Shay's lip curled. 'Jesus, you disgust me, do you know that? Not only do you do his dirty work for him, you crawl back on your hands and knees and beg for more. You should be fucking ashamed of yourself. I never want to set eyes on you again.' Turning away from her abruptly, he stalked off in the other direction.

Darcy felt tears running down her cheeks. Heartbroken, she turned and found herself encircled by the iron-strong grip of Judd's arms and she started shaking like a leaf at the look in his eyes. Dashing the tears from her cheeks, she hoped to God he hadn't overheard anything.

Judd felt fury pulsing through his veins. With everything he had thrown at Darcy and all he had done to break her spirit, she had never exposed her vulnerability, and had never shown she cared. There had been no tears and no recriminations and Judd had grudgingly respected her for it.

Now, however, he realised the truth. Darcy had never shown she cared because, quite simply, she didn't. She might be petrified of him but she had no feelings for him, not ones that mattered. And that hurt. His ego took a tumble and Judd had no idea how to handle it. Forcing Darcy to face the stage, they both watched Savannah came out on stage again to sing her second song. Now dressed in black jeans and a black leather jacket, she was calm and composed. She sang the ballad Darcy had chosen for her faultlessly, her voice strong and melodious, the best it had ever sounded. Through the swirling red mist in front of his eyes, Judd noted that Savannah's performance was understated, classy and a hundred times better than her first one. He realised that it was down to Darcy that his daughter had pulled off such a slick routine and for some reason this tipped him over into a wrath that was so hot and vengeful, Judd was almost a mass of lava.

Waiting until Savannah had sung her second song to loud, approving applause, Judd snatched hold of Darcy's arm and marched her out of the club. Hailing a cab, he ignored her stammered questions and threw her in the back of it where she sat, quailing. Arriving at her flat, he practically carried her into the lift and manhandled her through her front door.

'I'm sorry about Shay Maguire,' she began, her legs shaking. 'I didn't know he'd be there tonight . . . I didn't invite him. He must have been sent by whoever he now works for but I don't know who that is. Shall I find out? He wouldn't tell me . . . he hates me . . .'

'You're rambling,' Judd said, cutting her off callously. 'Worse than that, you're boring me.' He took a step towards her. 'You have no idea what you've done, have you?'

Darcy shook her head, scared stiff.

Judd laughed cruelly. 'I didn't think so. Let me spell it out for you. No one sleeps with me and falls in love with someone else, get it?'

'I'm not . . . why would you . . . who on earth . . .'

'You really don't know, do you?' he jeered. 'Poor Darcy, so

fucked up and lost, you don't even know you're in love with Shay Maguire.'

She blinked at him, stupefied.

'It would be touching if it wasn't so fucking sad,' Judd sneered.

Darcy gaped. *This* was what had got Judd so worked up? He was pissed off because he thought she was in love with someone else?

With chilling precision, Judd removed his Armani suit jacket, laid it over the back of a chair and rolled back the sleeves of the monogrammed shirt his private tailor in Jermyn Street had made for him.

Terrified, Darcy stumbled backwards. With a thumping heart, she watched Judd casually remove his Rolex, her nerves crackling with tension.

Judd gave a mirthless laugh. 'You need to be taught a lesson.'

Flexing his fists, he advanced upon Darcy purposefully. Then he calmly set about beating her senseless.

Lexi shifted uncomfortably, trying to remove Sebastian's stapler from under her left buttock. She sighed as Sebastian pounded away inexpertly. Now that meeting at Brockett Hall was out of the question, they had moved on to Sebastian's office. Lying on Sebastian's desk with her breasts covered in chocolate body paint and the door wedged shut with a chair was hardly the glamorous, wildly exciting ride she'd been expecting. All Lexi could pin her hopes on was the fact that Sebastian had to inherit Daddy's billions one day. She just hoped he'd ditched Martha by then so she could get her hands on the money.

As she wrapped her toned legs and Gucci heels around Sebastian's pale back, Lexi felt a small pang of guilt about Leo. He was a great guy; gentlemanly, funny and a fantastic lay but financially speaking he just wasn't in the Harrington league.

Letting out an Oscar-worthy shriek of delight as she pretended to come, Lexi slithered around on Sebastian's paperwork, hoping she didn't get a paper cut in a nasty place. The smell of the body paint was making her feel faintly nauseous and she couldn't wait to get home and scrub herself clean.

Certain Lexi had never had sex this good in her life before, Sebastian smugly unplugged himself. 'I have work to do,' he told her, zipping his trousers up. He meant it. If he didn't get some of Jett's legal issues sorted for his father, he was sure his finances were going to suffer drastically. His father had already hinted that his cushy lifestyle at Jett was about to take a nosedive if he couldn't focus on his job and get his act together. Sebastian, freaking out at the thought of losing his expense account and his vastly inflated salary, nevertheless couldn't resist shagging Lexi on his desk. She'd surprised him in the office that afternoon with a tube of chocolate body paint, but now he had paperwork to be getting on with. Half of the new artists that had been signed to Jett were still technically out of contract, as Sebastian hadn't yet tied up the legalities, and if any of them backed out, he knew his ass would be on the line. Still smarting from Savannah's cheap trick the other week, Sebastian knew he had to be on his toes. The last thing he needed was his bitch of a half-sister screwing things up for him.

'When shall we meet again?' Lexi asked, sitting up and pulling her dress over her head. She took her diary out of her handbag and, glancing down, she prodded her stomach. Christ, she hoped she wasn't putting on weight. Her dress had felt a little tight when she'd put it on that morning; probably because of all the gym sessions she'd missed now that she was seeing Sebastian more regularly.

'Next week?' Sebastian offered vaguely, not even sure of his movements for the next few days, let alone the following week. He knew Lexi liked to have their dates booked in so she could cover her tracks and make sure Leo didn't suspect anything. For his own part, Sebastian wanted to keep this arrangement going for as long as possible. Lexi wasn't exactly wife material but she sure gave good blow jobs.

Lexi flicked through the pages of her diary, determined to get their relationship established as something serious. 'Have you thought any more about speaking to Martha about a divorce?' she asked casually, removing some papers from underneath her bottom. They were legal documents of some kind but seeing that they were smeared with chocolate body paint, Lexi hastily stuffed them into the shredding pile at the end of the desk.

'Not as such.' Sebastian averted his eyes. Lexi was always going on about him finishing it with Martha but so far he'd managed to be non-committal about it. What Lexi didn't realise was he didn't *want* to divorce Martha. She might be whiny and annoying but it suited him to be married to someone who didn't question his every move. Sure, she might occasionally get upset – the failed pregnancy had been a serious low point – but Sebastian had a feeling Lexi would be far more high maintenance.

'I see.' Lexi's voice was cool. She frowned as she checked the pages of her diary again.

'Things are different right now, what with Martha wanting to fall pregnant.'

Barely listening, Lexi swallowed. Counting back with her heart in her mouth, she prayed she'd made a mistake. Maybe she had swine flu or whatever the latest virus was or maybe she was just feeling a bit under the weather. But Lexi knew she was kidding herself. No, the reality was that she was well and truly pregnant. Gritting her teeth, Lexi realised the baby must be Sebastian's; she and Leo had barely slept together over the past few months. It had probably happened that first time in Sebastian's Porsche – God, how *common*!

Lexi reeled. This couldn't be happening to her but she could only think the stomach bug she had suffered after the Valentines' Ball had made her pill stop working. Christ, she didn't want children – she hated them. Children made women fat and ruined their bodies with stretch marks and saggy boobs. Worse than that, when they arrived, they did nothing but scream, shit and puke. Lexi couldn't even bear it when she came into contact with other people's children. She found them smelly, sticky and pointless. She liked the way French women had children; they were in and out of hospital with no fuss, they received prescriptions for toning their pelvic floor and their tummies, and nursing was frowned upon because it 'ruined the breasts.'

She cursed herself; she'd done some foolish things in her time, but this had to be the worst. How would she explain it to Leo? What would Sebastian say? He was bound to think she'd done it on purpose. She took a deep breath.

'Speaking of pregnancies,' she started, squaring her shoulders, 'I think we might have a small situation here.'

Sebastian fixed frosty blue eyes on her then started when he saw her face. 'You've got to be fucking kidding me.' Despite his aggressive tone, he was pale beneath his freckles.

She shook her head, her glossy hair hiding how vexed she was.

'Jesus.' Sebastian sank down on to his office chair. How could the silly bitch have got herself pregnant? He expected women to take care of such things as safe sex. When he got the chance, Sebastian fucked indiscriminately, never worrying about the consequences. Like father like son, after all, he thought grimly, suspecting his father would take a much dimmer view of his son siring a bastard child than he had about doing such a thing himself.

Lexi noticed Sebastian's appalled face. How did he think *she* felt? She was the one with a baby growing inside her, a baby that would engorge her breasts until the veins popped, stretch her skin until it split and, as a final insult, force its way out of her body, causing havoc and untold damage as it went. Lexi felt sick. All she could think about was nasty pregnancy symptoms women talked about in all those real life magazines – swollen ankles, excessive flatulence, painful haemorrhoids. She shuddered, sensing that vomiting on Sebastian's Gucci loafers wouldn't help her cause right now.

'It's definitely yours, before you ask,' Lexi said. 'I've barely been near Leo.'

Sebastian was thinking rapidly. Part of him felt elated that his sperm had managed to do the job they were meant to do and part of him felt aggrieved that he had impregnated the wrong woman. If Martha was pregnant instead of Lexi, life would be a whole lot easier. At least it proved what he'd thought all along, however; it was Martha's fault they hadn't had a baby yet. Sebastian felt vindicated and not in the least bit sympathetic towards his wife's fertility issues.

Sebastian linked his fingers together as he leant on the desk. This news could very well tip Martha over the edge. Having an affair was one thing but getting his mistress pregnant when his wife couldn't conceive a much longed-for child would put him straight in the divorce courts, an expense he could do without.

Should they abort the child? For some reason and much to his surprise, the thought filled Sebastian with distaste. This was his child, his son or daughter, residing in Lexi's almost flat stomach. No, that was out of the question so Lexi was going to have to go through with the pregnancy, whether she liked it or not. An idea occurred to Sebastian but it was so out there, he didn't even know if he could get his head around it at this stage.

'I need to think about this,' he told Lexi shortly. 'And I still have work to do.'

'Well, I'm glad you have your priorities sorted,' she answered sarcastically. She paused by the door. 'I'd like to think you'll start paying me some proper attention from now on.' With that, she left.

Sebastian watched her, beginning to think Lexi had just become his biggest headache. As if he didn't have enough to worry about, he thought, glancing round his desk for the contracts.

'Can I take these papers for shredding?' Heidi asked, coming into his office and gathering up the pile at the end of his desk. She gave him a disdainful look, wondering why all the Harringtons felt the need to have sex on their desks. 'Your father's on a mission to get the whole office tidied up.'

'Yes, yes . . . take them away,' Sebastian said, flipping through the remaining piles on his desk. Hearing the door closing, he sat back and contemplated his life. Sebastian was sure his problems had only started when his bratty sister Savannah had arrived. Even now, she was swanning around the house thinking she was something special just because she'd managed to sing on key for five minutes and secure a few magazine interviews.

Where the *hell* were those contracts? Sebastian turned his desk upside down frantically. If he couldn't find them, he was a dead man as far as his father was concerned. And if that was the case, he might as well emigrate because the news of his bastard child would most likely see him being written out of the family will.

Sebastian sighed. Why did his life always go tits up?

Chapter Fourteen

'Again,' Pia demanded, slamming her phone down on the piano. Her dark eyes flashed as she turned them on Iris, who winced. Pia had just taken a call from Judd Harrington which involved her screaming down the phone then holding it out as Judd responded in kind. Finally she had told Judd to go to hell before taking out her rage on Iris by making her sing challenging scales over and over again.

'Er . . . I think my voice is going to crack if I carry on for much longer,' Iris said in a hesitant tone. 'That high note is pretty harsh.'

About to yell at her to get on with it, Pia closed her mouth and took a deep breath. 'You're right. Sorry. I don't want to undo all our good work just because Judd is being an asshole.'

Iris leant on the piano. 'Is everything all right?'

Pia pursed her dark lips. 'Not really. Judd is a very forceful man and we've always got on well.' She fixed her eyes on Iris. 'But let's say he's trying to go too far this time and I'm not willing to play his stupid games any more.'

'Do these games . . .' Iris lifted her amber eyes to Pia's. 'Do these games involve me in any way?'

Pia's expression became blank. 'Why do you ask?'

'Because my brother Shay was on the phone the other day.'

'Did you tell him about Ace?'

Iris turned pink. 'No. I know I should but I just can't bring myself to tell my family yet.' Her hands twisted nervously. 'Ace is . . . it's complicated.'

Pia said nothing. Iris seemed utterly besotted with Ace and she was worried. Pia knew about Judd's plans and she didn't want Iris distracted. Or hurt.

Iris was keen to move away from the subject of Ace. 'Anyway, Shay finally told me why he's been acting like a bear with a sore head.'

'Go on.'

Iris took a swig of water and told Pia about the debacle with Darcy. 'The worst thing is, I reckon Shay might have feelings for this woman. He sounded really gutted.'

Pia raised her eyebrows. 'That has Judd written all over it.' She glanced at the music she had picked out for Iris's next performance, her face clouding over as she remembered the way Judd had punished her for daring to have an honest opinion about Savannah's voice. She shuddered. She'd slept with him again against her better judgement and she wouldn't be doing it again. Humiliation wasn't her thing – neither was pain.

Pia turned away. She wasn't about to tell Iris that quite out of the blue, Judd had commanded her to sever all contact with Iris and withdraw all requests to get her demos played on air. Furthermore, he had refused to fund any more of the coaching sessions or anything related to Iris's PR or public performances. And Iris had revealed he'd taken back the Jeep he'd bought her.

Pia had no idea what had brought on the abrupt about-turn but, this time, she simply would not go along with Judd's craziness. She had always maintained a good professional relationship with him, as well as picking up where they'd left off sexually whenever he was in town but that was over now. This crazy feud with the Maguire family was tipping him over the edge and Judd's professional judgement was becoming questionable. What had always seemed like daring business acumen and aggressive competitiveness now smacked of bizarre obsession and vengeful recklessness.

'All I'll say is that I will personally be looking after your career while you're in LA,' Pia told her, knowing it would be best if Iris was kept in the dark. She scrutinised her protégée. Dressed in a pair of black jeans teamed with an off-the-shoulder cream sweater and some flat ballet pumps, Iris looked tanned and relaxed. Her blond hair was freshly washed and hung down her back in gold ripples, and a smattering of honey-coloured freckles had broken out across her nose and cheeks from the sun. Apart from the clothes, Pia thought Iris looked like a ravishing figure from a Pre-Raphaelite painting. And just like the owners of those priceless paintings, Pia intended to protect her investment for all she was worth. Iris was too damned talented to be the latest victim in Judd's twisted one-upmanship.

Before she could say anything else, Pia was interrupted by the arrival of Ace.

'Have I got news for *you*!' he cried, charging into the studio like an over-excitable puppy. Dressed in slouchy jeans and a red shirt that should have clashed with his dark auburn hair, he was waving a magazine in the air. 'Sorry, Pia, but I just had to show Iris this.' He spread the magazine out on the piano, revealing a glorious photograph of the pair of them, laughing together after Ace's recent NASCAR win at Richmond. Iris looked stunning in a bright yellow sundress, with her hair tangled up in a messy bun, and she was hugging Ace. Together, they were dynamite, Pia thought. Iris's bashfulness was the perfect foil for Ace's extrovert personality. His grey eyes were firmly fixed on Iris's bee-stung lips and they looked seconds away from tumbling into bed.

'Oh my God.' Iris clapped a hand to her mouth.

'I know.' Ace nodded proudly, his hand caressing the bare skin above the waistband of her jeans. 'How good do we look?'

'Not that.' Iris had turned pale beneath her tan. 'If my parents see this magazine at home, I'm dead. I still haven't told them about you, Ace. The last time I spoke to my mother, she went on about how haggard and ill my father looked and I couldn't do it. I even kept it from my brother and we're normally really close.'

Pia flipped the front of the magazine over. 'This is a US publication. You can probably get it at home but unless someone gets this delivered specially, I think it's unlikely they'd see these photos.'

Iris let out a gasp of relief, threading her fingers through Ace's.

Ace squeezed them. 'The best part is that I got a call from this high end brand that sell racing clothes for both Grand Prix and NASCAR. Their new line will mostly be targeted at female racing fans and girlfriends. They do cute race-style outfits as well as some really hot designer stuff.' Seeing the incomprehension in Iris's eyes, he got to the point. They think you'd be the perfect model to promote these clothes.'

'Me? A model?' Iris laughed. 'As if!' She saw Ace's serious expression. 'You're kidding me. They want *me* in an ad campaign?'

Ace nodded vigorously. 'They want to shoot you – well, us – in Monaco next month when the Grand Prix is on. My father has an apartment there so we can use that for the shots.' He turned to Pia. 'It will be great publicity for Iris, won't it, with her singing? It will really get her face and her name out there.'

Pia nodded, watching him carefully. As he sank his hands into Iris's hair and gave her a kiss that made Pia feel as if she should leave the room, she realised something with a jolt. Even if Judd had orchestrated the meeting, Iris and Ace's relationship was real. Iris was blissfully, giddily in love and from the way Ace was curving his body into Iris's and gently cupping her face, he was head over heels as well. They had been inseparable since the night of Iris's performance, with Ace sitting in on Iris's coaching sessions (having respectfully and charmingly asked Pia's permission beforehand) and, in spite of her intense guilt over her father, Iris had accompanied Ace to his NASCAR races, providing it fitted in with her singing schedule.

Catching Ace's eye as he pulled away from Iris, Pia saw a glimmer of guilt and guessed Judd was holding Ace to ransom the way he'd tried to do with her.

Unaware of the undercurrent between Ace and Pia, Iris was

flabbergasted by Ace's news. Shy and not remotely vain, she was astonished that anyone would think she could model professionally. She touched her hair apprehensively.

'What about my hair? Everyone says it's too long, and I don't know anything about make-up or clothes.'

Ace laughed, sliding his arm around her waist. 'You don't have to worry about that, the photographic team will deal with all that stuff. I'm up for some pampering, though, if you fancy it. After living with Jerry and his face packs, I'm totally in touch with my feminine side.'

Iris giggled. 'I don't need pampering, I need a bloody haircut. I haven't had one since I've been here.'

Ace shot Pia a wary glance, almost as if he expected her to blow his cover.

Pia couldn't blame him. She'd been Judd's bitch for years – in more ways than one – and it was about time she acted off her own back. She waved them both in the direction of the door. 'Go before I change my mind,' she said in a gruff voice. 'Take her to Rodeo Drive and spoil her, Ace. Spend some of your father's money,' she added with a grim smile.

Ace's eyes met Pia's. 'Rodeo Drive! Let's go, Iris. I know the best shops. Jerry drags me there all the time.'

Shooting Pia a grateful glance, Iris let Ace drag her out of the studio by the hand. Over the course of the next four hours, starting at the fabulously opulent Beverly Wilshire Hotel, Ace took her into one high-end shop after another. Gasping at the glittery array of designer goods, Iris went from Dior to D&G, from Prada to Valentino, having to forcibly stop Ace from buying anything she so much as picked up. As he gazed in the window of Cartier, Iris ran ahead of Ace to stare at all the gorgeous dresses in Chanel.

'Let's go in,' Ace said, joining her after a few minutes. 'Come on. Try some on . . . for me?' Not letting her answer, he went in and spoke to the assistants and they were led to a private area at the back and presented with glasses of champagne. Taking some quick measurements, four assistants hurried around the shop collecting dresses while two others offered them canapés.

'What did you say to them?' Iris muttered under her breath. 'Did you tell them you were related to royalty or something?'

'No.' Ace lounged back in his chair. 'I just handed over my father's special credit card.' He grinned. 'Money talks, as they say, so now they want to kiss our asses. You might as well try everything on and enjoy it because I'm buying or, rather, Daddy is and he has more money than God so don't even think about it.'

Speechless, Iris let herself be led away into the changing area. Trying on exquisite dress after exquisite dress, she came out and twirled around for Ace. The hours passed and as darkness fell outside, it was clear the shop was due to close but the shop assistants were more than happy to keep bringing her new choices. Ace's credit card helped but, secretly, they were enjoying dressing someone as young and lovely as Iris.

'I love that one on you too,' he said, half cut on champagne. He smiled naughtily at her, making two shop assistants swoon. 'You're so fucking sexy in everything. I think we should buy all of them.'

Equally drunk, Iris pretended to give him an exasperated look, fingering the silky fabric of the dress. It was her favourite and she daren't even look at the price tag. 'Don't be silly. I'm feeling guilty about choosing even one of these.'

Ace kissed her hand. 'Don't. You deserve it.' He pulled her on to his lap and kissed her thoroughly. Coming up for air, he tucked a strand of blond hair behind her ear. 'We never did get you that haircut,' he murmured, trailing his fingers down her neck.

'Never mind,' she said breathlessly, feeling his hands sliding under the dress. 'But Ace?'

He gave her an inquisitive look.

'If you're going to do that, I think we'd better buy this dress before you rip it in two.'

Laughing uproariously, Ace tipped her off his lap. 'You're right. I'll probably ruin it. I'd better get you the other ones as well.'

Ignoring her protests, Ace paid the bill with Judd's credit card and they left carrying three huge Chanel bags. The street was alive with twinkling lights and throngs of people laden with shopping bags.

'I can't let you do this,' Iris said, winding herself around Ace outside the store. She felt deliciously warm and fuzzy from the champagne and burying her face in his neck, she breathed in the musky scent from his skin.

'You can.' Feeling totally out of his comfort zone, Ace dumped the bags on the ground and shakily took a Cartier box out of his pocket. He lifted her chin. 'And you have to let me do this too.'

Iris was speechless as Ace clipped a diamond-encrusted heart around her neck.

'Just formally giving you my heart,' he said in a mocking tone. 'Don't ever give it back, will you?' His tone was light but the intent in his eyes was clear.

Not sure what to say in response, Iris stood in front of him, trembling. 'It's rude to return a gift,' she managed in a choked voice.

Ace swallowed. Jerry would wet his pants laughing if he could see how soppy he was being but Ace didn't care. He wanted Iris to know how he felt. 'I know I'm a bit drunk but just in case you think I do this with all the women you know I've been with, I haven't. Not ever.'

Iris nodded, believing him. She knew about the notches on Ace's bedpost; the only way his playboy past could be hidden from her would be if she'd spent the past decade on the moon. But Iris didn't care about his past; all she cared about was what they had now. She touched the heart around her neck, knowing she would never take it off.

Ace took her hand, giving her a cheeky wink. 'I can think of some other parts of my body you can have too but maybe not on Rodeo Drive.'

Iris grinned. 'We'd better go then before we get arrested.' Hand in hand and struggling with the bags, they staggered down Rodeo giggling.

* * *

Dressed up to the nines in a black leather jacket with a diamanté skull on the back and a pair of skin-tight white jeans, Charlie Valentine knocked on Darcy's office door. As much as he hated the idea of his greatest hits album, he'd had an idea about ordering the songs and including some live tracks from a few of his best concerts. Unable to track down Darcy on her mobile, he had decided to pop in and see her as he was in London shopping for a gift for Susannah's birthday.

Frowning when Darcy didn't yank the door open like she normally did, Charlie knocked again.

'She hasn't been in work for a few days now,' Heidi informed him. God, was that eyeliner he was wearing . . . and foundation? Heidi stifled a giggle. Her eyes widened as she checked out his outfit and, not for the first time, she wondered why men of Charlie's age thought they could get away with skinny jeans. She could practically see his meat and two veg!

'Is she on holiday or something?'

'I'm Judd's secretary, not Darcy's. She doesn't have a secretary,' she added, before he asked. 'She says she doesn't need one.'

Charlie pulled a face, his craggy cheeks creasing. 'Typical. She's such a bloody women's libber, isn't she?'

Heidi shrugged. She didn't feel nearly as antagonistic towards Darcy as she used to, not since Savannah's launch. 'Look, there are all sorts of rumours going round that Darcy has got the rough end of Judd's tongue, if you get my drift. Or rather, his fist.'

'You're not serious!' Charlie was reeling at the news that Judd might have hit Darcy. In his opinion, Darcy was far too ballsy to be treated like that.

Heidi sighed. 'I don't know any more than what I've told you. Look, have you tried her mobile?'

'She's not answering.' Not sure he believed the rumours about Darcy's absence, Charlie put his hands on his hips and gave Heidi 'the look'. 'When are you stopping for lunch, angel? Fancy coming out for a drink?'

'I don't have lunch, I'm too busy,' Heidi snapped. 'And just as a heads up,' she added, 'I prefer to date people my own age.' She gave him a pointed stare. 'Maybe you should try it.'

Outraged, Charlie watched her flounce off. Cheeky cow, he thought grumpily. He'd had girls far younger than her and they'd never complained about his age before. He stomped out of Jett's office, his ego wounded. Catching sight of himself in the mirrored glass outside, he peered more closely at his reflection. When he'd left the house that morning, Charlie had imagined he looked the dog's bollocks. But now, observing himself in the cold light of day, he realised he just looked . . . dated.

Disillusioned and thoroughly depressed, Charlie forgot all his good intentions to find a present for Susannah and headed for the nearest bar. What on earth was he going to do about his career? Since he'd left Lochlin and Shamrock, his life had been grim, to say the least. Judd was a complete nightmare and seemed offensively uninterested in Charlie's album. The only one with any savvy, in his opinion, was Darcy. So where the hell was she?

Locked in her flat, Darcy was huddled beneath a duvet, shivering uncontrollably. She had spent the past week staring at the bolts on the front door. Every so often, she had jumped up to check they were secure before taking up her position in her armchair again.

Judd hadn't been to her flat for over a week but he had sure left his mark when he was last here. Darcy touched her bruised face and winced. She had two black eyes that had been puffy and deep purple at first but they were now beginning to turn bluer with ugly yellow shadows. One cheekbone felt crushed and, like the delicate skin around her eyes, it was developing into an array of colours as it slowly healed.

Darcy had thought her nose was broken because it was so swollen that she could barely breathe the day after it had happened. It had bled for almost a day and, finally finding the courage to look at herself in the mirror, Darcy had barely recognised herself. But now she realised that, like her self-esteem and her dignity, it was simply bruised and battered. Her body ached all over and she had bruises on almost every limb. Her ribs were sore, one in particular which Darcy suspected might be cracked, but she couldn't bring herself to go to hospital because she was too ashamed.

Darcy had replayed the night of Savannah's launch in her head over and over again, wondering what she could have done differently. Presumably if she'd avoided Shay Maguire, none of this would have happened but, even now, she couldn't really understand why Judd had reacted so savagely.

Darcy wrapped her arms around her knees, wishing she could stop trembling. She hadn't spoken to anyone about what had happened because what would she say? She knew what people would think – that she had brought it all on herself by mixing with Judd in the first place. And they would be right.

Darcy had foolishly – no, *arrogantly* – thought she could cope with Judd's personality. She had mistakenly believed *she* had been in charge, never noticing the impact of Judd's constant putdowns and the gradual way in which he had taken over her life.

Hit by a flashback of Judd hurling her across the room, Darcy realised she had tears streaming down her face. She winced as tears trickled into her cuts. Suddenly another memory flashed into her mind.

Her mother, jerking her sweater up on to her shoulder to hide something, her eyes darting around warily. Now it all made sense. She recognised her dominant, charismatic father in Judd and as she caught sight of her bruised, battered face in the mirror by the armchair, Darcy recognised her own mother staring back at her. Her eyes were brimming with fear and self-loathing and it was a powerful wake-up call. She realised now that her father hadn't been the hero she'd thought he was. Like Judd, he had been a violent bully and she had refused to see it.

Darcy picked up her phone with fumbling fingers, but who could she call? She had lost touch with her mother years ago when she had left home and female friends were thin on the ground. Feeling totally alone, Darcy miserably flicked through the names on her phone, realising that most of her contacts were men – men she had slept with, men she thought would be useful to her career, or both. She paused as Shay's number appeared.

Darcy tentatively dabbed at her tears with a tissue, creasing up in agony. Unlike most of the other men in her life, Shay hadn't tried to use her – he had seemingly just wanted to get to know her. And what had she done to him? She had used information he had innocently provided her with to have him fired, just because Judd had demanded it. What kind of person did something like that?

Hearing a sound outside, Darcy's eyes darted to the front door, her heart racing. Gathering her duvet around her, she began to shake as a key was inserted.

'Darcy,' Judd called. Astonishingly, insultingly, his voice sounded normal. But Darcy wasn't opening the door to him, whatever he said. Safely on the other side with bolts and chains to protect her, she was taking the first step towards shutting Judd out of her life.

'Open the door!' Judd commanded, his voice becoming angrier. 'Come on, Darcy, stop mucking about. I'm not standing out here all day.'

'Go away,' she said, meaning to shout but it came out as a strangled whisper.

Almost leaping out of her skin as Judd's fist thumped on the door, she recoiled as he began to shout obscenities through the letterbox. Grabbing her phone with fumbling fingers, Darcy shot out of her chair and dived into the sitting room, safely hidden from view. She sent a frantic text to the only person she could bear to see, even though she didn't think he would help her in a million years.

Shaking like a leaf, Darcy huddled in the corner of her sofa, praying to God Judd would give up and leave her alone for ever.

On his way to interview a high-profile new band who had been signed for a ground-breaking sum of money, Shay frowned as he received a text message from a number he didn't recognise. About to head inside a nightclub in Camden, he opened it, wondering if Iris had a new phone. He made a mental note to phone her again soon anyway; he was sure she was hiding something. Reading the text and seeing who it was from, Shay's lip curled contemptuously.

'*Sorry for everything . . . please can you come over. Darcy,*' he read. Her Kensington address followed the message. Snapping his phone shut furiously, Shay carried on walking into the nightclub without missing a beat. What did she think he was going to do after conning him once already: come running? No way. His fingers had been severely burnt and there was no way he was dipping them in the fire a second time.

Shay stopped dead. As ever, the thought of the night that he had spent with Darcy poleaxed him, sending his senses reeling all over the place. He knew he shouldn't be attracted to her after what she'd done to him but he couldn't help it. She had got under his skin and, like a stubborn thorn, he couldn't get her out, whatever he did and however hard he tried.

Shay felt bile rising in his throat. What was wrong with him? More to the point, what was wrong with *her*? Did she simply get off on screwing people around and messing with their heads? For such an intelligent, switched-on woman, Darcy was royally fucked up if she wanted to be part of Judd's perverted world.

About to delete the message, Shay hesitated. It was his only connection to her and, twisted as it was, he couldn't quite bring himself to get rid of it. Instead, he sent Darcy a terse message back telling her he wanted no part of her games. Not now and not ever.

Whatever she was playing at, she was on her own, Shay thought, ducking inside the club and doing his level best to put Darcy Middleton out of his mind.

Drumming his fingers impatiently on the boardroom table, Judd was fuming. People were letting him down left, right and centre and it wasn't good enough.

Savannah, the apple of his eye over the past few months, had let him down spectacularly at her launch party and they had barely spoken since. The way he saw it, Savannah had been unrehearsed and unprofessional and she'd made a laughing stock out of him. And Judd hated looking like a fool. He had half a mind to kick her out of Brockett Hall without a penny but he had too many other things to deal with at the moment.

And what about Pia? Always so willing to go along with his plans in the past, she suddenly seemed to have developed a conscience where Iris was concerned. Iris Maguire was unquestionably talented but so what? There were more important things at stake here and Pia knew that. But even he could see that Iris was exceptional. And she worked so hard, her performances were slick and professional to the point of perfection. As Darcy had predicted, Iris's stutter and her self-effacing modesty had become her USP; audiences were bowled over by her unaffected charm.

Speaking of Darcy . . .

Judd's face twisted and he glanced at his watch, realising Sebastian was late for their meeting. Darcy had been, to date, a willing apprentice. But her recent conduct had led to her letting herself down spectacularly. How could she have allowed herself to fall for the Maguire boy? She certainly hadn't fallen in love with *him*, Judd thought, livid. Still, he was certain he had convinced Darcy to stay away from Shay Maguire in the future; all she had needed was some gentle persuasion.

Judd examined his knuckles impassively. Some women just needed to know who was boss. He didn't think Darcy would be stepping out of line again anytime soon. And although she was clearly holding him at arm's length for now, Judd knew he would be back in her life, and in her bed, within a few weeks.

With grim pleasure, he read through a report in today's newspaper which showed Shamrock's shares plummeting to an all-time low. The Jett Record Corporation was doing well, although Judd would prefer it if their shares had a higher placing on the overall list. Still, there was plenty of time for Jett to shine. Little Aidan's album was due for release soon and that was bound to get them some positive attention. Darcy had some idea about releasing the album around Christmas time but Judd wasn't prepared to wait until then. Competition for the Christmas number one spot was fierce and as endearing as Aidan was with his big brown eyes and his heart-rending background story, Judd couldn't see how he could compete with the reality TV winners or the charity records that would be released in November/December.

Judd wasn't a stupid man; he realised Darcy knew the business well enough to predict the consumer and monitor trends. But she never took risks, everything was carefully calculated on how the market responded to given criteria and that approach was far too formulaic for Judd. He craved excitement and unpredictability, he loved making a quick buck; long-term investments had never been his thing. Judd had made an enormous amount of money over the years and most of it had been based on gut instinct and knee-jerk reaction. The fact that he could have made even more money over a prolonged period of time was not something he chose to dwell upon.

Judd tossed the newspaper aside, wondering how Lochlin was feeling as he read it. Sick to the back teeth most likely, Judd hooted to himself. The poor bastard must be rueing the day he ever messed with a Harrington, and if he wasn't, he soon would be.

Judd took out his crumpled photograph of Tavvy. He hadn't seen her since he'd arrived in England, apart from a few agonising glimpses from afar. It was deliberate on his part; he wanted to see Tavvy when he had achieved his objective of bringing Lochlin to his knees. Judd stuffed the photograph back into his pocket. He hadn't given up on Tavvy, not by a long shot; he just needed to show her how worthless Lochlin was and how easily he would crumble under pressure. His spies at Shamrock had reported back that Lochlin looked like hell. Heidi's sister Laura, posing as a PA, had told him that Lochlin spent hours shut away in his office, refusing to talk to his teams and remaining uncommunicative and withdrawn. By all accounts, Lochlin was walking around like the living dead, grief-stricken at the thought of losing Shamrock.

Losing Shamrock was the least of his worries, Judd thought malevolently.

He looked up as Sebastian rushed in with flushed cheeks. 'About time,' he barked, giving his son a disparaging once-over. He was a mess; his tie was askew, his ginger hair looked unkempt and there was a splodge of ketchup on his shirt.

'Sorry I'm—'

'Get that shirt dry-cleaned,' Judd cut him off mid-sentence and shot his own perfectly starched cuffs. Not for the first time, he wondered how on earth he could have sired such a disappointing excuse for a human being.

Sebastian took a seat and shuffled his hastily collated batch of papers, trying to get them into some semblance of order. He still hadn't been able to locate a number of the contracts his father wanted to see and he hadn't a clue how to bluff his way out of it.

'So where are the contracts?' Judd asked in a dangerously quiet voice.

Sebastian cleared his throat. 'I've managed to track a few of them down and I've got them here for signing.' He rustled the paperwork self-importantly, clearly keen to gloss over the fact that he had had to 'track them down' in the first place. 'As for the others, I'm sure they'll turn up . . .'

'That doesn't inspire much confidence, does it?' Judd commented sharply, yanking the paperwork out of Sebastian's hands. He perused the sheets at high speed, signing where they were marked with a cross. 'You're sure the missing contracts will "turn up", you say? When, exactly? And where do you think they might be hiding?' He gestured under the table mockingly. 'Under here, perhaps?' He pointed to a cabinet in the corner. 'Or maybe they're in there, with all the Christmas decorations?'

Beneath his freckles, Sebastian blanched. 'Look, Dad, it's all in hand,' he stuttered, visibly sweating as he loosened his tie. 'I'll find the contracts and we'll get everything sewn up.'

'And if we don't? There are several missing. Charlie Valentine's, for one, and he's more than likely to go skulking back to Lochlin if he remembers there's a three-month let-out clause.' Judd tossed the names of some other acts into the melee, listening to Sebastian's lame excuses and stammered apologies. His expression became thunderous. 'Christ, Sebastian, do shut up! Just because you've finally found someone to fuck other than your boring wife, doesn't mean you can take your eye off the ball.' Ignoring his son's gaping mouth, he went on. 'You've lost contracts and you haven't signed off on a number of acts we've acquired. I've been running around covering your arse for months now and it's simply not good enough. Who the hell are you shagging anyway? Anyone I know?'

Sebastian was so scared, he accidently blurted Lexi's name.

'Lexi Beaument? That little tramp,' Judd jeered. 'It must have taken you all of five minutes to get her knickers off. But it doesn't excuse you being so fucking preoccupied over the last few months. It's only sex, Sebastian. Most of us get it daily and still manage to hold down a job.'

Sebastian quailed.

'Christ, can't any of my children do anything right?' Judd roared, losing his temper. 'You're all happy to spend my fucking money but none of you can be relied upon to deliver the goods. You, snivelling little Elliot, Savannah . . .'

Hating himself, Sebastian couldn't help feeling a stab of pleasure that his brat of a half-sister was finally out of favour. He could only imagine it was down to the disastrous launch night he'd heard about and Sebastian couldn't be happier to witness Savannah's fall from grace. His cheeks turned an ugly red as he recalled the indignity of that day on the golf course when one of the directors at Jett had pointed out the terrible swear word scrawled across his neck.

Sebastian gritted his teeth. The little bitch. He hoped Savannah was kicked out without a cent and that none of them had to see her again. He wasn't going to be bullied by anyone . . . Catching sight of his father's furious expression, he got to his feet.

'Er, do you need me for anything else?'

Judd gave him a withering look. 'What would be the point, Sebastian? You'd only fuck it up somehow.' He cracked his knuckles. 'Now fuck off and find those contracts, will you?'

As Sebastian shot out of the door like a petrified rabbit, Judd realised it was time to start bringing his plans to fruition. Clearly, he was the only person who could make that happen. More fired up than he'd felt for a long time, he picked up his phone and started making some calls. If Lochlin thought the vice around his throat was tight now, let's see how he feels after this, Judd thought cruelly.

Chapter Fifteen

'Fuuuuuuuccccck!!!!'

Ace yelled at the top of his voice as he came, collapsing in a sweaty heap on top of Iris. She gasped, trying to catch her breath and buried her face in Ace's salty neck.

'So . . . are you glad you came?' Ace panted, stroking a strand of blond hair out of Iris's eyes. 'Forgive the pun. I mean to Monaco.'

Winding her leg sinuously around his, Iris thumped him on the arm. 'Let me think about that . . .' She gazed through the vast, floor-to-ceiling windows that offered a panoramic view of Monte Carlo. She could see the glitzy harbour, full of over-sized white yachts huddled together in orderly rows, their tall masts pointing skyward. Down below was part of the road used in the Grand Prix and with the fabulously regal casino building just around the corner, along with a plethora of glamorous shops and restaurants, Iris could barely believe her luck. Aside from the heavy weight of guilt resting on her shoulders about her father, Iris couldn't think when she'd been happier.

'This apartment must be worth a fortune,' she murmured, kissing Ace.

'Millions,' he agreed in a genial tone, wrapping his arms around her. 'Dad's missing out on a huge rental fee letting us stay here during the Grand Prix so we'd better make the most of it.'

Iris felt her stomach flip over as Ace left a trail of hot kisses down her neck. Fresh from a spectacular second place win at the NASCAR Sprint All-Star race, Ace felt relaxed about his forthcoming races but irritated as coming second meant missing out on the $1,000,000 prize.

More than any other time he had driven in the All-Star, Ace had wanted to win the money and his driving had been reckless and crazy. Bryan Loveton, the winner of the match, had cut Ace up so badly on the final lap, Jerry insisted Ace should put in a formal complaint but it seemed petty in the face of defeat.

Stretching and giving Iris the benefit of his unashamedly sexy back view – taut shoulder muscles tapering to a narrow waist and the most perfect arse she had ever seen – Ace stood up and turned round, sporting an impressive erection.

Iris giggled and hid under the sheet. She couldn't take any more, her limbs were aching from all the sex but deliciously so, her mouth was bruised and she could barely walk. Dazed with love, she watched Ace yawn like a child as he flicked the curtains back and stared out of the window. Mrs Goldman, an elderly divorcee, caught sight of Ace's rock-hard body and equally firm erection and almost dropped her croissant in her black coffee as she sat on her veranda.

Raising her coffee to him with a cheeky smile, he waved back at her. Putting a cigarette in his mouth, Ace threw himself into a chair and lit it.

Iris had to pinch herself. She couldn't believe she was here in Monte Carlo. Judd's apartment reportedly pulled in an astonishing £25,000 a month, which shot up to astronomical levels during the Grand Prix period. The Grand Prix wasn't taking place until the following day but Monte Carlo was already bustling with eager tourists, drop-dead gorgeous models and hyped-up racing crews. Hotels were bursting at the seams and bars were doing a roaring trade from all the additional people spilling out on to the pavement, enjoying glasses of champagne in the sun. Extra security had been stepped up outside the casino area and there was an air of intense excitement and expectation in the air.

Iris couldn't wait to go for a stroll down by the harbour and she was dying to check out the sleek Aston Martins and Ferraris outside the infamous casino but she had to do the photo shoot for 'Racy', the clothing company Ace had secured the deal with, first.

Ace glanced at his watch, belatedly remembering that the photo crew were due to arrive any second. 'Shit, have you seen the time? You need to get ready.' He did a double take at the window, spotting what he thought was a familiar face in the window of one of the apartments nearby. Surely Allegra had no business being in Monaco?

Ace rubbed his eyes. He must have been mistaken. He hadn't seen Allegra for weeks and he was sure she would have been in touch if she knew they were in the same place. The girl he'd just seen *had* looked very much like her, though.

Iris gathered the sheet up around her and tore past him into the shower as she heard a knock on the door. 'Tell them I'll be out in a minute.' She gave him a lingering kiss and giggled. 'I reek of you . . . I can't be photographed like this.'

Ace growled, grabbing for her as she slipped out of his grasp. Pulling on a pair of purple boxer shorts, he let the crew in, and apologised for oversleeping, shrugging as he took in their saucy grins. Iris was gorgeous; what did they all expect any red-blooded man to do?

Emerging from the shower with damp hair and naked beneath a silky pink kimono, Iris apologised for keeping everyone waiting and obediently sat back to let them get to work on her. Within seconds, she had won over every single one of them and, apart from Ace trying to distract her by pulling funny faces in the background, Iris couldn't help enjoying being fussed over by a team of make-up artists. As her face was being made up with tinted moisturiser and rose-coloured cream blusher, someone else was working on her nails, painting them hot pink.

Watched by Ace, who had sent out for coffees and breakfast pastries for everyone, a hair stylist came over, telling Iris confidently that he would take away a few inches but that she would gain a fantastic style instead. Nervously, she let him snip away at her tawny-blond hair before running some styling product through it and blowing it all over the place with his hairdryer. When he'd finished, he fluffed his hands through Iris's hair and showed her the end result in the mirror.

Iris was stunned. She didn't look like herself at all! Her make-up was flawless and natural looking and her hair looked incredible . . . 'Wow . . . you've all made me look . . .'

'*Fucking* sexy,' Ace drawled proudly, noticing all the heterosexual members of the crew salivating over his girlfriend.

Leading her to a rail of clothes, a stylist handed her a yellow playsuit with a black and white check pattern around the legs.

'That's . . . tiny,' Iris said, gulping fearfully.

'You can carry it off,' the stylist told her, holding it up against her. 'Your figure is perfect and your colouring will look amazing with this sunshine yellow.'

'If you're sure.' Looking doubtful, Iris dived into the bathroom to try it on. When she came out, Ace whistled appreciatively. It showed acres of tanned thigh and the zip revealed a hint of cleavage but Iris wasn't used to wearing anything as small as this. Flanked by a very hung-over looking Jerry, who had a cap pulled down over his preppy blond hair, and Luisa, who was holding on to Jerry's arm as if they were a couple, Ace looked as pleased as punch as he gazed at Iris.

Nick, the photographer, was keen to get started, and he positioned Iris in the huge sitting room, with the view of the glittering Mediterranean behind her. 'What I have in mind is a fun shoot,' he explained quickly, nodding at a lackey to play some music. Beyoncé's 'Crazy in Love' boomed out. 'With you in all these different clothes, dancing around to the backdrop of Monaco with all it has to offer.'

'Dancing?' Iris echoed. Ace hadn't told her anything about dancing. Why did they have to pick the one thing she was absolutely rubbish at? She caught Lusia's eye but Luisa was too busy trying not to laugh at Iris's predicament.

'Yes, just go for it. Let your hair down and just go with the flow.' Nick got into position and waved a hand for her to start.

Feeling hideously self-conscious, Iris started to weave around on the spot.

'More!' shouted the photographer. 'Go for it!'

Iris threw in a few more arm movements, going red as Luisa lost control of herself and burst out laughing.

Nick glared at her. 'You think you can do better?'

Luisa stopped giggling. 'With the dancing, yes, but with looking like Iris, no way.'

'Shut up then.' He smiled, giving her washboard stomach an approving glance. He turned his attention back to Iris. 'Look, don't worry about looking cool; this is just about you looking as if you're in Monte Carlo for the Grand Prix, dancing around before you go out on the town.'

Iris tugged at the playsuit. 'I'm really sorry. I'm just . . . dancing really isn't my thing at all.' Realising they were all waiting for her to get it together, she took a deep breath. They were paying her an awful lot of money to represent their brand and she was going to have to think of a way to get over her stiffness and give them what they wanted. Thinking for a minute, she came up with an idea.

'Could I do an impression of Cameron Diaz, where she dances like a goofball in *Charlie's Angels*? I could give that a go because it's the only way I can let my hair down.'

Seeing Nick shrug, Iris flung her hips out and forgot anyone else was in the room. She must have been doing something right because Nick was galvanised into action, leaping round the room like a gazelle, his camera snapping away as he got shot after shot.

'You go, girl!' Luisa cheered, clapping her hands. Iris was a natural comic, far more suited to playing the fool than looking aloof and doing serious dance moves. One of the stylists was on the phone to the director of the brand, telling him in French how fabulous Iris was and how she was personifying their brand to a tee.

Ace laughed uproariously at the sight of Iris sending herself up and he nudged Jerry. 'I love this girl!' he cried. 'Don't you just love this girl, Jezza?'

Jerry nodded. He did. Iris was adorable and, grudgingly, Jerry admitted that she was perfect for Ace. She was sweet and fun and she clearly loved Ace wholeheartedly. And looking at Ace, Jerry strongly suspected he felt the same way about Iris, even if he didn't realise it, having never been in love before. Trust Ace to fall for the one girl he wasn't meant to, Jerry thought uneasily. Assuming he would be horribly resentful of any girl who came between him and Ace, Jerry was taken aback at how much he cared about Iris too, and he guessed it was probably because she *hadn't* come between them; she respected their friendship.

'Have you heard from your father recently?' Jerry asked, his eyes radiating concern. Iris came with a shelf life; that was her only downside and it was a shelf life that wasn't within Ace's control. Jerry couldn't help wondering what Ace was going to do when Judd phoned to call in the other part of their deal.

Ace's phone rang. 'Speak of the devil,' he muttered. 'Yeah, everything's fine,' Jerry heard him say. 'What? Oh, that, it's all in hand. Yeah, shocking, I know. I'm obviously better in the sack than you think I am. Right, bye.' Ace snapped his phone shut, his mouth set in a grim line. 'I just told him Iris will sign a contract with Jett.'

Jerry gaped. 'But—'

'I was trying to buy myself some time, Jez, that's all.' Ace's grey eyes were anguished.

Jerry gave his shoulder a squeeze. 'But you do know he's going to call at some point and get you to dump her, don't you?'

Ace stared at Iris, tortured. 'We have to think of something,' he muttered to Jerry under his breath. 'If you really are my best friend, Jerry, you have to help me come up with a solution.'

He forced his face into a sparkling grin as Iris bounded over.

'Was I all right?' she asked, giving Jerry a kiss on the cheek and grabbing Ace's hand.

'Fabulous,' Jerry told her, thinking Ace was doomed. There was no solution to this, not if Ace wanted to carry on driving for a living. And racing cars was who Ace was. Aside from wanting to win his father's approval, this was going to kill him, Jerry knew that for sure.

'You were sensational.' Ace pulled Iris into his arms. 'Fucking sensational.' Staring at Jerry over the top of Iris's blond head, they wondered what the hell they could do to stop the car crash.

Hiding out in a vastly overpriced apartment next door to Mrs Goldman, Allegra was watching everything through a powerful telescope. Sitting back, she narrowed her eyes, thankful she had her model's salary to fall back on as she followed Ace and Iris on their travels.

Allegra contemplated what she'd just seen. There was more to this relationship than met the eye; she would lay her life on it. All she had to do was get to the bottom of it. And finish it, once and for all.

At Brockett Hall, Martha was surveying the view despondently. It was raining hard and she could see a stray cat, soaked to the skin and shivering, using a dripping rhododendron bush as an umbrella. Feeling gloomy as she stared out across the fields at the sodden crops and the trees, drenched and bent sideways by the downpour, Martha found herself missing LA. People complained about the relentless predictability of the sunshine but at least it was reliable, at least you didn't wake up expecting sunshine and end up with thunder and lightning.

Catching sight of her reflection in the mirror, Martha felt a sob rising in her throat. Pale at the best of times, the lack of sunshine in the UK had left her looking like Caspar, the friendly ghost. Her face looked puffy and unhealthy and her hair was desperately in need of a cut. Like the stray cat huddled up against the rhododendron bush outside, Martha felt neglected and bedraggled.

Trying not to think about all the weight she'd gained recently, she helped herself to a Magnum ice lolly from the freezer.

'Hey. I thought I'd come and see how you were.' Sebastian joined her.

She met his eyes warily, unused to small talk with her husband.

Martha silently finished her Magnum, guessing Sebastian had fallen short of Judd's expectations yet again and therefore needed a sounding board, or more likely a metaphorical punch bag. She still suspected he was having an affair; the odd waft of perfume on his suits gave him away, as did the long, predatory-looking scratch mark she'd seen down his back in the shower the other day.

'Do you think some people aren't meant to have children?' she asked, out of the blue.

Sebastian eyes shifted uneasily. 'What?'

'I've been thinking about it and I think some people aren't supposed to have children for some reason.' Her voice caught in her throat. 'It's the only way I can make sense of what's happening to us, to think that, for whatever reason, it just wasn't meant to be.'

'Er . . . we need to talk,' Sebastian said in a sombre tone.

'What about?' Martha felt a wave of tiredness washing over her. Sometimes, being with Sebastian was such hard work, she felt as if she needed a vacation from him, just to clear her head.

Sebastian paced up and down the kitchen, tugging at the collar of his shirt as if it was choking him. After the toe-curlingly hideous dressing-down he'd suffered from his father earlier that week, Sebastian had realised he didn't have too much to lose at this stage. His career at Jett was hardly setting the world on fire and whatever he did he was never quite able to impress his father, professionally or otherwise.

Feeling Martha's eyes on him, Sebastian wondered how to even broach the subject of Lexi's bombshell. The news could send

Martha hurtling towards the edge of the proverbial precipice but time was running out and decisions needed to be made. Sebastian had come up with a crazy notion which seemed to have made sense in his own head but now, face to face with Martha, it suddenly seemed like the worst idea in the world. Either way, Sebastian knew his marriage was hanging in the balance and he couldn't for the life of him understand why he felt so panicked about it.

'How badly do you want a baby?' he blurted out in a far brusquer tone than he'd intended.

Martha stared at him. 'You know how I feel about it. I want a baby more than anything in the world.'

Sebastian hesitated then went for it. 'All right, what would you say if I said I knew someone who was having a baby who didn't want it. Someone who might give it up if we paid her.'

Martha attempted to make sense of what he was saying. 'Who? Wh-who has a baby they'd give to us?'

Sebastian waved the question away. He planned to tackle that particularly awkward issue later on. But if having a baby was the most important thing in the world to her, Sebastian thought he might actually be able to sort out the mess he'd got himself into.

'Is adoption an issue for you?'

She shook her head, wondering where all this was leading. Perhaps Sebastian wanted to do a Madonna and adopt an African baby or something. Not that she minded; she would happily embrace a child from any culture. 'I was thinking about surrogacy the other day. I thought it would be lovely if the baby could be part of one of us, at least.'

Feeling an unexpected rush of guilt, Sebastian looked down at his hands. He had that angle covered but not quite the way Martha imagined. Standing up, he found himself taking her in his arms, something he hadn't done in a long time.

Martha, stunned at the intimate gesture, wasn't sure what to do.

Sebastian took a deep breath and held her tight. 'You see, I know this woman who's pregnant and I don't think she wants to keep the baby. Now, I haven't asked her yet but she might be open to offers. We might even be able to keep it all under wraps and pass it off as our own . . . I don't know yet.'

Martha looked up at him with wide eyes. 'This woman . . . is it someone at work?'

'Not exactly.' Sebastian couldn't look at her, not at this point.

Her heart beating rapidly, Martha eased her arms away from him as an appalling idea occurred to her. All the nights he'd been home late, his evasiveness, the hint of perfume, the scratch on his back. 'You're not . . . this isn't . . . oh my God, Sebastian.' She backed away from him. She couldn't believe it. If it was anyone else but Sebastian, she wouldn't have even contemplated such a revolting notion but knowing him as she did, Martha knew she was right.

'Now, don't go all psycho on me,' Sebastian snapped, feeling cornered.

'You got some girl pregnant, didn't you?' she whispered, shaking her head disbelievingly. She felt her way blindly along the kitchen counter, moving as far away from him as possible. 'You screwed some girl, got her pregnant and you thought you'd found the perfect get-out clause.' Martha's face contorted with pain. 'Jesus Christ, Sebastian! You seriously think you can pay this girl off and shut me up by giving me the baby?'

'At least it's partly ours,' Sebastian offered tactlessly.

Martha's eyes clouded over with tears. 'You always told me it was my fault we couldn't have children and you were right. All those years of trying and we never managed it, yet you screw someone else and, bingo, a baby.'

Sebastian knew he shouldn't be congratulating himself in the circumstances but the fact remained; he had always maintained the problem was down to Martha and he had been proved right, unequivocally.

Martha stared at him coldly. 'At what point are you going to apologise for having an affair?' she asked. Talk about like father, like son. Martha knew exactly how Kitty must have felt over the years being married to Judd.

Sebastian sighed heavily. Trust Martha to want apologies and remorse. Couldn't she just accept that there was a baby up for grabs? Couldn't she just make the best of it, like he was trying to do?

'Who is she?'

He jumped at Martha's sharp tone. 'It doesn't matter.'

'It does to me!' she screamed. Hurt beyond belief, she ran at him and hit him haphazardly, thrashing around like a wild woman. She wanted to cause him pain, she wanted him to suffer.

Sebastian held her off with difficulty, shocked to the core that Martha had reacted so violently. Meek little Martha, always so subservient and dutiful. She had a backbone, after all, it had simply taken something she really cared about to bring it out in her. In spite of himself, Sebastian couldn't help being impressed with his wife.

Martha, on the other hand, had never hated Sebastian more in her life. How could he do this to her? She turned away from him, sickened. She had always been a loyal wife . . . she had tried so hard. And he had repaid her by getting some other woman pregnant. With the baby *they* should have had, Martha thought, anguished.

She felt a fleeting moment of sympathy for the baby. It was innocent in all this and it deserved the best chance in life it could have. What if the baby's mother really didn't want it? Would she allow it to be adopted by someone else? Would she – God forbid – might she abort it? Martha suddenly saw Sebastian's hateful idea in another light. But that didn't mean he was off the hook.

'Who is she?' she asked again, quietly. It shouldn't matter to her, but it did.

Sebastian dithered, really not sure if revealing Lexi's identity was such a good idea. But, if they went through with his plan, Martha would find out soon enough who was having his baby.

'It's . . . it's Lexi Beaument,' he confessed. Swiftly he held his hands up in case she went mental and attacked him again.

'Lexi Beaument?' Martha's face crumpled. Lexi was half her size and what most men would consider sex on legs. How on earth could she, Martha, compete with that?

Feeling horribly betrayed, she let out an anguished howl and dashed to the bathroom. Sebastian stared after her, realising he'd probably made a huge mistake.

The following day, Lochlin was rereading the share report in the newspaper with a sinking heart. It was official, Shamrock was on the slippery slope downwards, Jett was soaring into the stratosphere and, as far as he could see, there was nothing he could do about it.

What would his family think of him? Lochlin wondered, pouring himself a large Scotch, the only thing that seemed to pass his lips these days. Would Tavvy be disappointed in him? She knew better than anyone how hard he had worked to honour his father and make Shamrock a success. Would she blame him for letting it slip through his fingers? Tavvy had always been his biggest supporter and the one person he knew he could always trust and confide in but for some reason, Lochlin felt too ashamed to open up to how bad things had got. And it was creating a chasm between them, a gaping abyss he felt most tangibly at night, as the gulf between their carefully positioned bodies yawned and widened.

The other night he had heard her chatting on the phone, talking about renovating the barn for Noah's Ark to house more horses, and he had felt shut out and excluded. Lochlin realised she had probably told him all about it but he was so preoccupied, he could barely function.

He sighed. It wasn't Tavvy's fault. In the old days, he would come home from work and chat about his day, asking her advice and feeling his problems lift away from his shoulders with ease as they worked through them together. Since Judd's return, Lochlin had felt as if he needed to prove himself worthy of running Shamrock and, more significantly, of having Tavvy in his life. Confessing his failure to secure certain clients and to win new acts had become something Lochlin felt shameful about, certain that by comparison with Judd, he would be found lacking.

This unspoken competition with Judd appeared to have no rules and with both of them stubbornly clinging to each petty victory, it was a competition that looked set to be won only upon the death of the other. Lochlin lived each day in fear of losing everything – his business, his family, his home. He checked his phone again. So many days had passed without a word from Iris, Lochlin was convinced something must be very wrong. Uniquely bonded to her since childhood, he couldn't understand why his daughter might be avoiding him, not unless Judd was involved somehow.

Tossing back his Scotch, Lochlin wondered how on earth his family would forgive him if he lost Shamrock. Realising he had shut Tavvy out, Lochlin stood up, knowing he had to make things right with her. It was about time he went home and faced the music. His mouth curved slightly at the unintended pun and, ignoring the breathlessness that kept stopping him in his tracks, he did something he hadn't done in months.

Making peace with his father by silently apologising to the friendly face in the office portrait, Lochlin shut down his computer, said a firm goodbye to an astonished Erica and headed home early.

Dressed in a big jumper of Lochlin's and a scarf to keep her neck warm, Tavvy was giving Kitty the trial she had promised her at Susannah's party. She'd been putting it off for a while as Lochlin seemed so stressed out but as he was spending increasingly long hours at Shamrock's offices, she thought it was time she gave Kitty a chance.

Brushing Moccachino's rump with long, brisk strokes, Tavvy handed the brush to Kitty. 'See, it's easy. You have a go.'

Nervous at being around such a large and unpredictable animal, Kitty bravely took the brush in her gloved hands, doing her best to mimic Tavvy's strokes. Growing in confidence, she moved faster. 'This is actually really therapeutic!' she exclaimed.

'Isn't it? I've lost hours out here because it's so lovely looking after the animals.'

Kitty gestured to Petra, who was hard at work shovelling fresh straw into the stables. 'She seems very dedicated, if a little scary.'

'Heart of gold, social skills of a reclusive hermit,' Tavvy agreed. She outlined her plans for the new barn with extensive stables and a possible cat sanctuary.

'It sounds wonderful,' Kitty said, impressed. She was surprised at how much she enjoyed Tavvy's company but she admired her on so many levels. Tavvy had forged a new career for herself by setting up Noah's Ark, even though it had been completely out of her comfort zone. Kitty wished she had half of Tavvy's courage.

'Something on your mind?' Tavvy inquired, observing Kitty's taut shoulders. Her soft grey eyes seemed troubled and Tavvy wondered if she was too polite to say how much she hated working with her. 'If you've had a change of heart, I won't be offended, I promise. I mean, I feel passionate about Noah's Ark but I don't expect anyone else to.'

'If you offered me a job here, I'd take it like a shot.' Kitty stared up at Pembleton wistfully. 'I love it, Tavvy, all of it. Pembleton, for a start . . . it's just magical to me, like a real home. Brockett Hall is beautiful, of course, but it's rather like an ice sculpture. It's a very regal house but it has no soul.'

Tavvy shivered. She couldn't agree more. Brockett Hall had always seemed like a mausoleum to her, chilly and slightly creepy, but she had her reasons for feeling that way. 'Have you ever been to Foxton Manor, Leo Beaument's place? You'd probably love it, it's very traditional and cosy and it has a lovely lived-in feel about it.'

She blew on her hands. 'Poor Leo, there's a rumour going round the village that his wife Lexi is cheating on him but none of us want to believe it's true.'

'Oh, it is true.' Kitty nodded, throwing a straw bale into the shed. 'I went out for a drink with him a while ago and he told me about it.'

Tavvy straightened up. 'You went out for a drink with Leo?'

Kitty blushed. 'We didn't arrange it or anything, we just met up one afternoon.' She felt upset remembering how devastated Leo had seemed. 'He was doing his best to hide it but I could see Lexi's affair was tearing him apart.'

'Poor Leo. He deserves better. Did he say who Lexi's sleeping with?'

Kitty shook her head. 'Oh no, it was only a brief chat. And we're just acquaintances; he wouldn't confide in me or anything.'

Tavvy looked at Kitty from under her fringe, wondering why her new friend was at such pains to play down her friendship with Leo. 'Coffee time,' she announced, deciding she and Kitty deserved a break. 'Petra brings her own, probably because mine is so terrible.'

Kitty followed Tavvy inside Pembleton, delighted to find a coffee maker. She set about making coffee; if Tavvy's was as bad as she said it was, Kitty didn't want to offend her by throwing it down the sink. The coffee machine glugged and puffed and soon they had two steaming mugs in their hands.

'Oh, thank God you know how to work that,' Tavvy cried. 'Shay left it behind and I gave up trying to get it to work. Wow, this is good, much better than my efforts.'

Making them both jump out of their skins, Caitie charged in brandishing a magazine. 'Have you seen this?' she screeched. She stopped short when she saw Kitty. 'Oh my God, you're Elliot's mother.'

Kitty held up her coffee cup by way of greeting. 'Nice to meet you.'

Tavvy snatched the magazine out of Caitie's hands. 'Stop staring, darling, it's very rude. Kitty's helping out with Noah's Ark for a while. I need the help and Kitty needs to get out of Brockett Hall now and again.'

'Does Dad know?'

Tavvy pulled a face. 'No, he doesn't. Any more than he knows about you and Elliot playing Romeo and Juliet in Hugo's play.'

Caitie turned puce. 'How . . . when . . . ?'

Tavvy took a crumpled flyer out of the biscuit tin. 'This was delivered a few weeks ago. I've been hiding it from your father ever since.'

'Shit.' Caitie had the grace to look apologetic. 'Sorry, Mum. I've been wanting to tell you for ages . . .'

Kitty laughed. 'So that's what Elliot's been doing all this time!' She smiled. 'Good for him.' She glanced at Caitie. 'I bet he's brilliant. Is he brilliant?'

'He is, actually.' Caitie turned the pages of the magazine. 'Anyway, look, it's Iris . . . in Monte Carlo at the Grand Prix.' She looked at Kitty with accusing green eyes. 'With your son, Ace.'

Kitty's coffee mug paused in mid-air. 'What?' Leaning over Tavvy's shoulder, she gaped at the photograph. Ace, looking bronzed and sexy, had his arm thrown around Iris's shoulder as they wandered along the harbour by all the flashy yachts in Monte Carlo. Iris, her hair shorter than usual and cut stylishly, was wearing a short, violet dress. The breathtaking backdrop of the glittering azure-blue of the Mediterranean Sea was almost eclipsed by their beauty; Ace and Iris both looked besotted with each other and the searing sexual chemistry between them was so tangible, it seemed as though it would take a crow bar to prise them apart.

'Bloody hell,' Tavvy said, overcome with shock. 'And that . . . that's your son, is it? Ace?'

Kitty nodded. 'That's Ace.' She scrutinised the photograph. She'd never seen Ace looking so happy before; his grin was so wide it looked as though his face might split. She wondered how her son and Tavvy's daughter had ended up together and a terrible thought occurred to her.

'Isn't he a serial shagger?' Caitie demanded, crossing her arms and fixing her intense green gaze on Kitty. 'He's very good looking but me and Jas Googled him and he has a dreadful reputation.'

Kitty pulled a face. 'He *is* a bit of a playboy, yes.' What could she say? Ace's sexual antics were legendary, there was no point in her denying it.

Tavvy stared at the photograph. Ace and Iris looked perfect together; they were the picture of youthful sexiness and they had that secretive look about them, that delicious, sexual intimacy that told the world they had spent hours coiled around one another in bed. Tavvy knew it was wrong but she couldn't help thinking that if Ace and Iris ever had children, they would be absolutely ravishing.

Oblivious of the tension in the room, Shay wandered in. 'Hi. Thought I'd cook for you all tonight. I've brought steaks . . .' He caught sight of Kitty and did a double take. 'Blimey, Mum, you're living dangerously, aren't you? Does Dad know you're sleeping with the enemy?' He corrected himself. 'Or having tea with his wife, at any rate? Sorry, Mrs Harrington, no offence meant.'

'None taken.' Kitty stared up at Shay, thinking how handsome and capable he looked.

Tavvy frowned and handed him the magazine. 'Seriously, Shay, Kitty is the least of our worries.'

Shay looked at the photograph, going cold all over. What the hell was Iris doing with her hands all over a Harrington? No wonder she'd been evasive on the phone!

'I wonder . . . look, I don't mean to alarm you all, but I think Judd might have something to do with this,' Kitty stated, voicing her fears. She refused to believe Iris and Ace had randomly found each other in Los Angeles. LA was a very big place and singers and racing drivers rarely frequented the same social scene. No, this little stunt had Judd stamped all over it. More worryingly, Kitty thought, was what he intended to do now that he'd got the pair of them together.

Tavvy clapped a hand over her mouth. 'You're joking. Good God. Lochlin is going to have a seizure. He's been trying to get hold of her for days. No wonder she's not answering her phone.'

Shay was reading the accompanying article. 'Has anyone actually read this?' They all shook their heads.

'We were only looking at the photo,' Tavvy said, putting her hand to her chest.

'It says that Iris has signed a deal with the Jett Record Corporation. The very thing she'd promised Dad she'd never do when he let her go to the States.' Shay slammed the magazine down in a rage. He couldn't believe Iris would do this. What the hell was she thinking? He could only imagine this Ace Harrington had turned Iris's head and convinced her that a record deal with Jett was her best bet.

Tavvy put her head in her hands. This was Lochlin's worst nightmare. She couldn't imagine how betrayed Lochlin would feel if he ever found out. But he was going to, there was no way they could hide this from him for ever and Tavvy felt a tremor of fear shoot through her.

Caitie zipped through the article. 'I don't believe it,' she declared. 'Iris would never do this to us.' She put the magazine down. 'And there was me worrying about Dad finding out about me and Elliot being in the play together but Iris going out with Ace Harrington and signing a deal with Judd's record company. . . .'

Staring at her mother's stricken face and her frantically waving hands, Caitie's voice died in her throat. Spinning round, she saw her father standing in the kitchen doorway, his face aghast.

Looking grey, Lochlin blinked at Tavvy. His stressed-out mind, already at breaking point, tried and failed to make sense of what he was seeing and hearing. Caitie, in a play with Elliot Harrington? And who was Tavvy sharing a cup of coffee with? Surely not Judd's wife, Kitty? Lochlin's eyes travelled from Kitty to the open magazine on the table, witnessing the betrayal in glorious technicolour. Iris, beautiful, talented Iris, with one of Judd's son's all over her. Iris, who'd signed a deal with Jett.

Croaking, Lochlin tugged at his shirt collar as sweat poured down his body.

Shay stepped forward with anxious green eyes. 'Dad? Are you all right?'

Lochlin shook his head, gasping and clawing at his chest. Feeling the nagging pain that had been bothering him for weeks now travel to his neck and arms, it gathered pace until the pressure was almost too much to bear. Fuzzily seeing Caitie and Tavvy rushing towards him as in the distance Kitty reached for the phone to dial an ambulance, Lochlin heard their voices as if he was drowning.

Collapsing into Shay's arms, Lochlin passed out.

Chapter Sixteen

Slumped over Lochlin's hospital bed catching a few minutes' sleep, Tavvy woke up with a start. Her eyes darted immediately to the heart monitor and she let out a shaky sigh of relief when she realised the cheery lights and noises were flashing and beeping as they should be. Lochlin's face was peaceful and it looked like he was sleeping soundly. She peeled away the slightly musty-smelling hospital blanket they'd given her and lifted the curtain fractionally. It was bright and sunny outside, even though it was late afternoon, but Tavvy was barely aware of the time. Lifting her unwashed, lank hair out of her eyes, she tied it back with a grubby elastic band she'd found in her pocket.

Rubbing her eyes, Tavvy wondered when she'd last slept for more than ten-minute stretches since Lochlin's heart attack. Having been at the hospital for four days now, keeping vigil, there had been no change whatsoever in Lochlin's condition. Shay and Caitie had been in and out but she had sent them away, giving them tasks to keep them busy – like contacting Iris, for a start. No one had been able to reach her for days. Now she'd seen the photograph of Iris with Ace Harrington, Tavvy fully understood why Iris had been keeping her distance but Tavvy staunchly refused to believe Iris had signed a record deal with Judd's company, Jett.

She sighed and clutched Lochlin's hand. She refused to believe her husband would not survive the massive heart attack he had suffered, even though the doctors had told her to 'prepare herself', whatever the hell that meant. Tavvy reached out and stroked a wave of hair back from Lochlin's forehead. His skin had a ghostly pallor to it and he seemed to have shrunk somehow. The fragile, wasted form in the bed was a million miles from the robust, fun-loving man with broad shoulders and a raucous laugh she'd loved for as long as she could remember.

'Hello, Mrs Maguire,' said Rosie, a pretty Irish nurse with a stout behind. She bustled in with Lochlin's meds, chattering brightly to him as if he could hear every word. 'Top of the morning to you, Mr Maguire! If only you could see how sunny it was outside. We'll soon have you back on your feet so you can go and enjoy it, so we shall.'

Wiping her eyes, Tavvy gave Rosie a watery smile. She knew Lochlin would approve of being attended to by such a pretty Irish girl.

Checking the machines and scribbling on his chart, Rosie kindly patted Tavvy's shoulder. 'You mustn't blame yourself, you couldn't possibly have known that he'd been having all these mini heart attacks for weeks now.'

Tavvy nodded, sniffing. As nice as everyone was being to her, she couldn't help feeling she should have known how ill Lochlin had been. Why hadn't she realised he was suffering so badly? She was his wife, for heaven's sake! But then, they had both been hiding so much from each other.

Rosie, seeing Tavvy's stricken face and recognising the signs, started to get bossy. 'All right, my darlin', it's time you went home for a bit. You've been here for days. Change your clothes, grab a sandwich.'

Tearfully, Tavvy rubbed Lochlin's hand, willing him to respond. 'I just keep reliving the moment he walked in the door, Rosie . . . his face . . . it was so grey . . .'

'There, there. I know how wearing it can be to sit by someone's bedside day and night.'

Tavvy burst into noisy tears.

'Definitely time for you to go home and have a break.' Rosie gently lifted Tavvy out of her seat and led her to the door. 'I promise I'll call you the second anything changes, darlin'. Maybe pop into the office, like you were planning, if you need something to do.'

Hesitating, Tavvy knew Rosie was right. She *did* need a break. Stepping outside, she took in great gulps of fresh air. She decided to drive to the office, after all. She couldn't face the thought of being at Pembleton, so achingly part of Lochlin.

The late afternoon traffic was grid-locked but she made it just as night began to fall. Not even sure what she was looking for, she headed upstairs to Lochlin's office and found a peaky-looking Erica packing up for the day.

'Tavvy, I wasn't expecting you.' Erica gave her a sympathetic hug. 'How are you bearing up?'

'I'm fine . . . I think.' Tavvy brushed her hair out of her eyes vaguely. 'It's been difficult but it will all be worth it if Lochlin pulls through. I don't really know what I'm doing here.'

Giving her a quick once-over, Erica noticed Tavvy's face was etched with worry lines and she had deep violet shadows beneath her eyes. She unlocked the door to Lochlin's office.

Tavvy wandered inside, inhaling the air that seemed to be imbued with Lochlin's woody aftershave mixed with the faint whiff of the black coffee he always drank. And Scotch, by the looks of things, she thought, picking up an almost empty bottle that sat on a cabinet. Gazing up at the imposing portrait of the Maguire family, Tavvy felt a pang, wondering how worried Lochlin's parents would feel if they were alive. Poor Colleen had died after the tragedy and then a broken-hearted Niall had died over in Ireland some time later.

Taking a seat at Lochlin's desk, Tavvy switched his computer on and half-heartedly tapped a few keys. She wanted to help, but she didn't know where to begin.

Erica came in and gave Tavvy a curious look.

'Things have been pretty awful here,' she said. 'I don't know how much you know but Lochlin has lost a number of existing acts and has barely attracted any new ones since the end of last year. Share prices have dropped to an all-time low. Shamrock is worth far less than it used to be. I'm afraid it could be the end.'

Tavvy put a hand to her mouth in disbelief.

Erica glanced at her watch. 'I'm so sorry, Tavvy, I'll have to leave you to it. I've barely been at home in the past fortnight and my boyfriend's going to forget what I look like.'

Tavvy smiled at her. 'Off you go, Erica. I'll be fine.'

Barely knowing where to begin, Tavvy took off her coat and determinedly got to work. After phoning the hospital for an update, she decided to start with the accounts. She managed to get into Lochlin's computer by chance and set about reading through his emails and files. Her brow furrowed as she painstakingly tried to piece together various threads relating to legal issues, share prices and lost revenue. She was soon drowning in paperwork. As it got later and later, she didn't even realise great tears were splashing down on to Lochlin's keyboard. When she heard a noise outside, Tavvy hoped to God the bailiffs hadn't arrived. Wincing as the light was abruptly switched on, she was dazzled and couldn't believe her eyes when she saw a pair of broad shoulders outlined in the doorway, topped by dark hair.

'Lochlin?' she whispered.

'Wishful thinking, I'm afraid,' Shay answered with a wry smile as he stepped into the office. Seeing Tavvy surrounded by printouts and document files, he scratched his head. 'What on earth are you doing, Mum?'

Tavvy groaned. 'I wish I knew. I realise now I know plenty about music but absolutely nothing about running a record label.'

'Well, luckily for you, I do.' Gently, Shay extracted a bunch of papers from her hands before lifting her out of her chair. 'Now, step away from the computer and go and do what you do best.'

'What's that?' Tavvy gave him a bemused look.

Furiously tapping at the keyboard, Shay fixed his green eyes on the screen in front of him. 'Well, firstly, I think you need sleep and a shower. But after that, when you're ready, you need to write some more songs, of course.'

'Songs?'

'For Iris's album,' he answered absent-mindedly, pausing before typing the password 'Trinity' into the box provided. He smiled as the file of private information popped open. He knew his father so well; he had always called his three children 'the trinity'. Shay began to search through the files at high speed, filled with growing trepidation as he realised the extent of Shamrock's demise.

'Have you spoken to Iris, then?' Tavvy was so tired, she thought she might faint.

Shay shook his head grimly. 'Not yet but when I do, I'm going to give her a rocket up her arse for banging that bloke Ace and then I'm getting her on a plane and bringing her back here. To sign a deal with Shamrock.'

Tavvy's legs felt as if they might give way. 'But . . . what about the deal with Judd's company, the Jett Record Corporation?'

Shay grabbed a pen and started scribbling figures down on a notepad. 'I did some digging and that's a load of rubbish. I phoned Pia Jordan in Los Angeles and we had a very interesting chat. She and Judd have now parted company and she told me she'd be very surprised if Iris has signed anything with Jett.'

'But that magazine—'

'Pia reckons Ace told his father that to shut him up and that Judd leaked it to the press.' He rubbed his eyes tiredly. He'd been on the phone all evening before driving into London and he was worried sick about his father.

'How could Judd do that?' Tavvy whispered. 'He must have known what that would do to Lochlin.'

'I think that was the whole point.' Shay grimaced. 'We shouldn't have believed it, Mum. *I* shouldn't have believed it. There's no way Iris would sign with anyone else, even if she is head over heels with that racing driver moron.' He put his elbows on the desk and leant forward. 'Look, Mum, what's the history with Judd Harrington? Anything you can tell me might be helpful at this stage, especially now I'm trying to pick up the pieces.'

Tavvy sank down on to a nearby couch. 'We should have told you in the first place but Lochlin was trying to protect you . . . oh, it doesn't matter now. Put it this way, in my pop star days, there were always parties going on. I met Judd at one of them and we . . . we started going out.' She shivered at the memory. 'God knows what I saw in him . . . he can be very charismatic and persuasive when he wants to be. I soon realised what a bully he was and that was before he started giving me drugs.'

Shay gaped. 'Christ, no wonder Dad's been so over-protective with Iris!'

'Well, quite. I'm afraid I didn't exactly set a good example and poor Iris has suffered as a result.' Tavvy listlessly rubbed the mascara stains off her hands. 'I started off knocking champagne back at all these parties and then went on to a bit of weed and then when my career took off and it all got a bit crazy, Judd introduced me to cocaine.' Her amber eyes clouded over. 'He became my dealer and I relied on him for everything. I guess it was his way of trying to control me. Don't get me wrong, I think he loved me but he was so petrified I'd leave him, he kept me on a short leash. It was only when I met your father I had the courage to leave Judd and get help.'

Shay felt sickened. 'My God. He's an absolute monster! I had no idea it was anything like that.'

Tavvy flopped back against the couch. 'Oh, there's worse, Shay. Much, much worse. But . . . I'm done in. I need some sleep now.'

'Of course.' Shay jumped up and flung his jacket over her, tucking a cushion under her head for a pillow. Within seconds, Tavvy was fast asleep.

Shay brushed a strand of hair out of her eyes. He wasn't about to enlighten his mother about all the terrible things Pia had told him about Judd because it meant the situation with Iris and Ace was graver than they had all feared. He had sent dozens of texts but so far Iris hadn't responded to any of them.

Pushing Iris from his mind, Shay worked late into the night, comparing historical sales figures and making a list of anything he could think of to save Shamrock. It wasn't going to be easy.

In fact, he thought, digging out his mobile phone and dialling a number, unless someone at Jett had made some monumental mistakes somewhere along the line, Shamrock had well and truly had it.

'Leo? It's Shay. No, no change . . . Look, sorry to call you so late but I need your expert legal brain . . .'

Feeling detached as he sat in his Porsche with Lexi, Sebastian stared down at the fuzzy black and white photograph she'd given him. It didn't even *look* like a baby, it looked like an alien with a big white head attached to some freakishly skinny limbs. Sebastian shuddered. He felt absolutely nothing as he looked down at what was either his son or his daughter curled up in Lexi's womb.

'Well? What are we going to do about it?'

Lexi flipped open the mirror above the passenger seat and grimaced at the cluster of spots that seemed to have erupted on her chin overnight. God, pregnancy was a bind! Nausea and vomiting were bad enough; now she had acne to contend with.

Having finally visited her GP, Lexi had been sent for a scan. It turned out she was right; she had conceived back in March.

Glancing at Sebastian's weak chin and bright red hair, Lexi wondered what on earth she'd seen in him. He was rich, of course, which was the whole point, but the sex hadn't even been that good. Sex had been out of the question since the pregnancy announcement; mainly because Lexi could barely go five minutes without wanting to vomit into her Gucci handbag.

Sebastian's next words shocked Lexi so much she feared she might go into premature labour.

'How much would I have to pay for you to have this baby and give it to me?'

Lexi forgot her posh accent. 'You what?'

Sebastian thrust the scan photo into her hands. 'You heard me.'

She struggled to get her head round his suggestion. 'Let me get this straight. You want me to . . . to carry this baby for the next six months, give birth to it and then just hand it over to you?'

'For money.' He nodded, his eyes icy blue and emotionless.

'Has Martha agreed to this?' Lexi spluttered.

Sebastian looked away. 'Not as such. But she'll come round.' He gave her an impassive stare. 'Think about it. She wants a baby,' he pointed to her stomach like a crude schoolboy, 'and you have one in there.'

Lexi shook her head decisively. What sort of woman accepted a child from her husband's mistress? Martha seemed like a wet fish but surely even she had more backbone than that? Not that Lexi cared, she'd made her mind up. 'I'm aborting it. I have an appointment booked for tomorrow.'

'Cancel it. You're not aborting this baby.' He put his face close to hers. '*Capisce?*'

Lexi recoiled. She didn't know how Martha put up with him, even if he *was* rich. Falling pregnant seemed to have put Lexi's life in perspective all of a sudden and Sebastian, with all his faults and vulgarities, had come clearly into focus. *Capisce* indeed. *Arsehole.*

'We're at stalemate then, aren't we? I don't want this baby but I'm sure as hell not carrying it for you and your bloody wife.'

Sebastian produced a chequebook.

Trying her hardest to look disinterested, Lexi could barely believe it as Sebastian wrote a cheque for one hundred thousand pounds. She'd had no idea her baby was worth that much!

Quite a little earner, she thought, glancing down at her tummy which was beginning to curve outwards slightly. Lexi thought rapidly. Could she warm to the idea? Maybe having a baby and handing it over to Martha wasn't so crazy after all. But if she was going to do it, Lexi was going for gold. Sebastian was hardly likely to open with his best offer, so the way she saw it, she had him over a barrel with a broom up his bum! And she was going to take advantage of it. He was heir to a multimillion-pound fortune, for God's sake.

Lexi primly handed the cheque back, confident she was making the right move. 'I think that's an insult to me, *and* to your child.'

'What?' Sebastian seethed inside. The little tramp. He gritted his teeth. Lexi was nothing but a gold-digging slut and now she was playing hardball. That was his fucking bonus she'd just knocked back. Did she think he was made of money? As the penny, or rather the cent, finally dropped, Sebastian realised Lexi did indeed think he was made of money. That was no doubt what had attracted her in the first place and having abandoned all hope of becoming his second wife, she now wanted his cash for the baby he'd accidentally created.

Seeing Mrs Meaden, the village gossip, wandering around outside, Sebastian ducked down. Martha still wasn't talking to him and she'd even taken the step of moving his clothes into one of the spare bedrooms. Under normal circumstances, Sebastian would have promptly moved his things back and bullied Martha into letting him back into the marital bed, but he guessed he needed to keep her sweet if his plan was to work.

'How much do you want?' he asked Lexi, not bothering to play games.

Pleased he was seeing sense, Lexi smirked. 'Let's see. I've already carried this baby for three months and I have another six months to go. I may get fat, develop stretch marks and get saggy boobs.' Lexi glanced down at her magnificent, surgically enhanced chest with some fondness. 'And God alone knows what it might do down below, although I could always request a caesarean. I'll be checking in to the Portland, by the way – only the best for *this* baby and there's no way *I'm* sharing a ward with a bunch of NHS chavs. I won't be able to work during this time, so I suppose I must also add a sum of money for loss of earnings, I believe Leo calls it.'

'You don't work now!' Sebastian roared at her.

'Ah, but I *could*,' she pointed out with an amiable smile. 'At least, I could have done, before this baby was conceived.'

Sebastian, itching to slap her but knowing he couldn't possibly, glowered at her instead. 'I repeat, how much?'

Lexi opened the door of the Porsche. 'Two hundred and fifty thousand pounds,' she stated coolly.

Sebastian spluttered as she got out of the car. 'You've got to be fucking joking!'

Sticking her head back into the car, she said, 'And in future, that figure goes up by ten grand every time you speak to me like that . . . *capisce?*'

Slamming the door, Lexi stalked away triumphantly in her Gucci heels. With a newly found bounce in her step, she wondered how many Gucci shoes quarter of a million would buy her. Getting pregnant with Sebastian's baby wasn't turning out to be such a disaster after all, Lexi thought as she sashayed away without a backward glance. The only thing she had to do now was tell Leo the bad news.

'I thought you should know, Lochlin Maguire suffered a massive heart attack a few days ago,' Heidi announced, coming in with Judd's post.

Judd cut off the person he was talking to on the phone by slamming it down. 'You'd better be telling me the truth.' His sapphire-blue eyes lit up with delight.

'Of course I am. Why would I joke about it? According to my sister Laura, the one we planted in Lochlin's office, he went home early one night and had a huge heart attack at home.'

'Is he . . . dead?'

Seeing Judd's eyes shining with hope, Heidi took an involuntary step backwards. 'No. He's in hospital. But it's touch and go whether he'll pull through or not, apparently.'

His face falling with disappointment, Judd tucked his arms behind his head. 'What a shame. Poor Maguire. I wonder what caused him so much stress and worry?'

Heidi added some appointments to Judd's diary, feeling slightly sick. Having access to his email, his BlackBerry and all his private paperwork, she was well aware of Judd's agenda to ruin Lochlin Maguire, even though she had no idea what was at the root of his vendetta. But the poor man was in hospital, no doubt as a result of the intense pressure Judd had put him under, and here Judd was, looking as if all his Christmases had come at once.

'The entire office clubbed together to send Lochlin flowers in the shape of a Shamrock and some Guinness-flavoured chocolates,' Heidi told Judd mutinously. She wondered who would send flowers if Judd dropped dead. His kids couldn't stand him and his once loyal sidekick Darcy still hadn't returned to the office. Leaving Judd to his gleeful musings, she left the office and made a quick call to her sister Laura. Even if Shamrock was falling apart, Heidi thought she'd prefer to work for Lochlin than Judd.

Spinning on his chair, Judd hadn't even noticed Heidi leaving the room. He was ecstatic. This was better than he could have possibly hoped for. Lochlin, in hospital and possibly not going to make it – Judd could never have predicted such a fortuitous event, not even if he'd tried. He spun round to survey the view of London in an unexpected heat wave, sighing with pleasure. In the small patch of grass at ground level outside Jett's office, he could see girls who had stripped off their pencil skirts and shirts from Pinks to reveal multicoloured bikinis. Some were even braving it in their underwear. Outside a bar, men had taken their ties off so they could enjoy their pints of beer without being confined in the heat, and women were gossiping over glasses of chilled Pinot Grigio.

Life was good, Judd decided smugly. He might not have

everything under control – namely, the women in his life – but Lochlin almost dropping dead made up for everything. In fact, it was spurring him on to get the rest of his life in order.

Feeling in a sunny mood, Judd pressed the button on his intercom and cheerfully told Heidi to put together a severance package for Darcy and to courier it to her flat. 'She obviously didn't notice the clause I included where I could get rid of her if she failed to show up to work for more than a week,' he observed with some pleasure. Ignoring Heidi's incredulous outburst, he added, 'And put Sebastian on a formal warning.'

'Sebastian, your son?' Heidi stammered.

Judd's mouth tightened. 'That's right, Heidi, my good-for-nothing son who barely earns his salary as it is. I'd love to pay him the minimum wage but I think I could get myself in legal knots on that one.' He thought for a moment then his eyes brightened. 'Perfect. Write off his outrageous bonus to expenses,' he advised Heidi heartlessly. 'Tell him it's because of his previously mentioned poor performance and that if he wishes to discuss it, he can make an appointment with me.' He spun his chair round again, already moving on to his next assassination.

Judd decided idly he might put his mind to figuring out what Elliot was up to. All that stuff about football teams didn't ring true to him. Still, there wasn't much he could do from his office so Judd put that one on the back-burner until later. Remembering the unfinished business he had with Ace, he speed-dialled him, pleased when his son answered on the first ring.

'What's up, Dad?' Ace's voice was barely a whisper.

'Have you heard about Lochlin?'

There was a brief pause. 'Iris's father? No. Why? Has something happened?'

Intrigued, Judd wondered why Iris hadn't heard the news. He decided not to inform Ace about Lochlin's heart attack. Iris was bound to feel guilty if she'd been incommunicado recently; Judd didn't want to spoil the surprise.

'Oh, nothing important,' he responded breezily. 'How are things going?'

'Good, good.' Ace sounded non-committal. 'Actually, I have to go.'

Judd leant forward on his desk. 'Not so fast. I released a press statement in a magazine about Iris signing a contract with Jett.'

'You did what?'

Judd was beginning to wonder if Ace was ill. His voice sounded hoarse and he kept repeating everything like an idiot. 'You said she'd agreed to sign a contract with us – she did, didn't she?'

At the other end of the phone, Ace started to bluster. 'Kind of . . . at least, we discussed it and I'm sure I can convince her at some point.'

Judd was so incensed, he almost dropped the phone. 'Are you saying you fucking lied to me?' His voice was dangerously quiet. There was silence at the other end. Judd quickly collected his thoughts. There could only be a few reasons why Ace would have lied to him about Iris and the Jett contract. One reason might be that he hadn't dealt with it at all and he was basically buying himself some time. The other, more plausible, reason would be that, in spite of his explicit warnings not to fall in love with a Maguire, Ace had gone ahead and lost his heart to Iris.

Judd drummed his fingers on his desk, his mind swiftly zipping through his options. If Ace really had fallen for Iris, he would happily slaughter him. But what would that achieve? He couldn't exactly blame Ace. Iris was as desirable as Tavvy and he understood how easy it would have been for Ace to seduce her and find himself in love with her. But the fact remained that Judd couldn't stand being lied to. Irritated that all he seemed to be doing lately was showing people who was boss, he realised with a flash of genius that he could easily get Ace to kill two birds with one stone.

'Dump her,' he stated tersely.

Ace's horror was tangible, even though he was nearly six thousand miles away. 'No, Dad, you don't understand . . .'

Judd went for the jugular. 'I mean it, Ace. Dump her right now. And if I find out you haven't, there will be hell to pay. If you want to carry on racing for that team and living the way you do, you'll see sense.' As a final, brutal convincer, he added, 'And if you don't want to be removed from my will, do as I fucking say for a change. You're always letting me down and it's just not good enough. Dump Iris Maguire or your life as you know it is well and truly over.'

Hearing his son gasp in shock, Judd summarily cut him off. Sitting back, a grin the Cheshire Cat would be envious of spread across his face. The women in his life were a bunch of unreliable sluts but as far as his sons were concerned, they were well and truly under control. Admiring a particularly voluptuous blonde outside with curves like a Rubens portrait, Judd felt smugly certain he had Ace firmly by the balls.

Iris emerged from the shower wearing a small emerald-green towel, her wet blond hair coiled around her neck. With her long tanned legs and tiny waist, she looked like a sexy mermaid.

'Everything all right?' she asked, rubbing her hair dry with another towel. The diamond-encrusted heart was around her neck, where it always was because she refused to take it off.

Ace said nothing. He was lying on the bed wearing a pair of cheeful bright red swimming shorts that made him look like an extra on *Baywatch*. Inside, he felt as though he was dying.

'Who was that on the phone?'

'It was . . . my father.'

Iris sat on the edge of the bed, wondering why Ace looked so gloomy. 'What did he want?'

Ace gazed at her. More than anything, he wanted to be honest with her and tell her the truth behind the whole sordid scheme. But he was too afraid of losing her.

'Nothing,' he said, forcing a smile on to his face. 'He was just checking on me.'

Iris combed her wet hair. 'Again? Wow. He really likes to keep tabs on you.'

Ace turned away, unable to meet her eyes.

As Iris blasted her hair with the hairdryer, Ace watched her tawny hair flying around her golden shoulders. He didn't care about the money and he certainly didn't care about the will. It wasn't even that he wasn't prepared to give up his racing career, it was that without it, he was nothing.

Ace had been racing since he was a small boy; it was all he knew how to do. He was street-smart but he hadn't achieved high grades at school because racing was all he had ever cared about. The only jobs he had had before amateur and professional driving were at the racetrack itself, which he saw as the building blocks for his career. If he didn't drive, what would he do for a living? Without the danger and the thrill of putting his life at risk on the racetrack, who would he be?

Restlessly, Ace headed to the window and lit a cigarette. If he gave up his career for Iris, how would they live? How would he support her singing career? Worse than that, without driving, he couldn't imagine how he would fill his days. And what about letting his father down? That was the last thing Ace wanted to do. All his life he had craved his approval and affection and this ridiculous situation seemed to be the only way to win it.

He spun round, on the verge of telling Iris everything. Watching her remove the green towel and begin to massage body lotion into her beautiful, lithe limbs, he closed his mouth again. How would she react to the truth? What would she think of him? Even if she loved him, and he truly believed she did, how could she possibly love him once he told her that their relationship had started out as a sham? It was a risk Ace couldn't take – not yet.

He hated himself for being cowardly but while he and Iris were safe in their own little bubble, he could almost pretend his father's ultimatum didn't exist. Iris was also in denial; she hadn't answered her phone in over a week because she was avoiding her father's calls, too consumed with guilt to face him and too honest to be able to hide the truth from him if they spoke.

Remembering something, Ace tossed his cigarette out of the window. 'You should check your cell . . . I mean, your mobile phone, or whatever you call it.'

Iris looked up, startled by his uncharacteristically sombre expression. 'Why do you say that?'

'Something my father said.' He shrugged uneasily. 'About your father. I could be wrong but I think you should check your messages, just to be on the safe side.'

Unnerved by his seriousness, Iris immediately dug her phone out of her handbag and turned it on. Astonished, she discovered thirty-seven messages from Shay, as well as a few missed calls from her father a fortnight ago. Flipping up Shay's texts, she read them all but they gave nothing away, stating only that she should get in touch as soon as possible.

'Something's wrong,' she said, panicked. 'I have all these messages from Shay . . . oh my God, Ace, something's happened, I know it.' Not even bothering to check the time difference, Iris dialled Shay's mobile, barely noticing Ace's reassuring hand on her shoulder.

'Shay, it's me, what's happened?' Iris immediately turned pale. 'What? Where is he? Is he . . . ?' Tears filled her eyes. She stood up, pacing around the room with the phone glued to her ear. 'He saw what? Oh no.' She glanced at Ace, who was beginning to feel rather sick. 'It's not true . . . I mean, me and Ace, we're together.' Horrified, Iris's hand fluttered to her chest to touch the diamond heart. Her voice was barely a croak. 'I didn't, Shay, I promise. I am seeing Ace but I didn't sign a contract with Jett, I would never do that.'

Ace felt his stomach flip over. Whatever had happened had something to do with the lie he had told his father, the one he had announced in a magazine. Ace clutched his mahogany hair. If he had caused whatever had happened, he would never forgive himself. Why the hell hadn't he told Iris about lying about the Jett deal? That way, at least she could have warned her family.

Iris finished her call and slumped down on the bed. 'It's my father. He had a massive heart attack and collapsed.'

'Oh, baby,' Ace murmured tenderly, feeling utterly mortified at the news. 'I'm so sorry. I know how much you adore him.'

Iris burst into tears and buried her face in her hands. 'My family have been trying to reach me for days!' She wept uncontrollably. 'I've been so selfish. I just wanted a few more days for ourselves and then I was going to tell my father about us. And n-now it's too late!'

Her face blotchy from crying, she haltingly told him about the magazine article and the mention about the recording contract with the Jett Record Corporation. 'I don't even know why it said that,' she sobbed, barely able to breathe. 'I would never do that to my family, never. I've been so happy with you, Ace, I didn't want the bubble to burst but I've let my family down so badly.'

Ace gathered her into his arms, devastated. It was all his fault.

Iris was gulping, struggling for air. 'I have that performance at the peace concert next week . . . Pia pulled tons of strings to get me that. But I have to get home as well now. What am I going to do?' In anguish, Iris pulled away from him, her amber eyes swimming with tears. 'Ace, I've ruined everything.'

He stared at her, repulsed with himself. Iris wasn't the one who had ruined everything; it was him. He was in so deep now, he couldn't even see an exit route – at least, Ace sucked his breath in, not one that meant Iris wouldn't hate his guts for ever.

Promising he'd book a flight to London for her, he put an exhausted Iris to bed, then headed downstairs to tell Jerry everything.

'Fuck. How's Iris taking it?' Jerry snapped the top off a beer and handed it to Ace.

'Badly.' Ace raked his hair back and leant his arms on the bar. 'She blames herself for her father's heart attack but if it's anyone's fault, it's mine. I'm the one who lied to my father about Iris signing a deal with Jett.'

Jerry rubbed his chiselled chin sympathetically. 'Yes, and he's the one who leaked that information to the press. Your father put you in this position in the first place, Ace, he has to take responsibility for that.'

Ace scoffed audibly. 'Take responsibility? My father? That's never going to happen.' He picked at the label on his beer bottle. 'However you look at it, my father pimped me out and now he wants me to kick Iris to the kerb, all so he can get his petty revenge on Lochlin Maguire. If he's sick, then so am I for going along with it.'

'But you love her,' Jerry said, finally saying it out loud for the first time. He looked at Ace, whose head was bent over his hands. 'You love Iris and that's what matters.'

'Is it, Jerry? I'm not so sure. When the truth comes out, she's gonna hate me, there's no two ways about it.' Ace necked his beer. 'How would you feel in her shoes?'

Jerry thought about it. 'I don't know. But I reckon it would sound best coming from you. So whatever happens, you have to get to her first, and soon.'

Ace nodded. 'Yeah. I will. But tonight, can you just do me a favour?'

'Anything,' Jerry told him, meaning it.

'Get drunk with me so I can forget about this fucking mess I'm in?'

'Done.' Jerry knocked his bottle against Ace's and drained it.

Outside in her car, listening to every word, Allegra's eyes were gleaming spitefully in the darkness. Thank God she'd installed that bug behind the bar at the party all those weeks ago! Now she knew everything. The news that Ace was in love with the Maguire girl wasn't ideal; after all, Ace was positively allergic to commitment. At least, that's what Allegra had always told herself but now it seemed that might not be true. That aside, nothing could beat the elation of finding out Daddy Harrington had pimped Ace out to seduce Iris before unceremoniously ditching her. Allegra had no idea what Judd was up to but she knew one thing for sure: no self-respecting woman would stick around when they found out the love of their life was only there because he'd been ordered to be by his father.

Allegra tore off her headphones. All she had to do was get to Iris first and tell her everything. Or maybe she didn't need to 'tell' her as such, she thought cleverly. However she did it, Ace and Iris would never survive the bombshell being dropped by an outsider and Allegra's work would be done. She could act the sympathetic role of ex-girlfriend and turn up just when Ace needed a shoulder to cry on. Or a faceless body to fuck, she thought, willing to take any shred of contact Ace might offer her.

Tearing away in her car with all the evidence she needed to destroy Iris Maguire once and for all tucked safely in her handbag, Allegra knew she couldn't fail.

At the hospital, having finally spoken to Iris, Shay was slumped over his father's body. When he'd arrived, Lochlin had looked so wan and feeble, Shay had been certain he had gone. He had rushed over tearfully, but advised by Rosie, the kindly Irish nurse in attendance, that Lochlin was simply a bit dehydrated, Shay had gratefully kissed her before dropping into the seat next to the bed. Knowing he needed to make his peace immediately, just in case, Shay was earnestly telling his father how he felt.

'Come round, Dad, please. I've been a stubborn fool . . . we both have.' He rubbed his eyes. 'Sorry, I didn't mean that. I'm the idiot here. An idiot who loves you more than anything.' He choked on the words. 'I'm sorry about everything, all right? About moving out, about the new job . . . You know I'd rather be working at Shamrock. Look, you have to pull through, you just have to. We all need you, Dad.' When there was no response, Shay squeezed his father's hand in frustration. 'Look, just open your eyes, can't you?

Squeeze my hand back, anything, so I know you're all right.'

Lochlin remained motionless, the machines and tubes beeping and pumping away rhythmically.

Shay stood up, tears streaming down his face. Catching sight of Charlie waiting patiently outside the room, he came out. 'Sorry about that. It's all been a bit emotional. I feel like such a useless bastard right now.' He glanced at Charlie, wondering why he was wearing such subdued clothes. Instead of his usual mix of leather and diamanté, he was wearing a pair of grey skinny jeans which looked surprisingly good on him and a baggy black jumper with a small skull and crossbones motif on the collar. Even his hair looked as if it had been toned down, the blond nowhere near as brassy as it used to be.

Charlie waved away his embarrassment. 'Forget it. I'm just glad I'm not the only one here to make grovelling apologies. Has there been any change?'

Shay shook his head and wiped his eyes. 'No. They say it might not mean anything but how long are we supposed to wait until there are signs of life?' His face crumpled. 'Mum's a total mess but I've tasked her with writing Iris's album so that's keeping her busy for now.' He gave Charlie a sideways glance. 'Just a thought . . . if you could come back to Shamrock, would you?'

Charlie gaped. 'I'd love to but I signed a contract with Jett, there's no way I'd be able to get out of it.'

'Don't be too sure. Leo's looking into things for me and there might be a loophole.'

'Then count me in. I'll fax my contract over to him. To be honest, I was so angry at the time, I barely looked at it so God knows what it says.' Charlie looked shamefaced. 'I can't believe I left Shamrock in the first place.'

It was Shay's turn to wave away embarrassment. 'All water under the bridge now. Just to warn you, if you came back, you'd have to write some new material, none of that greatest hits shit, if you don't mind. I like your new image, though.' He pulled his phone out and frowned at it. 'Damn it, the bloody nerve of the woman. I can't believe she's sent me another text.'

'Who?'

'Darcy . . . Darcy Middleton. Better known as Judd Harrington's mistress.' Shay's face darkened.

'I didn't know you knew her well enough to be on texting terms.'

Shay flushed, not wanting to go into details.

Charlie bit his lip. 'The thing is . . . I think she's in trouble.'

'What? What do you mean?' Shay felt his stomach lurch.

'I was at Jett the other day and Heidi, she's Judd's secretary, she said there was a rumour going round that Judd had beaten Darcy up. She hasn't been in the office for over a week now.' Charlie held his phone up. 'And she's not answering my calls so you've had more contact than me.'

Shay flinched. 'I thought she was trying to set me up again. She had me fired from my job . . .'

'I know. You have every right not to trust her.' Charlie frowned, wondering why Shay looked so distressed. 'It's not your fault, is it? She got herself caught up with Judd and he's obviously more of a bastard than we all gave him credit for. It's not your problem if he's knocked her about.'

Shay glanced back at his father, lying there so helplessly. He had warned his family about Judd and, thinking he was being dramatic, they'd all ignored him and got themselves entangled with the Harringtons, one way or another. 'I have to go,' he muttered, wishing he'd listened to his father. 'Can you stay with my father, Charlie? Just for a bit?'

Charlie nodded. 'I can stay as long as you like. Go and do what you need to do.' He nodded at Lochlin's prostrate body. 'I have a lot of making up to do. It could take some time.'

Leaving him to it, Shay tore out of the hospital and into the first cab he could find. Calling up Darcy's message, he scanned through to the end to get her address and gave it to the taxi driver. It seemed to take for ever as the cab wove in and out of the busy

London traffic but he finally arrived and, telling the taxi to wait, he took the lift to her floor. He hesitated outside Darcy's flat. Was he insane, coming here?

Shay knocked on her door gently. If she really had been beaten, even an unexpected knock might freak her out. There was no answer; the flat inside was eerily quiet. Shay swallowed, wondering if Judd had come back and finished the job.

'Darcy?' he called, leaning closer. 'It's Shay.' He heard a slight movement inside the flat and, hugely relieved, he rested his dark head against the door. 'Charlie told me you were in trouble. I'm sorry I didn't come sooner.'

He heard a sob from the other side of the door. 'I don't blame you. After what I did to you, I can't even believe you're here.' There was a bitter edge to her voice. 'Hey, we're quits. I've been fired too. Judd couriered my severance package over, saying it was because I hadn't turned up to work.'

Shay was stunned. 'Did he beat you?'

'It doesn't matter.' Darcy trailed her fingers down the door. 'Is it . . . is it really you?'

The tremulous quality to her voice made Shay want to tear the door open but he knew he was going to have to be patient. 'Shall I say something only I could know?' Taking her silence as a yes, he carried on. 'That night in the jazz club, they were playing my favourite song, "Linger In My Arms A Little Longer", by Louis Armstrong. It's your favourite song too and when you told me that, I remember thinking it was serendipity or whatever they call it that we'd met.'

On the other side of the door, Darcy started to weep.

Shay put his hand on the door. 'We talked about jazz music, for hours . . . and . . . and you have a heart-shaped mole in the small of your back . . .' Hearing the bolts being slowly pulled back and the chain being unhooked, Shay moved backwards, not wanting to frighten her.

When Darcy cautiously opened the door wrapped in a grubby

cashmere cardigan that had seen better days, Shay couldn't help gasping. The colourful bruises covered the skin from her eyes to her collarbone and by the awkward way she was moving, he guessed there were many more cuts and bruises beneath her clothes.

Darcy's hazel eyes met his nervously. 'Wh-why are you here?'

Reaching out, Shay tenderly touched her cheek, wincing as she recoiled in pain. 'I'm here to take you home.'

'Home? This is my home.' Darcy looked dazed.

'Is it?' He tucked a strand of greasy dark hair behind her ear, not caring that she hadn't washed it for days. 'Home is where you feel safe and you can't possibly feel safe here now.'

Darcy started to shake all over.

Shay pulled her gently into his arms. He looked down at her, his green eyes full of compassion.

'I thought he was going to k-kill me,' she said hoarsely. 'I honestly thought I was going to die.'

'Ssshhh.' Shay smoothed her hair away from her face.

'He just kept hitting me and he wouldn't stop . . . I begged him but he wouldn't.' Her legs buckled at the terrifying memory.

Shay didn't need to hear any more. Gathering her up in his arms, he shut the door to her flat and, ignoring her protests, carried her to the taxi and deposited her safely inside.

'What about all my stuff?' she asked, stupefied.

'I'll send someone to get it for you. Let's just get out of here.'

Jumping in next to her, he tucked her under his arm and held her. Overwhelmed, Darcy wept into Shay's neck all the way to Bluebell Cottage.

Chapter Seventeen

Wearing a bikini made of the Stars and Stripes flag, Savannah was lying languidly by the pool, topping up her tan in the freakishly hot English weather that had made an appearance in the past few days.

Drinking Diet Coke by the bucketload, she had pulled her red hair up in a ponytail and was wearing huge sunglasses, which hid the discontented frown on her face. Savannah was bored rigid. Relations with her father were frosty to say the least and it had slowly dawned on her that her ill-fated launch spelt the end of her pop career. Her father, the vindictive bastard, had cancelled all her promised appearances and magazine interviews.

Savannah took a crumpled business card from her handbag. Conrad Lafferty. She'd met him that day after lunch with her father in the restaurant and he'd promised her the world. Didn't they all, Savannah thought bitterly, tossing the card back into her bag. Her father had done exactly the same thing and look where that had got her. In a matter of weeks, she would no doubt be out on her ear again; jobless, homeless and definitely penniless.

'I thought you might want another one of these.'

Martha, holding out an ice-cold can of Diet Coke, blocked the bright, warm rays of the sun momentarily. Wearing a creased pink T-shirt and a long black skirt which reached her ankles, she looked hot and uncomfortable in the sweaty heat. Her mousy brown hair was scraped up in a hair band and there were loose, sweaty tendrils stuck to her face, which was the picture of desolation.

'Hey, thanks.' Savannah took it and cracked it open with a hiss. 'Join me?'

'Thanks.' The lounger creaked beneath Martha's weight. Her skin looked sallow and unhealthy and her eyes were rimmed with red from crying.

Savannah noticed that Martha had piled on an awful lot of weight recently; all her clothes looked tight and her face had become rounder.

Savannah considered the possibility that she had found out about Sebastian's affair with Lexi and she felt an unexpected stab of guilt. She wouldn't have wanted to be the one to enlighten Martha about Sebastian's pathetic behaviour but it might have been better than her catching him at it, if that was what had happened. Martha was practically family, after all, and regardless of what Judd might have in store for her, Savannah knew she wanted to keep in touch with Martha and Elliot at very least, maybe even Kitty too.

Fucking hell, Savannah thought to herself in amusement. Was she going soft?

'Sebastian is a total bastard,' Martha blurted out.

Savannah lifted her face to the sun and said nothing. She could have told Martha that.

'This time he's gone too far. This time, I really don't know if I can forgive him.' Martha leant forward, her lounger almost tipping up. 'He's asked me to do something so . . . so . . . unbelievable I don't even know how to handle it.'

Savannah took her sunglasses off. 'Go on.'

Martha gave a shuddering sigh. 'First of all, he's been having an affair with Lexi bloody Beaument!' She dissolved into tears. 'That stick insect with the big boobs. She's already got a rich husband, why did she have to go after mine?'

'I'm so sorry.' Savannah patted Martha's pale arm, wincing as it made Martha's bingo wings flap. 'Hey, cheer up. Lexi's just a stupid bimbo. Sebastian will lose interest in her soon enough.'

Martha's lip wobbled. 'She might be a bimbo but she's having Sebastian's baby.'

'Shit!' Savannah sat up. 'God, Martha, that's awful.'

'You don't know the half of it. He wants *me* to keep the baby.' Martha dashed her tears away with her arm. 'Can you believe it, Sav? He drops the bombshell that he's been shagging someone else and in the same breath he suggests that we keep – sorry, *buy* the baby because it's half his and Lexi doesn't want it.'

Savannah couldn't believe how crass Sebastian had been. How insensitive to inform Martha of his infidelity and then shove someone else's baby in her face! He truly was his father's son!

'What do you think?' Martha asked her searchingly. 'I hate myself for even considering Sebastian's sick little plan, but I can't help thinking about that poor defenceless baby.' She chewed her fingernails. 'What if Lexi gives it away to an adoption agency? It could end up anywhere.'

Grudgingly, Savannah could see the sense in Sebastian's suggestion. Martha wanted a baby but she couldn't have one and Lexi had a baby that she didn't want. Savannah wasn't sure if the baby being half Sebastian's made the situation harder or easier for Martha to bear but, either way, it was a fact. Her own conception had hardly been as pure as the driven snow either.

'You've got a point about the baby,' she offered diplomatically. 'I mean, look at me. I wasn't adopted but life was pretty tough for me in New York.' She turned her gaze back to Brockett Hall, feeling wistful rather than bitter. 'My mother did her best but she was a mess to begin with.' Savannah gave Martha a half-smile. 'Whereas you were cut out to be a mother, Martha. You have so much love to give.'

Martha sobbed. 'Do you really think so?'

'I really think so.' Savannah slid her arm around Martha's heaving shoulders. 'Look, the way I see it, you're never going to forgive Sebastian for this. So you have two choices: you either divorce him, and take him for everything he's worth, or you stick around and take on this baby.'

Martha blinked at her. When Savannah put it like that, it all made sense. Suddenly, she felt an overwhelming urge to keep the baby Lexi was carrying so she could lavish it with love and attention. She nodded bravely.

'You're right, Sav. This is my chance to be happy, just not in the way I thought I was going to be.'

Pleased, Savannah put her sunglasses back on. 'And while we're at it, can I give you a bit of honest advice? Stop letting Sebastian bully you into the ground. Lose some weight, show him what he's been missing.'

Martha looked down at her corpulent body. She truly hadn't realised how plump she had become. 'How?'

'I'll help you.' Savannah grimaced. 'I have fuck all else to do now that Daddy dearest has ditched my pop career. Two things you're gonna need.'

Martha's brown eyes were alight with enthusiasm for the first time in ages.

'One, get a backbone,' Savannah ordered. 'I'm gonna be so hard on you, you're gonna be screaming for mercy.' Seeing Martha sit up straighter and pull her shoulders back, Savannah grinned. 'Two, you need to get a tan. You're so lily-white, you're fucking blinding me. White looks fat, tanned looks skinny, got it?'

Martha recoiled in horror. 'I can't get my body out, it's so fat and horrible.'

'Well, there's only me here and I'm not looking. So I suggest you get your clothes off.'

Martha shakily got to her feet. She pulled her T-shirt over her head and dropped her voluminous skirt to the ground so she was standing in her tight, slightly grey underwear. Then she stretched out on the lounger.

Savannah smiled. Doing nice things for people felt far better than being mean. Perhaps her father might figure that out one day and give it a go but somehow she doubted it.

* * *

Parking the Ferrari outside L'Absinthe, the restaurant Leo had mentioned, Kitty wondered why he had sounded so distraught on the phone. Hearing the crack in his voice, she hadn't hesitated, throwing on a new heather-pink wrap dress she'd treated herself to and some black heels. Remembering her reliable Land Rover had suffered a gear box failure the other day, Kitty had no choice but to borrow one of Judd's cars and she had always had a secret hankering to take the Ferrari for a spin. She wouldn't have dared if Judd hadn't been staying up in London for a few days but knowing he was safely out of the way, Kitty had enjoyed zipping through the country lanes in the flashy car.

Dashing inside the restaurant, she saw that it was small and intimate, with dark green walls and a wide fireplace which probably looked achingly romantic all lit up in the winter. Joining Leo in a cosy booth, Kitty gave him a bright smile.

'It's lovely to see you again,' Leo said, jumping up to kiss her cheek. 'Thank you for coming out to meet me.' His Labrador-brown eyes were dejected and his blond hair looked dishevelled. 'You look really pretty,' he commented, in spite of his misery.

Kitty blushed. She didn't know what it was about Leo that made her act like a pre-pubescent schoolgirl. Perhaps it was because he was a gentleman – the total opposite of Judd. 'How are things with Lexi?'

'Not great.' Leo looked away. 'I hardly see her. I spend most of my time in the office.' He longed to tell her about Lexi's pregnancy but he didn't think he could in the circumstances.

'What on earth is this?' Kitty asked, mystified as she held up a bizarre tong-shaped implement. It looked rather like an over-sized mascara curler or, worse, one of the horrible gadgets they produced in the doctor's when you went for a smear test.

'They're snail tongs. You put the shell in there, then you hook the snail out with one of these.' Leo held up a long, thin fork.

'Oh my, do I *have* to eat snails?' Kitty looked pained.

'Of course not.' Leo smiled, enjoying her Boston accent. 'You can eat whatever you like. The boeuf en Daube is excellent, as is the bouillabaisse.' Breaking open a freshly baked bread roll, he laughed. 'Beef stew and fish soup. Doesn't sound so exotic in English, does it?'

Didier, the restaurant owner, came over to greet Leo with much kissing and back-slapping. He splashed Bordeaux into their glasses. 'On the house,' he insisted.

'Thanks, Didier.' Leo smiled. 'No starter for me, but I'll have the *boeuf*.' He raised his eyebrows at Kitty, who nodded. 'Make that two.'

'Very good, *Monsieur* Leo.' Didier winked at him indiscreetly.

Leo rolled his eyes. 'Bloody French, they think everyone's at it.'

Kitty went scarlet.

Leo noticed a thread hanging from the sleeve of his jumper. 'Christ, it's unravelling, just like me.' He said it flatly rather than in a self-pitying way and gently Kitty reached out and snapped it off.

Glancing down at the plateful of aromatic *boeuf* Didier had presented with a flourish, Leo wondered if he'd lost the ability to talk normally these days. He was pleased to be spending time with Kitty; he had fancied some company and he couldn't think of anyone he'd rather chat to but he wasn't sure Kitty could handle knowing about Sebastian. Picking up his fork, he realised he was famished.

For some time, neither of them spoke as they ate their beef and made their way through several glasses of wine.

'Any news about Lochlin?' Kitty asked. 'I was there when it happened.'

'Of course, Tavvy told me.' Leo drained his wine. 'It's not your fault, you know. The doctors told Tavvy this had been brewing for some time.'

'It's such a shame,' Kitty said with a sigh. 'He's obviously been under a lot of pressure and I just know Judd is behind it.' Finishing her meal regretfully, she put her knife and fork down. 'Wow. That was exquisite.'

Didier appeared at the table. '*Merci, madame*,' he said with a bow. 'If you would like dessert, the chocolate soufflé for two is superb. It'll take some time but it's worth the wait.'

'Sounds good.' Leo nodded, seeing Kitty's eyes light up. Watching Didier saunter off to the kitchen, he shook his head. 'He's convinced we're a couple. Maybe he's heard all the rumours flying round the village about Lexi too.'

Kitty sympathised. Having suffered years of not-so-discreet talk about her marriage at social events in Los Angeles where even her friends would whisper behind their hands, Kitty knew what it was like to be at the centre of a scandal. They both drank some more wine before the chocolate soufflé arrived with much fanfare, a wobbling tower of perfection with soft peaks of chocolate and a glistening top. Sinking their spoons into it, they watched as it deflated slightly before diving in.

'Lexi's pregnant,' Leo confided abruptly, his tongue loosened by too much Bordeaux. 'And it's not mine.'

Kitty was horrified. 'Oh, Leo, why didn't you say before now? That's terrible.'

He shrugged. 'It is a bit, isn't it? She has a thing for lawyers, it seems.' He let out a short laugh before realising what he'd said. Paying the bill, he helped her into her coat and they walked outside.

'Are you . . . are you sure it's not yours?' Kitty flushed at her question, knowing it was indelicate.

Leo nodded, his shaggy blond hair falling into his eyes. 'Very. I expect the hair colour will be a giveaway.' He stopped, realising he'd said too much, again. He cursed Didier and his free Bordeaux. He took out a cigar and lit it, puffing smoke into the air. 'Er, I got Didier to call us a couple of taxis and he's offered to drop the Ferrari back tomorrow. I hope that's all right.'

Kitty nodded and clung to his arm. She felt extremely drunk but she was happier than she'd been in a long time. Breathing in a waft of Leo's cigar smoke, she gave him a clumsy kiss on the cheek, leaning against him as he held her close in a hug.

Sliding into one of the cabs, Kitty couldn't help thinking Lexi was insane to cheat on Leo with another man. He was kind, gentle and funny, and incredibly attractive too. Why on earth would Lexi sleep with someone else? Unless it was for money, perhaps. A few things occurred to Kitty in quick succession. Leo had said Lexi had a thing for lawyers. He had also said the baby's hair colour might be a giveaway.

Sitting bolt upright in the back of the cab, Kitty realised in an instant who Lexi had been having an affair with. She gulped. But that wasn't the worst of it. Not only did it mean her son was the man responsible for Leo's abject misery, but if Sebastian did indeed turn out to be the father of Lexi's baby, she, Kitty, would become a grandmother in a few months' time. Clutching her seat belt, Kitty tried hard not to become reacquainted with the chocolate soufflé she'd just eaten.

Back from his stay in London with a high-class hooker, Judd decided it was high time he found out what the hell Elliot had been up to all these months. He had wanted to speak to Savannah but apparently she was out jogging with Martha somewhere so Judd had turned his attention to his youngest son. Heading out to his garage, he spun round as he heard the sound of tyres skidding across the gravel on his driveway.

'What the fuck?' Judd gaped as his prized red Ferrari ground to a halt and a man with dark, slicked-back hair got out. 'Who the fuck are you?' Judd snarled rudely.

'Didier,' said Didier, looking unruffled.

'And what are you doing with my Ferrari?'

Didier gave a Gallic shrug. 'Returning it.'

Judd fought the urge to smash his fist into Didier's genial face. 'What were you doing with it in the first place, fuckwit?'

Deadpan, Didier raised his eyebrows. 'I think you misheard me.

I said my name was Didier.' He handed Judd the car keys and Judd strode around his Ferrari with eagle eyes, checking for dents.

Kitty dashed out on to the gravel, shocked to see Judd back so early. Widening her eyes at Didier, she pleaded with him not to give her away.

Didier winked. Leo was a very old and loyal friend and he wouldn't dream of dropping him in it. 'Your wife instructed us to pick it up and give it a service. That was nice of her, wasn't it?'

Judd shot Kitty a suspicious glance. 'Very.' Looking up, he saw a black Lotus slide into the driveway. A blonde with lips like a couple of lilos leant out and waved to Didier.

'Who's that?' Judd demanded, beginning to think he was in some kind of freak show.

'There's my . . . er . . . my *business partner*,' Didier invented, jumping into the passenger seat next to his girlfriend. The Lotus disappeared as quickly as it had appeared.

'Since when does a mechanic drive a Lotus?' Judd stormed. 'He looked far too bloody good looking to fix cars for a living, and that woman looked as if she'd be more at home on a Pirelli calendar.'

Kitty didn't know what to say.

'I'm going to find Elliot,' Judd informed her curtly. 'He's a lying son of a bitch – playing football indeed.'

Kitty trembled as Judd shot off down the driveway. She knew exactly where Elliot was – he was practising *Romeo and Juliet* with Caitie Maguire on the other side of the village. Kitty dashed inside to phone Elliot but his mobile was switched off.

Spotting Mrs Stafford, the old lady who'd pointed out Iris Maguire all those months ago, sedately wheeling her tartan trolley through the village, Judd pulled up alongside her suavely and slid down one of his windows.

'Hello there. I wonder if you can help me.' He fixed his sapphire-blue eyes on her.

'I'll try.' Mrs Stafford tittered girlishly. It was that *lovely* man from the big house with the moat, she thought, tidying her hair.

'I'm looking for my son, Elliot.'

Mrs Stafford's eyes twinkled. 'Oh, the handsome boy with the blond hair? He's bound to be at the village hall, rehearsing with young Caitie Maguire.'

Judd turned puce. 'Caitie Maguire?'

'Yes. Or Juliet, as I should call her.' Mrs Stafford giggled. 'Young love – so sweet, don't you think?'

'No, I fucking well don't!' Judd roared, firing up the Ferrari's engine loudly and almost giving Mrs Stafford a heart attack. Tearing over to the drama hall on the other side of the village, he flung the doors open and made a dramatic entrance.

Everyone looked up. On stage, mid-scene, Elliot gasped. Catching sight of Judd's red hair lit up by the streaming sunlight, Caitie stared at him in fascination. This was *him*, this was Judd Harrington. The man who had set Iris up with his son, the man who'd sent his mistress to destroy Shay and, worst of all, the man who'd caused her father to have a heart attack.

'This is bad,' Elliot whispered, his heart thumping crazily in his chest. 'This is really, really bad.'

'Can I help you?' Hugo frowned at Judd from behind his black-rimmed glasses. Doing a double take, he couldn't help thinking the intruder would make a wonderful Iago. 'It's just that we're rather busy rehearsing a key scene.'

Judd strode into the hall, giving Hugo a scathing glance. His gaze fell upon Elliot, who was quailing inside. Standing his ground, he lifted his chin as bravely as he could.

Jas gazed at Elliot open-mouthed, wishing she could do something. She knew how terrified he was of his father and now his secret was out. Skye and Abby Valentine exchanged delighted glances, watching with bated breath to see what happened. Skye could barely contain herself; seeing Caitie Maguire get her comeuppance was going to be worth every second of playing boring old Lady Capulet in this stupid play.

'Dad, I can explain,' Elliot began.

'You're Elliot's father!' Hugo gushed, missing the undercurrent. He dashed over and pumped Judd's hand. 'You must be *so* proud.'

'What, of my son prancing around like a fairy?' Judd snarled. 'Hardly.'

Hugo recoiled. 'Prancing around like a fairy?' he echoed, his eyes clouding over in dismay. 'Your son is one of the most talented young actors I've come across in a long time.'

In spite of his fear, Elliot couldn't help feeling chuffed to pieces but the feeling soon dissipated as he felt the full extent of his father's wrath.

'Really?' Judd scoffed. 'And who's he playing? Fucking *Tinkerbell*?' He narrowed his eyes at Elliot. 'I'm sure you'll look lovely in tights.'

Elliot bit his lip.

Hugo looked affronted. 'Tinkerbell? I don't mean to be rude but this isn't *Peter Pan*, this is *Romeo and Juliet*.'

'I couldn't give a flying fuck what it is.' Judd stepped forward towards the stage so there was hardly any distance between him and Elliot. 'Explain yourself.'

Elliot knew whatever he tried to say, nothing would appease his father's anger; if anything, it would incense him further. But he couldn't just stand here like a dummy so he opened his mouth to say something – anything. He was taken aback when Caitie heroically stepped forward.

'You have no right to speak to Elliot like that,' she chirped up, pink in the face.

'Oh, really?' Judd said in exasperation. 'And who the fuck might you be?'

Feeling vulnerable in her cut-off jeans, black vest top and bare feet, Caitie took a step forward. 'There's no need to swear at me. I'm Caitie Maguire,' she said in a loud voice.

Judd's eyes turned to ice. He gave Caitie a quick once-over, taking in her dark curls and green eyes which were sparkling with determination. 'You look nothing like your mother.'

'How astute of you.' She stared him down. 'Quite obviously, I take after my father.'

'Oh, yes, how is your dying papa?' Judd asked her cruelly. 'Popped his clogs yet?'

She gasped but refused to be baited. 'Actually, no. Unfortunately for you, he's doing very well and he's about to come round any day.' She gulped her tears down and flung her shoulders back.

Elliot had never been prouder of her and forgetting his fear of his father, he put his arm round her supportively.

Judd gave Elliot a withering stare. 'Got girls fighting your battles for you now, have you?' He shook his head disappointedly. 'Fucking hell. You're more of a wet than I gave you credit for.'

'Now look here,' Hugo leapt to Elliot's defence.

'And now the poofter's joining in!' Judd crowed, clapping his hands.

Elliot seethed. He'd had enough. He was sick and tired of his father's feud with the Maguires and he was fed up with being treated like he was nothing. 'Get out,' he hissed through his teeth at his father.

Judd stopped laughing. 'What?'

'You heard me. You're disrupting everything and I already know what you think of me. No doubt you'll kick the shit out of me when I get home so you might as well let us all get on with the rehearsal.'

Elliot had no idea where he had found the courage and he was pretty sure he'd be disinherited, or worse, by the time he got home but he didn't care any more.

Judd was shaking with rage. He wanted nothing more than to rush on to the stage and beat Elliot senseless but he knew there'd be repercussions from such a public loss of control. Elliot's punishment would have to come later and, by God, was Judd going to enjoy it.

'I'll see you at home then,' he said in a scarily quiet voice. 'But don't think you're going to get away with this.'

'Oh, as if I would,' Elliot retorted jadedly, knowing he had burnt his bridges. 'We all know no one's allowed to challenge the great Judd Harrington.'

Judd sucked his breath in and clenched his fists. Turning on his heel, he strode out of the hall, leaving the doors flapping in his wake.

Everyone let out a collective sigh of relief. Hugo sat down suddenly, fearing he might faint and Skye and Abby were talking nineteen to the dozen. Elliot put a hand to his mouth.

'Your father is *such* a bastard.' Caitie was shaking all over. 'I thought he was going to run up here and kill us both with his bare hands.'

Jas joined them, her brown eyes wide with shock. 'You were so brave, both of you.' She turned to Elliot. 'What are you going to do now? You can't go home, surely.'

Elliot realised his hands were shaking and shoved them in his pockets. 'I . . . I didn't think that far ahead, actually.' He shook his head. 'But I guess I won't be welcome at home, not for a while, anyway.'

'Come home with me,' Caitie murmured distractedly.

He was touched but her plan was flawed. 'That's very sweet of you but your house is the first place he'd look for me.'

'There's always my house,' Jas offered rather shyly. 'We have about thirty spare rooms, and I'm pretty sure your father wouldn't think to look there.'

'That's a great idea,' Caitie commented, looking preoccupied. 'It's surrounded by Rottweilers; your father wouldn't get within two miles of it without being savaged.'

Elliot considered the idea. 'I suppose I could . . . All right, thanks, Jas. Just until things die down.'

Jas blushed. 'Glad to help.'

Caitie, barely registering what was going on, stared after Judd thoughtfully. Coming face to face with the man who had hurt so many members of her family made her more determined than ever to find out why Judd Harrington wanted revenge. It was something to do with her mother and with Uncle Seamus, she was sure of it. And she wasn't going to rest until she found out.

Wearing one of Shay's faded blue T-shirts as a dress with one of his belts nipping in the waist, Darcy was wandering around Bluebell Cottage restlessly. It was a cute little place with doll's house windows but she had been holed up in it for a week now without venturing out. Outside she could see the ground was carpeted with bluebells, their bell-shaped heads and bendy green stalks forming a dazzling sea of glorious colour. Now that the rain had cleared again, the sun was filtering through the cracks in the trees but as much as she longed to, Darcy daren't go out and sunbathe.

'Do you feel safe here?' Shay had asked her and, surprisingly, she did. Darcy thought it was unlikely Judd would find her but it wasn't just that. It was being around Shay that helped. At the same time, she was a bundle of nerves around him. Instead of lying awake at night in fear for her life, she was tossing and turning restlessly because she knew Shay was in the next room and memories of the night they'd spent together were sending her senses spiralling. Darcy couldn't possibly let on to Shay about her feelings so she was doing her best to hide them.

Seemingly embarrassed in the role of the white knight, Shay had backed off and he was behaving like the perfect gentleman. Darcy felt so vulnerable and exposed, her barriers had shot back up, double the thickness.

Since they'd been sharing the cottage, Shay had been supportive but understandably wary. He had been doing most of his work for Shamrock from the cottage, setting up conference calls, having the post redirected by Erica and using his laptop for everything else. He worked day and night, but he kept himself to himself and told her nothing.

Darcy listlessly trailed her fingers along the window sill. She had been shocked when Judd fired her; she didn't care about the money because she had been savvy over the years and she had put money into various investments, as well as owning several houses. But she had never been fired before and, being a workaholic, Darcy hated being at a loose end with nothing to fill her days.

Starting fearfully as she heard a car pull up outside, Darcy relaxed when she recognised the distinctive, wheezy drone of Shay's battered Jag.

'One suitcase of clothes,' Shay said, coming in and dumping a vast Louis Vuitton case on the armchair. Wearing a pair of frayed blue shorts and a white T-shirt that showed off his tanned legs, he looked as if he'd just come off the beach. 'And all the other things you asked for so you can feel human again.' His green eyes flickered briefly over the expanse of bruised, toned thigh visible under the short T-shirt she was wearing but he quickly glanced away again.

'Oh, thank God.' Darcy fell on it gratefully. Rummaging through the bag, she could see that Shay had remembered every single thing on the extensive list she'd written.

'You can help me cook, if you like,' Shay said, leading the way into the kitchen. 'I bought us some lovely prawns. I thought we could have them with some Chablis.'

'I'll just get changed and then I'll do whatever you want me to.' Flushing slightly as she realised her words sounded faintly suggestive, Darcy disappeared upstairs. Feeling a pang as she removed Shay's belt and pulled his T-shirt over her head, she scolded herself. After all, she'd wanted her own clothes back, so why was she acting as if it was her first day back to work after a glorious holiday? Quickly changing into a pair of tailored white Joseph shorts that covered most of her fading bruises, a pale grey T-shirt and some white Marc Jacobs ballet pumps, Darcy came downstairs to find Shay smothering some huge prawns in garlic butter.

Expertly chopping some coriander, he glanced at her. 'Don't take this the wrong way but I think I preferred you in my stuff.'

'Bloody hell.' Darcy stuck her finger in the garlic butter and sucked it. 'After all that moaning about me stealing your gear.' She couldn't help agreeing with him; there had been something strangely intimate about wearing his clothes. 'Wow, that's so *good*. And so strong!' About to say it was a good job they were both eating it, Darcy stopped herself. Shay might have taken her in when she was in need of a friend but she honestly couldn't see him laying a finger on her ever again.

Shay wiped his hands on a tea towel. 'I hope you don't mind me asking but why do you think you ended up with a man like Judd?' He poured her a glass of chilled Chablis and slid it across to her.

Darcy thanked him and leant on the counter. 'I've been thinking about this and I can only think it's because of my father.' She sipped her wine contemplatively. 'I adored him, you see, and I admired him so much because he was successful and dynamic. I didn't just admire him; I wanted to be just like him, working for myself and not taking shit from anyone.' Darcy swallowed, her eyes filling with tears. She brushed them away impatiently. 'Foolishly, I didn't realise he was beating my mother. He never laid a finger on me.' She traced her thumb down the stem of the wine glass. 'And then most of the men I met after that were exactly like my father. With the odd exception.' She lifted bruised eyes to his. 'Contrary to what you might think, Judd didn't expect us to end up in bed together that night. As far as he was concerned, I went over and above the call of duty. That's why he snapped.' Omitting to mention she suspected Judd knew she was in love with Shay, Darcy turned away.

Shay was taken aback. He'd had no idea the beating Darcy had sustained was anything to do with the night they'd spent together.

Darcy watched Shay whip the prawns out from under the grill and throw a handful of fresh linguine in some bubbling water. 'Christ, is there anything you can't do?' she said, sounding bitchier than she'd intended.

'Plenty,' he answered sharply, shoving the latest figures for

Shamrock towards her with his elbow. 'My dad's still in hospital on life support, Shamrock is going down the pan and I haven't so much as broken the back of the financial and legal issues.' Dishing linguine and prawns into two dishes, he took them over to the table.

Feeling guilty, Darcy perused the paperwork and sat down. 'These look much better than they were. You can't expect miracles overnight.' She was shocked Lochlin had allowed things to get this bad; Judd's arrival and subsequent onslaught must have affected Shamrock more than they'd all guessed. 'Have you heard any more news about your father?'

Shay shook his head and gulped down some wine. 'No. Even Mum's struggling to stay positive, but we can't give up hope. Dad's a fighter and he'll pull through. He has to.'

'Poor Lochlin.' She sensed his derision and defended herself. 'I mean it, Shay. I never wanted anything like this to happen.'

'Sorry. I'm sure you didn't.'

Darcy rubbed her arms. 'I was stupid getting involved with Judd in the first place but I had no idea he was such a bastard until the end.'

'No one did.' Shay paused. 'Look, let's forget what's behind us and look ahead.' He pointed to the reports. 'I just want to start making some progress with these. Leo is coming back to me about the contracts and all the legal stuff but until he does, I'm stumped.' He passed her a bowl of salad and they both started as their hands connected.

Darcy whipped her hand away and stabbed a fork into one of the prawns. 'Why don't I help you with Shamrock?' She tasted the prawn. It was delicious, oozing with garlic butter and melt-in-the-mouth.

Shay slowly topped up their glasses and said nothing.

'You don't trust me,' Darcy said flatly. She put her fork down. 'Of course you don't; why would you?'

'Do you blame me?'

Darcy winced. Surely her years of experience in the music business and her expert knowledge had to count for something?

'Right, I can see I'm going to have to convince you I'm on your side.' Darcy took a swig of wine to buy herself some time. 'Well, let's see. I can offer you my experience and my knowledge of the music business for a start but more importantly, I know Judd and how he works.'

Shay listened.

'Judd has some thoughts about discrediting Shamrock in the press so I know exactly how we can bat those away and turn the tables.' Warming to her theme, Darcy continued. 'I have some contacts in the business that could really help you and I might even be able to persuade some of the acts Judd is about to sign to come to Shamrock. The way you need to tackle Judd is to realise he's all style over substance, and long-term objectives don't feature in his plans. He's bells and whistles and not much else.' Darcy pulled a face. 'He's not so scary when you think of him like that, is he?'

Shay was impressed but he deliberately remained poker-faced. 'I guess I can see how you could be useful.'

'I could work from the cottage as your aide and only communicate with you. No one needs to know we're working together. I can be your silent partner, if you like.'

Shay looked incredulous.

Darcy shrugged. 'Two heads are better than one, as they say, and frankly what have I – or you, for that matter – got to lose?'

It all made sense but pride was standing in Shay's way. About to knock Darcy back, he stopped himself. This was exactly what had been behind his father's downfall; an inability to trust other people and to accept help. Shay didn't want to make the same mistake.

'All right,' he relented. 'You can help. I could do with another pair of hands, especially yours. But if I suspect there's anything shady going on . . .'

Excited, Darcy tucked her dark hair behind her ears. 'If I do anything remotely shady, you have full permission to kick me out of the cottage to fend for myself. But seriously, do you think I have a death wish?' She pulled up her T-shirt to show him her bruised stomach. 'I've learnt my lesson the hard way.'

Shay caught his breath. He hated seeing Darcy's injuries. His green eyes slid back to hers. What was it about her that made him want to gather her up in his arms and kiss the life out of her?

Biting her lip, Darcy started clearing the dishes away. She didn't want Shay feeling sorry for her and she regretted showing him her bruises just then. She changed the subject back to work. 'Right, well, I have so many ideas for Shamrock. For a start, there's this whole list of acts I can show you that Judd rejected, not because they weren't good enough but because his arrogance gets in the way of his judgement.'

Shay watched her, fascinated. She had this way of wrinkling her nose when her mind leapt around at a hundred miles an hour.

Darcy was still in full flow. 'I have an idea for the sales figures too, and for Charlie's comeback. We can save an awful lot of money if we use this contact I have in a graphics firm, and we need some good PR about Shamrock in the music press. I could smooth things over between you and Dev.' She blushed then glanced at Shay, noticing he'd gone silent. 'What?'

'Nothing. I'm just glad to have you on board.' Shay was telling the truth. Rescuing Shamrock all on his own was a daunting prospect and having someone to bounce ideas off was going to be a godsend, especially someone as clued up as Darcy. Now all he had to do was get a handle on the ridiculously soppy thoughts that seemed to be clouding his brain.

Darcy cradled her wine glass in her hands. Thank God Shay was willing to give her a chance. Now all she had to do was focus on work and stop thinking about the fact that the more time they spent together, the more she was falling in love with him.

* * *

Iris stood on the stage, shaking like a leaf. Standing in front of the audience of thousands with cameras pointing at her face and letting her know that millions were watching her live, she couldn't think of the words to her song, even though she'd sung it hundreds of times now.

She gripped the microphone stand with trembling fingers. She had agreed to the performance because she didn't want to let Pia down and because Shay had insisted that she do it. He said there was no point in rushing home because there was no change in her father's condition and she needed to think of her career.

Iris took a deep breath. She wasn't thinking about her career, it was more that she felt she owed it to Pia, after everything she'd done for her. She'd pulled massive strings to arrange for her to sing at this concert and it was a prestigious event, honouring one of the great peace figures of the world. Iris knew she'd be mad to turn it down in terms of the publicity, but she also felt she'd let down enough people in the past few months. She had a flight booked in two days' time. She was going to miss Ace so much, she wasn't even sure how she would function but she couldn't think about that now.

The introduction to her mother's song 'Obsession' began. Iris rubbed a hand over her eyes and tried to collect herself. She opened her mouth to sing but all that came out was a croak.

Watching it at home with Jerry, Ace's heart was in his mouth. Silently, he willed Iris to do well. Standing in the wings, Pia and Luisa were holding hands, hoping to God Iris could pull off the performance with everything else she had on her mind. Even the audience seemed to be silently cheering her on.

Iris heard the introduction again and missed her cue once more, clutching the microphone as her knees buckled.

Sitting at Lochlin's bedside at five o'clock in the morning watching a tiny TV Rosie had stolen from somewhere, Tavvy and Caitie were knocking back strong coffee to stay awake.

'Oh my God, she's going to stutter,' Tavvy said to Caitie, gulping down another cup of disgusting black coffee from the hospital machine. 'She's going to cave – look at her, she looks terrified.'

'To be sure, she's a pretty little thing,' Rosie the nurse commented, more interested in Iris's flowing blond hair and cream Grecian gown than the fact she was dying on stage. 'Oooh, I love her shoes.'

Caitie rolled her eyes. 'No one's going to remember her shoes if she chokes, Rosie. Her career could be up the shitter here.'

Rosie waved away Caitie's negativity. 'She'll be fine, darlin', wait and see.'

Back in LA, Iris cleared her throat and accepted a cup of water from a stage hand who rushed on with it. Composing herself, she bent her head to the microphone and spoke in a soft voice. 'I'm so sorry. I'm . . . my father is in hospital at the moment and I'm really worried about him.' Her voice broke. 'I don't know if you're watching in England, Dad, or any of my family, because God knows what time it is there, but if you are, this one's for you.'

The audience gave a collective 'aaah' and around the world hearts melted. In the hospital, Tavvy promptly burst into tears and Caitie handed her a handful of tissues. At the side of the stage in Los Angeles, Pia and Luisa found themselves hugging each other in relief.

Iris nodded for the band to start again and this time, she didn't miss her cue. Pouring her heart and soul into the song, she sang the words yearningly and emotion poured from her. Recognising the song as the number one hit by Tavvy Maguire, the audience began to sing along, crooning the chorus with Iris.

Standing in the centre of the stage, her long cream gown blowing in the cool night breeze, Iris put everything else out of her mind and did her best to do the song justice. Holding her microphone out so that the audience could sing along, Iris moved from one side of the stage to the other, smiling. As she hit the hugely challenging note at the end, the audience fell silent in awe, bursting into riotous applause at the end.

'Thank you so much,' she said, bowing graciously. 'Sorry about before and thank you for giving me another chance.' Waving, she ran off the stage.

In the hospital in England, Tavvy, Caitie and Rosie flung their arms around each other and danced a jig. Lochlin lay motionless on his bed, his machines bleeping away, and Tavvy clutched his hand tearfully, wishing he could have heard Iris.

'He would have been so proud,' she sobbed.

Caitie brushed his hair away from his face. 'He will be proud of her, when he comes round,' she said gently.

'So he will.' Rosie nodded, patting Tavvy's shoulder. 'You mustn't give up hope.'

In their apartment in Beverly Hills, Ace leapt off the sofa and punched the air.

'Fucking hell. I thought she wasn't going to make it there for a minute.' He hugged Jerry.

'When are you going to speak to Iris?' Jerry asked, knowing he had to put pressure on Ace to do it sooner rather than later. Iris was leaving for England in a couple of days.

Ace groaned, pushing his mahogany hair out of his eyes. 'Soon, Jez, I promise. There just never seems to be a right time to come out and say it.'

Jerry handed him another beer. 'How do you think she'll react?'

'Fuck knows.' Ace shook his head. 'I'm petrified she's going to hate me but she's the only woman I've ever wanted a future with.' His grey eyes clouded over with regret. 'So I have to do it, I have to tell her about my father.'

'And what's he going to say when he finds out you've done that?'

Ace shuddered. He didn't even want to think about it.

At the peace concert, Iris had hugged Pia tearfully, saying goodbye and promising to call as soon as she was back in England.

'You'd better,' Pia said gruffly. 'I have big plans for you. I know you have to go back for your dad but when you're ready and once you have that deal in place at Shamrock, we can launch you officially.'

Iris's amber eyes were apologetic. 'I can't believe I croaked and missed my cue. I'm so sorry.'

Pia grinned. 'Hey, the audience forgave you. If anything, I think it made you even more adorable. Just don't stop practising, all right?' She gave Luisa a polite nod, forgetting the fact they'd been hugging a few moments before and left.

'Are we going to Ace's apartment?' Luisa asked.

Iris nodded. 'If you don't mind. I want to spend as much time as I can with him before I leave.'

'Do you think Jerry fancies me?' Luisa mused as she headed in the direction of Beverly Hills. 'We had a drunken kiss in Monte Carlo but nothing's happened since. I'm going to jump him tonight and see what happens. I mean, he sleeps with tons of women. What's wrong with *me*?'

She was so busy chatting, she didn't even notice the car following them a hundred yards behind, weaving in and out of the traffic all the way to Ace's apartment. Allegra's eyes gleamed. She had a big surprise in store for Iris tonight and she didn't want to miss a second of it.

Iris and Luisa parked outside Ace's apartment and headed indoors.

'You were great,' Ace told Iris, kissing her passionately.

Luisa jumped into Jerry's arms and he was too taken aback to let her go. 'I've missed you,' she said, planting a juicy kiss on his mouth.

'I choked . . . it was awful,' Iris groaned, throwing herself into a chair. 'All I could think about was my father.'

Ace felt Jerry's eyes on him. 'Speaking of fathers, I really need to speak to you about mine.'

Iris rubbed her eyes. 'Shoot.'

'Er, not here,' Ace said. 'In private.' About to lead her away, they all jumped as a recorded message started playing.

'Where's that coming from?' Jerry said.

Luisa frowned. 'It sounds like you two talking, you and Ace. Wherever it's coming from, let's listen.'

They all went quiet. As Ace worked out what he was hearing, he went pale. He was too late. Someone – God knows who – had got there before him and now Iris was going to hear about the deal in the worst possible way.

On the recording, Jerry could now be heard speaking. 'Yes, and he's the one who leaked that information to the press! Your father put you in this position in the first place, Ace . . . he has to take responsibility for that.'

Sounding tinny on the recording, Ace then spoke, scoffing loudly. 'Take responsibility? My father? That's never going to happen.' There was a pause. 'However you look at it, my father pimped me out and now he wants me to kick Iris to the kerb . . . all so he can get his petty revenge on Lochlin Maguire. If he's sick, then so am I for going along with it.'

Iris gasped and Luisa's mouth fell open.

Ace's heart was pounding so hard in his chest, he thought it might be audible.

Iris's amber eyes, when she turned them towards him, were wide with pain. 'Ace? It's not . . . please say that's not true . . .'

'It's . . . fuck, I can explain . . .'

Luisa's hands shot to her mouth as she saw Iris's face crumple.

'H-how could you d-do this to me?' Iris stammered, her bee-stung lips quivering. 'You're only with me because your father told you to seduce me?'

'You bastard!' Luisa yelled, hurling herself at Ace.

Jerry pulled her back. 'It's not how it looks,' he said roughly. 'You have no idea what Ace has been going through.'

Luisa narrowed her eyes. 'What *Ace* has been going through? Please do not expect me to feel any sympathy, Jerry! This is horrible.'

Ace grabbed Iris's hand. It felt limp in his and he couldn't bear it. 'It's not . . . it started out that way . . . well, that's not even true.' He shook his head. 'My father asked me to seduce you but when I saw you, I wanted you for myself, not because my father made me do it.'

Iris thought she might throw up on the spot. She'd thought Ace was the love of her life, and all along their relationship meant nothing, it was just some sick scheme of his father's. Suddenly, Judd's motive for giving her an all-expenses-paid trip to LA became painfully obvious. It had nothing to do with her talent, he had simply sent her here to make her fall in love with Ace.

'So my brother isn't the only one your f-father was trying to d-destroy,' she said, shaking all over.

Hearing her stutter over her words, Ace felt his heart clench. He couldn't lose Iris, he just couldn't. 'My father's a sick bastard,' he told her passionately. 'But I'm not him. He tried to get me to make you sign with Jett . . . he ordered me to dump you but I refused.'

Iris stared at him, thinking he was suddenly a stranger to her. 'Should I be grateful? Should I be thanking you for sparing me the humiliation of being dumped on command?'

Ace felt as though he was drowning. He had no idea where the recording had come from or who had set it up; all he knew was that Iris was slipping from his grasp right in front of him and there didn't seem to be anything he could do about it.

Tears ran down Iris's face. 'How c-could you?' she whispered. 'I thought you l-loved me.'

'I do,' he insisted hoarsely. 'Please, Iris, however this started out, I fell for you the moment I met you. Jerry will tell you.'

Jerry nodded dumbly, shocked by the hatred on Luisa's face.

'*Usted bastardos*,' she hissed at both of them. 'This is disgusting. I feel sick.'

Ace wanted nothing more than to gather Iris up in his arms and take her pain away. Taking a step towards her, the look of sheer anguish on her face stopped him in his tracks.

Iris could barely look at him; all she could think was that her world was caving in. Everything had been a lie, the way they'd met, the invite to the party – everything. Iris could see that now. Their relationship was nothing more than a sham, a joke that was totally on her. Her eyes were tortured as she faced up to the fact that she had almost lost her father and now she had lost Ace. Because after this, there was no going back. There was no way she could forgive Ace and there wasn't a chance in hell she could forget what had happened.

'No. It's not over,' he mumbled, seeing it in her eyes. Tears ran down his face. 'Iris, don't do this. It's not over.'

'It is,' she murmured, feeling a pain in her chest. 'It really is.' Turning, she spun away from him and ran out of the door. About to run after her, Luisa was stopped by Jerry. 'Look after Ace,' he yelled as he dashed out after Iris. 'Just look after him and don't believe any of this.' Finding Iris blinded by tears and fumbling to start her car with frantically shaking hands, Jerry flung the car door open.

'Ace loves you,' he told her fiercely. 'And trust me . . . he's never loved anyone in his life before.'

Iris shook her head. 'He doesn't . . . he c-can't. Not if he could do that.' She stared at Jerry helplessly. 'Who is he, Jerry? I don't even know him. I thought I did but if he's capable of this, he's no better than Judd.'

Jerry grabbed her hand. 'He is! He *is* better than Judd! He's scared of his father, all right? He thought if he didn't go along with this, his career was over because Judd pays for everything. But it's more than that. Ace has spent his life trying to impress that man, to win his approval. He lives this stupid playboy lifestyle because that's what Judd wants.'

'What a hardship,' Iris said in a flat voice.

Jerry raked his hand through his blond hair. 'He fell in love with you the moment he saw you, I promise you! And his father told him to dump you when your father had his heart attack and Ace refused. Do you know how much courage that took? Do you know what Judd is capable of? That man is a monster, Iris. You have to believe me.' Pain registered in Jerry's eyes. 'Believe me, Iris. I know he loves you more than anything in the world.'

Iris stared past him. 'I fell in love with him . . . I thought we had this big future together. I risked everything for him, Jerry. I turned my back on my family and for what? For nothing. It was all just a scheme of Judd's to get back at my father because he wants revenge.'

Jerry didn't know what else to say. 'He's never loved anyone in his life before,' he repeated. 'And he fell for you. You have to believe him, you have to give him a chance.'

Luisa dashed out and jumped into the car with Iris. 'I think you'd better go and see Ace. He's in a bad way. Come on, Iris, let's get out of here. Don't touch me, Jerry.'

'Tell Ace not to call me,' Iris told Jerry, heartbroken. Tearing off the necklace he had given her, Iris put it in Jerry's hand.

Jerry watched them pull away with a heavy heart.

Sitting in her car out of sight, Allegra smiled to herself. What a dramatic little scene, far better than she could have hoped for. All she needed to do now was bide her time then turn up just when Ace was too weak to push her away. Allegra drove off feeling elated.

Heading back inside, Jerry found Ace slumped over the piano, Iris's sheets of music soaked with tears.

'I've lost her,' he choked, not even seeing Jerry through his tears. 'Haven't I?'

Wishing he could tell him different, Jerry put his hand over Ace's. Letting out a howl of grief as he saw Iris's necklace, Ace put his head down on the piano and wept.

Chapter Eighteen

Charlie Valentine sat in his studio and for the first time in years thought about writing some new material. He wanted to be taken seriously this time round; his days of diamantes and tight trousers were over. Well, almost, he thought, glancing down at his snug jeans. But at least he didn't look like an ageing rocker any more; his hair had been dyed a more subdued honey-brown colour which his twin daughters assured him was 'cool, but not twatty', which was good enough for Charlie, and he had a new wardrobe of clothes Susannah had helped him buy which were edgy but not too young for him.

Tentatively, Charlie brushed the dust off his guitar and played a few chords. He felt jittery about writing new material but he was determined to make a proper comeback with a new image and something fresh on stage. If Shay and everyone at Shamrock thought he could do it, then he was going to have to believe in himself too.

'Shit, this used to be so easy,' he muttered to himself. Back in the day, songwriting had been a doddle and some of his best tunes had been knocked out in under an hour. Of course, songwriting had never given him the thrill that performing did but nothing could do that.

It was only in later years that writing had became more arduous and putting a song together had started to feel more like a chore than a joy. Charlie knew the cause of it deep down: he had become disillusioned with the music business and everything it stood for and his dissatisfaction showed when he tried to pen a song. Realising people loved him for the old-style music he used to play,

Charlie knew he was taking a huge risk by trying something new but it was time for a change.

Trying a few more chords on his guitar, he started to note them down. As he gained confidence, Charlie soon found that the floor around him was covered with sheets of music paper with scribbles all over them. Glancing at his watch, he realised he'd been shut in his studio for over four hours without noticing the time, something he used to do years ago. He *was* talented, after all. In a flash, Charlie realised he'd got caught up with all the rock and roll bullshit and had lost sight of what was important to him. Writing music, touring, women . . .

Susannah poked her blond head around the door. 'Fancy a drink?'

He grinned. 'I'd love one.'

She came into the room bearing a tray with various cups and glasses on it. 'I wasn't sure what you were drinking in the studio these days so I've brought you a mug of tea, a beer and a tequila shot.' She was wearing a tight red T-shirt with her blond hair around her shoulders and a pair of tight black jeans that made her legs look endless.

'Tea is fine, thanks. It might not be very rock and roll but I'm parched.' Charlie took it and drank it quickly.

'How's it going?' Susannah asked, perching her bottom on a speaker. 'I can't remember the last time I saw you in here – I mean, properly writing songs.' She peered at the sheets of music on the floor with scribbles all over them. 'Wow, you've done so much already! Chas, I'm so proud of you.'

Charlie strummed on his guitar, wondering why he had forgotten how fabulous his wife's legs were. 'Thanks. I feel like the old me again.' He tugged at his newly dyed hair. 'Well, not quite the old me, maybe a new me.'

'I hope so.' Susannah gave him a lingering kiss. 'I love the hair but I'd hate you to start shagging groupies every two seconds again.' Looking rather sad, she left him to it.

After all his years of womanising and messing Susannah about, Charlie suddenly felt like a heel. Christ, how had she put up with him all these years? he wondered, shamefaced. Bedding silly girls just to boost his ego and help him play out the rock and roll dream – how pathetic. And Susannah had stood by him, through all of it, waiting patiently while he got his kicks elsewhere, never once turning her back on him, even when everyone else thought he was a loser and a has-been.

What a woman. Realising belatedly that his wife was a truly amazing person, Charlie felt humbled. Inspired, he grabbed another sheet of music. 'Susannah's Song', he penned across the top.

This is going to be the most incredible song I've ever written, Charlie told himself, as some lyrics and music popped into his head at the same time.

Charlie wasn't the only one writing music. Back at Pembleton, Tavvy was rapidly putting the finishing touches to the songs she'd put together for Iris's album. She was confident the melodies were strong and perfect for Iris's key and she'd put her heart and soul into the lyrics. Everything she'd been feeling about Lochlin and Judd and the things that had happened that year had gone into Iris's album and it had been cathartic to get her emotions out.

There were also two extra tracks with music but no lyrics as yet and even though Iris claimed not to be able to write songs, Tavvy was sure she could if she put her mind to it. She had no idea how Iris would sum up her experiences in LA but she suspected once Iris sat down and focused on her time there, she'd be able to come up with something.

Gazing out of the window, Tavvy couldn't help feeling as if she was in a dream. She knew Iris was due back shortly but she had no idea what was going on with Ace Harrington or whether Iris intended to go back to the States or not. For now, Tavvy was just focusing on seeing her daughter again and hoping against hope that Lochlin would pull through.

Please, please get better, Lochlin, Tavvy pleaded silently. Nothing felt the same without him; Pembleton, the home they'd spent years building up together, felt empty without his solid presence. She felt as if her right arm was missing, as if she was stumbling around like half a person without him. It was only now he wasn't here that Tavvy realised how distant they had become from each other, how they had gone from being two people who had always thought of themselves as soul mates to a couple of almost strangers, residing in the same house but no longer sharing, confiding or connecting.

At least Iris was coming home, Tavvy thought, awash with relief as she cleared away her music sheets. Sounding shaky and tearful, Iris had called to say that she was catching an earlier flight that would arrive later that afternoon, so Tavvy had said they should all meet at the hospital so the doctor could give them a progress report.

The wild, overgrown garden looked heavenly, Tavvy thought absent-mindedly. Basking in early June sunshine, the garden was awash with lilac rhododendrons in full scented bloom and blush-pink tulips that bent in the light breeze.

Seeing her at the window, Kitty came in and gestured to the coffee machine. 'Shall I fire her up?'

'Actually, I think I need something a bit stronger,' Tavvy confessed, pulling the fridge open and taking out a bottle of white wine. 'Join me?'

Useless at drinking during the day, Kitty agreed, knowing Tavvy needed a drinking partner. 'The barn's looking great,' she commented, sipping her wine gingerly.

Tavvy took a gulp of hers. 'I'm so sorry I'm not out there more often. My priorities seem to be Lochlin, sorting this album out for Iris and not much else.' She looked down at her hands and seeing them shaking, tucked them under the table self-consciously. 'And now the album's done, all I can think about is Lochlin.'

'You're doing more than enough,' Kitty assured her. Gently, she asked the question she knew Tavvy dreaded. 'Any news?'

Tavvy shook her head, her eyes filling with tears. 'God, I'm such a wet at the moment. It's just hard coping with Lochlin not being here. Pembleton . . . it's just *him*, you see. Everything about it reminds me of him.' She put her hands on the table, trying to stop them shaking. 'They've asked us to go into the hospital later for a "talk". What do you think that means?'

'It's probably just an update on Lochlin's progress,' Kitty said, patting her hand briskly. She felt nothing but sympathy for Tavvy but she also knew she was going to fall apart if she sat here thinking about Lochlin and drinking herself into oblivion. 'You need another project. The barn is well under control so what about this midsummer party you said you host each year. Isn't that in a few weeks' time?'

The Midsummer Ball was an event Tavvy hosted each year, usually held in a marquee in the woods near Bluebell Cottage. It was a magical night and Tavvy would always go to enormous trouble decorating the marquee with twinkling lanterns, flowers and foliage. It would usually feature whatever play Hugo was putting on, in this case *Romeo and Juliet*, and there would also be singing and dancing of some kind as well as some incredible food. They had a ritual bonfire at the end of the night at the edge of the clearing and under normal circumstances Tavvy threw herself into the planning earnestly.

She sighed. 'I guess I should go ahead with it and Shay has instructed me to because he's sure Lochlin will be better by then.'

Kitty very much doubted it but she did her best not to let her misgivings show on her face. 'At least it will give you something to do now that you've finished Iris's album. And I can help out too, if you need me to. Just give me a "to do" list and I can get on with it.'

Tavvy nodded. 'Thanks. I guess the irony of Caitie and Elliot playing the leads in *Romeo and Juliet* isn't lost on any of us, is it?'

Kitty shook her head. 'No. It's not. My life seems to be full of surprises at the moment, not to mention the odd scandal.' She lifted her grey eyes to meet Tavvy's. 'If I tell you something, will you promise to keep it a secret?'

Tavvy sat up, pleased to have something else to think about. 'Of course.'

'Lexi Beaument. The man she's been sleeping with is my son.'

'Not Ace?' Tavvy gasped, her befuddled brain wondering how Ace was managing to keep up affairs on two different continents.

Kitty's brow frowned. 'Not Ace. *Sebastian*. Lexi has been sleeping with Sebastian.'

'Oh dear.' Tavvy shuddered. From what she could remember, Sebastian Harrington was a rather ugly specimen with bright ginger hair and Judd's brusque manner. 'Er . . . poor Martha.'

Kitty raised her eyebrows. 'You don't know the half of it. Lexi's pregnant and Sebastian wants to buy the baby for Martha.'

Tavvy's mouth fell open.

Kitty nodded. 'I know. You don't have to say a word. But, there's more.' She took a gulp of wine for Dutch courage then blurted it out. 'Aside from the fact I could be a grandmother by the end of the year, I think I might have a thing for Leo.'

Tavvy jumped up and pulled the fridge door open. 'I think we're going to need more wine,' she said gravely, holding up another bottle.

Martha stopped for a break and bent over, panting like mad. She and Savannah had taken a new route for their jog and although Savannah didn't realise it, they were only a few yards from Foxton Manor where Lexi lived.

'Come on, you can do it!' Savannah yelled. Not even breaking a sweat despite the baking hot sunshine, she jogged on the spot, determined not to let Martha slack. Wearing a bright green vest and a tiny pair of black shorts with her red hair in a long plait, she looked fit, athletic and irritatingly gorgeous.

'I need a break,' Martha gasped, feeling a desire to slap Savannah hard. Taking her role as personal trainer and dietician very seriously, Savannah had Martha running five miles a day and sticking to a hard-core diet, but she hadn't stopped praising Martha for her commitment.

Much to her surprise, Savannah was enjoying her new role immensely and it occurred to her that if all else failed, personal trainer was a possible career route for her. There had to be any number of overweight housewives around here she could train back to normality – that was if she was going to stay in the area, of course, Savannah thought wryly. Her future was looking very uncertain right now.

'What are you going to do if Judd kicks you out?' Martha asked, admiring Savannah's long, toned legs, and thinking her own were at least a little slimmer. 'I'll miss you if you leave. You've been such a good friend to me.'

'Aw, don't go all soft on me,' Savannah said, her cheeks going pink at the compliment. 'You'll be just fine without me.' Then she spotted a figure heading towards them. 'Houston, we have a problem,' she muttered.

Martha straightened up, the colour draining from her face.

Lost in thought, Lexi was almost level with them before she realised who they were. Starting, she turned beetroot. She was wearing a pair of pink tracksuit bottoms and a black halter-neck top but Martha could have sworn she looked a size bigger than she had the last time she'd seen her. But then, she was pregnant, Martha reminded herself with a trace of bitterness.

Seeing Lexi like this, her tummy blossoming into motherhood, hit Martha hard. She could feel her bottom lip trembling and although she didn't want to make a show of herself in front of Lexi, she couldn't help feeling overwhelmed at coming face to face with Sebastian's mistress.

Savannah put her hands on her hips, her stance aggressive. 'Do you want me to deal with her?'

Petrified, Lexi backed away.

Martha didn't blame her; she wouldn't want to be on the wrong side of Savannah either. She pulled herself together, determined not to look weak and emotional. 'No, I'm fine, thanks. Look, why don't you leave us to it? I'll catch you up.'

Savannah shrugged. 'All right. But make sure your muscles don't get cold, otherwise you'll seize up.' She jogged off in the other direction, impressed by Martha's strength and composure. Personally, she thought Lexi deserved a good slap, pregnant or not, but maybe Martha's way of handling things was better.

Lexi fiddled with her top, pulling it over her bump. 'I thought I'd come out for some air,' she explained haltingly. She swept back her glossy curtains of hair, her shaking hands betraying her nerves. 'I've been feeling so sick lately.'

Biting back a sarcastic response, Martha returned her gaze coolly.

'Have you told your husband yet? About the baby, I mean.'

Lexi looked pained. 'Yes, I have. Leo was very . . . fair, in the circumstances.' She had actually found it a very difficult conversation. Being a lawyer, and an exceptionally good one at that, Leo had drawn up a document stating that whatever the result with the baby, they should get divorced. If the baby was his, he would provide generous support to both her and the baby, including finding somewhere for them to live. If not, Lexi could keep her clothes and jewellery and she should accept a one-off payment.

Lexi knew Leo was being businesslike about the arrangements because he was so hurt and, unexpectedly, she had felt a pang of regret. He had been so good to her. For the first time, Lexi had realised she'd made a huge mistake letting Leo go.

'I'm not sure we have anything else to say to one another,' Martha told her stiffly, realising it was the truth. She didn't want to befriend Lexi, nor did she care what happened to her after the baby was born. 'Just . . . look after the baby, all right? That's all that matters.' She did a few quick lunges before pounding down the path after Savannah.

Lexi was stunned that Martha had been so pleasant. She started, feeling a fluttering movement inside her, and she wondered if it was the baby moving. Telling herself it was too early, she realised that even if it was the baby kicking, she had no one to share the news with.

Lexi headed back to Foxton Manor, running her hands over her changing body with distaste. Everything felt different; her boobs felt as if they might explode, her trousers were getting tighter by the day and, lifting her top to examine her stomach, dear God, was that a tiny stretch mark developing?

Repulsed, Lexi walked more quickly, desperate to go home and smother herself in Mama Mio Tummy Butter.

Jerry glanced at Ace worriedly. Listening out for the weather reports because the race had been cancelled before due to rain, they were just about to head outside to complete the Michigan Lifelock 400 race. Jerry had no idea why the officials were stressing about the weather; it was a magnificent day outside with bright blue skies and brilliant sunshine. Frankly, he was more concerned about Ace.

Since Iris had walked out a few days ago, Ace had sunk into a depression, barely able to string a sentence together and not remembering to eat or drink. After they had flown to Michigan, Jerry had done his best to keep Ace's spirits up by making him his favourite scrambled eggs with smoked salmon, but after valiantly managing a mouthful, Ace had rushed to the bathroom and vomited. He had spent the past few days in bed, only rising this morning because Jerry had sternly pushed him in the direction of the shower before their race.

His mahogany hair still damp from the shower, Ace hadn't been able to wash away the violet shadows under his eyes, nor did his racing suit disguise how lean his frame was. He was literally wasting away and Jerry couldn't bear it. He had a strong feeling Allegra was behind the twisted little stunt with the tape recording. She probably thought she could walk back into Ace's open arms. But Allegra would keep. It was Ace who was important now.

'How are you feeling about the race?' Jerry asked.

'I couldn't care less about it,' Ace said. He stared at the track without interest, his grey eyes lacklustre. He barely noticed members of the Chevrolet and Toyota teams clapping him on the back and wishing him luck as they strolled down to their cars. His shoulders were rigid with tension and he had a strange, almost defiant expression on his face.

Jerry felt a tremor of fear. He had seen that expression once before.

Discovering that Judd had once hit his beloved mother, Kitty, a young and outraged Ace had challenged his father about it. Receiving a deafening punch to the ear that had affected his balance and his peripheral vision for a week, Ace had spun his car out of control on the Las Vegas Motor Speedway track and had ended up on crutches for three months. Ace was wearing the same expression now; his chin high and his mouth twisting rebelliously.

'Hey, why don't you sit this one out?' Jerry suggested, suddenly desperate to stop Ace from driving. 'Say you're ill or something.'

'Why on earth would I do that?' Ace frowned. 'This is exactly what I need, Jerry. Something to take my mind off . . .' A flicker of pain crossed his face. 'I can't even say her name. Can you believe that?' He shook his head, staring straight ahead. 'I lost her and I can't blame anyone but myself because however much I want to say it's my father's fault, it's not, is it? I'm the one who went along with his stupid fucking plan. I'm the one who was too gutless to tell Iris about it in the first place.'

Jerry grabbed his arm. 'You fell in love with her! You couldn't help it. You didn't do it on purpose. You weren't to know Iris wasn't going to be another one of the bimbos we meet every day in this job.'

'But I did, Jerry. That's the problem. I did.' Ace zipped up his suit restlessly. 'The first time I met her, I knew Iris was different, and I went ahead and did it anyway, because I wanted her. How fucking selfish is that?' He picked up his helmet grimly. 'Still, the joke's on me, isn't it? I'm the one who's ended up without her and now nothing matters any more.'

Striding past Jerry, he headed down to the track and stood by his car.

Jerry stared after him anxiously. There was no way Ace was going to make it round the track in one piece in his current state of mind.

'Jerry?'

He turned at the sound of a familiar, breathless voice. 'Luisa! What are you doing here?'

'God knows. I've had to tell all sorts of lies to get in here. If anyone asks, I'm your personal masseuse and you can't function without me, *entendido*?' Catching her breath, Luisa grabbed Jerry's arm. 'Iris has gone back to England but I've been thinking about what happened with Ace and Iris. And as much as I still hate both of you, I believe they love each other.' She nodded, her black curls bouncing off her shoulders. 'And only for that reason, I think we haff to get them back together.'

Jerry grinned at her accent then looked sombre again. 'How are we supposed to do that? Iris doesn't want to see him or speak to him ever again and Ace is a total mess.'

'I don't know!' Luisa punched him on the arm. 'We haff to think of something, though. They're meant to be together, like Romeo and Juliet or whoever.'

Jerry heard an announcement calling all the drivers down. 'I have to go. Look, I'll speak to you afterwards. And Luisa, Ace is so sorry about all of this. And so am I. I tried to talk him out of it, I really did.' He lowered his dazzling blue eyes. 'But then he fell for her and it was like something was set in motion.'

Luisa gave him a brief smile. 'Unlike you and me, eh? We haff no chemistry whatsoever, we're not even friends with benefits.' Suddenly Luisa wondered why that was. Not out of vanity as such, but because she'd never quite been able to figure Jerry out.

'But . . . we're friends, aren't we?' Suddenly, it seemed important to Jerry that Luisa didn't hate him any more.

Luisa nodded. 'Go. You need to do this stupid race.'

Jerry dashed down to the track. This particular race consisted of two hundred laps with the cars jostling for position and it was always absolutely thrilling. Keeping his eye on Ace, Jerry leapt into his car. They set off and hurtled round the track, some spinning out of control, others zipping round expertly.

Rushing to the viewing gallery, Luisa shimmied her way to the front, her heart pounding. She watched the cars zigzagging in between one another, bumpers shunting, tyres screeching. The commentators were making their usual joking comments over the loudspeakers.

'And it's Jeff Gordon for Chevrolet in the lead, followed by Greg Biffle but he's run out of fuel . . . surely not! No, he has . . . he's run out of fuel, how crazy is that?'

Another commentator joined in. '*And there's Kurt Busch for Dodge, always a good bet . . . but what's Ace Harrington doing? He's all over the place today . . . he's cutting corners and driving like a maniac.*'

Luisa fixed her eyes on Ace's car. He *was* driving like a maniac. Ace had always driven recklessly but today he looked almost out of control and his car was weaving all over the track as if it had a mind of its own. What is he *doing*? Luisa thought, as she watched him hurtling towards a barrier. It was as if he was driving towards it on purpose . . .

'Slow down!' Luisa yelled, making the other spectators in the viewing gallery jump. She waved her arms around like an idiot. 'Stop, you stupid fucker!'

But Ace didn't stop. In what seemed like slow motion, his car carried on charging towards the barrier at high speed and Luisa wasn't even aware of her own shrieks as she watched Ace's car crunch into the barrier with a sickening crash. There was a collective gasp as people rushed to the front of the gallery to get a better look.

Pushing past them, Luisa fought her way through the crowds to get down to the track. Frenziedly she pelted down to the edge but she was held back by officials. Screeching at the top of her voice, Luisa watched Jerry pull over, his car at an angle across the track. Jumping out, Jerry took his life in his hands as he dodged in between random, speeding cars.

Tears streaming down his face, Jerry banged on the windows but Ace remained immobile in the car. Held back by two officials, Jerry struggled against them redundantly, screaming Ace's name before collapsing into their arms with a sob. Ambulance crew swarmed around the car and managed to free him from behind the steering wheel. They slid Ace out of the car window and placed his unmoving body on a stretcher.

Her heart in her mouth, Luisa shrieked at Jerry to go with him and, nodding, he pulled free from the officials and leapt into the ambulance. It immediately shot away from the track and there was a shocked silence as the ambulance turned on its siren and headed towards the hospital.

It was early evening in England and Iris had just arrived at the hospital. Utterly worn out and emotionally drained, she was hardly in the right frame of mind to visit her father but there was no way she was going to be a no-show.

Not even sure where she was going, Iris realised she felt bereft – bereft but also detached. The only way she could describe it was that she felt grief-stricken but strangely empty. Ace's betrayal seemed as though it had happened to someone else a long time ago, but Iris knew she was kidding herself. She could almost convince herself it was just a nightmare, except it wasn't; it was real and she had a stabbing ache in her heart to prove it.

Having left her luggage at the airport to be collected later, Iris carried only a handbag and some of her father's favourite flowers – a huge bunch of irises. Wearing a pair of white skinny jeans and a black T-shirt, her blond hair was piled on top of her head messily but she didn't care what she looked like. Now she was here, all she wanted to do was rush to her father's side. Finding his room finally, she saw her mother and Shay there already, standing around a bed connected to an array of tubes and machines.

Seeing her father looking so helpless and frail, Iris burst into tears. 'Oh my God, I can't believe this has happened. I can't believe I wasn't here. Can you ever forgive me?' She sobbed incoherently. 'It's all over with Ace . . . I love him but it's all gone wrong . . .'

'Iris!' Tavvy fell on her neck and hugged her until Iris thought her bones might crack. 'I'm so glad you're back, darling. Please don't be sorry. What's happened with Ace?'

'I can't even talk about it,' Iris managed, overcome with gratitude when Shay pulled her into his arms. 'It's . . . it's over . . . so I betrayed everyone for . . . for nothing at all, as it turns out.'

'Hush,' Shay said, kissing the top of her head. 'It's good to see you and I mean that. Christ, I barely recognise you with that tan and the flash new hairstyle.'

Iris gave him a weak smile. 'Has there been any change?'

Shay's eyes clouded over. 'Not yet. But the doctors are coming in to speak to us later.'

Tavvy gave Iris a worried once-over. She had no idea what had happened with Ace but Iris looked like a ghost of her former self.

'Did Ace . . . did he hurt you in some way?' Tavvy asked.

Iris gulped down a sob. 'Very much. But he's also one of the sweetest, most genuine people I've ever met. That's why this is so painful.' She grabbed some tissues from the bedside.

A kindly looking man with grey hair and a lovely bedside manner arrived. He introduced himself as Dr Kemple and then asked, 'Is everyone here?'

'My daughter Caitie is on her way,' Tavvy fretted, checking her watch. 'She must have got held up.'

Dr Kemple checked his notes. 'I really need to have this chat now, if possible. I have three other patients to see this evening.'

Tavvy nodded. 'All right.' Her amber eyes were wide with fear. 'What's the prognosis?'

'Well, I'm afraid it's not as good as we'd hoped for,' Dr Kemple said carefully. 'We've tried a number of different treatments but nothing seems to have worked and in situations like this, unfortunately, we have to think about the long-term effects of keeping someone on life support for this long . . .'

Tavvy let out a cry and promptly sat down on a nearby chair. Iris, tuning the doctor out, took the seat next to her father and grabbed his hand. Shay ran a hand through his dark hair.

'Is there really nothing we can do?' he asked, devastated.

Dr Kemple's face became serious. 'We can talk about organ donation if you'd like to, although I know this can be a very tough thing to think about at a time like this . . .'

Tavvy clapped a hand over her mouth.

Iris started. 'I felt his hand move!'

Dr Kemple nodded understandingly. 'It's an involuntary reaction,' he explained. 'It can happen at any time but it's just nerve endings, I'm afraid. It doesn't mean he's about to come round or anything.'

'He did it again!' Iris jumped up. 'I swear, he's squeezing my hand repeatedly. Feel it, Dr Kemple!'

Dr Kemple put his folder down and picked up Lochlin's hand. 'No, I'm sorry, it's just . . . hang on.' He stared at the machines and squeezed Lochlin's hand. 'If you can feel that, Mr Maguire, please do it back.' Lochlin's hand clearly moved. 'Goodness me. This is unprecedented.'

Tavvy rushed over to his bedside, closely followed by Shay. 'Iris, what did you say to him?'

'What needed to be said. That I was sorry for everything.'

Shay grinned. 'Typical. I've been coming here day after day, chatting to him and reading him stuff from the tabloids and you waltz in and bring him round in a few seconds!'

Iris looked appalled. 'No wonder he didn't bother coming round. He reads *The Times*, remember?'

'Now, this is a very good sign,' Dr Kemple said, 'but I don't want anyone to get their hopes up. I'm only being realistic here; this sometimes happens and then the patient can go downhill again. There might have been brain damage, we just don't know at this stage . . .'

Suddenly Lochlin opened his eyes and smiled, wincing when he realised he had a tube in his throat. When it had been removed, he croaked painfully. 'As if I have brain damage,' he said, pulling a face as he spoke for the first time in weeks. 'I'm fine. Why wouldn't I be?' He let out a hoarse laugh as Tavvy smothered his face with kisses.

Ushering Shay and Iris out into the corridor, Dr Kemple and his team got to work on Lochlin, checking his vitals and making sure he was stable enough to be removed from the life support machine.

Face flushed from running, Caitie dashed up to Shay and Iris. 'I'm sorry I'm late, I was in the library.'

Shay let out a mocking laugh. 'In the library? You?'

Caitie elbowed him. 'Oh, shut up. I was doing some research, actually, but I'll tell you about it later.' She glanced at Iris. 'But that's not why I'm late. Look, I got delayed because I saw this thing on the TV and I was trying to find out if there was any update online.'

Iris frowned, wondering why Caitie was looking at her so strangely. 'What are you talking about?'

Caitie nibbled her fingernails and bought herself some time. 'How's Dad?'

Shay was attempting to look through the window in the door, his hands cupped around it. 'He's awake, can you believe it? Iris came back, said a few words and he bloody woke up! He seems fine but the docs are just giving him a once-over.'

Caitie whooped. 'That's amazing! Thank God for that. He's been on those nasty machines for so long now, I was starting to lose hope.' She turned to Iris. 'Look, this thing . . . you probably don't even care but it was about Ace.'

'What about him?' Iris asked warily. She wondered if the day would ever come when hearing his name wouldn't feel as if her heart had been ripped out.

'He . . . look, I don't know how to say this, but he crashed his car and they don't know if he's going to make it.' Caitie twisted her hands distractedly. 'And they're saying . . . but this is unconfirmed . . . they're saying he might have done it on purpose.'

Turning round, Shay held his arms out just in time and caught Iris as she fell against him in a dead faint.

Chapter Nineteen

Finding himself at home on a Saturday night for once, Judd wandered into the sitting room. The house was unusually quiet and Judd had no idea where any of his family were. Savannah's iPod wasn't on full blast like it normally was and even Martha, usually a permanent fixture in the kitchen next to the biscuit barrel, seemed to be absent. Sebastian was keeping a low profile since the board meeting even though Judd knew he must be furious about his bonus.

He strolled to the drinks table and poured himself a Scotch. Staring out to the glittering, still water in the swimming pool, Judd felt a shiver go down his spine. Christ, was he ever going to be able to forget that night? Sometimes he thought being back here was more of a torture than a triumph.

Averting his eyes, he thought about Elliot. Elliot hadn't been seen since Judd had gatecrashed his rehearsal and it seemed as if he might have moved out of Brockett Hall – a wise move, in Judd's opinion. As far as he was concerned, the longer the little fairy stayed out of his way, the better. As for him becoming an actor . . . Judd almost spat with contempt.

Spotting an envelope on the mantelpiece, he opened it and pulled out an invitation to Tavvy Maguire's Midsummer Ball. Printed on cream card, it was edged with dark green ivy and studded with silver stars. '*Prepare to be dazzled*,' he read, '*with a performance from Charlie Valentine before Romeo and Juliet act out their romantic tragedy before your eyes. There will be champagne cocktails on arrival, followed by a sumptuous banquet. Your evening will end with an enchanting performance by Iris Maguire . . . Dress to impress.*'

'Fuck me!' Judd sneered out loud. 'Sounds like a blast.'

'It's probably a good job you're not invited then,' Kitty commented quietly from the doorway.

Judd glared at her. Kitty looked different somehow, she seemed calm and composed. Her grey eyes were clear and direct; the guarded fear that was usually present in them was noticeably absent. Even her physical appearance had changed. Gone were the frumpy dresses and flat shoes; Kitty was wearing a pair of jeans which made her look almost slim, a pretty navy top and surprisingly high sandals. Her blond hair was swept up in tortoiseshell clips and she was even wearing a jaunty touch of red lipstick.

'I don't think you'd be welcome there, do you?' Kitty came into the room but she kept her distance.

For once, instead of being afraid to come into his personal space, Judd had the distinct impression his wife simply didn't want to be near him. 'And why would that be?' he demanded, taking a swig of Scotch. He sat on the edge of one of the sofas and turned his scornful blue eyes in her direction.

Kitty contemplated him. She had spent the last however many years fearing for her life, too petrified to challenge Judd, let alone leave him. And although her stomach still lurched when he gave her a particular look, Kitty knew something had changed inside. Bringing Savannah into their home with such casual disregard for her feelings had been the final straw. It was as if he'd hurt her so irrevocably, any feelings of love had finally evaporated and she was finally free, metaphorically speaking.

Maybe her feelings for Leo had something to do with it too. Kitty had no idea how he felt about her and even though she didn't dare hope he might be falling for her, she suddenly realised there were actually men out there who could be funny and sexy and, most importantly, respectful. She had spent so many years convincing herself Judd was still a good husband, that whatever his faults and however many affairs he had, he still looked after her. It had taken a long time for her to realise the only reason Judd held on to her was because he couldn't bear to let any of his possessions go. His desire for her to stay with him wasn't because he loved her or because he would miss her; it was a question of ego, pure and simple. Which explained why Judd was still so obsessed with Tavvy Maguire: she was the one that got away and he hated that.

'Judd, why did we come to England?'

Irritably, he got to his feet and topped up his glass. 'You know why. So I could set up the Jett Corporation and take the music world by storm.'

Kitty ignored his sarcastic tone. 'Be honest, for once. You came back for revenge . . . you came back for Tavvy Maguire.'

Judd's head whipped round. 'What are you talking about?' An ugly flush swept across his face.

She sighed. 'Everyone knows the truth.' Kitty had never seen Judd so ill at ease before. There was a hint of anxiety around his eyes and his jaw was tense. 'At least . . . I think the only person who doesn't know is Tavvy herself.'

'And how can you comment on what Tavvy does or doesn't know?' Judd was thrown off balance by Kitty's words. All at once, she seemed like a stranger to him, poised and unruffled and not in the least afraid of him.

'Because she's my friend,' she answered simply.

Judd started. That was the last thing he'd been expecting Kitty to say. 'Since when?'

'It's actually none of your business who I'm friends with.' Kitty walked over to the window. The view stretching out from Brockett Hall was magnificent but gazing out at the clipped lawns and carefully planted flowers, Kitty felt nothing. She knew she wouldn't miss it when she left because it was intrinsically a part of Judd and her feelings for him were dead. She turned round to face him. 'You never think you've gone too far, do you? You've got away with murder for so long, you think you're untouchable.'

Judd flinched. Not sure if Kitty was speaking literally or figuratively, he downed his Scotch.

Kitty didn't notice. She'd been building up to this speech for a long time and she wasn't going to allow Judd to put her off or interrupt her. 'You've alienated everyone around you. All of us have stood by you through thick and thin and you've never appreciated it.' She walked towards him slowly. 'You've made a fool of me time and time again and I was so scared of you, I let it happen. And what about your children? You say Sebastian is a disappointment but he's the mirror image of you! I'm astonished you haven't spotted the similarities.'

'You're making a big mistake,' Judd started.

'Oh please!' Kitty let out a derisive laugh. 'I've made many mistakes in my life but this definitely isn't one of them.' She shook her head. 'Little do you realise but Sebastian is that chip off the old block you've always wanted, you just don't recognise yourself in him. You've driven Elliot away and you've even made it clear Savannah doesn't reach your ridiculously high standards.'

'She's an ungrateful, gold-digging slut,' Judd roared.

'No, she's not,' Kitty shot back. 'She's caring and considerate and a damned sight more grounded than you.' She looked around the sitting room regretfully. 'So what are you left with? A mausoleum of a house that has no soul, no warmth and, shortly, no family living in it.' As she walked to the door, Kitty glanced over her shoulder. 'I'd like a divorce, by the way.'

Judd spluttered. '*You?* You want to divorce me?'

Kitty was, as ever, caught off guard by his audacity.

'Is that so hard to believe? You're hardly the model husband, are you? You've cheated on me, you've hit me and you've played games with everyone I care about.' She saw him redden and knowing him as well as she did, she knew he was building up to an explosion. 'And before you start talking about money, I'm well aware you'll say I no longer have a home and you'll cut me off without a dime.

Which, as it happens, you can't because the law is on my side. But apart from that, my father is going to help me start over.'

Staggered, Judd resorted to scorn. 'Poor Kitty! Going back to Daddy with your tail between your legs?'

Feeling her blood boiling, Kitty gave him a withering look. 'While you waste time throwing stones, you might want to know that Ace has been in an accident.' Seeing the shock register on Judd's face, she refused to weaken. 'They're not sure if he's going to pull through – not that you'd care after the stunt you pulled with him and Iris Maguire. They say he might have done it on purpose. Why might that be? I wonder.' Gulping down a sob, Kitty turned with as much dignity as she could muster and left the room.

Judd stared after her, trying to take it all in. The last time Ace had been in a serious accident was after a terrible row about hitting Kitty. Was it possible Ace had deliberately crashed his car because of Iris Maguire? Judd squashed the thought down, unfamiliar with the concept of guilt. Ace's bad driving was hardly his fucking problem. The boy was clearly lacking in backbone, just like all his other children. As for Kitty, she could have her fucking divorce but Judd wouldn't make it easy for her.

There were a few things he needed to get shot of, Judd decided, looking around Brockett Hall. Jett, for one; it had somehow lost its appeal now Shamrock wasn't being led by Lochlin. Darcy had fallen by the wayside, and so had Pia. It was time for some fresh blood . . . or maybe something from the past needed a revival, he mused. Brockett Hall had been a satisfying acquisition but there were far more important things on his agenda.

Looking down, Judd realised he was still holding the invitation to the Midsummer Ball. Kitty might think he wouldn't be welcome but he was damned if he was going to miss it, not now.

No, he would make an appearance, Judd thought, his blue eyes gleaming as he relished the thought of finally coming face to face with Tavvy. With any luck, Lochlin would have gasped his final breath, and his wife and everything else that was dear to him would be up for grabs. And with what Judd had planned, the Maguires had better be ready for him because his crusade to destroy them could only end one way.

Looking down, Judd realised he'd ripped the invitation to shreds. Tossing the fragments to the floor, he stalked towards his office to set the final wheels in motion. Starting to throw his belongings into a box, Judd realised he really did have nothing left to lose.

Sitting under an oak tree during the final dress rehearsal for *Romeo and Juliet*, Skye and Abby were gossiping. It was such a hot summer's afternoon, Hugo had led them outside for the rehearsal and there was a buzz of activity as everyone scurried around making sure they were word perfect.

'Have you decided what you're going to do to ruin Caitie's night?' Abby asked, wrestling with a cardboard cutout. It was supposed to resemble the streets of Verona drenched in late evening sunshine, but it looked more like London after the Great Fire. 'Just remember, her father is still in hospital, even if he *is* on the mend, so you'd better make sure whatever you decide to do isn't obvious otherwise you're going to look like a prize bitch.'

'I'm aware of that, thank you,' Skye snapped, surreptitiously sewing some silver spangles on the short red dress she was planning to wear as Juliet once Caitie was out of the picture. 'And no, I haven't decided what to do yet. Can't you think of something?'

'You said I was too stupid so I've given up trying.' Abby gave the dress a critical once-over. 'Would Juliet *really* wear something like that? I thought it said in Hugo's notes that she was about fourteen and very innocent. I heard Caitie has this incredible ethereal dress but if you go ahead with your plan, you're going to turn Juliet into some slutty hooker.'

Skye frowned. Since when had Abby used words like 'ethereal'?

'I'm just making Juliet a bit sexier, that's all.' She held the dress up. 'Don't you think it's gorgeous?'

Abby looked dubious. She thought her twin was way off the mark with the red dress. Juliet was from the olden days and she shouldn't look as though she was about to go clubbing in Aiya Napa.

Dreamily, Abby watched Elliot and Caitie rehearsing the famous scene in the crypt, with Elliot, as Romeo, bent over Caitie's prostrate body, begging Juliet to rise. His blond hair flopped into his eyes as he passionately said his lines and Caitie looked fabulous with her dark curls spilling out across the grass.

Watching them from the side, Hugo could barely contain himself as Elliot bent to kiss Caitie's lips.

'*Here's to my love!*' Elliot quoted, with a look of utter desolation. He smoothed Caitie's hair back tenderly.

> *O true apothecary!*
> *Thy drugs are quick. Thus with a kiss I die.*

Giving Caitie a slow, romantic kiss, he fell to the ground next to her.

'Oooh, just like that, Elliot!' Hugo cried, clapping his hands. 'The audience will be in raptures.'

Abby couldn't help agreeing. 'I know we're supposed to hate Caitie but I can't help thinking she and Elliot have the most wonderful chemistry. They pretty much sizzle as a couple on stage.'

'God, whose side are you on, Ab?' Skye grumbled, hating to admit it but grudgingly thinking her sister was right. 'Wouldn't Elliot have great chemistry with me?'

Abby rolled her eyes. 'Hardly. He's a great actor but you two aren't exactly on the same page, are you? No, trust me, Elliot and Caitie are good friends and they click.' She gave a knowing nod. 'But unless I'm very much mistaken, Jas is probably more Elliot's cup of tea.'

They watched as Elliot and Caitie took a break, with Elliot and Jas talking nineteen to the dozen and Caitie frantically texting someone on her mobile.

Skye glanced at Abby, wondering where she was suddenly getting her insight from. 'Who are you and what have you done with my dozy sister?'

'Oh, shut up! I can be clever when I want to be, you know.' Abby gave her a push.

'I've just had a thought,' Skye said softly. She turned back to watch Caitie, her lip curling as she saw her practising her lines again. 'I know exactly how I can take Miss "I think I'm about to get an Oscar" down a peg or two. Just you wait, Ab, this is going to be brilliant.'

Caught up in her twin's enthusiasm, Abby clapped her hands. 'Bring on the Midsummer Ball!'

Switching on the fan in his father's office, Shay skimmed through the latest reports from the accountants with increasing pride. They weren't out of the woods yet by any means but things were starting to pick up. Could they pick up in time? That was the question. Having left his well-paid consulting job to save Shamrock, Shay had called upon every single contact he knew in the business to shamelessly promote the record label and its acts but, most importantly, he had signed up a whole host of exceptional new bands and singers. Despite the fact that Leo's marriage was falling apart, he had helped out with the legal side and his assistance had been invaluable; without him, Shay knew they wouldn't have been in such a strong position.

Back at Bluebell Cottage, Darcy was working like a woman possessed, with her BlackBerry in one hand and her mobile phone in the other. Determined to show her loyalty to Shay, she was going all out to secure new business, to find the best marketing tools and to figure out the most effective ways to promote the business.

Considering how opinionated she was, they made a surprisingly good team, Shay thought to himself. They rarely disagreed when it came to picking new acts and promoting them; if anything, they were perfectly in sync. They were so frighteningly in sync in fact, Shay had taken to working in the office for at least part of the day so he could keep his mind focused on the task in hand instead of allowing his mind to wander off and think about kissing Darcy's full, sensuous lips . . .

Erica came in balancing some post, a stack of CDs and a mug of black coffee in her hands. Shay brought himself back to the present sharply.

'These CDs have been sifted by the A&R guys and this is the post that needs your immediate attention.' Erica put the mug of coffee down on the desk.

As he gave her a brief smile, she was treated to a view of his achingly perfect cheekbones. Staunchly, Erica reminded herself that her boyfriend Tony was very sweet and caring and much more likely to propose to her than Shay Maguire ever was. 'Everyone at Shamrock is so impressed with how you're starting to turn things around, you know.'

'Thanks. I think there's a long way to go yet, but I can't help being pleased with how it's looking so far.' Shay skim-read through an email from Dev, his old boss at *Music Mode* magazine, pleased Darcy had admitted her part in his dismissal. Dev was keen to make it up to Shay and had generously offered space in the magazine. 'They've given us a four-page special in *Music Mode* this month, with interviews with bands we've signed and a special promotional piece about Shamrock.' He showed Erica the mock-up, which was entitled '*Shamrock: The Phoenix Rises*'. 'I told them to go with the theme of the phoenix, to focus on the company being reborn and coming back stronger than ever.'

'Wow, that's a powerful piece.' Erica read it quickly. She couldn't believe how Shamrock's profile had improved since Shay had been on board. If only Lochlin had hired him sooner, things might have turned out differently.

Shay raised his eyebrows. 'Let's just say a few people there owed me some favours. *NME* and *Q* have also been in touch to write a piece because they've heard about us signing Stiletto Heels, that brilliant girl band who were signed to Jett until recently, as well as Charlie Valentine and that terrific kid Aidan. Judd was going to release his album in a few months but he's clearly a prime candidate for the Christmas market.'

Erica sifted through the CDs the A&R team had sourced. 'Some of these look promising, but how did you manage to get the acts that were already with Jett?'

'Leo found a loophole in their legal documents.' He grinned impishly. 'Judd should fire his son Sebastian at the earliest opportunity because he failed to get several acts formally signed off. There's a cooling-off period and Shamrock were able to swoop in and grab the acts. When they all realised that Judd had no intention of building a long-term career for them, they leapt at the chance to come here.' He sipped his coffee. 'I did actually hear on the grapevine that Judd is considering selling off Jett. I just wish we had the money to buy it because I'd be in there like a shot but that's not going to happen at the moment. Christ, how satisfying would it be to take Jett away from him?'

Erica sat on the edge of his desk. 'One step at a time. You're doing such a lot already. It's like these new bands you've signed up, when your father was here, it was as if Jett was one step ahead of Shamrock, as if they had inside information. But now it's the other way round.' She gave him a curious glance. 'It's almost as if *you* have inside information.'

Shay looked away evasively. He hated being so clandestine, especially with Erica, but Darcy's presence had remained very much a cloak and dagger affair. So far, she hadn't put a foot wrong but Shay wasn't sure he wanted the world to know about her involvement, at least not yet. But Erica was different. 'Can you keep a secret?'

She nodded, intrigued.

'I *do* have inside information. Darcy Middleton is working with me.'

Erica gaped. 'Darcy Middleton? Judd's mistress, the one who had you fired? Shay, what are you thinking? Lochlin would be furious if he knew you were working with her.'

'I know.' Shay halted Erica with his hand. 'It sounds crazy but Darcy really is on our side.'

'How do you know?' Erica couldn't believe Shay was dancing with the devil. Or the devil's plaything, at any rate. 'How do you know you can trust her, Shay?'

Shay gathered up his post and the CDs and shut down his computer. 'I just know, all right? Look, I need to head home because Darcy's working on Charlie's relaunch. He's writing a new album and I've heard some of it already. It's incredible.'

Erica frowned, wondering if Shay's liaison with Darcy was purely professional. From what she'd heard about Darcy Middleton, she was a prize bitch and if Shay was tangled up with her on a personal level, it might affect his judgement where Shamrock was concerned. Watching Shay gulp down his coffee and head for the door, Erica stared after him in dismay. She just hoped he knew what he was doing.

Shooting back to Bluebell Cottage, Shay was stunned to find Darcy working outside for once. She was stretched out on a lounger with her dark hair piled on top of her head, wearing a Missoni bikini with an abstract print in browns and pinks. Her long limbs were smothered in suntan oil and she was wearing a pair of huge sunglasses as she sipped what looked like a freshly made Mojito.

She looked up, hurriedly shutting her laptop. 'Hi. I wasn't expecting you back so soon.' She gestured to the bright sunshine overhead. 'I decided this weather was too lovely to miss and I don't want to develop agoraphobia, just because of what happened.'

'I see.' Shay eyed her laptop. 'What are you doing?'

Darcy averted her eyes. 'Just working on Charlie's album. Did you manage to sort out much at the office?'

Shay met her gaze. 'Yes, thank you.' What was she hiding from him? He felt his stomach shift uncomfortably. Perhaps Erica was right, perhaps he had been too quick to trust Darcy.

Hating himself, he couldn't help allowing his eyes to travel down her half-naked body. The tiny bikini didn't leave much to the imagination and seeing her narrow waist and shapely legs brought the night in the hotel sharply back into his consciousness. Shay remembered the feel of Darcy's silky limbs wrapped around his, her nails down his back . . . her lips on his, but furiously, he reined himself back in.

Itching to gather Darcy up in his arms but not trusting her as far as he could throw her, Shay stalked into Bluebell Cottage to take a long, cold shower.

'Are you sure you're all right?' Caitie asked Iris worriedly, watching her make a cup of tea with trembling hands. Tea was splattering over the work surface as Iris desperately tried to stop shaking. 'Why don't you tell Mum you don't want to sing at the party?'

Iris shook her head. 'After she wrote that amazing album for me? No way.' She picked up the song sheet with the new song she was due to sing at the Midsummer Ball. 'Irresistible' was going to be tough for her to get through; singing about being desperately in love would be almost impossible but she owed it to her mother.

Iris was glad she was thousands of miles away in England, otherwise she knew she would have caved and rushed to Ace's bedside when she'd heard about his accident. Because whatever she told herself, she couldn't seem to stop loving him. She touched her neck where the heart chain used to be, feeling bereft.

'Don't you think you're being too hard on yourself?' Caitie said, removing the mug from Iris's hands. Calmly, she removed the tea bag and splashed in some milk. 'You didn't fall in love with Ace Harrington on purpose.'

Iris wrapped her hands round the mug of tea for warmth, even though it was blisteringly hot outside. 'I just miss him, Cait. I know I should think he's a complete bastard but I can't help it. As pathetic as it sounds, I thought he was "the one".'

Caitie's romantic heart swelled. All along, she had imagined herself and Elliot to be cast in the real-life roles of Romeo and Juliet but the truth of it was that Ace and Iris had inadvertently become the embodiment of the tragic leads. As it was, Caitie knew she'd barely given Elliot more than a passing thought recently because she'd been too caught up getting to the bottom of the mystery. And she had almost solved it too.

'You and Ace are the real "star-cross'd lovers",' Caitie mused out loud. 'Torn apart by family feuding and petty revenge.'

'Don't you feel that way about Elliot?'

Caitie shook her head, her green eyes serious. 'No. I thought I was in love with him but now I realise I just got caught up in the whole Romeo and Juliet thing.' She looked sheepish. 'I think I might have neglected him a tad too. I've been pretty obsessive about this mystery. I looked up everything I could find about Uncle Seamus recently in the library.'

Iris frowned. 'And?'

'Long story short . . . Mrs Meaden hinted there'd been a murder here years ago – yes, yes, I know it sounds dramatic and unlikely, but still.' Caitie bit her already short fingernails fretfully. 'When I looked up what had happened to Uncle Seamus, all I could find out was that he'd died mysteriously.' She gulped. 'At Brockett Hall.' She lifted troubled eyes to Iris's. '*Brockett Hall*, Iris. In the swimming pool, at some party. Some guy tried to say Judd did it but he was such a crackhead, no one believed him.'

Iris stared at her. 'What are you saying? Are you saying you think Judd Harrington killed Uncle Seamus and got away with it?'

Caitie got to her feet. 'Maybe.' She grabbed the edge of the table. 'And if he did, what the hell's he doing back here? He must want something pretty badly to come back, don't you think?'

'What do you think he wants?'

Caitie's eyes were wide with fear. 'Dad dead, maybe? Mum back as his girlfriend . . . or as his wife?'

Iris recoiled in shock. 'You're not serious!'

'We're home!' Tavvy sang, appearing in the doorway with Lochlin on her arm. She faltered. 'Why are you two looking so weird?'

Exchanging a tremulous glance, Iris and Caitie leapt up to greet Lochlin.

Astonishingly, he looked revitalised, as though he'd been pampered at a health spa rather than just having spent weeks in hospital hooked up to a life support machine. His face was fuller after some decent meals and his green eyes sparkled optimistically, the way they used to.

'Have you missed me?' he asked, holding his arms out.

Iris dived into his embrace. 'More than anything. Do you really feel better?'

'I feel fantastic,' he answered. 'Strong and healthier than I have in a long time. Probably because I've been on a Scotch-free diet.'

Tavvy grinned. 'They're calling him the Miracle Man in hospital. They said your father should be in an early grave but somehow he's clawed his way back and it's like he's been given a second chance.'

Lochlin nodded exuberantly. 'I've had an epiphany. This heart attack has been the kick up the arse I needed.' He grinned at his daughters. 'A phoenix from the flames and all that, just like Shamrock. I really want to talk to Shay. Is he at Bluebell Cottage?'

Caitie nodded. 'He's been really cagey lately. We reckon he's up to something but he won't talk to any of us.'

Lochlin gave a slight frown. 'That's no good . . . I've learnt that the hard way. Oh well, I'm sure he'll talk when he wants to. I can't wait to tell him how proud I am of the way he's turned Shamrock around. Judd Harrington must be feeling sick to his stomach right now.' His eyes twinkled. 'Now, who's going to make me a cup of tea?'

'I will,' Caitie offered, sticking the kettle on. She caught Iris's eye and could see she was thinking the same thing: *was* Judd sick to the stomach? Or did he have something far more dastardly planned now that Shamrock was reclaiming its place in the music industry?

Overcome with hopelessness, Jerry squeezed Ace's hand. No response . . . just like before. Ace's mahogany-coloured hair looked stark against the crisp white pillow and his cheeks were pallid.

'Nothing?' Luisa asked, lifting her head. She was curled up in a chair in the corner of the room, where she'd been since the accident.

Jerry stood up, clutching his hair until it stood up in blond tufts. The week at Ace's bedside had taken its toll on him; he was shattered and he couldn't take the strain of not knowing if Ace was going to be all right.

'The smell of those flowers is making me gag,' he snapped irritably. They could barely move for the cards, teddy bears and gifts Ace had been sent by well-wishers and fans. Joe Wilson and the rest of the racing team had sent a massive card signed by all of them and a crate of Ace's favourite beer, and there were piles of signed panties from women who presumably thought used underwear would bring Ace round.

Forgetting Luisa was in the room, Jerry grabbed Ace's hand and burst into tears. 'Please wake up,' he pleaded. 'Please! I can't stand this.'

Luisa sat up, the truth finally dawning on her. 'Oh my God,' she said in an awed voice. 'You love Ace.'

Jerry's head whipped round, his eyes agonised.

Luisa nodded. 'No wonder we never got together! You're gay.'

Jerry looked stricken. 'No, you're mistaken . . . I'm not . . .'

'Don't worry, Jerry. Your secret's safe with me. Does Ace know?'

'Of course not,' Jerry spluttered. 'We've been best friends for years, it's not the sort of thing you can blurt out over a beer, is it? Oh, by the way, I bat for the other team and every time you walk around naked, I go crazy.'

'But you don't just fancy him, you *love* him,' Luisa prompted.

'Like a brother,' Jerry said lamely. 'All right, maybe not like a brother. But he must never know, do you understand?'

Luisa gave him a small nod.

They both jumped as Ace let out a groan.

Jerry went scarlet. 'Ace? Ace, can you hear me?'

Ace groaned again, more strongly this time. His hand twitched and his eyelids fluttered slightly.

Jerry was so deliriously happy he didn't even care at that moment whether Ace had overheard his confession.

'I'll go and get someone!' Luisa cried, running outside to find a doctor.

Within seconds, a crowd of people dashed into the room, milling around the bed. Jerry was sure there were far too many nurses in the room and that their uniforms weren't meant to show *that* much leg or cleavage. Stethoscopes were pressed to Ace's chest and vitals were taken and two of the nurses appeared to be wrestling with Ace's chart at the end of the bed. One of them snatched it away and self-importantly started to update some details.

'Mr Harrington?' One of the doctors leant down to speak into his ear.

'Ace . . . my name's Ace . . .' Ace murmured.

The doctor gave Jerry a reassuring nod. 'That's a very good sign. He knows who he is.'

Ace opened his eyes. 'Of course I know who I am.' He gazed at all the people in the room. 'I just don't know *where* I am.' He caught sight of a flower arrangement in the shape of an angel. 'Christ, I'm not *dead*, am I?'

'No, you're not dead,' Jerry said, laughing and crying at the same time. 'You crashed your car at the Michigan.'

'The Michigan?'

Gingerly, Ace propped himself on his elbow, bewildered as he watched medical staff going into overdrive. Once they seemed satisfied, Jerry managed to shoo them out of the room, forcibly shoving one of the busty nurses out as she tried to come back in to take Ace's temperature.

'Was she really a nurse?' Ace asked woozily. 'I think I'd better phone Hugh Hefner and thank him for sending her from the Playboy Mansion.'

Exhausted, Jerry sat on the end of the bed. 'Ace, what were you thinking, crashing like that?' He fixed his blue eyes on him. 'I don't know what you remember but they're saying . . . they're saying . . . it looked as if you did it on purpose.'

Ace fell back against the bed. He remembered the race with absolute clarity. He remembered feeling so bleak when he got in his car that he genuinely didn't care if he lived or died. The way Ace saw it, there was nothing left to live for. He'd spent his life attempting to impress Judd, trying desperately to be the playboy racing driver and make his father proud, but not being able to give Iris up had left him dead in his father's eyes, Ace knew that.

But worse, far worse than that, Ace had lost Iris. The only girl he had ever loved, the only girl who understood him and loved him without caring what he did or what his name was. In fact, Iris had loved him *in spite* of his name and in spite of what it might do to her family if she stayed with him.

Ace turned away from Jerry. The race had gone past in a blur as thoughts of Iris had swirled around his head and he remembered very clearly making the biggest decision of his life, a decision so startling he had lost control of his car and swerved into the barrier. The sense of utter relief the decision had brought as everything slotted into place had slipped away as his car crashed and buckled.

Jerry blinked at Ace, wondering what the hell was going on in his head. 'Did you do it on purpose? Because if you did, I'm going to kill you. It's so fucking selfish, I can't even tell you how *angry* I—'

'Of course I didn't do it on purpose!' Ace interrupted. He rubbed his head. 'Christ, I feel like I've head-butted a wall. Seriously, Jerry, what do you take me for?' He spotted someone over Jerry's shoulder and turned ashen. 'Luisa! What are you doing here? Is Iris . . . ?'

'No, she's still in England,' Luisa told him, her dark eyes regretful. 'I'm sorry, Ace. I have called her several times but she refuses to talk about you.'

Ace fell back against the pillow, crushed.

'You're all right! Thank God you're all right!' Pushing past Luisa, Allegra shot into the room and rushed to Ace's side. Wearing a crotch-skimming acid-orange sheath that showed off her long tanned legs, she stood tall at five foot nine with an additional four inches in her heels.

Ace gave her a wary look. 'What are you doing here, Allegra?'

She kissed him effusively. 'I've come to see you, of course, silly.' She gave him a feline smile. 'I heard about your accident and here I am.' Possessively, she smoothed a lock of hair out of his eyes.

'I bet you did,' Jerry said, eying her mistrustfully. 'You're like the proverbial bad penny, aren't you, Allegra? You always turn up, no matter how many times Ace gets rid of you.'

Allegra coloured. Recovering herself, she flicked her long chestnut hair back. 'Play nicely, Jerry,' she said in a quiet voice. She turned back to Ace. 'I just thought you might need some company now that girl Iris is off the scene, my angel.'

Ace looked puzzled. 'How do you know she's off the scene?'

Allegra started. 'It was . . . it's been in all the papers.'

Jerry shook his head. 'No, it hasn't. No one knows about it.' He folded his arms. 'The only person who would know about that is the person who made sure that tape was played into the house that night. Christ, I *knew* it was you.'

Allegra turned scarlet.

Ace groaned. 'Why didn't I guess? You've been following us, haven't you? I've seen your car . . . and I swear I saw you in Monaco.'

Jerry grabbed hold of her arm. 'You set this whole thing up, didn't you?'

She yanked her arm free, her eyes spitting fire at Ace. 'So what if I did? You ditched me for that skinny English girl, what the fuck was I supposed to do? You can't just throw me away, you can't just shut me out, Ace.' Allegra looked desperate. 'I'm your girlfriend, I don't care about that bitch Iris . . .'

Ace turned away tiredly. 'Fucking hell, I can't handle this.'

Spinning Allegra out of the door, Jerry was astonished when Ace flung his legs over the side of the bed and made to get up. Thankfully, a doctor came in, just in time.

'Mr Harrington, you've suffered concussion, not to mention exhaustion and dehydration. You need to rest,' the doctor told him sternly. 'And your legs have taken a severe battering. Nothing is broken as such, but you've pulled ligaments, bruised most of your muscles and a few of the smaller bones are fractured.'

'God, I'll be able to race again in the future, I hope?' A terrible thought occurred to Ace. 'Fucking hell . . . I will . . . *walk* again, won't I?'

The doctor smiled and nodded. 'Absolutely. You're just going to be sporting crutches for a while but I'm sure you'll carry them off with panache.'

Coming back into the room, Jerry saw that Ace was prodding his legs to see if it hurt. 'Ouch! Can I fly to England?' He looked up at the doctor, his grey eyes pleading. 'Like, tomorrow?'

Jerry put his hand to his head. 'Fly to England? Does that mean . . . ?'

Ace nodded. 'I made a decision just before I crashed my car, Jerry. I have to get Iris back.' He rubbed his hand over his stubbly chin. 'I'm not doing anything my father asks me to ever again and if that means living in a trailer park and shopping in K-Mart, then so be it. I'll even give up being a NASCAR racing driver – whatever it takes.'

'No need,' Jerry told him quickly. 'Remember the NASCAR Sprint Showdown? Bryan Loveton was disqualified for taking drugs so you were awarded first place instead.'

'But that means . . .'

Luisa laughed. 'It means you just won a million bucks!'

'Plus a few lucrative advertising deals,' Jerry added drily.

Ace gasped. 'Thank God. I can finally be free of my father.' He turned to the doctor. 'What's the prognosis, Doc? Can I fly or not?'

Seeing three sets of eyes staring at him expectantly, the doctor didn't have the heart to say no. 'But you must be careful,' he warned Ace. 'You've had a big shock, you need to take it easy.'

Tearing off his white gown and accidentally giving everyone in the room a full frontal, Ace grinned. 'Whatever you say, Doc, whatever you say.' Dressing hurriedly as he sat on the bed, Ace couldn't stop talking. 'I don't know if she'll ever forgive me but I have to try, don't I? I've got to convince her I love her and that nothing my father says matters any more.' He straightened up, his grey eyes sombre. 'I mean, no disrespect to you guys, but my life is nothing without Iris, you know?'

Jerry squeezed his shoulder. 'Have faith, Ace. We'll get her back.'

Luisa nodded rapidly, not so sure. She knew Iris and, as much as she loved Ace, forgiving him for his betrayal was something else. 'Between the three of us, we must be able to convince her, right?'

They all looked at each other apprehensively, none of them sure Iris was going to be easily won over. Grabbing a wheelchair, Jerry plonked Ace in it and they all headed out to book their plane tickets.

Chapter Twenty

Trembling with nerves, Caitie watched the guests beginning to arrive, providing splashes of colour in their bright summer frocks and high heels. Men had opted for crisp white or blue shirts and dark trousers, and children were tearing around ruining their best party clothes and hiding under the food tables.

The marquee had been set up in the bluebell-strewn wood near Shay's cottage and it had been transformed from a boring white tent into a magical wonderland. The ceiling had been covered by a deep blue canopy studded with silver stars, with lengths of sparkling thread dangling down, with crystals attached. The marquee walls were covered by masses of lush green foliage and white pillars containing bunches of pink and white lilies, deep purple irises and sprigs of fragrant lavender. The only light was provided by small lanterns which were strung along the sides and across the huge stage area at one end.

Caitie caught sight of Iris. Wearing a floaty, empire-line midnight-blue gown which had a silver belt and silver stars all over the bodice, she looked utterly beautiful. Vulnerable but stunning. With fragile straps and a low v-neck, the gorgeous dress showed off her slender arms, and around her delicate throat she wore a tiny crystal star on a long chain. Iris's tawny-blond hair was caught up in diamanté combs, with just a few tendrils hanging down, and her amber eyes, highlighted by smudgy silver and navy make-up, looked huge.

Caitie sighed, hoping Iris was going to be able to get through the night. She watched Susannah and Charlie Valentine arriving. They looked a million dollars together; she in a tasteful red gown that set off her freshly dyed blond hair and heavy eye make-up and he in a dark suit with a diamanté-studded T-shirt beneath it and black baseball boots. Still sporting his brown hair, Charlie looked years younger and stylishly trendy.

The twins followed behind them wearing bright blue mini dresses with brand new matching Louboutins with six-inch heels and signature red soles. They headed straight to the food tables to have a nose and to score themselves some illicit glasses of champagne.

Mrs Meaden had provided most of the food and a handsome glazed ham studded with cloves had been chosen as the centrepiece and it was surrounded by piles of fragrant white and pink roses on a silver platter. As well as dips and the usual party fare plates heaved with sausage and bacon rolls, smoked salmon and crème fraiche blinis and mouth-watering slices of rare beef fillet with horseradish cream on crisp toast. For the children, there were iced fairy cakes, mini pizzas and breaded cod in cute shapes.

'Hungry?' Elliot asked, joining Caitie.

'Not remotely. Too nervous. You?'

He gulped. 'Petrified. Shall we go and rehearse again?'

Caitie nodded and took his hand. 'Come on. We've still got about an hour before we have to go on.' She looked him in the eye. 'We can do this . . . can't we?'

'We're gonna have to,' Elliot replied, his mouth set grimly. He hadn't risked the wrath of his father for nothing; this performance was going to have to bring the house down.

With Leo standing nearby, Lexi sat close to the food table, unable to stop herself from snacking every two minutes. No one had told her pregnancy would make her so *hungry*, she thought, demolishing a round of chicken and grape sandwiches in record time.

'Can I get you anything else?' Leo asked politely.

Gulping down a blini laden with smoked salmon, she shook her head. 'Do you think I'll ever be a size eight again?' she moaned, grabbing her waist miserably.

Leo sincerely doubted it but he knew better than to bait a pregnant lady. 'I'm sure you'll be back to your best as soon as you've had the baby.'

Lexi sighed. She'd been on to the Isabella Oliver website, as well as Crave, to order some outfits because she knew all the celebs bought their maternity clothes there, but in the meantime, she was wearing a size ten dress which was bursting at the seams. The pink stretchy material made the most of her gigantic cleavage but it also drew attention to her blossoming stomach and backside in the most unflattering way.

Lexi sulked, wishing she could just get it over and done with. She was gaining weight rapidly, developing stretch marks in the most unexpected places and her brown hair had gone from glossy to greasy in the space of a few weeks. Oddly enough, being pregnant was like having a permanent period.

'So much for having a pregnancy glow,' Lexi said to Leo crossly, forgetting sausage rolls gave her heartburn as she tucked in.

Leo spotted Kitty at the marquee entrance. Wearing a pretty beaded cream dress, she was obviously nervous to be arriving alone. Making his excuses, he left Lexi to it.

Lexi fumed, wiping her hands on a napkin. Since signing Sebastian's contract to pay her a cool quarter of a million pounds for bastard Harrington, she was set, financially speaking. However, when it came to attending scans and doctor's appointments and her pregnancy yoga classes, she was on her own. Surprised to find she cared, Lexi had taken to brandishing her huge engagement ring and matching diamond band to avoid the 'single mother' tag and the pitying stares of her peers.

Lexi was still appalled at herself for sleeping with Sebastian in the first place. Without money to make him appealing, he really didn't have a great deal going for him. His wife had lost even more weight since she'd last seen her, Lexi decided huffily. Wearing a navy satin dress with a corseted top, Martha's curves appeared more hourglass than chubby and even though she could still do with losing another stone, her brown hair and tanned skin looked healthy and she seemed to have a glow about her.

On, the irony, Lexi thought jealously, munching on a fattening slice of pizza. I'm getting fatter and greasier and bloody Martha Harrington is going the other bloody way.

In actual fact, Martha was feeling on top of the world. Wearing the new navy dress she had treated herself to as a reward for losing so much weight, she was feeling pretty damned good. Savannah's regime was tough and Martha would kill for a sausage roll right now, but she was sticking to her guns, and allowing herself carrot sticks, fruit and nothing else.

'I can't believe I'm so excited about the baby now,' Martha said to Sebastian, accepting a white wine spritzer from him. 'I mean, I'd rather it was ours but at least we have a baby on the way.' She had almost, but not quite, managed to put Sebastian's betrayal out of her mind and she was trying to think of Lexi as a paid surrogate and nothing more. She was surprised she didn't feel like scratching Lexi's eyes out, but somehow Martha felt quite calm about the whole thing. 'Have you arranged payment for Lexi?'

'It's . . . all in hand,' Sebastian said evasively, hoping Martha wouldn't press him too much on that issue. He had no intention of telling Martha the extortionate sum of money Lexi had demanded for their child. Not only would Martha freak out, Sebastian also knew Lexi would have no qualms about aborting the baby or, at the very least, putting it up for adoption if he said no. But since his father had pulled the huge bonus he was relying on to fund the baby deal, Sebastian had been frantically selling off valuables without Martha's knowledge. For once in his life, he was being responsible and he didn't like it one bit.

His beloved Porsche had gone and, unbeknownst to Martha, he

had been taking the train into work, something Sebastian detested, because he felt he was mixing with the dregs of society. He had sold off a ton of shares he'd been given by his father in place of a pension and, most shamefully of all, he had sold a family heirloom in the shape of some emerald earrings that should rightfully go to Martha on her thirtieth birthday. As that was some years away, Sebastian hoped he could either buy them back or explain away their disappearance by faking a robbery or something.

He felt Lexi's eyes on him and, noting her contemptuous stare, he threw one right back at her. How dare she look at him as if he was shit on her shoe! Completely forgetting he had cheated on his wife and got another woman pregnant, Sebastian drew himself up self-righteously. If it wasn't for Lexi, he wouldn't be selling off valuables like some sort of peasant, he thought indignantly.

At least his father appeared to have made a quick exit. According to his mother, Judd had emptied Brockett Hall of all of his personal possessions and no one had seen him for a few days. Sebastian fervently hoped he was free of his father's iron grip but secretly he was panicking about his work situation. Being Judd Harrington's son only carried weight when Judd was actually in the vicinity; the Harrington name didn't count for much anywhere else.

'Having a good time?' Savannah drawled, joining them. Wearing a slinky silver halter-neck dress that left nothing to the imagination as it clung to her toned thighs and narrow waist, the light from the lanterns bounced off her like a diamond. With her red hair curled and held off her face by a thin silver headband, she looked like a model with her titian wave of hair hanging down her back.

'Hasn't Dad kicked you out yet?' Sebastian asked her with a nasty smirk.

Martha hit him on the arm. 'Sebastian! Stop being horrible. Savannah's family, you know, like our baby will be.'

He closed his mouth, realising his follow-up comment about

Savannah's illegitimacy would be rather inappropriate in the circumstances.

Deciding against sparring with Savannah, he headed to the bar for a drink. Things with Martha were on an even keel and Sebastian didn't want to jeopardise the one part of his life that actually seemed normal. After forcibly insisting he and Lexi undergo a series of humiliating tests to ensure neither of them had contracted sexual diseases (Sebastian was sure Savannah had put her up to it), Martha had informed Sebastian that he was 'allowed' to move back into the marital bedroom. He wasn't going to rock the boat with a spiteful scrap with his half-sister when things were on the mend.

'For the record, Judd hasn't thrown me out yet,' Savannah told Martha evenly, impressed that Sebastian had walked away without a word. 'But only because he's been too busy, I'm sure. No one's seen him for days, anyway. I heard he was selling off Jett and going back to the States, but who knows? I'm sure he'll find the time to kick me out at some point.'

Martha looked horrified at the thought of losing her confidante. 'What will you do?'

Savannah glanced at her watch quickly. 'One thing being around Daddy dearest has taught me is to always be one step ahead. So regardless of what he was planned for me, I have something else up my sleeve so it doesn't bother me either way if he boots me out of Brockett Hall.' She glanced over her shoulder, as if she was looking for someone. 'I just hope my gamble pays off.'

Martha pulled her into a hug. Unused to the physical contact, Savannah hugged Martha back. She wouldn't miss Judd and Sebastian, she was sick of their arrogance and bullying ways. But she *would* miss Martha, as well as Kitty and Elliot because they felt like a real family to her, something she'd never experienced before.

She pulled away, not wanting to get too emotional. 'I really admire your courage, taking Sebastian back and preparing to love this baby.'

Martha shrugged. 'I've got you to thank for that. I wouldn't have had the guts to stand up to Sebastian in a million years before you came along.'

Savannah gave Martha a warm kiss on the cheek. 'Listen, if I don't get to say goodbye, just promise me you'll keep up the good work with the exercising and healthy eating, all right?'

Martha looked puzzled. 'What do you mean, if you don't get to say goodbye?'

Savannah waggled her finger in Martha's face. 'Just promise me!'

'All right, I promise.' Martha watched Savannah disappear outside, wondering what she meant.

Outside, Savannah bumped into an extremely good-looking guy with dark auburn hair and crutches. He had arresting grey eyes, very much like Kitty's but sexier and they were darting around restlessly. Wearing a black tuxedo with a snow-white shirt and an undone tie, he was possibly the most handsome guy Savannah had ever set eyes on. Which was a shame because she was absolutely certain they were related.

'You must be the other brother,' she remarked, holding out her hand. 'I'm Savannah, your half-sister . . . Elliot told me all about you.'

Giving her a crooked smile, Ace shook her hand. 'Nice to meet you, Savannah. I've heard a lot about you too.'

Savannah's cool blue eyes flashed. 'From Elliot or Sebastian? Your opinion of me could be at one end of the spectrum or another depending on who you've been talking to.'

'Elliot speaks very highly of you,' Ace assured her, trying not to be rude as he urgently looked around for Iris. 'Sebastian says you're a bitch but I'd take that as a compliment, frankly.'

Savannah grinned. 'And which type of Harrington are you, I wonder. There are two distinct types, I've found. Are you a good guy, like Elliot, or a bad guy, like Sebastian? And our father,' she added sardonically.

'A good guy, I hope.' He nervously fiddled with his bow tie, trying to do it up. 'You'll know either way by the end of the night, I guess.'

Savannah slapped his hands away. 'Leave the tie. It looks sexier that way.' Giving him a wink, she walked off in the other direction just as Jerry and Luisa arrived to give Ace some moral support.

Leo found Kitty standing alone by a tree outside the marquee and immediately went to her side.

'Leo!' Her expression lit up when she saw him but as soon as her smile faded, Leo realised her face was etched with worry. 'How are things with you and Lexi?'

'Very much over,' he told her, leaning against the tree next to her. 'All we need to do now is confirm who the father of the baby is.'

Kitty met his gaze. 'I'm so sorry about Sebastian,' she said, pink with embarrassment. 'I can't believe my son has caused you so much pain.'

Leo took out a cigar. 'Do you mind if I smoke?' Seeing her shake her head, he lit the cigar and puffed on it. 'I honestly think if it hadn't been Sebastian, it would have been someone else.'

'Do you? Why?'

'I don't think we ever had much in common.' Leo scratched his head, messing up his shaggy blond hair. 'We had fun and I truly loved her but I didn't really know her. She's all about the money and I didn't have a clue.' He shrugged. 'She was always going to leave me for another guy at some point, it's just that no one richer had come along until your family arrived.' He smiled to soften the blow. 'What about you and Judd?'

'Very much over,' Kitty said, echoing his words. She gave him the ghost of a smile. 'I asked for a divorce and Judd's agreed. He won't make it easy for me, I'm sure, but I feel free, at last.' A look of terror crossed her face. 'I'm on my own for the first time in years and it's scary. Judd's gone – he's cleared out all of his stuff and I haven't seen him since I asked for the divorce.'

Concerned, Leo stubbed his cigar out. 'Where will you live? I mean, I'm assuming Judd isn't reasonable enough to let you stay at Brockett Hall until the divorce is finalised.'

'God, no!' Kitty's grey eyes widened as reality set in. 'I hadn't even thought about it, but you're right. I don't have anywhere to live now. Neither does Elliot. He's been staying with a friend since Judd blasted him at his rehearsal.'

Leo took her hand. 'Look, feel free to say no but you could always move in with me. All of you, I mean,' he added hurriedly. 'I'm putting Lexi up in a house – her choice, incidentally – so I'll be on my own.' He reached out and tentatively stroked Kitty's face. 'I'd really appreciate the company. That is, I'd really appreciate *your* company.'

Kitty caught hold of his hand. 'What if you're the father of Lexi's baby?'

'I can handle it if you can. And to prove it, Martha and Sebastian can move in too, if they want to.' Leo smiled. 'I just want whatever will make you happy.'

Kitty was overwhelmed. '*You* make me happy. Judd never did, not once in all the time we were married. Apart from having the kids, I've been unhappy for such a long time now.' She pulled a face. 'My own silly fault but at least I've come to my senses finally.'

Leo leant in and gave her the sweetest kiss. He didn't know how he knew but his gut was telling him he and Kitty were meant to be together. And Leo was prepared to take it slowly and do things properly this time. Kitty was worth it. 'Where's Judd tonight? Not planning to make an appearance, is he?'

Kitty shivered. Knowing him as she did, she would be very surprised if Judd didn't have something dreadful planned for tonight. She just hoped no one got hurt.

Inside the marquee, the lights went out all of a sudden. The stage lit up and Charlie, sitting at a vast piano, spoke into the microphone. 'Good evening, ladies and gentlemen. I want to sing you something new I've been working on,' he said. 'It's called "Susannah's Song" and it goes something like this.' Playing the romantic intro, Charlie started to sing, locking eyes with Susannah who was flabbergasted. Thrilled to have a song written for her, she blew him kisses. People at the front of the stage held their lighters aloft and swayed in time to the music as Charlie sang his heart out. At the end, the round of applause left him in no doubt that he was back and better than ever.

Jumping off the stage, he ran out into the audience and swung a weeping Susannah round. 'I'm going on tour again, but will you come with me?'

'After that, of course I will. As long as you promise, no more groupies?' Susannah gave him a kiss.

'No more groupies,' he agreed, kissing her in return. 'And not just because they all have blue rinses and Zimmer frames these days.'

Laughing, Susannah let him spin her around the dance floor.

'God, aren't our parents embarrassing?' Skye grumbled, finding their public displays of affection nauseating. ' "Susannah's Song" . . . how gross.'

'I thought it was quite sweet,' Abby said, rubbing her tummy. 'And just imagine if they both go on tour together. We'll have the house to ourselves.' She moaned softly.

'What's wrong with you?' Skye asked, trying to catch a glimpse of Caitie. If her plan was working, Caitie should be showing signs of discomfort any time now and Skye couldn't wait. She hugged herself, excited at the combined thought of taking Caitie Maguire down a peg or two and getting to play Juliet, the role she had coveted for months now.

Abby winced. 'Er . . . I did something rather naughty just now.'

'Which was?'

'I was having a nose at Caitie and Elliot's dressing room and I noticed this amazing cupcake.' Abby's stomach let out a fierce growl. 'It had cream icing and a pink "J" piped on top and it was so pretty with all these edible pieces of gold leaf on it . . .' She felt

Skye's furious gaze. 'Don't look at me like that! I was hungry, all right? We skipped lunch to fit into these dresses and I was starving. This cupcake looked so delicious, I couldn't help myself and I—'

'You ate it,' Skye finished in a monotone.

'I did.' Abby clutched her stomach again, wishing it would stop making such weird noises.

Skye pushed her. 'You bloody idiot! Why on earth did you eat it?'

Abby looked wounded. 'Why are you being so mean? I'm suffering enough as it is. It must have been off because I feel as if the world might fall out of my bottom at any minute.'

'That would probably be because of all the laxatives in the cupcake,' Skye told Abby heatedly. 'The ones intended for Caitie Maguire, in the cupcake I made especially for her so she'd eat it, and spend the rest of the night on the toilet.' She pushed her twin irritably. 'Leaving the way clear for me to play Goddamed Juliet, just as I'd planned all along. Didn't I tell you it was all in hand? Didn't I mention the fact that I'd come up with an amazing idea to get my own way?'

'That?' Abby gaped and let out a loud fart. 'That was your incredible, foolproof master plan to get your own back on Caitie Maguire?' She scoffed at her twin. 'Lacing a cupcake with laxatives? Wow, how clever, how inspired. It must have taken you ages to think of *that*.'

Skye pursed her lips. 'You're the one who's about to get incredibly well acquainted with the portaloos, so who's the smart one here?'

'Oooooh!' Abby heroically clenched her sphincter. Skye had a point. 'Come on, you've got to help me!'

'No way.'

'You *owe* me. You're on toilet paper duty and God help you if there isn't enough . . .'

Skye recoiled as Abby's bottom let out a fearful wail and, grabbing her arm, she hurried her to the portaloos.

* * *

'*Since arm from arm that voice doth us affray,*' Caitie quoted, looking sensational in a white lace dress. Leaning over Abby's poorly painted balcony, her nerves made her utterly convincing as a vulnerable but courageous Juliet.

'Hunting thee hence with hunts-up to the day.
Oh, now be gone, more light and light it grows.

'*More light and light, more dark and dark our woes,*' Elliot responded, looking up at Caitie, his blond hair flopping into his eyes. Having spent hours in Jas's parents' huge mansion with Jas as Juliet, Elliot was word perfect. He had honed his English accent and Romeo's impetuous intensity and passionate nature to a tee but, inside, he was trembling with nerves and certain he was making a fool of himself.

Their performances were going down a storm with the watching audience whose faces were rapt with attention and pleasure.

Hugo was beside himself with pride as his two protégées brought the famous lovers to life with understated brilliance and he could barely stand it as they acted out the final scene in the crypt with such emotional integrity, he could feel his heart pumping in his chest.

Skye, back from the portaloos, was unintentionally hilarious as Lady Capulet. Having spent far too much of her time concentrating on rehearsing the role of Juliet so she could step in for Caitie, she could barely remember her own lines. Jas, having overheard Abby cursing Skye for the laxative cupcake intended for Caitie, took advantage of her additional role as prompt by calling out the wrong lines which Skye regurgitated to much cat-calling and sarcastic applause.

Poor Abby missed the entire thing as she was still locked in the portaloo and Skye couldn't help being relieved her twin hadn't witnessed her appalling performance, otherwise she'd never live it down. She gave Jas a furious mouthful as she came off stage, seething as Jas smiled benevolently at her and, with a straight face, apologised profusely for feeding her the wrong lines.

As Hugo, pleased as punch and revelling at being on stage again, delivered the Prince's final words, a sombre feeling settled over the audience, particularly over the Maguire family.

> *Go hence to have more talk of these sad things,*
> *Some shall be pardon'd, and some punished.*
> *For never was a story of more woe,*
> *Than this of Juliet and her Romeo.*

Taking an extravagant bow, Hugo clasped his hands together at the riotous applause that followed. He beckoned for the cast to join him and Caitie and Elliot came out and took bows, delighted when the audience cried for more. Skye took a huffy bow and flounced to the back of the stage.

'Would you be terribly upset if I confessed that I don't think I'm in love with you, after all?' Caitie said to Elliot in an aside as they took yet another bow.

Startled, he glanced at her. 'Not at all.' Catching sight of Jas at the side, Elliot felt as though he'd been hit by a thunderbolt. 'That's actually a relief because I . . .' He paused. 'I think I have feelings for Jas.'

'*Really?*' Instead of feeling jealous, Caitie couldn't help thinking they'd make a lovely couple. 'You're right . . . you're perfect for each other and I couldn't be happier for you both. Why didn't I see it before?'

Elliot laughed. 'Why should you? I didn't.'

Caitie grinned. 'Sorry I neglected you. We made a good Romeo and Juliet, though, didn't we?'

He kissed her cheek. 'The best.' He shrugged. 'Mom reckons Dad's gone back to the States and do you know what? I don't feel a thing.' Glancing over her shoulder, Elliot started. 'Oh my God. That's my brother, Ace.'

Caitie spun round. 'He'd better not be here to upset my sister again . . . wow, he's *gorgeous*!' She stared at Ace curiously. 'No wonder my sister's head over heels in love with him, he's the most beautiful thing I've ever seen. Why do you think he's in England?'

'I know why he's here,' Elliot stated. 'He phoned me this morning.'

Caitie gave him an inquiring look.

Elliot looked sheepish. 'He's here to get Iris back. Don't look like that, Cait! He loves her and he never meant to hurt her.'

'Hmmm. I'll hurt *him* if he so much as damages a hair on her head – or whatever the expression is.'

Elliot flicked his hair out of his eyes and propelled Caitie towards the side of the stage. 'Ace is head over heels in love with your sister and from what you've told me, she's miserable without him too.' Elliot grinned. 'Now, let's go and help him get her back.'

Chapter Twenty-One

Shay grabbed Darcy by the hand. Trying to ignore how stunning she looked in the emerald-green dress that brought out her hazel eyes and dark hair, he showed her a press statement Erica had faxed over to him earlier that night.

'Look at this!' He thrust it into her hand. 'It says that someone bought the Jett Record Corporation from Judd, which basically means he's admitted defeat! Not that surprising really; between us, we've managed to put Shamrock right back on the map. I can't wait to tell my father.' Shay slapped his hand on the article. 'The weirdest thing about this is that it was bought by a company called Phoenix, which is the angle I was going for with Shamrock, you know, the phoenix rising from the flames and all that.'

Darcy read the article quickly, her body language oddly closed. 'I didn't know you'd chosen that angle. How strange . . .' Handing the article back, she twisted her hands awkwardly. 'Look, about the Phoenix thing—'

'Oh my God, my father made it! Let's go and see him.' Delighted, Shay grabbed her hand and they wove through the crowds to get to Lochlin. Absurdly pleased that Shay seemed to want to be close to her, Darcy followed him.

Wearing black tie and looking incredibly dashing for someone who'd suffered a major heart attack some weeks back, Lochlin opened his arms to Shay as soon as he saw him, gathering him up in a bear hug.

'Shay! Good to see you.'

'You too, Dad. You look way too bloody healthy. Jesus, *I* look older than you!' Shay laughed. 'Mum, what have you been doing to him?'

Standing protectively close to Lochlin, Tavvy looked gorgeous in a silky cream dress with a long fringe around the bottom, her blond hair loose around her shoulders. 'He's been looking after himself for once,' she commented, squeezing Lochlin's hand lovingly. 'He's like a new man.'

Darcy, sure her presence would go down like a rowdy drunk at an AA meeting, held back. The last thing she wanted to do was cause a scene. Staggered when Tavvy stepped forward and drew her into a hug, Darcy reacted stiffly at first, before gratefully relaxing into her arms.

'You poor thing,' Tavvy murmured sympathetically in her ear. 'I hope you don't mind but when Shay finally plucked up the courage to tell us about you, he told us what happened with Judd.'

Darcy shrank back and flushed. 'I'm so ashamed . . .'

'Don't be.' Tavvy affectionately put her hands on Darcy's shoulders. 'I've been in your shoes and I know just how persuasive and scary Judd can be. You have nothing to be ashamed of, I can assure you.'

'Besides, there's been far too much bad feeling around here,' Lochlin added, his expression briefly solemn. 'It's about time we all moved on and let go of the past. One thing my heart attack taught me is to forgive and forget because it's not worth getting all bitter and twisted about things that are best left in the past.'

Shay nodded. 'Caitie just told me Judd might have gone back to the States because no one's seen him for days. Fingers crossed, eh?'

Tavvy looked overcome with relief. 'Thank God!' All of a sudden, she felt safe again.

'Here.' Lochlin handed over a set of keys to Shay.

'What are these?'

'I'm formally handing you the reins,' Lochlin explained gruffly. 'To Shamrock. You deserve it, son.'

Shay was so moved, he could barely speak. 'But . . . aren't you coming back to work now that you're back on your feet?'

Lochlin shook his head. 'I'd love to work alongside you, Shay, but to be honest my heart just isn't in it any more. I think that's why Shamrock unravelled; I was having second thoughts even before Judd arrived. I just felt too guilty to let go.' He glanced at Darcy. 'Thank you, Darcy, for all your hard work. I'm sure it must have been very difficult to tear yourself away from Judd.'

Seeing Lochlin gazing at her kindly, Darcy hoped to God she wouldn't disgrace herself and burst into tears. She wasn't used to people being nice to her and receiving this kind of reaction from Shay's parents after everything she'd done was overwhelming.

One person was giving Darcy the cold shoulder, however, and that was Erica. Clinging to her boyfriend Tony, she was shooting daggers at Darcy.

Despite Erica's hostility, Darcy realised this was probably the best time to tell everyone her news. 'Er . . . there's something I need to tell you all.'

Erica gave her boyfriend a knowing look as if to say, 'I told you so.'

Doing her best to ignore her, Darcy forged ahead. She was well aware people didn't trust her and that not everyone was as forgiving as Lochlin and Tavvy – or Shay for that matter. Darcy met his shamrock-green eyes with foreboding, hoping against hope she had done the right thing.

'It's about that company buying the Jett Record Corporation.' She drew some papers out of her handbag. 'Phoenix is me . . . I'm Phoenix. I bought Judd's company.'

Erica sucked her breath in. 'You snake! You bought Jett so you could destroy Shamrock once and for all.'

Darcy shook her head. 'No. I bought Jett to be rid of *Judd*, once and for all.' She thrust the papers into Shay's hand. 'That's what I've been doing at the cottage, as well as helping you. Predictably, now that he no longer wants it, Judd sold Jett for peanuts but to fund it I've sold my flat and five other properties I owned, as well as some shares.' She cast her hazel eyes to the ground. 'I did it to buy Jett. For you.'

'Darcy . . . that's . . . amazing,' Tavvy managed. 'I didn't realise you were so . . . self-sufficient.'

Darcy shrugged. 'I've always had this massive fear of not being able to support myself.' She looked away. 'I didn't want to rely on a man to look after me so I invested nearly all of my money over the years. But none of that matters. I just wanted to prove that I'm not that person any more . . . I'm not Judd's right-hand woman.'

Shay stared at her in disbelief. 'You did this for me? Why?'

'To prove my . . . my loyalty to you,' Darcy said. She stopped abruptly. She wished she could be more truthful and admit she had bought Jett for Shay to prove how much she loved him. What was the point? Judging by the way he was looking at her, Shay would always see her as soiled goods, ruined by Judd and tainted for eternity.

'Wow.' Shay stared down at the papers, skim-reading through them. 'You sold your flat in Kensington to do this? And everything else you own?'

She nodded.

'How do we know you haven't just done that to pull the wool over our eyes?' Erica accused. 'How do we know this isn't some elaborate scheme for you and Judd to get back at the Maguires somehow?'

'Erica,' Tavvy said, touching her arm. 'I really think Darcy's telling the truth.'

Darcy shook her head helplessly. She didn't know what else to say to convince them all. 'Shay? You believe me, don't you?'

Truthfully, Shay was speechless. Before he had time to explain that he was simply overwhelmed at her magnanimous gesture, Darcy dashed away, with tears in her eyes.

'Shit! Now she thinks I don't trust her.'

'I'm sorry, Shay,' Erica said, feeling like a total bitch. 'I honestly thought Darcy might have been trying to get one over on us all again.'

'I know. It crossed my mind too, so don't feel bad about it.' Shay raked his hand through his hair. His disbelief had been just as damning as Erica's accusation but Darcy had caught him off guard with her admission about Jett. It explained what she'd been doing for all those hours at her laptop and it showed her enormous sense of commitment to Shamrock to take Jett out of the running completely.

And what about Darcy calling herself 'Phoenix'? Shay thought, amazed at how in sync they were. He hadn't even mentioned to her that he had told *Music Mode* to use that imagery so unless she had seen the mock-up for the interview, he had no idea how she would have known about it.

Shay dumped his drink on a table and headed out to look for her. Finding Darcy outside Bluebell Cottage, he saw that she was staring up at the star-studded sky with trembling lips.

'I've tried so hard to prove to you that you can trust me,' she said in a broken voice.

'I know.' Shay moved closer to her. He glanced up at the twinkling constellations in the inky sky, deciding a round of 'Rude Stars' probably wasn't the best idea. 'Did you know Darcy is an Irish name?' he said, instead.

Darcy looked up at him curiously.

'It means "the dark one".' He reached out and traced a finger around her wide mouth. 'So you have an Irish name and you chose to call yourself Phoenix without knowing I'd used the phoenix to describe Shamrock's comeback. Those two things tell me that you and I have more in common than we think.' Darcy could hardly breathe. 'Add to this the fact that I can't stop thinking about you, I think the stars are trying to tell us something.'

Darcy couldn't believe what she was hearing. 'Aren't there scores of half-witted debutantes left out there for you?' she mocked, feeling her skin prickle with anticipation.

'You can't put me off that easily,' Shay told her, his green eyes alight with amusement. 'I know that whenever you feel vulnerable, you turn into an absolute bitch.'

'Sorry,' she said shortly, unable to look him in the eye. 'I'm just not used to this stuff.'

'What stuff? Hearing that someone is ridiculously, head over heels in love with you?'

Darcy's knees buckled.

'And, for the record, there probably are dozens of debutantes and other women out there but I don't want them. I want you.' Shay slowly trailed his fingers up her side, feeling her jerk against him.

'But I'm prickly and rude and ambitious . . .'

Shay pulled her closer. 'Those are the things I love about you,' he told her. 'What's wrong with being ambitious? And as for being rude and prickly, that's just who you are. But you're also utterly fascinating.' He threaded his fingers through hers, the way he'd done all those months ago in the nightclub when they'd first met.

'Do you really think Judd has gone back to the States?' Darcy clung to his young but very broad shoulders.

'Hopefully. Good riddance, is all I can say.' Shay ran a finger across her mouth again. 'But who cares about Judd? All I care about is you . . . or rather, you and me.'

She marvelled at his ability to understand her; she had never met anyone in her life before that 'got' her, not the way Shay did. 'Do you . . . do you really want me?'

Shay smiled. 'I really want you.'

'That's good because I need somewhere to live now I've sold off my Kensington flat.' She linked her arms around his neck. 'Do me a favour and do what I've been wanting you to do since I moved into Bluebell Cottage, will you?'

'What's that?'

Darcy ran a hand over his taut thighs. 'Take me back there and make mad, passionate love to me before I explode, for fuck's sake.'

Shay didn't need telling twice. Scooping Darcy up into his arms, he picked his way through the bluebells and ducked inside the cottage.

'I just need to go and check on that new foal that was delivered yesterday,' Tavvy said to Lochlin, linking her fingers through his. 'He's slightly lame so no one wants him, can you believe that?'

Pulling her closer, he gave her a lingering kiss. 'It's very sad. Don't be long. I feel as though we've wasted too much time as it is.' Lochlin slid his arms around Tavvy's waist, the silk of her cream dress thin under his fingers. 'I can't believe I shut you out like that.'

She nodded, her amber eyes meeting his. 'I did the same. I guess we didn't want to worry each other but it . . . it feels as if we've been given a second chance, doesn't it?'

Lochlin stroked her tawny hair back from her face. 'It does. We must never let anything – or anyone – come between us again.' He swallowed. 'Let's hope Judd really has gone. Let's hope we can be free from him, once and for all.'

Reluctantly, Tavvy slid out of his grasp. 'I hope so. I feel as though a weight has been lifted off my shoulders.' She smiled. 'I won't be long. Meet you back here in ten minutes?'

Lochlin nodded, watching her slip out of the marquee. Coming round after his heart attack, he had felt like a changed man. Nothing seemed to matter any more apart from his family. Everything Judd had done paled into insignificance compared to the thought of leaving everyone he cared about behind. Which didn't mean Lochlin could find it in himself to forgive Judd. Too much damage had been caused for him to be able to do that, but nonetheless, Lochlin had found himself in a more peaceful place as a result of his heart attack.

He felt calmer, happier and, without wanting to sound like a cliché, glad to bloody well be alive. He couldn't help wondering at how inexplicably tangled the lives of the Maguires and the Harringtons had always been but Lochlin no longer found himself battling against it. Caitie had made a good friend in Elliot Harrington who was clearly nothing like his father, Shay was running Shamrock like a pro and, unlike Lochlin who had found himself jaded and longing to spend more time at home even before Judd Harrington had come back and laid down his gauntlet of revenge, his eldest son was bursting with energy, new ideas and fresh concepts. And with Darcy Middleton in tow – both professionally and personally, by the looks of things – Lochlin was sure Shamrock would go from strength to strength.

He helped himself to another soft drink. The only one of his children he was worried about was Iris. She had come back from LA with a wealth of experience and exposure but Lochlin knew she was also secretly heartbroken because of her failed relationship with Ace Harrington. He didn't blame Iris one bit for falling for Ace, nor for hiding the relationship from him. Lochlin knew better than anyone what it was like to fall in love with someone and for that love to cause you to risk everything you held dear. Lochlin knew that Iris's feelings – and Ace's, for that matter – must have been genuine. He only hoped they would be able to find one another in the future.

His gut tightened momentarily as he thought about the way Judd had manipulated them like a couple of hapless pawns in his twisted chess game. Shaking his head with regret, Lochlin checked his watch and realised Tavvy was a little late back from the stables. Uneasily, he put his drink down before scolding himself for being so dramatic. What possible harm could Tavvy come to?

In the stable with the new foal, Tavvy propped the lantern on the side and ran a hand along its quivering back. She was in the stable nearest to Pembleton, which was the only free space as the new barn wasn't yet finished. It was huge, if a little chilly. She wrapped a blanket over the foal. 'It's all right, angel. Nothing can hurt you now.' She heard a noise and, assuming it was Lochlin, she called out, 'I'm nearly ready, darling.'

'It's been a long time since you called me "darling",' drawled a familiar voice.

Tavvy's head snapped up. 'Judd,' she whispered. 'What are you doing here? I thought you'd gone.'

Emerging from the shadows, Judd's red hair was lit up by the overhead lights. 'Me? No way. I've come back to reclaim what's rightfully mine.' Wearing a crumpled white shirt outside dark trousers, he cut an imposing figure. Somehow, the uncharacteristically dishevelled clothes gave him an even more sinister air; it was as if he had totally lost control of himself. Judd was formidable when he was *in* control, but now . . .

'Wh-what's rightfully yours?' Tavvy echoed, spotting an almost empty whisky bottle dangling from Judd's hand. She stumbled backwards slightly, afraid. She put a protective hand on the foal's soft mane, her eyes darting round the stable to see if there was anything she could defend herself with.

Judd ran his sapphire-blue eyes down Tavvy's body. 'Yes. You, Tavvy. That's why I came back in the first place, that's what this has all been about. Darcy getting your son Shay fired, Shamrock being run into the ground, Ace and your delectable daughter, Iris.' His face contorted nastily.

'Don't say that,' she stammered, overcome with horror, as she realised she was responsible for all the pain her children, not to mention Lochlin, had gone through. All because Judd couldn't let her go.

'It's true,' Judd said, leaning against the stable wall. 'What did you think I came back for, Tavvy?' He pointed the whisky bottle at her. 'It's always been you – you're the one that got away.'

Tavvy felt as if someone had thrown a bucket of ice-cold water over her. She didn't want to believe Judd but knowing him as she did, his words rang true. Not many people would bear a grudge for so long but it was perfectly plausible to envisage Judd sitting in the wings for the past twenty-five years, plotting and scheming, hell-bent on getting revenge and clawing everything back.

Before she had a chance to think another thought, Judd had made it across the stable and pinned her to the wall. The foal trembled and scuttled to the corner on shaky legs, its eyes wide and alarmed. The blanket fell to the floor, leaving the foal shivering with cold and fear.

'We have unfinished business,' Judd slurred, his face close to Tavvy's. He held her down with one arm across her throat and chest. His free hand rested on her hip.

Tavvy recoiled from the stench of whisky on his hot breath, struggling desperately against his rock-hard grip. 'No, we don't. Whatever we had was dead and buried long ago. Why can't you just accept that?' She turned her face away in revulsion as Judd's hand slid down her thigh.

'You were mine!' he hissed. 'You were mine and Lochlin stole you away from me. And I hate losing anything that belongs to me.'

Tears slid down Tavvy's cheeks. 'I didn't belong to you, Judd; I never did. You controlled me with drugs and violence, and Lochlin . . . Lochlin rescued me and brought me back to the land of the living.'

Judd sneered. 'Unlike Seamus, eh?'

Tavvy gaped. 'What are you talking about?'

He let out a soft laugh. 'Oh, come on, Tavvy! You know what I'm talking about. Poor little Seamus,' Judd mocked, his hands moving over her body crudely. He enjoyed the way she squirmed and flinched, wishing Lochlin could see him now. 'Seamus got in with the wrong crowd and they led him astray appallingly, got him into drugs and all sorts.'

'You killed him, didn't you?' Tavvy whispered, writhing against his forceful hands. 'Seamus was never into drugs . . . Lochlin didn't believe it for a second and neither did his family.' She looked around blindly, desperate to get away, and wondered if Lochlin might wonder where she had got to.

Still holding on, Judd stared past her, looking the past in the face finally. 'It was New Year's Eve, nineteen eighty-four. God, I remember it like it was yesterday! You and Lochlin got married in that sickeningly romantic Christmas ceremony. Oh yes, I was there, Tavvy.' He pulled a face. 'All snow and candlelight. It made me want to *vomit*.'

Tavvy gasped, shrinking back even further. The thought of Judd watching over their wedding ceremony made her flesh crawl.

'My parents were hosting their usual New Year's Eve party at Brockett Hall,' Judd was saying, not even noticing Tavvy's appalled expression. 'The party was wild, out of control. Stupid young Seamus wanted part of the action.' His lip curled scornfully. 'So when he wanted to play with the big boys, who was I to say no?'

'You gave him drugs,' Tavvy guessed. It was the only way Seamus would have taken drugs – because the older boys he admired so much were doing it. The trouble was, Seamus hadn't even been a drinker and he didn't know his own limits. 'You gave him drugs and he overdosed . . . that's what happened, isn't it? She eyed him with disgust. 'I always knew you had something to do with it. Lochlin suspected it too.'

Judd shrugged. 'It's not my fault if the stupid kid took all the tablets in one go. Or that he was so sure he could see a pot of Irish gold at the bottom of the pool, he dived in to get it.' Judd's eyes glazed over, a smile playing at his lips. 'He hit his head on the bottom of the pool . . . there was so much blood.'

'You left him to drown. Oh my God. You saw him struggling in the pool and you watched him die.' Tavvy felt physically sick.

Judd's blue eyes slid back to hers. 'An eye for an eye, as the Bible so eloquently puts it. Lochlin took something of mine and I took something of his. His beloved baby brother. And, as it happens, his mammy and pappy too, because they couldn't handle losing poor little Seamus.' Judd let out a laugh. 'And all that's left now is for me to get you back. Because now, Tavvy, I have nothing left to lose. I've lost everything so nothing matters any more. Nothing apart from having you.'

Forcing his mouth down on hers, Judd kissed her, unzipping his trousers with his free hand. Tavvy struggled, crying out as he pushed her dress up around her thighs and beating at him with her fists. Before she knew what was happening, she heard a howl and Judd was roughly pulled off her. Holding Judd by the scruff of his neck, Lochlin glanced at Tavvy, shaking with rage.

'Are you all right?'

Wrapping her arms around her body, she nodded, relief flooding through her.

'You fucking bastard!' Lochlin shouted, sinking his fist into Judd's face. 'How dare you touch my wife!' He hit Judd again, blood flying in the air. 'And that's for killing Seamus, you motherfucker! I can't believe you got away with it, but you won't this time, I promise you that.'

Stunned, Judd fell back into the straw, blood gushing from his nose. He gazed up at Lochlin with hatred in his eyes. 'Lochlin fucking Maguire. You have a habit of turning up just at the wrong moment, don't you? Always the knight in fucking shining armour.' He wiped an arm across his face, smearing blood across it. 'I just can't get rid of you, can I? I can't believe you're still alive.'

Lochlin panted, clenching his fists. 'That's more than you're going to be in a minute, you murdering bastard.'

'Lochlin, your heart!' Tavvy warned him, putting out a restraining hand. 'He's not worth it, Lochlin, he really isn't. This has to end now and I think we both know who should be going to prison here.'

Judd jerked his head round to face them. 'How touching it is seeing the two of you together,' he said maliciously. 'So touching it makes me want to throw up.' Turning back to the stable door, he saw a crowd of people staring at him.

Judd could see Kitty's blond head next to Leo Beaument's, her grey eyes wide and distant, as if he were a stranger. Iris Maguire was looking at him oddly, not so much with hatred but with pity and it was almost more than Judd could bear. After everything he had done to her and Ace, Iris simply looked as though she felt sorry for him.

'I called the police,' piped up Caitie, her dark head appearing in the doorway. 'I did tons of research and I sent it off to the police. Just because some crazy guy said Judd did it and no one believed him, he got away with murder, literally.' She narrowed her eyes at Judd. 'You deserve to go to prison for what you did to my brother and sister, let alone anything else.'

Savannah came in with Conrad Lafferty on her arm, her long red hair hanging over one shoulder. 'Oh, Daddy,' she said mockingly, her identical blue eyes meeting his. 'What *have* you done now?'

Judd gave Savannah a withering look. 'You're hardly one to talk, you gold-digging bitch.'

Conrad gave Judd a disapproving stare. 'I was going to reassure you that I intend to take very good care of your daughter, Mr Harrington, but I see you don't actually give a shit.'

Going red, Judd looked him up and down before turning back to Savannah. 'Christ, if that's your new boyfriend, you must have horrendous daddy issues.'

She looked at him with equal disdain. 'Get your head out of the gutter, Daddy. Conrad is my new business partner. Anyway, you're hardly one to talk about morals, are you? Didn't you kill someone?'

'It was all so long ago now . . . no one cares.'

Catching everyone by surprise, Judd spun away and grabbed the lantern from the side. 'Keep back, otherwise I'll drop it!' he yelled.

Tavvy quickly led the trembling foal out, but Lochlin stayed put. Petra took the foal to one of the other stables so it was safe and warm again. The other animals could sense the tension and began to kick and call out in their stables and cages.

'Don't be an idiot,' Lochlin bellowed at Judd, watching the

lantern swaying dangerously close to the straw. 'There's no need to do this. It's over but it doesn't have to end this way.'

Judd held the lantern aloft, his eyes flashing madly. 'Oh, it does, Maguire. It does.' Hurling the lantern to the ground, he and Lochlin all jumped back as the straw caught fire and flames leapt high in the air.

'Everyone out!' shouted Lochlin, flapping his arms. Jesus, he thought. This whole stable could go up and it was attached to the house. As smoke spiralled into the air, Lochlin looked around frantically. 'There are hoses by the kitchen and buckets for water!' he shouted over his shoulder, glad when he was joined by someone.

'DCI Lipton,' the man said by way of introduction. 'I'm here to arrest Mr Harrington. Jesus, what's he doing? Trying to kill himself?'

Lochlin watched flames licking at Judd's feet and wondered how he could appear so calm in the face of death. 'Looks that way.'

'Mr Harrington,' DCI Lipton called urgently. 'You need to step away from the fire and come outside.'

Judd looked down at the flames as though fascinated. 'Why should I come out? You're here to send me to prison, aren't you?'

'I'm sure we can talk about it . . .'

'Nothing to talk about!' Judd shouted, laughing like a crazy man. 'I did it but there's no way I'm going down for it.' His eyes were manic. 'I always said this fight would be to the death, Maguire!'

Lochlin raked his dark hair out of his eyes, coughing and spluttering. 'This is stupid, Judd. Come out before you kill yourself!'

Fearing for Lochlin's life, Tavvy ran back into the stable, her arms thrashing through the billowing grey smoke. 'Get out of there!' she screamed to Lochlin through the blaze. 'I can't lose you . . . please!'

Judd retched into his sleeve, choking on the dry air. Flames flickered at the edges of his trousers and sparks leapt up and ignited the sleeves of his shirt. Suddenly the fire leapt out of control and Judd started to scream.

Lochlin couldn't believe what he was seeing. 'Judd! You're mad . . . please come out!' He squinted as the smoke wove itself around him, making it almost impossible to see.

DCI Lipton ran out and grabbed a hose, aiming it at the stable as Leo took hold of the other. The fire was burning out of control; the stable went up in flames and the edge of Pembleton started to catch fire too.

Taking one last look at Judd, Lochlin was about to tear out of the stable and leave him to his fate. But, for some bizarre reason, he simply couldn't bring himself to do it. As much as he wanted to leave Judd to burn to death and as much as he probably deserved it, Lochlin couldn't have Judd's death on his conscience. Too many people had been hurt already for Judd's life to end this way.

He heard Tavvy's voice shrieking at him from a distance to come back as he blindly threw himself at Judd, yanking him by the arm. Pulling him down under the smoke, he charged towards the fresh air, dragging a flailing Judd behind him.

As the stable exploded with a loud bang, the wood crackled and bowed and Judd and Lochlin were sent flying. Judd spiralled through the air like a spluttering Catherine wheel and he and Lochlin crashed to the ground. Rolling over and over until they fell against the side of Pembleton, smoke billowed out above them and flames crackled and spread, bursting into a magnificent blaze that engulfed the roof of Pembleton and one side of the half-timbered building.

'Up there!' someone shouted, turning a hose on to Pembleton's roof and side. Panting, Leo followed suit and played water over it continuously. Conrad threw his jacket over Judd, and held on to him until the paramedics arrived and took him away with a police escort.

Savannah, distressed at seeing her father hurt in spite of everything he'd done, rushed after him. 'Dad!'

'Fuck off!' he screamed at her. 'You're a traitor, just like the rest of them!'

Wiping away a tear, Savannah realised her concern for Judd was wasted. She leant against Conrad and resolved never to spare a thought for her father again.

Tavvy put her arm around Lochlin as they watched the fire on the roof, their hearts in their mouths. Pembleton was too precious for them to lose, especially like this. Lochlin held Tavvy's hand tightly, glad she'd stopped him from tearing Judd limb from limb. Just for a moment, he'd almost got sucked into Judd's games again . . . he'd almost lost control and thought more about the satisfaction of revenge than about the things that were important to him.

'Thank God you were there to keep me sane,' he told Tavvy. He coughed harshly, his eyes streaming and bloodshot. 'Otherwise, I don't know what I might have done.'

Tavvy smiled weakly. 'You've learnt your lesson as far as Judd is concerned, Lochlin. You didn't need me there to tell you what to do; you saved Judd all by yourself. And not many people would have done that after hearing about what he did to Seamus.'

'Or what he did to you,' Lochlin said roughly, pushing the unsavoury images from his mind.

'Don't you worry about me; I'm tougher than I look.' Tavvy stood by Lochlin's side as they both prayed their home would be saved.

'Not Pembleton,' Caitie whispered, clutching Iris and burying her head in her shoulder.

'It's all right,' Iris told her gently. 'Look, they've managed to put the fire out. The roof and the side are a bit damaged, that's all.'

Cringing, Caitie opened her eyes. 'Thank God!' She glanced at Lochlin. 'Why did you save Judd, Dad? After everything he's done to us, you could have just left him to die.'

Lochlin kissed the top of her dark head, his eyes sore from the smoke. 'Because too many people have been hurt. I couldn't let him die, not like that.' His green eyes crinkled at the edges. 'Let's just say I'd rather he got his comeuppance in jail than in the morgue.'

Elliot came running out of the marquee. 'I was just helping Abby out of the toilet – Jesus, what the hell just happened?'

Caitie quickly filled him in. Elliot's mouth tightened. When was he ever going to stop being ashamed of his father?

'Don't worry,' Savannah assured him, her spark returning. 'I told him what we thought of him.' Her eyes flashed. 'I don't think he wants to see any of us ever again.'

Elliot ran a hand through his blond hair as he surveyed the fire damage. 'What a mess.'

Iris realised her hands were shaking. 'I haven't even done my performance yet. But I don't expect anyone is worried about that.'

Tavvy shook her head. 'No, if you're up to it, Iris, I think you should do it.' She gripped Lochlin's arm. 'We need to celebrate. It's over. Finally. We can clear all this up in the morning.'

Lochlin gave them a wry grin. 'And maybe for quite a few months afterwards.'

Caitie took Iris's arm. 'You have to do this performance, Iris.'

'Why?'

Caitie averted her eyes from her sister's puzzled gaze. 'Just . . . because. I'm dying to hear the new songs, for a start.'

Iris frowned. She knew when Caitie was up to something and she had guilt written all over her. Nonetheless, she allowed herself to be led away back into the marquee.

'Where's Shay? He's missed all the drama.'

Caitie rolled her eyes as she hurried Iris to the stage. 'Probably shagging Darcy.'

'She must love him to have bought him Jett.' Iris yanked her arm free of Caitie's. 'Look, why are you in such a hurry? What's going on?'

'Nothing. Absolutely nothing. Just go and sing.' Giving her an innocent smile, Caitie gestured to the stage.

Doing as she was told, Iris found herself standing in the middle of the stage, trembling with nerves. After all the drama, she had come hurtling back down to earth with a thud, remembering how lonely she felt without Ace. Everything reminded her of him, even being on stage.

'Are you all right?' Caitie hissed from the side of the stage.

Iris nodded. She managed to get through 'Irresistible' and, although she had tears running down her face at the end, she quickly brushed them away, hoping the audience thought she was simply moved by the song.

Trying to find it in herself to sing 'Obsession', Iris caught sight of her parents in the audience, cheering her on. Mrs Meaden and Ian from the village shop were clapping excitedly, as were Leo and Kitty. Iris focused her mind on the words of the song and gave it her all.

Halfway through the track, she became aware of another voice, singing off-key into a microphone. Glancing behind her, she couldn't see anyone. Puzzled, she carried on singing. She heard the voice again and frowned, wondering why it sounded so familiar.

'*Have to . . . I have to, I have to have you . . . my obsession, you're my obsession . . .*' sang the voice, now the only one as the crowd strained to hear it and Iris stopped singing altogether. She saw Caitie at the edge of the stage then someone else emerged from behind the curtains at the back. Hobbling on crutches, the person took ages to move to the front, all the while singing extremely badly.

Iris squinted in the dim light, making out a head of mahogany hair. She put a hand to her mouth and her heart began to pound erratically. It couldn't be . . . surely, it wasn't . . . catching sight of Jerry's blond hair and Luisa's bouncing black curls in the background, Iris realised it couldn't be anyone else. Ace was hobbling towards her, a microphone wedged under his armpit, the volume up full blast.

'*Have to be with you . . . my obsession . . .*' Ace sang in totally the wrong key. Finishing the song, he hobbled to her side. 'You told me once that whoever sang that song to you was "the one".' Dropping the microphone and a crutch, he cupped her neck and gave her one of his heartbreaking smiles. 'You never said I had to do it in tune.'

Iris shook her head, her lips quivering. 'Ace . . . I can't believe you're here.' She gazed at his face, noticing a cut above his eyebrow. Resisting the urge to throw herself into his arms and kiss his pain away, Iris reminded herself why she had run from him in the first place.

He hurt me, she told herself. Badly. He used me and he only went out with me because his father asked him to seduce me. Iris hardened her heart but it was a half-hearted effort.

'I love you,' Ace said simply. 'From the moment I first saw you, I knew you were the one. And I can honestly say that I didn't care what my father had asked me to do, I just wanted to be with you.'

Iris hesitated. Feeling his warm fingers caressing her neck, she almost caved. 'How do I know for sure?'

'You know.' Ace kissed her fingers. 'In your heart of hearts, you know I love you. You took risks to be with me and now I'm taking risks to be with you.' He stroked her tawny-blond hair, sinking his hands into it. 'My father will never speak to me again but I'm done trying to impress him. The only person I care about impressing from now on is you.' He looked out across the audience. 'Although didn't my father just try and burn a house down and confess to killing someone? I guess he can't judge me from jail.'

They all nodded wryly.

'But enough about my father. Can you ever forgive me?' Ace's grey eyes met Iris's pleadingly. 'I'm willing to spend the rest of my life showing you how sorry I am.'

There was a collective gasp from the audience.

'How romantic,' Mrs Meaden sighed, nudging Ian.

Ian sulked. Just as he'd thought he might be in with a chance with Iris again, along comes another bloody handsome bastard sweeping her off her feet with passionate words and over-the-top gestures.

Oblivious of anyone in the audience, Iris slid her hands around Ace's waist. 'I want to believe you . . . I really do.'

'Then believe it. Because I'm telling the truth.' He gave the heart necklace back to her. 'Am I making enough of a fool of myself?' he asked her softly. 'Because I'll do this every day if you want me to, or anything else that will prove how much I love you. Put it back on . . . please.'

The audience sucked in their breath simultaneously.

Iris stared at Ace. She wanted to believe him more than anything but her heart felt so bruised, she didn't know if she could put herself through it again. But she missed him . . . so much. Inhaling his familiar scent, it was all Iris could do not to throw her arms around his neck and kiss him until her lips hurt.

Hopping on one leg, Ace brushed a tendril of tawny-blond hair out of the way so he could lose himself in Iris's amber eyes. 'You're . . . irresistible,' he said with an ironic smile. 'But I've never been in love before so you have to forgive me for being so crap at it.' He decided to go all out and just lay himself bare. 'All I can tell you is that I literally can't live without you. I've tried and I can't do it because I love you too much to be without you.'

Iris melted. She pulled his face towards hers and kissed him. The kiss went on and on and they only came up for air when the noisy cheers of the watching audience finally burst their bubble.

'So, are we back together?' Ace asked teasingly, running his hand down her body. God, he'd missed her. He couldn't wait to touch her all over again. Somewhere he didn't have to stand on dodgy legs with crutches, Ace told himself in amusement.

Iris contemplated him gravely, clutching the necklace tightly. 'We're back together, as long as you promise me one thing.'

'What's that?'

Iris stroked his mahogany hair, curving her body into his. 'Don't ever, *ever* sing again.'

Ace saluted her. 'Deal.' Accidentally losing his other crutch, he grabbed her waist. 'Don't let go,' he whispered, wobbling as his damaged legs started to give way.

'Never,' Iris said, knowing she had tears streaming down her face. 'I thought you were supposed to sweep me off *my* feet? At this rate, I'm going to have to carry *you* off the stage.'

Ace nuzzled his face into her neck, feeling his legs buckle weakly. 'Let's just stay here all night,' he murmured, his mouth finding hers again. 'I can't think of anywhere I'd rather be.'

Losing herself to the kiss, Iris couldn't agree more.

Chapter Twenty-Two

Six months later, mid-December

Holding his guitar aloft and coming off stage, Charlie grabbed a towel and wiped his sweaty face. It was the last night of a gruelling tour but he was ecstatic. The turnout had been amazing; full stadiums in every city and adoring fans singing the words of his new tunes and cheering him on.

'You were great and the blue rinse brigade *love* you,' Susannah teased. 'And at least I don't have to worry about groupies.'

'Oh, shut up.' Charlie was delighted with his new fan base. Some of them might be a bit older than the sexy young rock chicks he was used to but he wasn't about to complain. 'Hey, how about going home early, Suse? The twins must be bored rigid on their own.'

Susannah doubted the twins were in need of company but she was more than ready to go home after a few months away. It had been fun touring with Charlie but she missed home, so days later they packed up and headed back to the mansion.

Pulling up outside, Charlie heaved his guitar out of his Mercedes convertible. 'Home, sweet home. Can't wait to put on some slippers and light my pipe.'

'I think you mean you can't wait to put on your Hawaiian shorts and have a puff on your bong.' Susannah giggled. 'I can't see you ever turning into a proper geriatric, Chas.' She frowned as they went in. It was quiet – and extremely tidy. The Christmas decorations were up already, with silver and cerise tinsel strung from every beam, and lights twinkled around paintings and window frames.

Charlie picked a flyer up from the hallway table. He read from it aloud. '*Host your party at the infamous Valentine Mansion*,' it said. '*Have a dip in the heated indoor jacuzzi and sleep in the Gothic bed. Prices start from twenty thousand pounds.*'

Susannah shrieked. 'The twins have been pimping out our house, the cheeky so-and-sos!'

'I can't believe people would pay that much to host a party here,' Charlie said in wonder, feeling rather flattered. Seeing Susannah's furious face, he shook his head firmly. 'But it's bang out of order. Absolutely reprehensible.'

Skye and Abby chose that moment to make an appearance, clad head to toe in Burberry. Seeing her mother holding the flyer, Skye decided to blind them with success. 'We've made one hundred and eighty thousand pounds,' she piped up.

About to shout, Susannah blinked in astonishment. 'You made . . . *how much*?'

Charlie couldn't believe his ears.

'People really love you, Dad,' Skye cajoled, 'and they're willing to pay top dollar.'

Abby nodded smugly. 'We've been very entrepreneurial, if you think about it.'

Taken aback that Abby knew such a word, Susannah gathered her thoughts. 'We want in,' she said, receiving an agreeable, if stunned, nod from Charlie. 'I'll throw in some free cosmetics and Dad will auction off some of his old memorabilia for bigger charity events. As for the split, I'd suggest seventy, thirty because we're the parents.'

'Sixty, forty because it was our idea,' Skye countered.

Abby sighed. 'How about fifty, fifty? We are family, after all,' she added. And for the record, it was *my* idea. Not so thick after all.'

'Fifty, fifty,' Charlie agreed. 'Well, well . . . not so bad being a sad old has-been then!'

They all burst out laughing and cracked open a bottle of champagne.

* * *

Martha swept away a lock of Raef's auburn hair and let out a blissful sigh. Nothing had prepared her for the utter exhaustion she would suffer from the sleep deprivation when Lexi's baby was delivered, but neither had she expected to feel so overwhelmed with love. As soon as she'd looked into Raef's big blue eyes, that had been it.

Of course, the birth hadn't been without drama. Lexi had gone into an early labour, missing out on her private room at the Portland Hospital and finding herself sharing a grotty room with three other exhausted mothers in the local NHS facility. Leo had dutifully rushed to Lexi's side. But, thirty hours later, Raef's full head of ginger hair and sapphire-blue eyes had put paid to the need for a paternity test.

'Isn't he gorgeous?' Kitty swooned, leaning over and stroking Raef's soft, downy cheek. 'I can't even remember what life was like before he arrived.'

'Me neither,' Leo said, giving Kitty a kiss.

Martha looked down at Raef adoringly, certain he'd just given her a tiny smile. After everything that had happened at the Midsummer Ball, she and Sebastian had decided to stay in Brockett Hall, while Kitty had moved into Foxton Manor with Leo. Leo had been remarkably laidback about it all and he adored Raef as much as the rest of them.

Sebastian, having taken on a role in a much smaller legal firm, was finally finding out what it was like to have to work hard for a living but he had no choice. He had Martha and Raef to support, as well as paying off Lexi.

'Did you hear the latest about Lexi?' Kitty asked, grabbing a muslin for Martha's shoulder as she fed him his bottle. 'She's working out all day long to lose the five stone she gained and she's dating some footballer who earns fifty grand a week.'

Martha smiled. 'Good for her. Personally, I'd rather have Raef than all that money any day.'

Sebastian slouched in and tossed his briefcase on the sofa. Waiting for someone to ask how his day had been, he gave up and threw himself into an armchair.

'Raef's done really well today,' Martha informed Sebastian proudly. 'He's taken all his bottles and he had two big poos this afternoon.'

'Lovely,' Sebastian snapped. He didn't know what had happened since Raef had arrived but it was almost as if he was invisible these days. At first, he'd assumed Martha was punishing him for sleeping with Lexi but he now realised her disinterest in him had more to do with her ongoing love affair with Raef. Sebastian was astonished to find himself jealous of his own son. And wanting, for some bizarre reason, to win Martha back. Used to Martha worshipping him and hanging on his every word, the tables had turned and, perversely, Sebastian found himself wanting to make his wife fall in love with him all over again. He watched Martha prepare to put Raef down for his nap.

'I'll come,' he said eagerly, hoping Martha might fancy a kiss and cuddle once Raef was settled. Or even just a chat, he thought desperately. Martha shrugged as if she couldn't care less but Sebastian jumped up and followed her obediently out of the room.

'Who'd have thought it,' Kitty commented to Leo. 'Sebastian's besotted with Martha and Martha hasn't even noticed.'

Leo sat down and put his arm round her cosily. 'Nothing wrong with being besotted with the woman in your life,' he said, thinking this was going to be the best Christmas ever. 'As long as it's a two-way thing.'

'Oh, it's definitely a two-way thing,' Kitty told him naughtily as she unbuttoned his shirt.

Shay knocked on Darcy's office door at Shamrock. Going in, he showed her some reviews of little Aidan's album which had been released that week.

'They're brilliant. It was definitely the right time to release the album.'

Darcy looked up at him, feeling a flip-flop of desire in her groin. 'Dinner tonight?'

Shay sat on the edge of her desk and nodded. He and Darcy worked together at Shamrock's offices and still lived in Bluebell Cottage, being too busy to find another house and rather liking their little love nest. In spite of spending every waking hour with one another, they were still in perfect unison. Shay kissed Darcy's neck.

'Listen, I hope I've done the right thing but I have a surprise for you.'

'Really?' she murmured, her hands snaking round his neck. She gazed into his eyes, utterly in love with him and, these days, not afraid to admit it. 'What sort of surprise?'

'The kind I hope doesn't make you hit me.'

Darcy pulled back warily. 'I'm guessing you haven't bought me a pair of diamond earrings, then.'

'Er . . . no.' Shay hesitated, suddenly thinking he may have mightily overstepped the mark. Leading her towards the boardroom, he felt her quivering under his hands. 'Trust me?' he said, kissing her.

She nodded, shaking. She did but she couldn't help feeling slightly sick.

Opening the door, he led her in. Darcy started. Sitting in a chair at the side, looking thin but self-assured, was her mother.

'Oh my God.' Darcy's hands fluttered to her mouth.

'Darcy.' Her mother stood up. 'It's so good to see you.' Faltering, she stopped talking as Darcy held up a hand to silence her. Expecting a tirade of abuse, Mrs Middleton gulped. She was disarmed when Darcy rushed towards her.

'What are you doing here? How did you find me? Where . . . where do you live now?' The words came tumbling out without preamble but Darcy wasn't even sure what she was saying.

Mrs Middleton took a deep breath. 'Shay phoned and asked me to come.'

Shay winced, wondering if Darcy was going to tear into him.

Mrs Middleton carried on talking, needing to fill the awkward silence. 'I live down in Cornwall near the sea and I walk my two dogs on the beach every day. It's beautiful . . . you'd love it.' She stopped short, realising she didn't have a clue what Darcy would love after all these years. She stared at her daughter, waiting for a reaction, as did Shay, with bated breath.

Darcy surprised them both by bursting into tears. 'I'm so sorry, Mum!' she cried, tears coursing down her cheeks. 'Can you ever forgive me?'

Mrs Middleton didn't hesitate. She opened her arms and welcomed Darcy into them warmly. 'There's nothing to forgive,' she assured her, holding her daughter close.

Quietly closing the door, Shay left them to it. They had a lifetime of catching up to do and he hoped he'd have a chance to get to know her too. After all, he thought, she might just end up being his mother-in-law one day.

Savannah lapped up the adoring applause. Since she'd moved to Japan with Conrad, her life had changed beyond recognition. She didn't know what strings he'd pulled, but as soon as Savannah set foot on Japanese soil, she had been worshipped like a star. And in all honesty, it felt fabulous.

Having already released one album – a digitally remastered, retouched, enhanced affair that made her vocals sound as good as Iris Maguire's – Savannah was now hosting her own show, with her name up in glittering lights. It didn't matter one bit that she couldn't speak a word of Japanese; she had been welcomed with open arms.

Savannah dashed off set, loving the fact that six minions were immediately at her side, teasing her hair and touching up her make-up. Wearing a Pucci mini dress with a bold, swirly print and some funky shoes a well-known Japanese shoe company had sent her, Savannah had never been so well dressed, nor had she felt so much adoration in her life before.

For some reason, her red hair and lightly tanned skin were an instant hit over here; legions of fans had dyed their hair red, some with disastrous results, and sales of fake tan had gone up in their thousands. Savannah had already been asked to endorse a new fake tan brand and Conrad mentioned a six-figure sum that had sent Savannah's head into a spin.

'You're due on set in ten minutes,' Natsuki, her polite PA, informed her with a sweet smile. Putting a bottle of water in Savannah's hand, she bowed her head respectfully and ran off to check her BlackBerry for further appointments.

Savannah sank into her comfy make-up chair and drank some water, making sure her lipstick didn't get smudged. Glancing down at her phone, she smiled as she opened a brief but happy text message from Martha. She'd attached a picture of baby Raef wearing a Santa hat, his ginger hair poking out from underneath. Privately Savannah thought Raef looked rather like a pickled walnut but she was delighted Martha had finally found contentment, even if she hadn't ditched Sebastian in the process.

'Hey.' Conrad joined her and carefully moving a set of lurid eye shadows out of the way, sat on the edge of the counter. 'I have some good news for you. You've just secured another ad campaign. A big one, this time.'

'Bigger than Golden Glow fake tan?' Savannah asked, wide-eyed. Running her eyes over Conrad's well-cut grey suit, she couldn't help admiring his toned physique.

'Much bigger than Golden Glow fake tan.' Conrad smiled. 'This is with the biggest sports company in the world. They've picked up on the fact that you like to keep fit and eat healthily, so they want you to front their New Start campaign, which is all about taking small steps to changing your lifestyle.'

Savannah gaped. 'Are you serious?' She leapt out of the chair and threw her arms around Conrad's neck. 'I don't know how you do it.

We're making so much money, I can't even take it all in!' She drew back from him and met his piercing green eyes. 'I don't know how to thank you,' she said softly, running her hands down his back.

'Not like that,' he told her firmly.

'I'm not doing it for that.' Savannah meant it and she coiled her arms round his neck.

Conrad studied her. 'Are you sure? Gratitude can make a person extremely generous. I've never taken advantage of anyone in my life and I don't intend to start now.'

Savannah felt nervous for some reason. 'Is it taking advantage if I want it?'

Conrad ran his hands over her taut waist and slender hips. 'I guess not, but like your father suggested, perhaps you just have "Daddy issues".'

Her mouth twisted contemptuously. 'That's rubbish. I don't even think of you as old.'

He laughed. 'Gee, thanks!'

Savannah blushed. 'Oh, you know what I mean.'

'Miss Harrington . . . one minute!' called Natsuki.

Conrad released Savannah. 'Are you sure about this?' he murmured, close to her mouth.

'I've never been surer of anything in my life,' she told him confidently, knowing her feelings for him were real.

Sashaying on to the set, Savannah guessed she finally had something to thank her father for. If she hadn't tracked Judd down, she wouldn't have met Conrad and she wouldn't be the biggest star Japan had ever seen.

Giving the camera a smug little smile, Savannah tilted her face. She intended to lap up every second of her good fortune and her father was now nothing more than a distant memory.

Lochlin checked the plans for the kennels they were building behind the new barn. He was fairly sure they'd thought of everything but he guessed he should check with Tavvy. Trudging back to Pembleton, Lochlin waved at Petra who, wearing a huge navy body warmer, was drinking her flask of coffee by the stables. Kicking off his boots, Lochlin found Tavvy warming her hands on the Aga in the kitchen.

The kitchen was looking Christmassy already, with red and green tinsel strung along the cabinets and bunches of fresh holly and mistletoe tied with ribbons on the table. The air was ripe with Tavvy's third attempt at a Christmas pudding, the other two having burnt to a crisp and sunk in the middle.

Apart from the stench of singed currants, Lochlin couldn't help thinking the scene was pretty damned perfect.

'I think we can go ahead with these,' he told her, flapping the plans.

'Great.' Tavvy nodded at the kitchen table which was covered with song sheets. 'Iris faxed those through. They're good, *really* good. She just needed to believe in herself.'

Lochlin smiled proudly and picked up a photograph of Caitie. She was playing the part of Betty in Hugo's touring production of *White Christmas* and getting rave reviews.

'She looks beautiful, so she does,' he said proudly, showing the photo to Tavvy. 'She will be back in time for Christmas, won't she?'

'I hope so,' Tavvy said, checking her pudding for the fifteenth time. 'Her new boyfriend, Henry, is pining like mad for her and Elliot and Jas have been leaving messages on the answerphone daily in the hope that she's back.' She straightened up and glanced at Lochlin apprehensively. 'Honestly, do you miss it?'

He looked up with a frown. 'What? Shamrock? Oh, sometimes. Some days the alarm goes off and I almost go to jump out of bed, all fired up about the next big thing. But that's just force of habit, darlin', and I wasn't enjoying myself for a long time. I was just too stubborn to admit it.'

'You? Stubborn?' Tavvy mocked him. 'As if!'

He laughed. 'But I'm much happier spending time with you . . . being a man of leisure.' He pulled her closer. 'What man wouldn't be? Besides, I've had so much to do repairing the stables and sorting out the roof after the fire.' A shadow crossed his face briefly but Lochlin guessed he might always feel a tightening in his stomach whenever he thought about Judd.

Distracted by a distinctly acrid smell, Lochlin sniffed the air. 'I think your pudding might have met its maker again, darlin'.'

Tavvy shrieked and yanked the Aga door open. Pulling out yet another sunken pudding with singed edges, she dumped it on top of the oven. 'That's it. I'm going to call Shay and ask him to get me one from Fortnum's.'

Lochlin grinned. 'We only set fire to it, anyway. Just think,' he said to Tavvy, wrapping his arms around her, 'we'll have Caitie and Henry for Christmas dinner, as well as Shay and Darcy. Will Iris and Ace make it back in time?'

'They promised they would,' Tavvy said, poking her pudding in exasperation. She gazed up at Lochlin. 'It's definitely over now, isn't it? I mean, the feud . . . Judd . . .'

He nodded. 'Of course it is. He can't hurt us ever again.' Wrapping his arms around her, Lochlin finally believed that was true.

Standing in court being sentenced, Judd found himself in a state of shock. His case had played out like a soap opera for the past six months, with press attending every session and scribbling down the salacious details as they were tantalisingly revealed. A 25-year-old story had suddenly become hot news, played out as a tale of unrequited love and murderous revenge, and Judd had become something of a criminal celebrity. He was represented by London's best lawyer, Michael Cole, at the head of a shit-hot team large enough to rival O.J. Simpson's entourage. Michael had been given carte blanche to do *whatever* it took to get Judd off and, realising this was the biggest case of his life, Michael was fighting dirty.

Private investigators had been hired to dig dirt on judges who had been approached with bribes and, as far as Judd was concerned, he was home and dry. But then everything had gone wrong. An unknown judge had mysteriously ended up presiding over the court, Judd's defence team had been torn to pieces and the prosecution had produced another witness who'd been at the party all those years ago, this time a pillar of society who'd never taken drugs but who claimed to have seen Judd supplying Seamus with them. He had been utterly convincing and Judd's fate was sealed.

'I therefore sentence you to life imprisonment,' the judge was saying in a booming voice as the spectators cheered and crowed.

Judd barely heard what was going on. There was a strange noise in his ears and he felt very much as though he was drowning. As he was manhandled back down to the cells, he turned to his lawyer and yelled over his shoulder at him.

'You can pay that fucking salary back unless you get me out of here, you incompetent prick!'

Feeling slightly shaky, Michael Cole picked up the suitcase he'd stashed under his table and took out his passport. On the huge retainer Judd was paying him, he could happily afford to retire to a mansion in Barbados, and that was exactly what he intended to do.

Driven to a high-security prison, Judd was stripped of his Armani suit before being led down to a cell that was smaller than the downstairs bathroom at Brockett Hall. He couldn't believe he was about to play out his final years behind bars when Lochlin Maguire was probably eating mince pies with Tavvy.

Telling himself his money would at least buy him privileges in prison, Judd resolved that no one would be bossing *him* around.

'They like posh boys like you in here,' said the prison warden with a slight smirk.

'Anyone who goes near my arse will live to fucking regret it,' Judd snarled.

'*Really*.' The prison warden looked unimpressed as he unlocked a cell. 'This is Benjy.'

Judd glanced at the small unassuming man in the cell, sitting patiently with a book on his knee. He shouldn't give him any trouble. 'Are you my new cell mate?'

The prison warden let someone else in. 'No, *this* is your cell mate.' The door clanged behind him in a slightly menacing fashion. 'He's called Don. As in *the* Don. He's in for mass murder and extortion.'

Judd turned around slowly and found himself face to chest with a giant of a man, beaming from ear to ear.

'Stay away from me, you fucking fairy,' Judd barked.

Don put an arm round him and pulled him close. 'Now, come on, Judd! We're like one big happy family in here.'

Gripping the bars of the cell, Judd clenched his buttocks and wondered where the hell he could get hold of a mobile phone.

Iris rolled over in bed. 'God, it's so hot! LA in December, it's hardly festive, is it?'

'No, but your house back in England will look fucking gorgeous when we fly back later in the week so it doesn't matter.' Wearing a pair of jeans and not much else, Ace tossed his cigarette out of the window then clapped his hand over his mouth. 'Shit! I keep forgetting I can't do that in this apartment. Sorry if that hit anyone down there!' he called.

Their new place was on the very edge of Beverly Hills and it was nowhere near as glamorous as Ace's other apartment but it had three bedrooms, a huge sitting room and its own pool. Ace couldn't care less about the decor or the location. It was his apartment, his and Iris's, and they shared the rent. For the first time in his life, Ace felt grown up and responsible for himself. It felt good to be free at last, free from his father's control and free to make his own decisions. Ace finally felt as if he was in charge of his own destiny and he couldn't be happier.

'Have you seen this picture of Jerry?' Iris said, holding up the latest copy of *Attitude* magazine. Jerry was on the front cover in a pair of pristine white boxer shorts, his arms folded across his sculpted chest. His preppy blond hair was swept back to give his chiselled chin centre stage and his blue eyes were staring directly at the camera. Inside, he was dominating a sexy six-page spread in various poses with his clothes on – and off.

Ace peered at it. 'I can't believe I never knew Jerry was gay! Why didn't he tell me?'

Having discussed it with Luisa, Iris knew exactly why Jerry had never mentioned being gay to Ace before now. She also knew it was best for that particular piece of information to stay hidden for ever, not because it would bother Ace to know the truth but because Jerry would be mortified. Besides, he had a boyfriend now anyway and in spite of his fears, Jerry's NASCAR colleagues and fans hadn't batted an eyelid at the news.

Iris rolled over on to her front, exposing her naked back. Ace ran a finger down it adoringly, unable to keep his hands off her when her bare skin was on offer.

'And how about you?' he teased. 'A number one album on the cards, a massive contract with that clothing company.' He pretended to sulk. 'I'm feeling rather left out with all this commotion. Although I suppose I'm NASCAR's hottest driver right now, at least according to *US Weekly* and they *always* tell the truth.'

Iris kissed him and nuzzled his neck. 'I can't believe you actually came all the way to England to woo me with your singing.'

Ace lazily stroked her honeyed shoulders. 'Speaking of which, Pia called earlier. She said she's been in contact with someone in the UK and she's lined up a massive performance and presenting slot for you at some awards show in February.'

'February?' Iris's amber eyes were wide. 'That's not . . . it's not the Brits, is it?'

'Might have been.' Ace smiled, loving the way Iris's face lit up when she got excited. He noticed she was lying on some sheets of paper. 'Hey, do you want me to sing some of your music to you?' Unable to read music, he sang the words in some tune known only to himself.

She snatched the paper back and held her hands over her ears.

'You promised me you'd never sing again!'

He flipped her on to her back, leaning in to give her a slow, seductive kiss.

'Oooh, Ace,' she joked, blushing slightly. 'Is that a gun in your pocket or are you just pleased to see me?'

Ace went scarlet and sat up. Putting his hand over his pocket, he cursed himself for not taking the box out of his jeans.

Iris felt a shiver of fear shudder through her. 'Ace, what's wrong?'

He sighed and turned round. 'God . . . I've ruined everything now.'

'Ruined what?'

'My big surprise. I was going to do this on Christmas Day at your parents' but . . .'

'But what?' Iris watched him pull a small box out of his pocket and she gulped as he dropped to one knee.

'I know it's soon and you can say no but I couldn't help myself.' Ace opened the box to reveal a stunning heart-shaped diamond ring. 'Er . . . Cartier said I can return it if you don't like it but me and Jerry spent ages choosing it because you like hearts and it's probably way too big for your tiny fingers,' he gabbled. Tears sprang into Ace's eyes. 'But the thing is, I really want to spend the rest of my life with you . . . you know, if you'll have me but I'll understand if I've made a total ass of myself with this ring and everything . . .'

'Don't you dare take that ring back. I love it.' Iris held out her left hand, tears running down her face. She gazed at Ace. 'And of course I'll have you, you big idiot.'

With shaking hands, he slid the ring on. Linking his fingers through hers, Ace kissed her longingly.

'What's your father going to say?' he asked when they both came up for air. 'Aren't I supposed to ask his permission or something?'

Iris smiled. 'He won't mind that but he'll probably say, "Iris, you can't marry a fucking Harrington." '

He looked horrified.

'I'm joking!' she said, pulling him back into bed. 'Now shut up about all that family crap and show me why you want to marry me, will you?'

Faced with a request Ace had no trouble honouring, he did exactly as he was told.

Acknowledgements

First, thanks to everyone in my family for being so excited about my books being published. Dad, there are even ruder bits in this one, so please skip those scenes where possible. Special thanks go to my fabulous mum for always championing my novels wherever she goes – on the beach whilst on holiday, in shops and to pretty much anyone she meets. Ditto my mother-in-law, Steph. Please continue to recommend my novels to all and sundry!

Thank you to all the girls at EEBs for prominently displaying my books wherever they go. To Jeni, who always keeps me sane with wise words and texts to let me know that someone is reading my book by the pool. Massive thanks to all my friends in Brentwood and Canary Wharf and to anyone who has taken the time to contact me with lovely messages.

Thanks to my brilliant agent, Diane Banks, for her continued support and encouragement and for the in-depth discussions about probably very minor character details. Oh, and for the lovely lunches! And to my amazing editor at Headline, Sherise Hobbs, for the ruthless (but much needed!) cutting which has so improved the book. Thank you to the Headline team for the beautiful cover, and for all the hard work that goes into my novels.

Once more, the biggest thanks go to Anthony – for debating plot and character ideas that suddenly occur to me in the middle of the night (or during your favourite programmes) but mostly for being there when juggling books and babies became challenging. It's been quite a year but it was definitely worth it. Love always.